THE BROAD GLEAMING

Hope you enjoy
Reading
Best wishes

Copyright notice

Dedications

To Sean Strong and Moa Stridh who created the excellent artwork for this book. To Lottie Clemens who thoroughly proofread this work and did a brilliant job of polishing it. To Penny who recorded the audiobook of the original novella version of this book and helped to inspire new avenues for the story.

To all the friends and lovers who over my life have made a mark and then moved on. We may not speak, may never speak again but all the same, thank you for the time we had.

To my parents who have always stood firmly in my corner.

To My Once Upon A Time Wonder Woman.
Thank you for the little kind gestures, that probably meant more to me than they did to you. Thank you for believing, thank you for every blessed second. I'd do it all again In a heartbeat.

I wish for you, nothing but happiness.
Yours truly,
Fruit Loop

Table of Contents

Forward

I think that the convention when it comes to forwards is to get someone to write something warm and glowing about you so that the reader feels like they are in safe hands. Or else you get someone to write something about how talented you are so that the reader looks forward to the epic tale ahead of them.

It all feels a bit false to me, a bit humble brag. You don't need to know how warm, friendly, funny … insert flattering adjectives here … I am. Likewise, I could line up a list of people to talk about how talented I am and really, it's just marketing and advertising. I'm sure you'll all make your own mind up about this book, as have I.

This is my first finished novel, after being told I'd never be a writer, and more or less that my dyslexia disqualified me from that ambition, I've finally done it. It's took years to get here, and it's not been a straight journey, often I came close to giving up. But I finished, I got there.

But finishing – as important as that was to me – wasn't everything. What mattered to me was having a finished work that I could be proud of and believe me I am immensely proud of this book.

So … I thought I might tell you instead about what this book is about to me. Reading it you will think it's about one couple dealing with cancer and a young girl surviving domestic abuse and to a degree that's right, that's what the book is about on the face of it.

For me this book is about something slightly different. Half of the story is about a relationship where two people are on the face of I good for each other but live in their own little bubble.

Their question is, can this relationship exist outside that bubble? It was written for an ex-lover, who was always kind and warm and offered me support with my writing where others who came before her dismissed it as a waste of my time. The other half of the story isn't really about surviving domestic abuse as much as its about coming into one's own strength and finally taking your first steps on your own path, rather than a path that's been laid out for you.

should this matter to you? does my interpretation alter what your about to read? Certainly not, in the end we all bring ourselves to the books, movies and music we consume, and what really matters to you is what – if anything – this book will mean to you. I hope that if you have in the past struggled through dark times connected to the loss of a loved one, or else an abusive partner you can find some measure of comfort in this story.

Nothing lasts forever, not even pain.

Prologue

The Saint of Lost Causes.

A white stag stood beneath the crescent moon, in the middle of the frozen lake, scenting the air. Something was approaching, something big and grizzly, something stinking of death and blood. The stag stood its ground and watched the horizon. It was there somewhere, creeping closer, hidden by the snow. The stag lowered its head so that its nose almost scraped the ice and pointed its antlers towards the thing ahead. It steadied itself then galloped towards that scent of blood and death.

As the stag drew closer the thing took shape as a polar bear of giant proportions, its immense white body was covered in scars, and its white fur was matted in patches all over its body. The stag charged, it drove its antlers into the side of the polar bear and knocked it clean off its feet. It wasn't good enough; the beast was up and turning on the stag. One giant paw closed around its right antler and then the bear was up on its hind legs, pulling the stag into the air. There was a sudden shimmer of light, and the bear wasn't a bear anymore, it was a behemoth, a giant of a man dressed in animal skins with a bald head and a straggly beard.

'Does the not know friend from enemy?' the giant said, in a thick, Yorkshire accent. 'No, you know nowt flower, bigger and badder than you have sought to do me misfortune and I've skinned them alive with my little finger.'

There was another shimmer of light and the stag transformed into a painfully handsome man in a white suit. The handsome man still dangled from the giant's grip, only now he was being held up by a fistful of hair, rather than an antler.

'I don't know you as friend or enemy, and I don't care which you are, you came into my sacred place uninvited.'

'Bloody cheek' The giant grunted. "Appen I did have an invite, it may not have been from you, and I'll admit that, but I was asked here.'

'Put him down, Polly.'

The third voice didn't belong to the giant or the handsome man, and both of them turned to look at him. He was a slight figure, dressed in silk that swirled red, blue and green. He had spikey, light-blonde hair, pointed ears and elfin eyes with odd purple flecks.

'I said ... put him down, Polly ... I didn't go to all this effort to make a chew toy for you.'

'Aye well, 'appen I will this time ... but if your young'un goes for me again, I'll lay a wallop upside his 'ed that'll make thine eyes water Goodfellow.'

The elfin looking man – Goodfellow – rolled his eyes and watched as the giant lowered the handsome man down and placed him softly on his feet. The giant laughed and cuffed him on the back of his shoulder with a gargantuan hand.

'Little misunderstanding weren't it young'un ... no hard feelings.' The giant offered a hand and waited for a reply, but the handsome man was too busy ruffling his shiny, curly, black locks. 'Bloody well stop fretting with your hair will ya? There's nowt wrong with it, well nowt a nice short back and sides wouldn't fix at any rate.'

At that, the handsome man sighed, rolled his eyes and allowed his right hand to disappear in the grip of the giant. He felt his arm being shaken, almost out of its socket, and then there was another slap on his back.

'Good, and now introductions I think,' Goodfellow said.

'Aye, and bloody hurry about it un'all. It's parky out, I'm freezing my brass monkeys off … by the time you get through all the names I'll be nowt but a slab of ice.'

'Baldr, this is Polaris, the north star and the spirit of the hunt.' Goodfellow said. 'Over his long life he has also been known by the names, Orion, Mixcoatl and, in the beginning, Herne.'

'Of course,' Polaris broke in, 'back then the stag were my totem. Aye, them were the days. I remember when I was Mixcoatl they offered up human sacrifices to me. Nowt like that I tell ye … gets you good and drunk … but then, of course, laughing boy there banned it … said it was savage and …' Polaris stopped when he saw Goodfellow raise an eyebrow. 'Aye, well 'appen it was a bit brutal all in all.'

'Polaris, like me,' Goodfellow paused and coughed, it was an affected cough, as if what he was about to say next was sticking in his throat, 'is a bastard son of Prometheus, the Prince of Fire, which sort of makes us family.'

'Aye, we're all bastards and brothers here … now get a wriggle on, I'm cold and hungry enough to eat a scabby old horse.'

'Polaris, allow me to introduce you to Baldr,' Goodfellow said, pointing to the handsome man. 'Baldr is the spirit of mercy and empathy, and the master of music.'

Baldr and Polaris nodded to each other, it was a half-hearted, cold recognition of brotherhood and it was over in the blink of an eye.

'Shall we eat?' Goodfellow asked.

''bout bloody time un'all,' Polaris rumbled. 'Let's go someplace warm … not France though. Bloody poncy food … and farty little portions to boot.'

Goodfellow drew his fingernail through the air, creating a rip in the world around them. He pulled the rip wide apart until it was as tall as he was and through it came a thick smog and the sound of angry car horns. Goodfellow stepped through the rip, followed by Baldr and Polaris, who had to hunch down to fit.

On the other side, the three spirits emerged onto a crowded street. People walked around them, there were so many of them and all of them different. Different races, sizes, heights, accents but all of them sharing that big city 'fuck you and the horse you rode in on' attitude.

They had disguised themselves in the camouflage of the plain and ordinary. Baldr was wearing jeans, trainers and a hoody pulled up over his Jim Morrison mop of hair. Polaris was a lot shorter and less imposing, but still big enough to fill a doorway. The diminished giant was dressed in dirty work overalls and his beard was clipped a lot closer to his flabby chin. The most dramatic transformation came in the form of Goodfellow. His fae, elfin appearance was hidden under the false face of an old man. Goodfellow was dressed in a buttoned-up shirt, a dated tank top, a paisley bow tie, a pair of trousers with a neat crease ironed into them, and a pair of brown carpet slippers.

'Where are we?' Baldr asked.

'New York, or thereabouts,' Goodfellow said. He scanned the buildings and the people passing by. 'Definitely one of the five boroughs, maybe Brooklyn or Queens.'

'Come on,' Polaris grunted. 'Me belly thinks me throat's been cut.' He stormed ahead slapping his large belly as he walked.

'We'll need money,' Goodfellow said. As he followed behind the big man, a walking stick appeared from his sleeve. He set it down, leaned on it and began to walk with a bent back.

'You don't carry money with you?' Baldr asked.

'You still think like the flesh folk,' Goodfellow said. 'Rule one, young Baldr. Spirits don't carry anything, we just take what we need … observe,' he said, pointing to a shady-looking character just ahead. Goodfellow shook his wrist and a gold watch appeared on it, but Baldr could see through the watch, it wasn't really there, it was a fake, a glamour and nothing more.

'Excuse me young man,' Goodfellow said to Mr Shady, when he spoke his voice sounded virtually decrepit. 'Can you tell us if there is a proper, old-fashioned diner around here? We're tourists you see … me, my son,' he pointed to Polaris, 'and his young boyfriend, we're all here on our holidays, and we always wanted to eat in a proper American style diner.'

'Hey!' Polaris shouted. 'What's this that thou are saying about me?'

'Come on Polly, don't be like that … I'll admit it, I wasn't happy to begin with, but I've accepted it now.'

Polaris glared at Goodfellow with gimlet eyes, when he looked to Baldr he saw him smirking under his hoodie. The giant shook his head and turned away.

'Get on with it, old man. If I don't get some food soon, I'll chew your hand off.'

Goodfellow glanced down at the watch on his wrist to check the time, and in so doing he drew Mr Shady's eyes to it. Quickly, the thief placed one hand on Goodfellow's back and the other over his wrist.

'No problem pops,' he said, as his fingers began to deftly unfasten the watch. He took his hand from Goodfellow's back and pointed down the street to distract his gaze. 'Two blocks down, one block east.' At that, he took the watch and closed it in his fist. Mr Shady didn't feel another hand reaching into his coat pocket or, for that matter, his wallet disappearing.

'Well thank you, young man. It isn't true what they say you know, not all New Yorkers are arseholes.' Goodfellow smiled and walked away, leaving a bemused look on Mr Shady's face.

Inside Mooney's Diner the three spirits commandeered a booth in a quiet corner. Polaris squeezed into one side, taking up the entire seat to himself, while Baldr and Goodfellow sat opposite him. A waitress appeared almost as soon as they took their booth, she turned their mugs over and filled them with coffee then placed a jug of cream on the table.

'Does thou not have tea around these parts?' Polaris grumbled. His voice drew the eye of the young waitress who stood chewing gum and clutching the coffee pot.

'What kind of accent is that?' she asked.

'English,' Baldr replied in his flat Coventry drawl. He took down his hood and when the waitress saw him she melted a little. 'Well, it's just about English. This one doesn't speak proper like what I do.' Baldr smiled at that.

'Ignore yon baby-faced ingrate lass,' Polaris said, picking up the menu. 'This accent comes from Old York, the men are hard up there and that's the way we like it.'

'Yeah, hard men alright! I know your type. You from God's own county, I know your attitudes and lack of emotion. What's that saying you have up there … "I say what I like, and I like what I say",' Baldr laughed.

'Aye, plain honest to goodness talking lad, we're direct to the point and we have no time for southern softness,' Polaris replied. Baldr responded to that by screwing up his face in a scowl, when he spoke again he mimicked Polaris's voice,

'Now come on, lad. I know ya family's been wiped out in t'car crash, but remember where you are … this is Yorkshire, we don't cry over trivial matters like that. The death of ya family is hardly a reason to cry, it's not like County lost at cricket, is it?.'

Goodfellow, sitting in the corner and still disguised as an old man, began to roar with laughter. His top set of false dentures came loose and fell out of his mouth, he caught them mid-air and crammed them back in. Through the disguise, Baldr saw the true elfin face of Goodfellow tipping him a wink.

'Yeah, yeah. Very funny lads ... now is this young lass going to take our order or am I going to have to start chewing on the corner of this table?'

'Sure, what can I get you guys?' the waitress asked, stifling a snigger.

'This, this, and this,' Polaris said, pointing to pictures of two different breakfasts and a plate of pancakes. 'And what about you two?' he asked, looking across the table.

'I'll have a slice of pecan pie, that sounds nice and American,' Goodfellow said.

'Pie, for breakfast, really?' Baldr raised an eyebrow.

'Don't blame me, I wanted to go to France,' Goodfellow replied, 'there are no rules here, nothing matters.' He pointed at the waitress, 'do you know they sell squirty cheese in a can ... well, not her personally, but her people ... you're half French, aren't you offended by that?'

'Such is life,' Baldr responded shrugging. He allowed himself another small smile, and when he turned it on the waitress, she melted all over again.

'What about you handsome?' she flirted. 'What can I get for you?'

'Just a sandwich,' he said, handing her the menu. 'Whatever you recommend.'

Before long the table was piled high with food, most of it under Polaris's nose. Baldr tried not to watch the giant eat, and yet he couldn't help but stare out of the corner of his eye. The big man was shovelling in bacon, sausage, egg, and syrup covered pancakes into his mouth, in great galumphing chomps.

'Are you ready?' Goodfellow asked as he savoured his pecan pie. 'It begins soon.'

'Ready as I'll ever be,' Baldr said, eyeing his sandwich. It was packed with meat, swiss cheese and, salad, topped with basil and drizzled with oil. It smelled delicious, but the grunting and gurgling from the other side of the table had put him off.

'You sound like you have misgivings?'

'Well, I do Goodfellow, you forget … it wasn't so long ago that I was on the other side of this. It feels wrong, you know … like manipulation. And, of course, I know these people, I like these people.'

'Human guilt,' Polaris said with a mouthful full of food.

Baldr reached up and brushed a crumb of pancake that had been projected onto his shoulder, then looked calmly into the big man's face.

'You're beyond such things now young'un. Best not worry about the trifling wrongs, it's like breaking a bone-china cup … it's regrettable but nowt to hang your soul over. And remember what yon joker says: it's just a cog in the machine. We serve Yggdrasil around here.' He whispered that last declaration, then put his hands up to shield his eyes, placing his fingertips on his temples. Goodfellow mimicked the gesture.

'If I stop feeling guilty, then what would be the point?'

'You speak wisely,' Goodfellow said, he squeezed Baldr's shoulder but didn't look him in the eye. 'You can still empathise where we can't, but don't allow yourself to get caught up in guilt. You can't fix it, my friend, you can search to the ends of the Earth, but you won't find some magical happy solution that will tie up everything.'

'I can try.'

'Can you?' Goodfellow sighed and then nibbled on the crust of his pie. 'If I was to tell you that our waitress is going to finish her shift, walk out into the road and get run down by a taxi. If I was to say she'll die, just like that,' he clicked his fingers to demonstrate, 'if I was to tell you that you could save her, but only if you choose someone to take her place, could you look around this room and single someone out?'

'No, of course not.'

'There we are my friend, death can't be denied.' He finished his pie and pushed the plate aside. 'Now ... to the blood brothers. Time to divide the labour.' He reached inside his pocket and pulled out a bag of stones, each was carved with an odd little symbol. 'Pick a stone, any stone.' Goodfellow shook the bag at them.

Baldr reached in and took a stone. It was painted red and shaped like a heart, there was a crack running down the middle of it and on the other side was a symbol of a river.

'Charlie,' Baldr said. 'I've got Charlie.'

'Oh good, that means I've got Henry, he was always one of my favourites,' Goodfellow smiled.

'And what's he for?' Baldr said, pointing to the giant who was mopping up the remains of three breakfasts. 'What's his job?'

'He's going to keep an eye on you. Keep you safe.'

'Aye, I'm the ...' Polaris paused and let out a burp that shook the glass in the windows. 'I'm the muscle. I'll be keeping a close eye on you, young brother, we're kin now, me and the ...' he paused and turned to Goodfellow. 'I assume I'm to teach him to fight un'all?'

'I can fight,' Baldr said. 'I battled Nevermore the Raven.'

'Aye, and a bloody pig's ear you made of it young'un. You let that thing escape,' he paused and held up his giant hands. 'With these hands, I kill titans. A hundred years ago – which is as good as yesterday to me – I tore Cthulhu to shreds. I'll tell you this for nowt, it doesn't matter how many strange aeons pass, that squidy little bastard won't be rising from his death.'

'Polly got swallowed alive and had to punch his way out of the creatures' gut,' Goodfellow explained, rolling his eyes again.

'Aye, well it worked, didn't it? Fish face is dead, and I took one of his tentacles home with me.'

With that, Polaris looked around the diner, found the waitress, wolf whistled at her, pointed at the empty plates and shouted, 'Ere totty, washing up.' He began to shuffle his way down the bench and escaped the booth with a pop. Standing up, the giant ran his hand through his beard, stretched and turned for the door. He was about to walk away when he remembered something, paused, then turned back to the table to pick up Baldr's uneaten sandwich. Polaris stuffed it into his pocket, then left the diner whistling a jaunty tune.

'He's always in a better mood when his belly is full,' Goodfellow said, as he emptied the stolen wallet on to the table. 'The problem is he's very rarely full.'

Baldr could have told him that this was far too much money but then, didn't the waitress deserve a hefty tip?

The two remaining spirits – or Pookas, in the old tongue – slid from the booth and left Mooney's Diner side by side. They found Polaris standing outside, leaning up against the wall and picking his teeth with the nail of his little finger.

'Aye, that was a good feed Goodfellow,' he said with a satisfied sigh. 'They may all be soft gun-toting nancys around these parts, but they certainly know how to feed a growing man.' He slapped his belly again and nodded at Baldr. 'How come he didn't eat? Is our baby-faced little brother watching his figure?'

'Food isn't quite the same anymore. When you're mortal you experience the food, it's vivid and bright on your tongue even when it tastes like crap. These days it's like I'm eating the concept of food, it's like I'm eating it with my mind.'

'Exactly right,' Goodfellow said. He had pulled out an odd little pocket watch and when he opened it Baldr glimpsed starlight and moonglow. 'You know what it's like to be human and so you discover truths about your new life that the rest of us can't appreciate … explain to this lumbering antiquity what it means to be human!' As he spoke those last few words, Goodfellow's voice was far away. It was as if he was waiting for something.

'It's a head cold and a nose full of dry snot. It's laughing at something when you feel terrible or coming over sad when you feel fine. It's the way the right kind of glance from the right kind of person can destroy you or make your heart skip a beat. It does, you know ... our hearts lose their rhythm ... it's a million little things that are next to nothing when you examine them one by one but together ...' Baldr paused and looked at Polaris, who was staring off into the distance, not paying any attention to him.

'It's a waste of time,' Goodfellow broke in, he was still staring down into his pocket watch. 'He can't understand, blood and death are his, tearing flesh and breaking bones ... he is the thrill of the hunt, the joy of the kill. There is a place for him in this universe ... but there is a need for you, there's a need for empathy and gentle hands. Remember that.'

'She was nice her wasn't she, that young lass in there?' Polaris asked. He slid across the wall and sat down on a windowsill, it bowed under his weight. 'She had a fair face. Too thin mind, I could have got one of me hands around her waist. I like meat on the bone me.'

'Meat and gravy,' Goodfellow laughed.

'It's a shame anyway, it's a shame when the pretty ones die young.'

'Who's dying?' Baldr asked. There was shock in his voice.

'Is thou deaf, did yon trickster not tell ye?' Polaris answered. 'The waitress is going to get run down.'

'That was hypothetical.'

'Oh, little brother,' the giant laughed. 'What spirit is that?' he asked, pointing at Goodfellow.

'Goodfellow,' Baldr answered, 'the master of magic and mischief.'

'Aye, right enough, but magic and mischief are the means to an end. It's fate and freewill he concerns himself with, not hypotheticals. Our friend is a trickster, you should know that by now.'

At that, the waitress stepped out of the diner, a long coat covering her tight uniform. She put a cigarette in her mouth and lit it.

'So, what are we here for then?' Baldr asked. He directed the question to Goodfellow, but it was Polaris who answered.

'Likely, to witness her death, it's the polite thing to do when the flesh folk are due their endings. Maybe he wants you to ease her passing. You're the spirit of mercy, it seems like your job young'un.'

'Can't we stop it? If we know it's going to happen, we could intervene,' Baldr sounded desperate, he glared at Goodfellow who didn't even bat an eyelid.

After what felt like an age, Goodfellow sighed.

'Two things,' he said. 'First, that beast right there doesn't belong in civilised society,' he said pointed at Polaris, 'take him back to the wilderness where he can do no harm. Second, you can twist fate, but you can't cheat death. Death will always take its pound of flesh, only sacrificing another life can undo it.'

It happened then, the waitress stepped out into the road, her phone in one hand, her smoke clutched between the fingers of the other. The taxi came speeding around the corner and slammed on the breaks. There was squealing from the car, smoke, the smell of burning rubber and someone screaming across the street. Then, Goodfellow grinned his puckish smile and jumped out into the road. He placed his hands around the young girl's waist and threw her aside. The taxi hit him head on, and moments later he was a bloody mark at the other end of the street.

'Aye,' Polaris sighed. 'Well, I guess we're done here … shell we make a move young'un?'

'I thought we weren't able to save her?'

'*We* can't save her … but he can. He makes the rules and then finds ways to break them … He'll be days without a body now, and likely there will be some price to pay down the road. But if he can, he does … as long as it doesn't mess with the big picture.'

'So, what do we do now?' Baldr asked.

'Go home and get on with it … or … we could wait for him to get in the flesh again. A few days in a big city … we could kick up our heels, have a little tipple, right some wrongs, crush some skulls?'

'Let's get you back home,' Baldr said with concern. He put his hand on the giant's back and led him down the street. They passed Goodfellow's bloody remains and headed towards the hole in the world that had brought them here.

'Aye, I guess,' Polaris grunted. 'That wolf won't hunt itself, will it?'

.1.

Snowed in

Alison Wheaton sprang bolt upright in bed, gasping for breath, damp with sweat and dizzy with unreality. She had been dreaming of her sickness, and on waking she was convinced that she was still sick now, that the cancer which had taken her right breast was still in there, eating away at her. In her spiral of panic, she could almost feel that merciless enemy within; a poisonous octopus spreading its tentacles throughout her body. For a while, she struggled to catch her rasping breath until at last the wave of panic broke, and she began to take longer, deeper breaths, filling her lungs all the way to the top, before releasing the cold air.

She realised she could smell the room. The lilac, the sage, the pine, and Charlie. Most likely it was the lingering scent of him that calmed her. His skin, his sweat, his aftershave, his soap, and skin moisturiser. All those individual scents mixed together made a heady brew; a smell that held a special significance for her nowadays. As far as Alison was concerned, Charlie smelt like strength and shelter. The smell of him lingered on the pillow next to her. A turn to the left revealed the indent where his head had lain. She reached out to touch it and felt the slightly clammy pillowcase. Charlie was a messy sleeper. Sweaty and drooling, he snored and often tossed and turned. Sometimes he woke her with his snoring, which was often like a pig snorting. All the awkward sleeping habits that had irritated her to begin with didn't

24

bother her anymore. In the early days of her illness, shortly after finding the lump, she had lain awake next to him just to watch his messy sleep.

She picked up Charlie's pillow and pressed it to her face, inhaling that heady brew deep into her lungs, letting it fill her belly and nourish her. Just like that, the panic disappeared. The unreality that came with the dream dissolved and she remembered where, when, and how she was. She wasn't dying. Yes, she had come close to slipping away, but in the end, she had beaten the cancer. Now, six months on, she was fighting fit and stronger with each passing day. She wasn't in hospital either; she was on holiday. Well, not a holiday exactly. It was more a sabbatical. Alison always thought of a holiday as a two-week break from life and the real world. This break had already lasted a lot longer than two weeks and, in the end, maybe they would never go back.

The holiday-cum-sabbatical was a surprise. Charlie had made all the arrangements and had only told Alison after her treatment finished. His agent made them a very kind offer: the use of his log cabin in the picturesque, Icelandic town of Húsavík. He had said to Charlie, 'Take an extended break, give Alison time to recuperate. Spend some time together, just the two of you. Time for you both to reconnect after your trauma, and for you to work on your second novel. Take as long as you like.' Despite hearing the words 'work on your second novel' emphasised in his agent's voice, Charlie jumped at the chance and booked the flights while Alison was having reconstructive surgery. Two weeks later, he carried her through ankle-deep snow towards a lone log cabin perched on a hill and circled by a stone wall. There, they crossed over the threshold and began to live in a snug, 'just the two of them', little world.

Alison swung her legs down from the bed and scrunched her toes in the thick shag of the rug. Her dressing gown was draped across a rocking chair that stood beside their giant bed. She reached for it, and slipped it on over her nightgown, then popped her feet into her slippers that were shaped like bear paws. With Charlie's pillow tucked under her left arm, she crossed the room to the window and wiped the glass with the sleeve of her dressing gown. Outside, she saw Charlie chopping wood in the afternoon sun. He was wearing at least four layers and his coat was so thick that it made him look like the Michelin Man. She watched as he awkwardly brought the axe up, and then down onto the log and wondered if he had ever chopped wood before. She found she couldn't imagine him ever holding an axe at any point in his life. Now she thought about it, a hammer and saw would look equally ridiculous in his smooth hands. Yet there he was, not knowing exactly how it should be done, but giving it his best shot. Strength and shelter. That's what he was to her.

Smiling, she turned from the window to face the full-length mirror opposite the bed. This time last year she had been gravely afraid of mirrors. A mere glimpse of her reflection sent shivers down her spine. Every time she looked she was forced to notice how death was becoming her. It was there in the hollows of her eyes, her sunken cheeks, and the frailty of her body. Now, death was in full retreat and catching sight of her reflection had become something pleasurable, almost arousing. Day by day her face was a little fuller, her body a little stronger, and seeing that healthy progression always lit the fire burning inside her. Nowadays all she really wanted to do was fuck. Fucking was the definition of life. She never felt as alive as she did when her man was hot and throbbing inside her. She couldn't get enough of it. Alison had always had a healthy sexual appetite, but now sex had become an all you can eat buffet. And to save time she'd just pulled her chair right up to the hotplate.

Standing in front of the mirror she dropped the pillow, slid out of her dressing gown, then pulled her nightie up and over her head. Standing naked, but for her white cotton panties and bear paw slippers, she set about the daily examination of her body. She noticed that the skin at her hips was still a little loose. During her illness, the weight loss had been drastic and since then she had come to terms with the idea of living with a bit of loose skin here and there. Her chestnut hair was reaching down towards her shoulders and soon she would be able to tie it back. She couldn't wait for that day. She noticed the dimples had returned to her cheeks, and that cheered her greatly. From there, her eyes fell to her mismatched breasts. Her right, a reconstructed teardrop, its nipple tattooed in place. Her left, bigger, sagging slightly, and far more sensitive. The surgeon who had reconstructed her right breast had naturally offered to make the left match, but Alison had refused. By that point, she was sick of medicine, surgery, and recovery. She wanted her left breast to remain the way it was. She wanted it to be hers, sensitive to the touch and slightly sagging, the way it was meant to be.

Downstairs the door opened and slammed shut. Then, very faintly, she heard the sound of Charlie's panting reach her in the bedroom. She guessed that he must have chopped enough firewood, or at least grown sick of swinging the axe. She put the dressing gown back on and left the bedroom. Crossing the landing, she saw a vase of dried lilac that stood on the small windowsill and stopped to smell them. The purple blooms had a fragrant, sweet, floral scent, without being sickly or cloying. She remembered how they always used lilac air freshener in the hospital. However, it didn't smell like this. The air freshener had an artificial aroma and smelt of chemicals, barely masking the stench of death. The lilacs in the vase reminded Alison of the handsome male nurse who worked the night shifts. She recalled that he had a kind face and that he always managed to put her at ease.

Standing on the landing, she slowly drifted off into her own little world. The dream came back to her then. The hospital bed, her cancer in full bloom, the smell of lilacs, chemicals, and bleach, and under that someone's loose bowels, maybe hers? Was she lying there in her own shit? Could she remember that? Was the dream that vivid? Then a pair of blue eyes pierced through the darkness and decay. Big, blue, kind eyes and soft hands holding hers; a gentle voice telling her that everything was going to be okay, that the pain would go away, that it was a useless figment of her imagination and would blow away on the breeze of her breath.

Then there was a stag by her sickbed. A stag as white as the newly fallen snow, with antlers that looked like embracing arms, and she was being lifted onto its back. She, who was nothing more than skin, bones, a sunken face, and a nightie drenched in sweat. She, who weighed about the same as a broken promise or a wasted breath, was lifted and placed gently onto the stag's back.

'Hold on tight. Hold on as if your very life depends on it,' the calming voice whispered … and then … and then … then she had awoken in a state of panic and unreality. Coming back to herself from the dream she saw a dried purple blossom in the palm of her hand. She crushed it with a tight fist and blew it away. Turning away from the vase, she raced down the stairs to find Charlie.

He wasn't hard to find. Charlie was kneeling in front of the fire struggling with the logs, kindling, and a box of matches. He had removed his outdoor clothes and had discarded them in a heap at the edge of the shag rug. She watched as he held match after match to the kindling, each one flickering out, unable to light the fire.

'Light, you bastard,' he mumbled. The curse was like a talisman anointing the last match in the box, which, when held against the kindling, managed to finally light the fire. The flames took hold and before long Alison could see them reflecting off Charlie's bald head. 'Fucking Iceland,' he mumbled to himself as he hunched over the fire, warming his hands and face. 'It had to be Iceland, didn't it? Not the Umbrian valley in Italy or Reims in France. Fucking Iceland.'

Alison was by his side, leaning towards him to put her hands on his shoulders. Startled by her touch, he fell backwards onto the shag rug, where he lay like an upturned turtle. When she looked down at him, she couldn't see his head. He had fallen on the rug directly between her legs, meaning that he was presented with a prime view of her white, cotton panties. This gave her an idea. She untied her dressing gown and threw it to one side where it landed on top of Charlie's outdoor clothes. Then, she hitched her thumbs under the waistband of her panties and slowly pulled them off.

2

Wallflower

Three … there were three incidents, three flukes, three tiny little chances that finally brought her to her senses. The first happened a year ago when a complete stranger walked up to her and grabbed her by the wrist. He didn't pull her or squeeze, he just held her first in his hand, then in his eyes. He had kind and mischievous eyes and odd little pointy ears.

'It doesn't have to be this way,' he said and held his hand to her face where she had concealed the bruise. 'Once upon a time there was a bear in Starkey's woods … but no, that's no good, that won't do.' He seemed to be having a conversation with himself until his eyes lit up as though he'd finally thought of the right thing. 'Don't worry about the bear … instead, watch for "The Karaoke Glow".' He looked supremely pleased with himself as if he had achieved some great feat, and then promptly he turned and walked away into the crowd. He was gone in seconds and she found herself wondering … *Could he be one of those … no, that would be silly.*

I guess you look alright for a ginge. As Jessica sat applying fresh concealer to an entirely new black eye, those words recalled themselves from the depths of her memory. They had been amongst the first words he had spoken to her in that crowded club. He had found her in a corner, nursing a pink gin and lemonade while her friends tore up the dancefloor, doing that silly, jiggly bum dance at all the passing boys. Twerking they called it, twerking for the jerks with their collars turned up, who reeked of weed and Paco Rabanne. No, she wasn't that kind of girl. She was much happier in the corner.

Rather than swaggering over to the dance floor to press his groin up to one of her friends' vibrating arses, he came to her and struck up a conversation, introducing himself as Kelvin. He was older than her and maybe just a little rough around the edges, but he seemed fun. And then he came out with that line, 'I guess you look alright for a ginge.' Quite obviously, it was a back-handed compliment, something nasty disguised as something nice, a device to make her work for his attention. She was far too smart to fall for that but ... there was no one else talking to her.

She wasn't ugly, far from it. She had flawless, ivory skin, strawberry blonde hair and dark eyes. She guessed she was a little tall compared to other girls, and she was awfully awkward and clumsy, but she wasn't ugly. Yes, she considered her friends to be prettier than her, not to mention more vivacious, and obviously they were far more fun than she was. But she wasn't ugly, she could look in the mirror and see someone beautiful looking back ... some days, other days she only saw her flaws, magnified by her inability to keep a man on the hook for longer than a few months. She couldn't understand why they left. Back when she met Kelvin, she had only been eighteen, but some of her friends had had boyfriends since the age of fourteen. Because of this, some days she looked in the mirror and felt ugly.

The night Kelvin found her in that club she was a bright yet shy young woman studying to be an accountant at university. More or less, she had her head screwed on. From time to time she was lonely and somewhat tired of watching her friends cop off on the dance floor while she sat in her corner with her pink gin and lemonade. Just because she didn't like dancing didn't mean she didn't like copping off. So, when he told her she didn't look bad for a ginge, she replied with:

'Yeah, and I guess you look okay for a pensioner.'

Now that her latest black eye was well and truly covered, she packed up a few belongings, a couple of changes of clothes, and of course 'the book', and then she left. He was due home in a couple of hours, but he might not come back for another day. Either way, she wanted to be gone before he got back.

He had only gotten worse since he started to take that new drug, those little vials of brightly coloured liquids had changed him for the worse, and she hadn't thought that was possible. She knew where she was with him when he was smoking weed, she could handle him jabbering bullshit when he was on coke, she could even deal with the odd angry belt when he'd been on the whiskey. But she lived in constant fear ever since he started taking the new thing. When he drank those vials, it was like someone had connected him to the power line, and that was okay as long as he was riding the high and happy. When it wore off, he was lifeless then angry, bitter, and violent. Even more worrying was the fact that he was trying to get her into it too. He kept describing how it felt when the red and the green ran through his veins. He kept telling her he'd take her to the Midway and introduce her to the Lotus King, and that worried her.

She had quite rightly deduced that he had exhausted his line of credit with the dealer, the Lotus King, and now he was hoping to use her for more. She would be his new line of credit, he would get her hooked and then glom from her supply. And what next? Would he turn her out? Would he drop her off on some street corner and make her turn tricks to pay for their habit? Of course he would, he was just that kind of guy ... or at least he was now. Once upon a time he was the guy who treated his girlfriend like a combination of a maid, a personal assistant, and a sex slave, and that was bad enough, that was a level of disregard she had grown accustomed to and had begrudgingly learned to accept. Now, he was the guy quite willing to drag his girlfriend down with him, to get her hooked on his new drug, and then more than likely have her to turning tricks to pay his way. This was worse, and the ounce of pride that she had left made her stomach turn at the thought of it

Outside of Kelvin's dirty flat, the taxi was waiting for her. She climbed inside with her one bag and told the man with bloodshot eyes to take her home to Oakenbrook. Home to the father who barely looked over his newspaper and the mother who always looked down her nose at her. Home to the big house where she would follow in her mother's wake, dutifully repeating 'yes, Mother'. Home where the family motto was: *sic ego dixi vobis*, or for the layman: 'I told you so'. Home, to learn how to 'do lunch' and socialise with the right set, to find the right kind of husband and never use her degree in any practical sense. As they pulled away from the curb, she sighed at the thought of how much humble pie she would have to eat, it wouldn't be just a slice this time. There would be pie for days.

Kelvin hadn't always been like this. That is to say, in the beginning, she hadn't known him well enough to know he had always been like this. A little dig here, a sly remark there, she had thought it was banter, like pulling a girl's hair in the playground then running away because it's too scary to say, 'I like you', or because the other boys will laugh if they hear it. Maybe with someone else it would have been banter, but not with Kelvin, with him it was like the constant lapping of waves that over time shapes an outcrop of rock. He didn't believe that he could do better than Jessica, but he needed her to believe that he could.

What started with 'you don't look bad for a ginge', grew over time until the backhanded compliments weren't compliments, and the veiled insults were just insults.

'Your arse looks like it's getting fat, you should do something about that. It'll go all saggy and then where will you be?'

'You know your tits are too small for your height, if they were bigger, you'd look like a proper woman.'

'Did you not have time to do your make up this morning, you look fucking awful?'

And the subtext to all of this was, 'it's a good job you've got me, it's a good job I've settled for you, it's a good job I love you.'

In the very, very beginning, he had been sweet. In the very, very beginning, he had cracked jokes and been interested in her stories. In the very, very beginning, he had expressed regret for an ex-girlfriend who had sadly passed away. He admitted that he hadn't been the best of boyfriends but he put that down to being young and stupid and said he'd promised himself not to let love slip through his fingers again. This was what got Jessica, he got her hook line and sinker with that little line. It hinted at a soft heart, kept hidden, deep down, and she was excited to uncover it. And of course, there was no one else chatting her up.

As the taxi drove down through Coventry city centre and turned onto the Roman road, they passed Ingle Nook coffee shop and Jessica thought of the second fluke. It came three months after the first; she was sitting in front of the telly flicking through the channels when she came across a documentary called 'The Girlfriend Experience'. The documentary was about a local artist, called Hank, and his wife Becky. Becky had been a high-class call girl and Hank was her last client. The couple gave a very honest, touching, and eloquent account of their lives and what led them to fall for each other. At the beginning, Becky talked about how every time Hank's name was in the paper, they mentioned her past. They kept trying to use it to humiliate him, so they had decided to tell their own story. They talked about their respective difficult childhoods and disastrous love lives, but what really caught hold of Jessica was when Hank looked into the camera and talked about low expectations. He said:

'Woman and men end up in mentally abusive relationships because they're taught to have low expectations. Things happen in their lives, it could be a series of small things or, you know, big stuff ... but either

way, you learn that you're worth less than other people and so you expect less from them. It's okay when your friends take you for granted and it's okay when your lover treats you like shit because you're not equal to them. You believe that their time is worth more than yours, so you accept being at the bottom of their list of priorities. Once you accept being at the bottom of the list, then you'll accept the abuse. You might give as good as you get to begin with but that peters out, and then you just take the constant jibes because they confirm the worst things you believe about yourself. And the point of it all is to make you work for their approval, make you grateful for their attention. I imagine it's the same with physical abuse, I imagine a smack in the eye is ...'

The taxi pulled up outside her parents' home and after paying the fare Jessica tip-toed down the gravel drive. They would be in bed, of course, and if she disturbed them now, she'd have to sit through a midnight rundown of all her flaws and failings, and the prospect of that turned her stomach. She could almost hear her mother's voice telling her 'Don't slouch when I'm talking to you dear, it makes you look so knobbly and crooked. Better you should look gangly than knobbly and crooked.'

Using her key, she let herself in through the large double doors at the front of the mini-mansion and put the code into the security alarm. She took off her shoes and walked barefoot across the marble hallway and up the curved staircase. She crossed the landing to find her old bedroom, full of boxes. They were stacked three high and covering almost every inch of floor and she had to swerve between them to collapse on her old bed.

She lay staring at the ceiling and took a brief audit of her life. She was twenty and back home after two-and-a-half years of abuse at Kelvin's hands. Now that she thought about it, wasn't there a line she could draw from her parents' … well, not abuse exactly … but it had been under this roof that she had grown into a wallflower, the shy girl in the corner of the room who nursed her pink gin while her friends had fun with boys. It had been the disinterest of her father and the criticism of her mother that had laid the way for Kelvin.

The third little fluke was the book. It had happened six months after the documentary, she was killing time in town not wanting to go back and find Kelvin passed out on the sofa, or worse still turning the place upside down to find something to sell. She was in the Lower Precinct when she saw him, that odd fellow with the mischievous eyes and the pointy ears. He was standing by the fountain and he waved to her, then turned and walked away through the crowd. She followed him into an old bookshop and found him at the end of an aisle, writing in a book. She was just about to approach when he held up his hand to stop her. He closed the book, put it back on the shelf, and then winked at her before disappearing around the corner into the biography section.

She rushed to pick up the book before anyone else could. When she opened it, she found fifteen pounds had been hidden inside the cover just below the strange man's inscription. It was a simple little note that read: *To the wallflower. All my best Goodfellow.* He had underlined his name with a swipe of his pen that transformed into an arrow. She turned the page to find another arrow scrawled across the publishing information. She turned that page and found the dedication page, with another arrow pointing to the scant text. It read: *To Hank & Becky, To Jude & Sophie. To the low & broken hearted. It doesn't have to be this way*. She pocketed the money and used it to buy the book.

Back at the flat she shared with Kelvin she knew enough to hide it away, only getting it out when he wasn't around. She read it here and there whenever he was sleeping off a binge or out scoring. It was the story of a man whose wife who was intent on destroying him inch by inch, and how that man was saved by the unfulfilled and mostly unspoken love between himself and another woman.

Jessica – lying on her old bed in her parents' home – reached inside the carrier bag by her side and rummaged through her clothes to find the book. She held it up and read the title: 'The Karaoke Glow'. Opening it, she found the photo of herself that she had blue-tacked to the dedication page. It was a photo of her, standing tall and proud outside of Coventry Cathedral in her cap and gown, holding her degree across her heart. There were other pictures taken that day, of course. Pictures of her standing with her dull-eyed father on her left and her mother, with that sour pout, on her right, but those pictures had never meant as much to her. Those pictures didn't belong in her book.

She closed the book, and then her eyes, and in the dark she thought about that day, about how proud she had been of herself.

Before drifting away into sleep, she promised herself that she wouldn't be here any longer than she had to be.

'It doesn't have to be this way,' she told herself.

3

The Aurora Borealis

The afternoon rolled into the evening, and Alison and Charlie were still lying naked on the deep, shag carpet in front of the roaring fire. She lay with her head in the crook of his arm, staring directly up at the sky, to the northern lights that swirled above their heads. She watched the greens flow into reds, then the blues into purples. It was a hypnotic display that made Alison feel like she was at the bottom of the ocean, like a fish lying on the seabed, staring up at a strange and unimaginable world. As she gazed up at the ocean sky, she found herself idly wondering how many nights they had spent like this. Almost all of them, but over how long? Six months … nine? She thought it was closer to the full twelve. Now that her life could be measured in years rather than days, time didn't seem to matter as much. On her sickbed, every passing second had been painful, both emotionally and physically, but it had been precious too. She had trained herself to cherish her agony and every moment that she was able to spend in the company of her loved ones. Now, of course, there was so much time and so little pain and heartache, that she found she was able to lie on a rug, stare at the ocean sky and just let it slip through her fingers.

She placed her hand on Charlie's chest and felt his hairless, smooth skin, then traced her fingers up to the base of his Adam's apple where she found his strange birthmark once more. To him, it was an odd mark, a patch of discoloured skin, but she saw something in it. It was a Rorschach test, an inkblot that resembled a comet or shooting star falling across his neck. Lying next to him beside the fire, she found her mind racing back to the night they met. Specifically, the first time that she had seen his birthmark peering out from beneath the buttoned collar of his checked flannel shirt.

She had met him at an open mic night. He was reading a short story from his collection and she was struck instantly by him. Not by his beauty, but rather by the strangeness of him. He was a tall man with gangly limbs, pale skin, and short ginger hair that was thinning at the temples. When she approached him after his reading, he had to bend down to talk to her. She watched him lean forward and saw the mark disappear beneath the collar that was riding up against his neck. On impulse, she reached up and unbuttoned the top of his shirt to get a better look at it. Her initial thought was that he was indeed a strange man; gangly, ginger and pale to the point of being translucent, and as if that wasn't enough, here was this unusual birthmark.

Born with a star on his throat and, by some strange coincidence, he grew into a man who had a way with words. It had been his way with words that had attracted her to him as opposed to any of his physical attributes. Charlie was far too odd-looking to be considered handsome in the traditional sense, but his words and stories contained some kind of unquantifiable beauty. At first, Alison saw that beauty in his words, then soon after she found it in his warmth, generosity, and humour. Shortly after their first chance meeting they began dating and then dating quickly snowballed into a love affair.

Before long, she was unable to look at Charlie, of whom she had often joked was Jim Henson's idea of what a man should look like, without seeing someone beautiful.

Meanwhile, the light show was still swirling above Alison's head and now her belly was rumbling with hunger, yet still, the greater need was to lie in the arms of her muppet man and just be. She moved her head onto his chest and listened to the sound of his heart beating and his slightly nasal breathing. After a moment or two, she heard his piggy snort as he woke himself from the lightest of sleeps. She laughed as he made a startled sound, and then she kissed his chest, just below his right nipple.

'Sorry,' Charlie said half-asleep, in a groggy voice. 'I must have nodded off for a moment.'

'It's okay, go back to sleep.'

'No, I don't want to sleep.'

'Oh,' her voice became light-hearted and salacious. 'So, do you want to go again then?'

'Maybe in a bit.'

She watched as he closed his eyes and a placid expression spread across his face. Slowly and lightly, she traced her fingers up and down his body in a figure of eight and watched as his expressionless face dissolved into a smile. She leant forward and cast her eyes downward towards his lazy, sleeping cock, kissing a few inches above his belly button. She continued to move upwards, and when she reached his nipple, she teased it with the tip of her tongue. Glancing down again she saw his flaccid cock twitch slightly.

'I don't know what's got into you these days,' Charlie said, his eyes still closed. 'Not that I mind, but you're insatiable.'

'Well,' she began, as she ran her hand down his body to fully wake that sleeping part of him. 'You have to enjoy life while you still can.' With her hand wrapped around him, she kissed him on the mouth. It was a light peck which was followed by a second and third. At long last, she teased his mouth open with her tongue and felt the effects of her kiss as he twitched in her hand. She responded by tightening her grip on that most vital part of him.

'You're right,' he said, his voice trembling slightly now, 'we should enjoy life while we can, but do you think we could wait half an hour before we start enjoying life again? Because right now I don't think I have enough energy to enjoy it properly.'

'Okay,' Alison laughed. At that, she loosened her grip, but she didn't let go altogether. 'You have exactly half an hour.' She watched him close his eyes and then she turned her gaze back to the skylight and the view of the coloured, swirling lights. She felt a question bubbling up inside her and before she knew if it was a good idea to ask it, it had already slipped out of her mouth. 'Are you happy?' she asked.

'Of course,' came the answer. He said it quickly as if to prove that he didn't even need to think about it. She accepted his answer, but hot on the heels of her first unintended question came a second, deeper, more probing one.

'Has it all been worth it?' Alison asked. 'All the pain and heartache that we went through … you know, with my sickness. Was it worth it

45

in the end or was it too much?' With her free hand, the one that was not clutching his manhood, she pushed herself up off his chest and stared down at his bald head.

Charlie didn't answer her right away. In his usual manner, he considered the question and then opened his big, sad, dark eyes and fixed them on her. That bittersweet look was on his face again. He had often worn this very expression whilst attending her sickbed. During her clearer moments, she had understood this as the sweet agony that came from spending time with a loved one whose days were numbered. The agony of knowing that someday soon the suffering would end, and the guilt of hoping it never would. She wondered what this look of his meant now that her cancer was gone.

'I don't understand and probably never will,' Charlie began, every word he spoke was slow and measured. Alison suspected that this was an attempt to keep himself from breaking while answering her. 'How come I get to be here with you? Me, of all people. Me, the spindly, pale, ginger man.' Alison tried to interrupt him with some manner of kindness, but he put his finger to her mouth so that he could finish his answer. 'When we got together Hank asked me, "what is that vision of loveliness doing with you?", and I never knew how to answer him. I just laughed it off. I told him, and anyone else who asked, that "young naïve girls chase pretty boys, but they soon learn what pretty boys are worth: absolutely nothing." Anyone who believes that they can take a woman's affections for granted isn't worth a woman's affections. People used to say "gay" was a phase but that's bullshit. "Handsome" is a phase. The minute women learn that, they stop chasing pretty and start looking for other things.'

'And what are these other things?' she asked, knowing that the punchline was coming.

'One, someone they can talk to. Two, someone who'll do the hoovering, and three, someone who doesn't complain about eating pussy.'

At that, Alison burst into raucous, hysterical laughter. Tears rolled down her face and she was unable to catch her breath for a moment or two.

'As if,' she answered through her giggles, 'as if I could ever get you to do the hoovering.' Charlie smiled, and his smile became a laugh that was the distant echo of hers. When the laughter died, she asked, 'So is that what you really believe then?'

'I don't know if I believe it or not, but I couldn't come up with a better answer. I still don't know why it's me here by your side now, but rest assured I'm grateful it is. So yes, it's been worth it. It's been the greatest privilege of my entire life to be by your side and there's no amount of pain or misfortune that could ever change that,' he paused. The next thought was like a gem he was trying to polish, trying to get it to its best, sparkling and most perfect form. 'I'll never understand why I'm here by your side, but there's nowhere else in the world I'd rather be.'

Outside, something was howling. Maybe it was the wind. It sounded quiet and far away, a sound Alison noticed but didn't pay much attention to anymore. When she first came to Húsavík and the cabin on the edge of the woods, she was struck by the place. It had a wild, beautiful, and almost magical feel to it. The winds were bitter and harsh, and in the first few days they had filled her head with ideas. It was as if the wind was a voice that confirmed all the stories she had been told about the frozen North. Her father's stories had been light, comforting, and warm. He had told tales of the plump, cheerful man in the red suit, the man with the bottomless sack of gifts who lived in the snow with the elves and the reindeer. Charlie's stories, however, had been a much darker affair. Full of blood and death and merciless old gods, his stories had thrilled her, yet at the same time left her feeling somewhat cold.

Now, as the wind blew somewhere distant over the hills, Alison wondered in the back of her mind if maybe it was all true? Maybe, somewhere out there, Santa had his workshop. Maybe the All-Father was hanging from a tree. Maybe Thor was hitting his hammer in the storm whilst Loki set about bringing chaos to the world. Certainly, back home in Coventry, there were strange tales. Stories of secret places and impish pagan spirits. They called them Pookas back home … but … well, she hadn't really believed, she liked the stories – particularly the one about the dream weaver and his giant turtle Nix – but she didn't really believe.

In the beginning, the thoughts and images conjured up by the savage Húsavík wind had been great, vivid, and exciting. The possibility of magic outside in the snow-covered world had, for a time, haunted her dreams. She had often dreamt of the stag and a painfully handsome man who sometimes came to tell her stories. But time had weakened those powerful dreams to passing thoughts. Now these ideas were like the background noises within a house, the sounds you learn, first to live with, and then ignore. A ticking clock, a creaking floorboard, or a squeaky door hinge. In short, she had acclimatised herself to the wind outside – and, more to the point, the peculiar thoughts that the wind provoked – and familiarity had robbed those thoughts of their power.

'The thing is,' she said, 'your joke is more or less right.' She ran her thumb up the length of his shaft and gently drew back his foreskin. Smiling, she slowly began to stroke his ego in every sense of the word. 'Hank and your friends might not have understood why we got together.'

'Well, Hank was just busting my balls. That's how you communicate as men, the more you like each other the more time you spend trying to find new ways to take the piss out of each other.'

'Yes, fine,' Alison said, rolling her eyes, 'but can you not interrupt when I'm trying to romance you?' she looked pointedly down to direct Charlie's glance to what she was doing with her hand. The look on her face said, *Really, you're going to bring up Hank now?* 'I was going to say; your friends might not understand why we got together but mine do. Within the first month, they were all like, "yeah, I get it now!"'

'Get what?' he asked. Alison thought it a redundant question, nothing more than him urging her on. He liked having his ego stroked.

'Why we got together. They saw what I saw,' she paused and glanced down at her hand again, this time to adjust her stroke; slightly faster, slightly firmer. 'Talent of course. Charm and wit. You always appear confident but there's that vulnerable edge that shines through. But it's more than all that. It's the way you treat people. You always have time for them, you listen. And by that, I mean that you don't just nod your head and wait for your turn to talk, you really listen and that's rare. Well … maybe not rare, but most guys who listen are a bit … soft. You're a nice guy but you know where to draw the line. You don't let people take advantage of you and you're more than happy to put your foot down if you have to.'

While she talked, he slowly began to stiffen in her hand, and now the anticipation of what was about to happen, for the second time that night, made her tingle in that old, familiar way. Her hand moved faster, a natural response to her own arousal. She wanted him to break on her like a crashing wave, to roll over from his afterglow and take her. Ravish her again, and again, and again. To satisfy her true desire …to fill that empty space inside her with a child. Yes, now that she thought about it, wasn't that the reason her sex drive had gone through the roof? Coming back to life from the verge of death, she had craved the thrill of having life growing inside her, without recognising that craving for what it was.

'And, of course, I told them all about the sex,' she said provocatively. 'I told them about how hot you get me. I'm surprised you didn't notice one or two of them making eyes at you. I told them all about that little flick you do with your tongue and …'

He fell on top of her then, covering her mouth with a deep kiss and cupping her right breast firmly in his hand. At his touch, she felt another question burning up inside her. She wondered if it felt like a real breast to him, or if it felt different after the reconstructive surgery? Knowing that this question was the ultimate mood killer, she swallowed it before it could escape her. She stopped thinking and gave into his firm hands, probing fingers, and that little flick of the tongue that he had perfected. At last, the moment came, and he paused above her, ready, looking down into her eyes for permission.

'Let's make a baby,' she said. For the briefest of moments, a matter of seconds, she thought she saw something that resembled sadness in him, but it vanished when he entered her.

4

The Kite

In his dreams, he sees his mother's face. Once upon a time she was his world. His father had disappeared before he was born, but for all his money that was no great loss. There was talk about how the missing father used to knock his mother around, and maybe that's why she did so well out of the divorce. The out of court settlement – big enough to choke an elephant – was conditional on her silence. There was other talk, talk about how his father was some other man; the gardener, or the guy who decorated the en-suite bathroom, and if that was true then no matter. All it meant was that his father was some different man who wasn't around. If it was true, he didn't think any less of her, she had been his world, once upon a time.

In the dream he is fourteen, they're at the beach, and he is already as tall as her. She jokes and calls him her beanstalk while standing on her tiptoes to ruffle his hair. She also calls him lucky because of the shooting star birthmark on his throat. He is flying a kite while she sits on a blanket reading. He watches as a man approaches her and kneels down by her side. His mum is a looker and quite often men chat her up while they're out. He knows she dates, sometimes the neighbours watch him while she has an all-night date, and he's old enough to know she's having sex. He's asked why she doesn't have a boyfriend and she says that although she likes male company from time to time, she has no inclination to lumber him with a stepdad.

After a moment or two the man kneeling by her side shrugs and walks away.

She winks at him in that way that says 'you're the only man for me, you're my whole world'. This is the last moment, the very last blissful moment with his mum. All the rest is routine, the day to day stuff that eats up time.

His dream jumps forward six months and now he watches from the window as she climbs into her car to pop to the shops for some odds and ends. She never comes home. Instead, there's a knock at the door and he opens it to find two solemn-faced police officers who break the bad news. She is gone, killed by a lorry driver who failed to stop at a crossing. He does not know, will never know, but she dies with his name on her lips. Lucy Dunn, she of the golden hair and the bright red lipstick. She who taught him to love books rather than just reading to pass his English exams. She who taught him how to talk to girls, and to remember that as long as you had respect for your partner then sex was fun and nothing to be ashamed of. She who said, 'as long as you don't lie, cheat, manipulate, or abuse it doesn't matter what you do'. She's gone and now he is alone.

Almost alone. His grandparents had passed in quick succession when he was eight, and there were no aunts or uncles, but there is a godmother. Her name is Mary Ann Walker and she is his mum's best friend from back home. He had met her a handful of times, she's a small friendly woman with a giant husband and a timid, chubby boy for a son. For all intents and purposes, they are strangers, and now here he was unpacking a tenth of his belongings into their tiny spare room. Mary Ann keeps looking at him with those big, sad eyes. She only comes up to his chest, so she strains her neck to look up at him. Her giant husband Tommy treats him well enough, but he insists on calling him Charles and talks to him like he's an adult friend from work. There is the chubby shy boy of course, Hank, and it turns out they're the same age, but Hank is terrible company. He hardly ever looks over the horizon of his sketch pad and when he does, he mumbles.

He is miserable. Often, he cries because he misses his mum, sometimes he cries at the thought of being stuck in this house with these people or having to go to the local comprehensive school at the end of the summer where the kids are all rough and speak with a funny accent. Worse than all of that; he has been dropped into the middle of family tensions. From the very first moment he arrives he notices an atmosphere between Tommy and his son Hank. Tommy very rarely says anything nice or supportive to his son, he only ever grunts at Hank's art, which is always excellent and well worth the praise. Is this how fathers act? Never having had one he doesn't know, but he suspects not. But what right does he have to criticise the big man's parenting? Tommy went out to work every day and came home every night. His own father – the rich banker, or maybe the white-van-man – had never even shown his face.

Often, he walks in the countryside. He has walked the length and breadth of Castlegate trying to escape his grief but the memory of his mum's face – fading as it is – is never that far behind him. It is the height of summer and Hank has gone off with some sour-faced girl.

Hank doesn't seem to have proper friends, just fellow outcasts to kill time with. He suspects that when he starts this new school in September, he will know all the outcasts well.

Somewhere between Castlegate and Pickford he sits down by the side of the stream and, with his head resting on his knees, he watches the water pass by. From the distance there are voices, they are laughing and gleefully shouting 'fuck!' and 'shit!' after every other word. He sees three teenage boys approaching, two small ones and a larger one with a bulldoggish face.

'That's him, Donnie,' one of the smaller ones says.

'Here mate!' the bulldog-faced Donnie shouts. Before he knows what's happening, they are circling. 'Numb nuts here says you talk all posh like …'

'Well, I have a different accent if that's what you mean?' As soon as he says it, he knows it's a mistake. They circle tighter around him and howl in exaggerated, feminine voices.

'Oh … he has a *different accent.*'

'Another little ginger royal with a plum in his mouth. Another Prince Harry.'

'Do you think you're better than us Prince Harry?'

'Well, I don't know you,' he says, angrily. 'But if I had to take a wild guess, I'd say …'

There is a thwacking sound as Donnie punches him square in the back of the head. He is dizzy and reeling and the boys are laughing, calling him a faggot, a freak, a lanky streak of piss. He tries to pull himself up and falls flat on his face, then rolls down the bank into the

Pickford stream. He opens his mouth and gulps down three mouthfuls of the water. Suddenly there are other voices, louder, deeper, manly voices.

'Ah … get off me!' Donnie is screaming. 'I'll tell me dad!'

He stands up in the stream, the water flowing around his feet and, glancing up the embankment, he sees a quartet of old men. The two at the back look as old as the hills, a tall one stands hunched over his walking stick. Beside him there's a much smaller man with a large gnomish face and big floppy sun hat. In front of the two elderly men there was a blond hippy, whose ponytail was trailing halfway down his back. He had a beard that almost matched. In front of the hippy was Big Tommy. It is only now seeing Tommy in this odd company that he realises just how young Tommy is. Thirty-five maybe, and if that was accurate then there were twenty years between himself and Tommy, another twenty between Tommy and the hippy, and yet another twenty between the hippy and the elderly gentleman at the back.

'That's right,' Tommy says, 'go tell your dad, send him after me. He had no reach when he was eighteen, we used to call Picasso on account of all the time he spent on the canvas … and cos we knocked his face jagged.'

In this dream of way back when, Charlie remembers pausing and taking the whole scene in. Big Tommy had hold of Donnie by the wrists and now he was lifting him up so that he was forced to tiptoe. The other two boys have run away. Around Tommy's feet, there are two bags of compost.

'Now, you wanna tell me what you're doing?' he asks, 'almost eighteen, practically an adult and still marching up and down this village picking on kids younger than you?'

'He cheeked us, he said he was better than us.'

'He is better than you,' Tommy says. 'That lad has suffered through losing his old dear and you don't see him turn to thuggery. Besides … I was down the road, I saw what happened. You started in on him and instead of sitting there and taking it, he said something back. Good for him.'

'Fine,' Donnie says, looking sullen. 'Let me go.'

'When are you gonna grow out of this shit Donnie?' Tommy sounds tired. 'This is exactly why you got kicked out of the boxing club. I train proud, young, disciplined fighters … I don't teach people how to be better bullies. I had this exact conversation with your brother and look at him now. I mean … do all of you Dorley boys want to grow up to be your father?'

'There's nothing wrong with my old man!' Donnie yells.

As Charlie watches, the hippy walks down the embankment and offers him a hand. He's pulled up to the path where, without saying a word to him, the hippy examines the sore spot at the back of his head.

'There's nothing right with your old man Donnie. He's a lot like my father, the two of them are cut from the same piece of cloth, neither one of them worth their weight in shit and piss.'

'You can't talk that way about my old man. And you can't make me leave that ginger kid alone.'

The hippy is rubbing some sort of ointment into the back of Charlie's head. The pain doesn't seem so bad now, he looks up and sees Donnie thrashing around trying to escape Tommy's grip.

'You're awfully brave today Donald,' the hippy says, his voice is rich and soft, and unlike the flat Coventry drawl that is common around these parts. 'The last time I saw you, young man, you were what ... ten years old? You come darting into the garden centre, screaming and crying. You kept saying the bear was after you ... the bear in Starkey's woods. Said it was as big as a house and had claws like daggers. I had to give you a hot chocolate and ...'

'Shut up!' Donnie screamed.

'Well, maybe I don't need to tell the rest of that story ... just as long as you're on your way, and you don't bother this lad again.'

'Fine.' Donnie grunts and, finally free from Tommy's grip, he turns and marches away. As Charlie watches the boy with the bulldog face grow distant, he knows this isn't over, he knows he will have to pay one day. But now, the hippy is patting him on the back and Tommy is laughing. The older men at the back tut and chunter, and the taller one with the walking stick grunts about having to give Donnie's grandfather a clip round the ear and quite a few nights in the drunk tank.

'You can tell you're not from round these parts young man,' the hippy says, as he puts the ointment back in his pocket. 'No one from Castlegate would risk getting the Pickford waters in their mouth. They think it's cursed you see ... they think it comes from the spirit world. They say drinking the water is as good as inviting Puck into your life.'

'What spirit world?' he asks.

'Now, don't go filling his head with that nonsense Solomon,' Tommy says and heaves the compost back onto his shoulder. 'He's got enough to contend with, he doesn't need your nonsense on top of everything else … come on Charles, let's get you home so my wife can fuss over you and fill your belly with her terrible cooking.'

He runs to catch up. From behind him, the hippy and the old men are all shouting after Tommy. The little one in the sunhat is telling him there's a lovely basket of vegetables waiting for him. The tall one with the walking stick is asking him to drop the compost off in his greenhouse, the hippy is asking him if he'll be in the Tiger's Head later.

'Ah, I'd best come for a pint,' he shouts back. 'No doubt Picasso will be in there making me out to be a child beater. Don't want the gossips to get hold of that one, hey.'

Charlie is jogging now to catch up with Tommy. The big man's strides are twice as wide as his own and he walks at a great pace.

Tommy is silent for a while before, turning to Charlie and saying, 'You're not like Clive at all, are you?'

'Clive Morton?' he asks. 'My father? I don't know Mr Walker, I've never met him.'

'Well, that's for the best Charles. He wasn't worth much.'

'Did you know him Mr Walker?'

'My little lady says I shouldn't tell ya.' Tommy stops, drops the compost, and sits on the path. 'I think you should know. But … it's a shitty story, so it's your choice.'

'Tell me.' Charlie says, without missing a beat.

'He was a real piece of shit. When your mum married him, we saw him half a dozen times, and that was five too many. He was the kind of man who judged your value by your bank balance and so a poor working stiff like me always came up short. All he talked about was bonuses, this new car, and that holiday ... meanwhile there's me and the wife struggling to keep our little roof over our head. That might sound like jealousy, but you can just tell when someone's wrong ... Your mum was eight months pregnant with you when she turned up on our doorstep, covered with bruises. A week later there was Clive, standing in my garden, shouting the odds ... so I went outside, took my belt off, and beat him within an inch of his life.'

Charlie can feel a smile spreading across his face. He knows he probably shouldn't be smiling, but he can't seem to stop the upwards curl of his lips.

'Did you really?

'Yes. the moment I was done I saw myself behind bars. The only thing that stood between me and jail was that old man back there, leaning on the walking stick. Mr Shepard used to be the bobby around here, he took your dad aside and said something ... God knows what it was, but it kept me out of jail, got your mum her divorce and a good chunk of your old man's money.'

'People say mum had an affair with a workman, or a delivery man or something.'

'Bullshit,' Tommy replies. He stands up and lifts the compost back onto his arm. 'She wasn't that type of woman.'

'She had boyfriends.'

'I don't doubt that. But if you were someone else's boy she would have escaped Clive sooner.'

'I don't look like him.'

'So, Hank looks like … well, he doesn't look like me or his mother … but there's an old family resemblance in him.'

They are at the door to the Walker home when Charlie sees an inexpressibly sad expression wash over Tommy for a matter of seconds. The giant of a man grunts and then his face is fixed, and solid, again.

'Why are you so hard on Hank?' Charlie doesn't mean to ask it, but the words are off his tongue before he can help himself. Tommy doesn't answer, he just opens the door to his house and disappears inside. Charlie thinks, *it's because you've got no softness left. The world has beaten it out of you.*

Lying beside Alison in the bedroom of the little log cabin, Charlie stirred from his sleep and came partly awake under a sad cloud. Even now, even in this place, even lying next to his love, from time to time he still dreamt about his mum. Time had blurred her face, but sometimes it was refreshed by a photograph, a scent, a few lines of song. When he dreamt of her, as fuzzy as her face may be, it was always the same dream. It always began at the beach with Charlie flying his kite. That moment, after all, was his last blissfully happy memory of his mother, the glamorous Lucy Dunn. He held onto it so tightly that it hurt, but he would never let it go.

Once upon a time she was his world.

.5.

The Second Kiss

While Alison slept, Charlie woke from dreaming of his mother and the early days in Castlegate and slid out from their bed. He crept out of the bedroom, tiptoeing on his long, spindly legs. He crossed the landing, passing the lilac without really noticing it, and slowly pushed open the creaky bathroom door. Once inside, he dashed to the toilet and proceeded to take a marathon two a.m. piss. Of course, he was careful to relieve himself up the inside of the toilet bowl to avoid any unnecessary noise. It was quite possibly the longest piss he had ever taken. As he stood there leaning against the wall, he tried to remember if he'd been to the toilet at all today. Yes, of course he had, three times in fact. In his sleep-addled mind he was just beginning to imagine himself as a camel, with a special upside-down hump full of urine, when the fast-flowing stream died down into slow, steady drips. Finally, he gave his old fella a couple of shakes, put it back in his boxers, and turned to wash his hands.

The water was ice cold, then suddenly scalding hot. He struggled with a bar of bright, green soap under the gushing, boiling water until his hands smelled like apples and were covered in bubbles. The soap was Alison's favourite brand, and the scent of it reminded him of the first time he stayed the night in her little city centre apartment, the one that was a little too close to Stockwell for his liking. She cooked him lamb tagine and served it with a cheap bottle of white. He remembered that she had had one of those old stereo sound systems that held three CDs. Whilst they ate, drank, talked, and laughed, Bombay Bicycle Club, then Sigur Rós, and finally Valentine's Day played in the background. At the sound of Valentine's Day blasting from Alison's speakers, Charlie couldn't resist the urge to name drop. He told her all about how Jude Valentine had grown up around the corner from him and Hank. About how they'd scored free tickets and backstage passes to Jude's gig in Paris. It had been a gift for Hank because the band was so pleased with the artwork he'd done for their Eurydice single. Alison had gushed about how handsome Jude was, about how his blue eyes made her heart skip a beat.

'Of course, he's a brilliant musician as well,' she had said, blushing.

'It's okay, he has the effect on everyone.' Charlie had laughed.

They had a wonderful night together that ended with fantastic sex, but what stayed with him the most was lying next to her afterwards and smelling the sweet scent of apples on her skin.

After washing his hands, he crept back across the landing and poked his head through their bedroom door. Alison was fast asleep on her back, her hand resting on her belly. Suddenly, there was an icicle in his heart and he felt a pang of guilt. Looking at her lying there, so peaceful, her hand positioned expectantly above her empty womb, he couldn't bring himself to crawl back in beside her. Instead, he turned and sloped his way downstairs to the office at the back of the cabin.

He collapsed onto his leather chair and automatically turned on his laptop. The cold glow of the screen lit up his face in an unnatural light.

At the sound of the start-up noise, and urged on by Pavlovian conditioning, he reached for his pad and pen and started glancing at his notes. He stared at the few words he had written, and at that moment his scrawl may as well have been hieroglyphics. He was still thinking of their first night together. Now the memory came flooding back to him. He had worn an ironic Mr Tickle T-shirt, and on opening the door she had fallen about laughing. By then she was already making jokes about how he looked like a Jim Henson puppet. She was already calling him her muppet man, and he laughed along, blushing and getting butterflies at the thought of being anything to her.

'Mr Tickle … why didn't I think of that?' she had exclaimed. 'I can't change your nickname now, I already think of you as muppet man. We're stuck with it.'

'That's fine,' he had given a brief, reserved reply, then followed her into her flat. He remembered being lost for words for the first few minutes of every date with Alison. It was as if the sight of her made him shy once more and robbed him of the art of conversation. The words would always come flooding back as soon as he had acclimatised to her company. Then, of course, he would overcompensate and spend half an hour being too hyperactive before finally, he overcame his nerves and his charm and wit would return to him.

He remembered her hair that night: chestnut, silky, and worn in a braid. After they'd eaten, they sat on the sofa and talked. She found a pack of gum in her pocket, offered him a piece and then took one for herself. They chewed and talked. She played with her hair and slowly she undid the braid, untwisting it from the end and smoothing it out. He remembered spying her Yamaha keyboard and her violin case on top of a table in the corner of the room. No surprise there. She had told him she was a music teacher on their first date, she told him about the quartet she played in, yet there was something about seeing her instruments there made it more real and he couldn't help but ask her to play something.

'No,' she had said shyly. 'Maybe I will, a little later.' Her green-blue eyes shone up at him, and after that, he didn't press the subject.

When she had finished un-braiding her hair, she turned and kissed him. He hadn't known it then, but it had been the kiss of his life, all the others after reflected this very kiss. His theory was that every relationship had three kisses that really mattered: the first kiss, the last kiss, and then this one. The kiss of discovery, full of knowledge and truth, filling you with a sensation akin to vertigo.

For Charlie, the kiss of discovery between Alison and himself took place on their fifth date, sitting on her sofa whilst Valentine's Day played through her sound system. It tasted mainly of chewing gum, but he could make out the faint taste of cheap wine and beyond that, spicy lamb and apricots. It was slow. He held a hand against her back, and she had her hands at the side of his face, her fingers running through his thinning, ginger hair. As their tongues caressed each other, sparks flying around their now shared mouths, Charlie wasn't thinking about anything as prosaic or clichéd as the word love. It's common knowledge that Eskimos have fifty words that all mean snow. In a reversal of this paradigm, love is a word that means fifty different things. It's a fickle concept that changes from person to person and moment to moment. During that kiss, he didn't think 'oh my God, I'm in love,' but he could taste the possibilities on the tip of Alison's tongue, and he couldn't imagine kissing anyone else, not for quite some time.

After the kiss she took him to bed, and eventually they slept. He drifted off, holding her around her waist and smelling the apples on her skin. She made his sleepy mind think of summer, walking through the woods, listening to the twitter of birds, and watching squirrels dart up and down trees. Then came sleep, deep, and dark, and dreamless. He woke to find a naked woman leaning on his chest with a quizzical look on her face. He felt uneasy, his unfamiliar surroundings disturbed him and he found he didn't quite know where he was. It came to him just as the woman perched on his chest began to roll over to the other side of the bed – Alison, of course, he had stayed at hers last night. Standing up, she strolled away naked, muttering about how he was such a messy sleeper.

Minutes later she returned holding two cups, with her violin case under one arm. He remembered watching her struggle with the mugs in her hands and the violin, before dropping the case onto the bed. She offered him a mug of coffee, put hers down on the bedside table and took the violin out of its case. She tuned it, and as Charlie drank his morning coffee, she sat naked on the edge of the bed serenading him with a soft, beautiful song that he didn't recognise and couldn't place.

The memory passed, Charlie was snoozing in his office chair, his head falling forward towards the desk. He woke when, from out the corner of his eye, he glimpsed a flash of movement past the office door. It was something pure white, with a pointy crown, and it was clip-clopping down the corridor. He yanked himself out of the chair, his bare, sweaty flesh sticking to the leather like Velcro, making it difficult for him to move quickly. He bolted out of the office, raced down the hall, up the stairs, and into their bedroom to find...

No strange pale figure, but Alison still fast asleep on the bed. The quilt in the same place, pulled back enough to reveal that hopeful hand resting on her belly. It made him feel cold in his heart and guilt, like nausea in his stomach, all over again. As he stood above Alison, looking healthy and bright, another chain of memories bubbled up inside him.

Charlie couldn't find her in the little house they shared. He had been shouting her name, but she didn't answer. Finally, he found her sitting on their bed wrapped in towels, sobbing into her hands. She told him about the lump she had found, and right away he felt like he was going to throw up. He wanted to fall to his knees and sob, but he couldn't. He had to be strong, not because he could be strong, not because strength was a cornerstone of his character, but simply because there was no other choice ... Big Tommy had always said that a man does what needs to be done for his loved ones. Charlie hadn't heard those words as often as Hank had, but he had still heard them enough for the idea to take hold.

He remembered standing in the doctor's office . The doctor was talking about treatments, pointing at x-rays and scans, and offering platitudes about long journeys and how every case is unique and not a statistic. Meanwhile, Charlie pictured all those possibilities he had tasted on the tip of Alison's tongue during that kiss of discovery. They are soap bubbles that smell like green apples, floating in front of his face, bursting one by one.

His memory jumped to Alison, lying in her hospital bed, a skeletal frame with a pale and gaunt face. Her breathing was hoarse, she could barely keep her eyes open, and when they were open, they were glazed. He held her hand tightly while, from a million miles away, voices told him to be prepared. It could come at any time. He should say his goodbyes. He felt nothing but rage for those distant voices. He wanted to claw at them, tear out their eyes, and break their bones because they just didn't understand. It wasn't enough, not nearly enough time. There was nothing he wouldn't have given to make her well. Given half the chance, he would have offered up his heart and soul for just a little more time.

Again, Charlie came back to himself, this time with a shudder. Standing in the bedroom of the log cabin they called home, he shook off the ugly, bitter chain of memories and climbed back into bed beside Alison. He reached out and touched her to confirm her reality. She was there, she was real, she was warm and healthy, and at that, he sighed with relief. The coldness and the guilt dissolved as he realised that they were happy now. All that pain and misery had grown distant and yes, they were happy. Almost blissfully. Life might not be perfect, they might not get everything they'd once dreamed of, yet he thought given enough time they – she – could be content with what they had.

As he held her close, he closed his eyes and thought about that tree by the banks of the river Windrush. He recalled the warm breeze that had rustled the branches above their heads, and the sound of happy children splashing in the water. He thought about that place and felt a little better, a little stronger, a little more solid in his heart.

Cwtch

Jessica – sitting at the kitchen counter in her parents' house dressed in her pink dressing gown and matching slippers – was trying her hardest not to be noticed. A week had passed since her midnight dart back home and now things were starting to calm down.

The first morning had bought a 6.30 a.m. screaming fit, followed by a full day of migraines and criticism.

Prudence Kirkpatrick – Mother, always Mother, never Mummy or Mum – woke early intending to take a swim in the new, heated pool. They had converted the conservatory the month before, and since then Prudence had found twenty laps as the sun rose over her garden to be invigorating. She was crossing the landing when, from the corner of her eye, she saw that Jessica's bedroom door was slightly ajar.

She found it deeply unsettling. Jessica wasn't there, of course, she was still shacked up with that waster and she barely came home these days, once a month, if that. At least she never turned up with him … that Kevin, or was it Kelvin? It was one or the other, or else something equally plebeian, it was something that suggested oil under dirty fingernails and a pair of overalls. Why couldn't Jessica have stuck with that nice Wickham boy from down the way? Prudence sighed, walking slowly towards the door. Sure, he was as dull as dishwater, but it wasn't like Jessica could afford to be all that picky.

Prudence pushed the door open and, at first, saw only the stacks of boxes. The contents of the conservatory had been stored away in her only child's room on her orders. She had done it out of spite, of course, to prove a point. Next time Jessica came home for a visit she would be given the guest room, and that would send a subtle message. Now, as Prudence scanned the cluttered room, her eyes fell on the shape in the bed.

'Andrew, Andrew!' she screamed shrilly. 'Come quick, someone's broken in. They're asleep in Jessica's bed!'

Moments later, Andrew appeared by her side. Sleepy-eyed and brandishing a golf club, he crept into the room and used it to poke the long lump in the bed. When his daughter poked her head out from under the sheets, he grunted, dropped the golf club, and wandered off to bed without saying a word to either of them.

In this brief moment, Jessica's gaze had been drawn away from mother – who stood at the door, pale, clutching her chest – and concentrated on her father. She caught a rare glimpse of his face not shielded by the newspaper, or a stack of spreadsheets, or the three computer screens in his home office. *Oh yeah,* she thought, *that's what he looks like, kind of like a pug or a French bulldog* and before she knew it, she was laughing hysterically while her mother glared down at her.

A week later and Jessica was still in the doghouse for her secret home invasion, but mostly for the laughter. Prudence had given her chapter and verse for laughing at her while she thought she was in danger. Even now, out of the corner of her eye, Jessica thought she could see her mum … no mother, of course, gearing up to go over the appropriate times to laugh once again. She noted that her mother had her muted blonde hair done up in a bun and, despite it only being eight a.m., she wore understated makeup and had donned her cream trouser suit. Prudence looked ready for the day and seeing that, Jessica disappeared back behind her book.

'Don't slouch dear.'

'Yes, mother.'

'Yes, darling.'

The answer came from father and daughter simultaneously and again, that tickled Jessica. She bit her lip and held onto her giggle.

'Well?' Prudence asked as she pulled the book from her daughter's grip.

'Well, what?' she asked.

'I just knew you weren't paying attention to me!' Prudence exclaimed. 'Off into flibbertigibbet land again.' She sat down next to Jessica and exchanged her orange juice for a glass of water, doubtless because of the sugar. 'I was enquiring about your plans for the day. Daddy's got you a credit card, it came this morning … we could go get you a whole new wardrobe and have lunch... not in Coventry of course, some place … more suitable for our needs. If it gets late, we could find a hotel and stay the night … Daddy won't miss us, he's going to Prague for a business meeting. He won't be back till Monday.'

'Well …' Jessica said timidly. 'I was hoping to go see Granda' Evans today … only I haven't seen him since I've been back and …'

'Fine.' Prudence snapped. 'As you like it ... But Jessica, how many times do I have to tell you ... he is your grandfather, not your Granda' ... not your Bampi ... We're not common Jessica.'

Yes of course, 'Grandad', Jessica thought. *Heaven forbid that anyone finds out that once upon a time you were Prudence Evans from the valleys.* Another giggle bubbled up and she found it harder to hold onto this one.

'If you're going to see my father, ask him if he's given any more thought to coming and living in the annex. He's getting too old to potter around in that cottage.'

'Granda ...' she stopped herself in time and adjusted. 'Grandad is fine, he's still working.'

'And how would you know that Jessica? You're hardly ever around these days. And when you're not around you're seemingly incapable of picking up the phone.'

Jessica withered under her mother's glare and kept silent about the weekly phone calls she had with Granda' Owen. She said nothing and waited...

'And while we're having one of our little heart-to-hearts Jessica dear, do you really have to read this trash?' Prudence picked the book up and then threw it down on the table next to her daughter as if it were incrementing evidence.

'It's not trash,' Jessica objected. 'I really like it.'

'Oh, it's trash, and of course, you know it's about him, don't you?'

'Him, who?'

'That musician, that rock star with the big house down by the Oaktree.' Prudence spat the words 'musician' and 'rock star' as if they were a bad taste on her tongue.

'Well, it's not literally about him,' she said, she was a little less ornery now, her mood had been lightened at the juicy bit of gossip she was about to chew over. 'All that stuff about spirits and magic is obviously nonsense, but the girls at the golf club reminded me that his first wife did disappear not long before he moved in with that young … what's the polite term … mixed race, that mixed race girl. You know this book has caused us nothing but trouble.'

'How?' Jessica asked. For once she was genuinely interested in her mothers' gossip.

'It was bad enough when he moved in. And, of course, he bought the best house in Oakenbrook, these entertainers get the best of everything, if you ask me a lot of them don't deserve the money they earn. But anyway, from the moment he moved in we got gapers.' She paused and when she saw the blank look on her daughter's face she endeavoured to explain. 'You know, looky-loos, nosy little parkers coming into our nice little village from all around and further. They come and stand outside his gates to catch a glimpse of him. I learned to put up with that, even though it made me feel like I was living in a zoo.'

The right corner of Jessica's lip curled upwards as her mother began to build up a good head of steam. She only ever saw Prudence this happy and affable when she was dissecting strangers with the sharp edge of her tongue.

'We got used to it, and I guess he was polite enough on the rare occasions I bumped into him jogging. But then that author started writing his books and they were all set around here … Well, mainly they are set in Castlegate and Pickford, but he mentions Oakenbrook. Suddenly there are organised tours all over the place. Daddy and I can't take a Sunday stroll together without slack-jawed gapers ruining it and forget taking Marshall into the woods for his walk … they're all in there looking for spirits.' She pointed at the bloodhound asleep in its bed at the far end of the kitchen. At the grand old age of fifteen he was barely able to make it to the garden, let alone do a lap of Starkey's woods. Jessica imagined her parents trying to push the old dog around the woods in a pram and suppressed another giggle.

'I thought you said his books were trash mother?' Jessica asked offhand.

'They are, dear.'

'But it sounds like you've read them all,' she smirked.

'Well … I had to, didn't I? All the ladies at the club were talking about them and besides, you need to know what people are writing about your home. You can't prove a liar, a liar, if you don't know what lies they've told you.'

'It's hardly lying, Mother. He's a writer, it's his job to tell stories.'

Prudence hmphed,

'All I know is he's not the right sort of person. You know who he is, of course …' she paused and after observing another blank expression on Jessica's face, she pressed on.

'Oh, you know him' she insisted. 'He's that orphan boy that the boxer and his wife took in, you know the big chap who worked as your grandfather's assistant for a short while.'

'Tommy Walker?' Jessica asked.

'Yes, that's him ... what was his son's name?' Prudence asked, and then under her breath, she began muttering, 'Look how that family turned out, his son marries a slut, and the adopted boy writes those trash novels.' She paused again and took a long moment to appraise her daughter. 'But I guess we all have our crosses to bear' She said, as she looked away.

Jessica snatched up her book and left the kitchen in a storm, mumbling goodbye as she went.

Within the hour she was showered, dressed, and riding her bike through Pickford towards Castlegate. As she pedalled, she wondered if her mother even knew she was cruel, and if she did know, did she not have any control over her impulses? Did she absolutely have to say everything she thought, were those words like bees rattling around her head, stinging her brain until she let them out? Or was it a conscious decision, did she take her time to think of the absolute worst thing to say? Did she wait and watch for the crestfallen reaction, did she even notice it? Jessica was in two minds about it, some days she thought her mother was struck down with some form of nervous OCD twitch unique to her, other days she just thought she was a heartless bitch.

She crossed over the stone bridge into Castlegate and before long she was passing through the heart of the village, passing the post office, the old barbershop, the village green, and then the Tiger's Head pub. She came upon her Granda's cottage and the smell of it made her happy. It smelt hot and sunny, of bluebells, and honeysuckle, and freshly cut grass. She knew, of course, the floral scents didn't come from his garden, but rather the garden that backed on to his. From his open window, she could smell bacon frying in the pan and the tobacco from his pipe. She dismounted her bike with a joyful hop and opened the gate, listening to the familiar creak as she pushed it open. Walking her bike around to backdoor, she heard him singing a suggestive snippet of a song that she recognised as Dylan Thomas.

'O nobody swept my chimney, since my husband went his ways.'

She pushed open the back door and found Granda' Owen hovering over the kitchen sink, half of his face covered in shaving foam, his razor in his right hand, his left-hand hovering over a bacon sandwich and the mug of tea that had been placed precariously on the draining board. She stood quietly for a moment to take him in. Six foot five, grey hair slicked back over his head with his old-fashioned pomade; wearing the familiar braces, the white vest, his blue pyjama bottoms, and the heavy boots he wore while working. She watched him shave the right side of his face clean, then reach out with his left hand, tear off a crumb of his bacon sandwich, and pop it into the clean side of his mouth. She laughed and he noticed her then.

'Jessica!' He bellowed, in his deep, rich voice. 'Come for a cwtch off your Granda' is it? Well, come to me girl, let me get a good grip of my strawberry.'

She rushed to him and felt his sixty-nine-year-old strong arms close around her. His shaving foam was messing up the left side of her hair, and the smell of him, the smell of old spice, and sweat, and tobacco smoke made her feel like she was finally home. Tears fell from her eyes and then, before she could stop herself, she was sobbing out loud.

'Oh. What's this now, tears is it?' he wiped the shaving foam out of her hair. 'Is this over that man of yours? I won't lie to you, Pruney told me you'd left him. I was expecting your visit. Just as soon as you could get from under her gaze, of course.'

'Bampi,' she sobbed. 'He did horrible things.'

He took her hand and led her to the kitchen table, they sat next to each other and she felt his hand close on hers.

'You tell Granda all about it Strawberry, Bampi's always here for you.'

'He used to hit me' she began and felt a weight lift from her shoulders.

.7.

Lifted by the Wind

The magical Icelandic wind lifted Alison from where she slumbered by her lover's side and carried her into the most surreal of dreams.

She flew over Santa's workshop, a little Christmas Tinseltown hidden under an invisible dome. She barely had the time to take it in before it disappeared, and now she was looking down on something completely different. Below her, she saw a potbellied, bearded giant sitting at a table of ice, arm-wrestling a polar bear. The giant was drinking a beer with his free hand, his foot resting on a hammer that was chipped, tarnished, and bloody.

The scene shifted again. Alison found herself in the heart of a bleak tundra. A shadow fell across the ice, threatening to engulf the world. She watched from the wings of the wind as it took the shape of a wolf and howled at the moon. Quickly, she closed her eyes. She didn't want to watch that father shadow wolf swallow the moon.

'Be still,' a voice spoke from behind her. Of course, she wasn't alone, nor was she carried by the wind. She was riding the back of the white stag and the owner of the voice was behind her. 'Everything is well.' When she opened her eyes, she saw a tiny figure running across the tundra towards the shadow. 'Yonder is Polaris the Hunter. We need not fear that shadow ahead.'

79

At that, the stag beneath her turned away from the imminent battle and flew to the West. Beneath her, she saw trees lining the circumference of a frozen lake. In the centre of the frozen lake she saw what looked to be a crystal palace, and surrounding the palace there was a village of small log and stone houses, each with a smoking chimney stack.

The stag touched the ground at the edge of the trees easily, without jolting her. She dismounted and took a few steps forward towards the crystal palace. She looked over her shoulder meaning to ask the man who had travelled behind her what this place was but on turning she found she was alone. Where the stag had been, she saw a large, very old, brown, leather book. On the front of the book, she read three words: *All the Stories*.

She opened it at random and read …

Once upon a time, long ago in Mercia, the kingdom of your birth, there lived a woman called Godiva, who wasn't really a woman at all. She was, in fact, the spirit of desire, made flesh, ageless and beyond mortal death. Over the course of her impossibly long life, she had been named beyond counting. She had been called Titania, Idun, and Aphrodite, but her first and true name was Pandora, she was the sister of Pandemonium, the great, fickle spirit of mischief and magic.

Godiva was the wife of Leofric, who had once been named Epimetheus and was the spirit of twilight, heartache, and afterthought. Leofric was the Earl of Mercia and protector of the flesh folk who lived there. He had no great love for the little human animals and watched over them out of duty, this and nothing more. But,

Godiva craved power. She didn't care for the flesh folk either, but she loved the way that they loved her. She wanted their undivided attention and she would only get that by deposing her husband, robbing him of his body, and banishing him to the spiritual realm. To that end, she called on her brother Pandemonium, who now called himself Puck.

'Puck,' she said in her saccharine voice. 'My husband is an unfit ruler. He treats the flesh folk with thinly veiled contempt. For their sake, help me depose him.'

Puck, of course, was no fool, but he had always found it convenient to be thought of as the fool of all fools. Thus, he pretended to take his sister's concern for the mortals at face value.

'Of course, I will help you sister,' he said. Godiva saw the concern in his furrowed brow and straight face and was pleased as she listened to his plan. If only she had noticed the twinkle in his eyes...

'Go to your husband and ask him for a token of his love, something small that speaks of the depth of his feelings for you. Whatever he presents, you will look upon it sour and forlorn, then cast it aside. Do this three times, and then your husband will demand tribute from the flesh folk in secret. First, he will ask them for a crafted gift, and when that doesn't please you, he will demand all their gold and shiny stones with which to make a statue in your image. When you declare the statue a poor likeness, he will demand the flesh folk offer up their food to hold a feast in your honour. It is at this point we will act.'

Puck paused, scooped up a small mound of dirt in his left hand and spat into his right. He cupped his hands together and made clay, which he formed into the shape of a small horse. He spun his magic around the clay figure, first growing it to the size of a warhorse, then making it pure white, and finally breathing life into it.

'When the flesh folk go hungry you will speak to them. You will tell them that you despise your lord and husband for the cruel way he treats them. Tell them that as they suffer, so do you, and when they cry it's your tears that roll down their face. Tell them that you will banish your husband and take his place just as long as they prove their love for you. On Hunter's Moon you will ride through the streets of Mercia naked, and if every living man, woman, and child averts their gaze out of respect, then you will rule, but if just one person looks at you and sees you in all your glory then no spirit will rule, nor ever have a temple on Earth again. We will be driven behind a veil and when we walk the realms of men, we will be diminished in power and encased in flesh, blood, and bones.'

Godiva was a vain and shallow creature, she didn't doubt for a second the love of the flesh folk, nor did she really care about their fate. It was for this reason that Puck came up with his crafty plan to deceive and dethrone both Godiva and Leofric. Puck – being a soft-hearted creature deep down – had realised that replacing one heartless ruler with another was a waste of his energy. Moreover, he knew in his bones that no spirit was truly fit to rule, none save Prometheus the Prince of Fire. If Puck could make the flesh folk see them for what they truly were, then they would reject spirit kind's dominion over them. At long last, man and womankind would have free will. They could invite the Pookas in and choose to show them *devotion. Or else they could ignore them and live their ordinary little lives.*

Puck set about his plan. He summoned Loa, she of the elephant head, his totem of creation. At Puck's orders Loa created a root from starlight and moonshine, shaped like a man. Puck buried the root by the light of the full moon and called upon Ariel the Dove, his totem of enchantment. Ariel sat cross-legged by the buried root and whispered all manner of secret truths to it while it slept. When the next full moon came around the root had sprouted purple blossoms.

'Twice blessed by the light of the full moon and bursting with secret truths, I name you Mandragora,' Puck whispered to the flower. He picked the purple blossoms and rolled them in his hands, putting a little bit of his own magic into them. He filled a bag with the resulting sparkling, purple dust and then called on Ratatoskr the Squirrel, his totem of low trickery, born from his shadow and his own mischievous nature. Puck gave the dust to that low trickster and told him, 'Trick the flesh folk. When they least expect it blow this powder in their eyes, and then when Godiva marches through the streets astride my horse they will see her for what she is. Even if they close their eyes or look away, they will be compelled to see.'

Behind Alison the wind began to blow again, the old, leather book slipped from her grip and she was lifted from the ground once more. Up, and up, and up she went, into darkness and starlight, when from somewhere behind her the voice spoke again.

'Understand, dear heart,' it whispered, 'this is not the story of how Godiva banished Leofric. Or the story of how Puck cheated Godiva out of her throne. Rather, this is the story of how Puck put chains and limitations on all the spirits that once ruled the Earth.'

At that, the dream subsided into deep, dark sleep.

8

The Good Earth.

The pan was back on the stove and two thick slices of bacon were crisping up nicely. Jessica watched her Granda' Owen flip them with a fork before relegating them to the edge of the pan to make room for the thick slices of bread he'd carved. She felt oddly hungry now that she had cried out all her heartache on his shoulder. He had listened placidly, and without judgment of all the ugly details, his only flicker of reaction was a grimace and a clenched fist on the table when she talked about Kelvin giving her the odd pop in the eye now and again. When she finished the story, he had ruffled her hair and kissed her forehead.

'The thing with your mother taking an instant dislike to everyone is that, every once in a while, she's bound to be right.' He said, before rising from his seat to cook her breakfast.

As she looked at him now, bent over the cooker, she remembered her mother's jibe about how everyone had their cross to bear and recounted it to Owen. She used that to segue way into her theory about how the indifference of her father and the constant criticism of her mother had laid the groundwork for Kelvin. It was at that point that Granda' Owen plated up her sandwich and sat opposite her, waiting for her to take a bite.

'You're the spitting image of your grandma.' He said as she swallowed her first bite. 'I never get tired of telling you that my little strawberry, Bridget was quite a woman … I wish you could have known her.' He refilled his pipe and struck a match along the edge of the table. 'I know about your mum, of course, I always knew what she was, even from a little girl. Often, I wonder how a working-class Welsh man and a dirt-poor Irish woman managed to breed themselves a member of the English aristocracy. Maybe she was swapped at birth … maybe my real daughter is right now sitting in the Dorchester, eating with her hands, belching the alphabet and goosing the waiters?'

Jessica laughed and choked on her bacon sandwich. A piece of the fried bread was stuck and she started to panic just as one of Granda' Owen's large hands came across and slapped her on the back to dislodge it.

'Don't do that Bampi,' she gasped. 'Don't make me laugh while I'm eating.'

'It was funny because it's true,' Owen answered, 'I don't know where she gets her airs and graces from. Not when you consider where she came from, me a gardener and her mum waitress. And look at her older sisters, your aunts. Alwena has spent all her adult life working on the fish stall at the Market, and God love Dilwen, but everyone knows she's a goodtime girl … you know what I mean don't you girl? You know your aunty is a Madam, don't you?' Jessica's jaw fell open and she looked aghast at her Granda'. 'Oh, it's common knowledge my little strawberry. She runs a brothel on the outskirts of the city centre … well, massage parlour … but you know!'

'Is that true?'

'Every word of it my girl, your Granda' Evans is many things but he's no liar.' Owen answered with a false look of shock on his face.

'So, it's not like the time you told me that Mr Solomon who owned the garden centre was growing tons of weed in the greenhouses?'

'Oh, that was true unall my girl!' he pointed at her with his pipe. 'Where to's he now? Scarpered he did, had away on his toes when old Mr Shepard went and pegged it.'

'What's Mr Shepard got to do with it?'

'Well he was in the Police wasn't he, he was Solomon's connection, he used to bung Shepard a few quid and the odd water feature here and there in return for keeping his name out of trouble.'

'Oh, that's rubbish Granda'!' she had finished her sandwich and took the plate to the sink. There was still a splodge of shaving foam on the edge of the washing up bowl. She smiled, rinsed it away, and then washed up her plate. 'Mr Shepard must have been in his eighties then. He was retired for like, forever, and didn't Mr Solomon leave before Mr Shepard passed away? None of this adds up Bampi, he couldn't have been Mr Solomon's bent copper ... and besides, they just don't look the type.'

'Shepard always turned a blind eye to what your aunty was up to. He said it wasn't his place to judge.'

'That doesn't make him a bent copper though.'

'That's your trouble my girl. Far too trusting. You look out there at Castlegate and see a pretty little village and automatically think the best of everyone. Trust me my strawberry, it's a hotbed of sin out there. I should know, I've sinned with the best of them.' He punctuated that with a laugh and Jessica waved his nonsense away with an indignant hand.

She boiled the kettle and put a fresh cup of tea in front of her Granda'.

'What are your plans for the day Granda'?'

'Well, I'm not sure until I look at my appointment diary, I'll go and get it now in a minute.'

While he searched for his appointment diary, she took her tea outside and drank it on the bench overlooking his garden. A patch of overgrown grass, a couple of plant pots, a hanging basket, and nothing else. She found it disappointing when she considered the beautiful gardens he had worked on for other people.

'I'm up in your neck of the woods today Strawberry,' Owen said as he appeared at the side of the bench brandishing his appointment diary, 'up to that lovely Mrs Valentine to see about the zen garden she wants. If you want to spend the day with me, I'll drop you off at Pruney's when I'm done?'

'Okay,' she said, smiling. She hoped the day would be a long one.

It was a short, chugging journey up the lane in her Granda's old van, and when they drove past her parent's house she shrunk down in her seat. Once they had passed it, she recalled her mother's instructions and recounted the invitation to live in the annex.

'Not bloody likely.' He grunted. 'She can't pull the wool over my eyes. That annex is a conveyer belt, the moment I step on it I'll be whisked away to a nursing home and then a hole in the ground. Never in this world Strawberry, you can mark my words on that.' He sounded resolute, but Jessica noticed a certain uneasy expression creep across his face for a moment, it was there and then gone in the blink of an eye.

The van pulled up outside the iron gates of Jude Valentine's house and Owen leaned out the window and beeped the buzzer. Jessica had butterflies in her belly, Jude was such a fitty. Quickly, she glanced at herself in the rear-view mirror, she looked pale and lacked even a dab of lipstick or touch of eyeliner. The gates swung open and her Granda' drove in. As the tires crunched across the gravel, Jessica saw two women standing in front of the house waiting for them. One was a blonde woman, carrying a baby in her arms, the other had curly dark hair and caramel skin. She was the one her mum had described dismissively as 'that mixed race girl', but she was known to everyone else as the singer Sophie Mia Darling.

Owen pulled up in front of them and stepped out of the van, big and bold, with his arms opened wide.

'Ah, my fan club is it?' He joked, marching towards them. 'Sophie you look lovely my girl. And who's this with you?' he turned his attention to the woman holding the baby. 'As I live and breathe Rebecca Walker you're a vision, a sight for sore eyes. You remind me of the girls back home ... tell me, do you have any Welsh in you?'

'No.' she said wearily.

'Would you like some?'

'Granda'!' Jessica shouted as she leaped from the van. 'You can't talk like that nowadays!'

'Oh, joking I am,' he said dismissing Jessica. 'We go way back, young Becky used to work with your aunty for a short while … and her father-in-law used to be my assistant when he was a young wisp of a man.'

Jessica stared at Rebecca Walker, wondering which aunt she had worked with when she recognised her. She was the Becky from the documentary, and her husband Hank was the son of her Granda's old assistant. Her mind began to reel with all the odd little coincidences, life around these parts was like a web of connections, but of course, that's how it is when everyone knows everyone.

'This is my granddaughter.' Owen said, introducing Jessica who was standing, slightly slack-jawed, by his side. 'This is Pruney's girl, Jessica … but don't go holding that against her, she's lovely she is.'

The three women said their hellos and shook hands, and afterwards, Owen punctuated the moment by saying,

'Now, ladies there are two choices as I see it. Either my granddaughter can watch the baby in your arms while the pair of you ravish me, or you can show me to your garden and tell me what's to do.'

'Oh, Owen,' Becky sighed. 'You know if I was ten years older …'

'You'd take me up on the offer?'

'No, if I was ten years older, you'd be dead.'

Jessica blushed as her Granda' let out a bellow of laughter.

After that, Sophie led him around to the large back garden and there was a long chat about raised flower beds, and water features, and the Zen word was mentioned once or twice. Jessica watched her

90

Granda' carefully, he had flicked a switch in his head and now he was completely professional. He nodded while Sophie talked and made notes on a little pad, offering some of his own suggestions.

There was a natural downward slant to the garden, as the house had been built on a slight hill. Owen suggested adding a winding path, leading down to a hedged off area that would make a secret garden for them. There could be an archway and through it there would be a little bridge crossing a koi pond. He could install a water feature, that poured right into the koi pond, and a moat around a small island, with a wooden gazebo at its heart and a cute, little bridge spanning the moat. He finished by offering to add flower beds to the side of the curved paths, each one set a little lower into the natural slope of the hill, to make them look like steps on either side of the path.

Sophie was thrilled about the idea and Owen suggested they step inside and discuss her budget. The two of them went in leaving Jessica alone with Becky and the babe in her arms.

'What's his name?' she asked.

'Francis Arthur Walker Doyle … but I think Frank for everyday use,' she said, beaming at the little man in her arms. 'Frank or Frankie, we're not going to be nicknaming you anything else are we, no matter what silly Mr Tickle has to say about it?'

'Mr Tickle?' Jessica asked.

'Oh … just his godfather… he's a bit eccentric. Mind, they all are around here, aren't they? Look at your Grandad,' she said smiling. 'I think they must put something in the Pickford stream.'

'Yeah, Puck's in the stream.' Jessica said chuckling to herself. She looked around and saw Becky was eyeing her.

'I see you read Mr Tickle's books then?'

'Who?' Jessica waited for Becky to respond, but she just stood rocking the babe in her arms, wearing a knowing grin.

'It's just something Granda' used to tell me when I was a little girl,' she said, embarrassed. 'He used to say that it was a magic stream and if you traced it back through Starkey's woods to its source you'd find the gateway to the magical land of Pandemonium where the Master of Mischief lives.'

'Hmm!' Becky responded. 'I know a man who loves those spirit stories. Maybe I'll introduce you one day.' But before Becky could say much more, Owen was back. He took Jessica aside and had her jotting down measurements as he walked the length and breadth of the garden, estimating the size in wide strides.

'So, you have plans I take it?' her Granda asked once the pair of them were alone again.

'What?'

'What are you doing with yourself now, what are your plans? You know Pruney will be asking you that question nonstop and if you don't have your own plans, you'll have her plans'.

'Well ...' Jessica sighed. 'I was thinking about asking Daddy to get me an accounting job at his firm ... then maybe I could get a flat and ...'

'Really?' Owen asked. 'That's a flimsy plan if ever I heard one. The longer you stay under Pruney's roof the more she'll make playdough out of you. She'll model you into a Stepford wife, and marry you off to some dull as dishwater banker so you can spend your life talking small at cocktail parties … No, my girl, you need a better plan.'

'What if I came to live with you?' Jessica asked. 'We could tell Mother that I was there to look after you and that way she wouldn't be bothering you to come and live in the annex and I'd be …' She paused as she realised exactly what she would be, 'I'd be free … maybe I could be your assistant?'

'Well, about time girl!' he exclaimed. 'I thought it was going to take you all day to get to the heart of it. Of course, I could have suggested it but it's better you thought of it on your own, this way it's your fault when Pruney hits the roof,' he said, laughing.

There was a moment of silence as Jessica made eye contact with her Granda' and saw some hidden sadness there.

She rushed to him and he pulled her into another cwtch. They stood there for quite some time, hugging in a stranger's garden until Owen pulled away and said, 'It will be a pleasure to have you stay with me my strawberry. It will be like the old days when you were a little pigtailed girl. Do you remember sleepovers, and coming out on my rounds? You always used to say "Granda', can I work with you when I'm grown up?" and I always told you yes.'

'Yes, but Mother put an end to that didn't she?' Jessica said sullenly. 'When I told her I wanted to come and work with you she told me not to be an idiot. She said I had to play to my strengths, that I was good at maths and I should do something with that.'

'You were fifteen then girl! You're an adult now, and an adult can make her own choices.' Owen sat down on the grass and reached inside his pocket for his pipe, took it out and then thought better about lighting up. 'Besides, if truth be told I think this will be good for you. There's something about working the earth, something that's deeply pleasing. You sit in front of a screen totting up numbers, and I bet you come away tenser at the end of the day than at the start. It's the exact opposite when you work the earth. You come away tired, achy, dirty, but you leave behind your frustrations. You plant them with the pretty flowers.'

'That's my plan then.' Jessica said as she sat down next to her Granda', both of them looking down the slope of the lawn to the spot where the hidden Zen garden would be. 'The only thing to worry about now is who's going to tell Mother.'

9

Turning turtle

Standing in the kitchen waiting for the kettle to boil, Alison listened to the steady *tap, tap tapping* of Charlie's fingers. As she stood, she held a hot water bottle to her cramping belly to help relieve the pain a little. Not pregnant, not yet, but there was time now. Time was definitely on their side. Of course, she had noticed that Charlie didn't exactly rave over the idea of having children, not the way he had once upon a time, but then his head was full of the new book. He wasn't the type of man who accepted charity, he never took something for nothing, and his agent's deal had been to take time 'for you to work on your second novel. Take as long as you like.' He saw it as his duty to uphold his end of the bargain, and so, when he wasn't cooking, sleeping, chopping wood, or inside her, he was to be found in the little office at the back of the cabin tap, tap, tapping away.

About a month ago, Charlie had begun to seriously apply himself to the task at hand. For just a short while, she had felt a little bit lost without his undivided attention. Living in a remote frozen, little 'just the two of them' world, meant that there was little in the way of entertainment or distraction. A trip into Húsavík was an arduous task. It meant contending with the country roads, the deep snow, and a language she couldn't get her lazy, English tongue around. Often, she walked in the snow to the frozen lake. Sometimes she made snowmen, but she couldn't spend all day exposed to the elements. Sooner or later she always had to come back inside and sit and wait for Charlie to be done for the day.

The answer to her boredom came one afternoon when she was exploring the basement. There were two doors that led down to that secluded, little grotto. One was under the staircase that led from the bedroom to the main living area, the second was a pair of storm doors outside the cabin that been sealed shut by the thick fall of snow. Alison had walked past that odd door that set in the staircase every day for about a year without paying it much attention at all. She thought it hid a cleaning cupboard or a small cloakroom. On a day that her boredom got the better of her, she found it hid a second, curved staircase leading to the hidden basement.

Down there she discovered her much needed entertainment. Finding and flicking the light switch directly at the bottom of the stairs, she found walls lined with shelves as far as the eye could see. The shelves on the north wall were filled fit to burst with books. The narrow east wall had shelves either side of the curved staircase that were stocked with an extensive movie collection. The south wall housed records, CDs and a large sound system with big, beefy speakers. There was a tatty, old sofa sitting in the south-west corner of the room. It was tucked away in a nook made by a second, smaller staircase that led up to the blocked storm doors. A small TV and DVD player were mounted on the wall of the nook, making a cosy movie corner.

All of this was nice enough, but what intrigued Alison was what she found in the centre of the room. A cosy chair stood beside a rug, and on the rug, there was a large table, and on the table were boxes, boxes, and more boxes. Examining them she found that they were construction kits for a model town. She had picked one up at random and read the brand name 'Breidablik' above a pair of stag horns.

'Well, that's incredibly nerdy,' she had said to no one at all. Then, what came to her mind was the image of a little boy with her face and Charlie's cow eyes. She saw that little boy, rosy-cheeked and gripping a toy car in his little hands, pushing it around his own little toy town. Opening the box in her hand she found the instructions inside written in five languages, English being the fifth. That first afternoon of boredom, while Charlie tap, tap, tapped above her head, she found Jeff Buckley in the record collection, popped it in the sound system, and then sat and made a little log cabin. It looked remarkably like their own cabin, she smiled to herself at the thought of a tiny, little Alison and Charlie making time with each other on the rug in front of the fire.

Today, however, was not a building day. Today her belly cramped, her head ached, and she was just a little sad that she hadn't fallen pregnant yet. This past month they had made love and fucked like animals so frequently that at times, she had felt like a sperm bank. She had ached constantly in that slightly pleasing way. Naturally, she assumed that there would be a baby in her by now. How could there not be? No, today was not a building day, it was a turtle day. A day to retract into her shell, watch movies, and bleed.

The kettle clicked beside her and she poured the boiling water into two cups — her tea and his coffee. Adding milk and sugar, she picked them up and walked to his office where she found him at his desk, hunched over a stack of papers. Again, she was struck by how tall he was, it was the curved hunch in his back, his desk was a little low which meant he had to bend further than the average person. *You just about get used to the size of him and then he catches you off guard all over again,* she thought. She placed his coffee on the corner of his desk, as far away from his papers and laptop as she could manage. She watched him jump in his chair, shocked by the fact that he wasn't alone in the world. He sat up straight and turned to look at her. He was about to speak when the paleness in her face stopped him.

'That time of the month again?' he asked. She nodded yes, and he didn't say a word. Instead, he took the cup from her hand, placed it next to his coffee then swept her up into his lap, putting his large hand on her belly, gently rubbing away her pain.

'I think I'll pack up for the day,' he said, lifting his hand from her belly to reach across and close his laptop.

'Don't be silly,' she argued. 'Finish what you're working on.'

'No,' Charlie said firmly. 'It can wait. I'll come down to your movie corner, we'll get under a blanket and hibernate for the day.' She watched as he picked up a pen and scribbled a few notes onto a scrap of paper in his scruffy handwriting. 'Go on then, you go choose the films and I'll get the blanket. I'll see if I can find some popcorn and chocolate as well.'

She stood and picked up the cups. As she walked away, he leant forward and slapped her arse. She was surprised that she didn't spill a drop of tea or coffee and giggled the instant his hand moved away from her. Her muppet man, a scholar, and gentleman, the type of man who would hold the door open and slap your arse on the way through. The type of man who joked about her being the little lady, chained to the sink while bragging about his prowess with both the hoover and the tip of his tongue.

Moments later she was picking out films in the grotto when out of the corner of her eye she saw him coming down the spiral stairs. His arms were loaded with blankets, snacks, her slippers, along with a couple of bottles of beer for him. He put them down by the sofa then strolled to the middle of the room to examine the beginnings of her little model town, three little log cabins and half of what looked like a town meeting hall.

'You're still full of surprises aren't you babe?' he said, and she heard the grin in his voice. 'I never thought you'd take to something like this. Not in a million years.'

'Tip of the iceberg, darling,' she replied as her eyes scanned over the endless rows of DVDs. 'You'll never get bored with me around.'

There, in the middle of one of the shelves, she found the old classic 'It's a Wonderful Life'. Picking it up off the shelf and strolling across the room to the sofa where Charlie was already under the blanket, she found herself thinking, *it certainly is a wonderful life, even on turtle days.*

.10.

Into the Woods

It was a scorching summer Sunday in Castlegate, and Jessica was about her Granda's business. She had woken up early and run out to do a food shop, then prepared a healthy breakfast of yoghurt and fruit, followed up with grilled bacon for her Bampi. He grumbled a little about it not being fried but she paid no attention. She let it go over her head and when he was done, she told him that she was intent on keeping him strong and solid for as long as possible with a little healthy tweak here and there.

The work at the big Valentine house hadn't begun yet, but the planning and the logistics had. After breakfast, her Granda' sat writing out three lists. The first was a list of things they'd need right away for the construction and landscaping, things like the gravel and timber they'd need for the raised flower beds and the lining for koi pond moat. On the second list were all the things he'd need after the donkey work was completed, the peat and the sand. The slabs for the path that would lead down to the zen garden and the hedges and archway that would go around it, hiding it away. The third list was what he called ribbon and bow work, on it were all the flowers, the water feature, the little bridge to cross the koi pond and, of course, the gazebo. He put a star by these last two items as they'd need to be made to measure.

Jessica's job was to drop the lists of at Cactus Jack's garden centre – which she had already done – while her Granda' spent the day on the phone drumming up some casual labour. Finding herself at a loose end she took the time to enjoy a casual stroll. It was such a lovely day, the sun was roasting, the birds were twittering, and a fresh breeze was blowing over from the fields. She decided to walk away from the village with the vague idea of walking all the way to the Meridian Hotel to have tea and maybe take a turn around the grounds.

She was curious about the Meridian, as were all the locals of Castlegate, Pickford, and Oakenbrook. The three villages had long memories and still spoke of the time before the Meridian Hotel when the Cavendish Manor stood on those grounds. The old folks still talked of the lords of the manor, the father, Sir Norman, who often spoke of how his blood went back to the old Earl of Mercia, and whose arrogance and pomposity was legendary around these parts, and, of course, young Sebastian who went mad in the ruins of his father's house.

Jessica was fifteen when the ruins of the old manor were sold, and unlike the rest of her peers, she had never tried to creep in and carve her name above the fireplace in the old drawing room. It was a rite of passage for everyone else, but throughout her teenage years, Prudence kept a tighter leash on her daughter. As Jessica thought about it now, she realised how much of her youth had slipped through her fingers. She had missed out on being young and immature during that time of life when no one could reasonably expect any differently of her. There had been no time for shenanigans, no time for school discos or White Lightning at the park. In fact, her first alcoholic drink hadn't been until freshers' night at university, and by then the shy wallflower act was deeply ingrained.

As Jessica wandered along the road her mind began to flit back and forth between thoughts of tea at the Meridian Hotel and memories of the furore at her parents' house when she told them of her plans. Predictably, the idea of her daughter spending her time cutting grass, weeding, and generally scrabbling around in the dirt sent Prudence off the deep end.

'Obviously I'm wasting my time trying to make a lady out of her.' She had yelled addressing her own father. 'I mean it's bad enough that she came out as tall as she did. No girl needs to be that tall. But you won't be satisfied will you … Not until she has rough hands and dirt under her fingernails and she's as common as the rest of your tribe.'

'That's enough Pruney!' Owen had yelled back, his face beetroot red. 'Your mum would turn in her grave if she could hear you talk like this … she'd be ashamed of you, really she would.'

'How would I know?'

'It's not my fault you didn't have a mother Pruney … I didn't take her away from you she just died. You had your sisters … that's better than some have.'

'I grew up dirt poor with a father who had no time for me, with a whore and a butch lesbian raising me … can you blame me for wanting better for myself and my daughter?'

'Enough!' Jessica had yelled, coming in between her mother and Granda'. 'Enough ... I'm an adult ... I'll make my own choices!'

'You've never known what's good for you.' Prudence had muttered under her breath.

'Do you hear yourself?' Jessica sounded so tired and weary, even to her own ears. 'I can't remember the last time I had any encouragement from you or failing that a kind word, even a crumb of affection. Everything with you has a passive-aggressive edge ... worse than that you're not even interested in me. Not who I am, at any rate, you're only interested in what you can make out of me. You haven't even asked me why I've split up with Kelvin ... he was beating me mother, I was living in fear.'

'Well, whose fault is that? I told you he was no good and you still decided to shack up with him.' Prudence had stopped dead then, perhaps sensing for the first time in her adult life that she had gone far too far. Her eyes fell away to the floor in the manner of a guilty child.

'Congratulations, Mother.' Jessica had replied. She took her Granda' by the wrist and led him towards the double door of her parent's house. 'You were right again,' she called as she closed the doors behind her.

The sharp sound of a car horn brought her out of her replay of the argument and back to herself with a jolt. She jumped back onto the path just in time to avoid a passing jeep clipping her. She couldn't remember stepping out into the road. All of this was flying around her head, and somewhere there in the background she found herself thinking about the other rite of passage in Castlegate, she was thinking about the bear hunt.

Once upon a time the old, crazy farmer around these parts, one Lesley Starkey, claimed to have seen a bear in the woods at the bottom of his field. Of course, back then he had been known as Young Starkey, son of Barry, and it had been his grandfather Walter who still technically owned the farm. In addition to working on the farm for his father – who was far too busy waiting for old Walter to finally bite it to pull his own weight – Young Starkey worked for the Cavendish fox hunt. On one particular hunt, he had followed the hounds from one end of Castlegate to the other and finally across his grandfather's land and into the woods at the bottom, which were then known as the Pickford woods. Twenty minutes later, he had remerged as white as a sheet followed closely by a spooked pack of hounds.

'Bear!' he had shouted as he ran past Lord Cavendish. 'There's a bear in them woods!'

Young Starkey had told everyone ... absolutely everyone. The men in the Tiger's Head pub, the women leaning over their fences for a gossip, but most of all he told the kids. And when the kids grew up to be adults, he told their children and their grandchildren, and this was how the Pickford woods became Starkey's woods, and how generations of kids grew up in the shadow of the supposed bear.

The bear hunt was a time-honoured tradition, a group of teens would creep into the woods at dusk. They would sit around drinking pilfered vodka or sharing a joint of whatever ditch weed they could get their hands on. When it got dark, they'd walk around the woods and take it in turns to slink away from the group without being seen in order to roar from the shadows and leap out of bushes at each other. The aim was to scare the piss out of each other, and whoever screamed the loudest was known as 'the Starkey' until the next bear hunt.

Jessica had stepped out into the road because she was directly opposite Starkey's woods. Thinking about the argument had made the idea of afternoon tea at the Meridian grow distant. Afternoon tea at the Meridian was something her mother would enjoy. She could picture her, sitting rigid and nibbling at a mini scone, being careful to not drop a single crumb, of course. She felt the woods calling out to her, not the bear, there was no bear in the woods, but maybe there was some mischief to be found there.

Fully aware now and present in the moment she crossed the road safely and let herself through the kissing gate. The public right-of-way ran along the edge of the field and she saw it was thick with dog paw prints. The hedges were littered with crisp packets and empty drink bottles and oddly as she walked her foot kicked a stick of chalk out in front of her. She bent down and picked it up and after examining it for a moment slipped it into her pocket.

She followed the path into the woods, and she was barely fifty steps in when her eye was caught by something at the foot of beech tree. It was a discarded magazine from which a face was leering at her. When she got closer to it, she saw a naked blonde woman sitting with her legs wide open juggling her ample boobs.

'Well, there you are,' she said aloud to no one at all. 'There's no bear in these woods but there is the occasional hairless beaver.'

She laughed to herself and carried on walking along the track. Deeper in, she came to a crossroads where the right-hand path seemed to lead away to a darker, older, more foreboding part of the woods. She spied a red squirrel on the left side of the track and decided to follow it.

A memory bubbled up inside her, she was five and walking in the woods with her mother and one of her mother's friends. She had spotted something moving in one of the trees and had tried to climb it, her mother warned her not to, but she didn't listen and when she fell, she scraped the skin of her knee. She remembered running to her mother bloody, crying, and arms outstretched for a hug. Prudence had taken hold of her and firmly held her back.

'No Jessica. No hugs, you'll get blood all over me. I told you not to climb that tree, didn't I?'

Sobbing, Jessica nodded her head, but then her mother's friend had turned her around and wiped her knee clean with spit and a tissue. Then she had been lifted up and pulled into the warmest hug of her short life. She couldn't remember that lady's name but she was a plump woman with a kind face. As this came flooding back to Jessica, she realised that it was in that strange woman's arms that she first realised something wasn't quite right. She was only five, a little bit of a girl and there was so much to learn about the world. Until that moment she didn't know mums could be soft and warm.

She had been leaning with her back against a tree and, suddenly overcome by that heavy, buried sadness, she slid all the way down the tree, collapsing into a heap on the ground. She sat there sobbing and let the woods go on around her, the birds were tweeting, the critters were scampering through the undergrowth, and the wind was rustling the branches. From somewhere deeper in the forest little feet were moving towards her, breaking twigs, and splashing in puddles and finally clambering up onto a rock beside the tree. Jessica didn't hear the owner of those feet approaching, she was too busy sobbing into her hands. A stampeding elephant could have galloped past and she would have been none the wiser.

She stopped crying long enough to take a deep breath and dabbed her eyes dry with the heal of her palm. *There's always more bottom,* she thought to herself. *I keep thinking that I've reached rock bottom but there's always more waiting for me.* She sniffed and dug inside her jeans pocket for a tissue to wipe her nose. Unable to find one, she was just considering wiping her nose the sleeve of her coat – *oh Jessica that's so common* – when a little hand shot out and offered her a handy pack of tissues. Jessica nearly jumped out of her skin but, for a moment, she didn't look around. She did no more than stare at the little hand and the packet of tissues.

'My mummy makes me keep them with me,' a little girl's voice announced. 'She says only little boys walk around with snotty noses and I'm too lovely to be a little boy.'

'My mother said something similar only it wasn't as polite.' Jessica answered. Still not looking up at the owner of the little hand, she took the pack of tissues, fumbled one out and honked into it. Halfway through she looked up and saw the little girl and stopped dead. She was quite possibly the prettiest little girl Jessica had ever seen. Big blue eyes stared out at her from underneath a wool hat, knitted to look like a fox's head, complete with pointy ears, black buttons for eyes and a nose, and whiskers. She had perfect porcelain skin, dimples, and long curly hair that poked out from beneath her hat.

'Why do you have sad eyes?' the little girl asked.

'Oh, it's nothing.' Jessica blurted, slightly embarrassed to be caught in this state by this little, pixie princess. 'I just got myself upset about nothing is all.'

'No,' the little girl shook her head. 'You have deep down sad eyes like Uncle Charlie. Uncle Charlie didn't get enough time … he was really, really sad when I was tiny but he's getting better now … Daddy's helping him, Daddy's good at helping people … Daddy used to have deep down sad eyes but mostly he's happy now.'

The little girl stopped and tilted her head as if listening to some far-off sound. Jessica stood up, dusted the dry earth from her bum, and then looked around, replaying the little girl's comments in her head. She was struck by the childish honesty and innocence of it. It's always left to the child to point out that the Emperor is naked because adults refuse to see it.

'Are you lost?' Jessica asked. She looked around for the little girl's parents, flatly refusing to address the naked Emperor. 'You're not here alone, are you?'

'Of course not,' she replied in a 'what a stupid thing to say' tone of voice. 'My Daddy's here, he's coming now.' She pointed to a shape moving some way down the track. The little girl jumped down off the rock and began to kick through the undergrowth as if looking for something. 'Maybe he could help you with your sad eyes … but don't tell him I said that. He says I see too much and I should learn how to be discreet … actually,' she said, thinking carefully, 'it's best you don't tell him anything I've said.'

'Twinkle!' A voice yelled from about fifty yards away. 'Twinkle, where have you got to? I told you not to get too far ahead.' The voice sounded loving but frustrated, like a father's voice, like a real honest to goodness daddy.

'I'm here Pop-Pop… I found a red woman.'

'Twinkle, is that your name?' Jessica asked, wondering who on earth would call their daughter Twinkle.

'No.' The girl laughed, 'He calls me that because I'm his starlight … Mummy is his moonbeam, and Frankie the baby is the chip off his old block … I don't know what that means though.' Twinkle confessed.

'It means they're alike.'

'Oh,' the little girl said with a furrowed brow. 'Mostly he says that when Frankie is breastfeeding.'

Jessica couldn't help but laugh. When she laughed the little girl – who was unaware she had said anything funny – responded the way she always did to laughter. She smiled, and when that little girl smiled confidence, warmth, and happiness radiated from her skin. Jessica thought that looking at her was like looking at a negative of herself at that age. Twinkle was blessed, she would never grow up to be a wallflower, she would always know her own worth.

Something occurred to Jessica, 'Frankie …' she said aloud. 'Is his full name Francis Arthur?'

'How do you know that?'

'I met your mummy a few days ago … She was at Mr Valentine's house.'

'Oh, Uncle Jude.' She said and sniffed wrinkling up her little button nose. 'I wasn't allowed to go because of the grown-up business.' She paused and looked over her shoulder at the shape of her Pop-Pop, getting bigger as he made his way towards them.

When she spoke again she was whispering,

'I'm not supposed to know because I'm only eight … but Uncle Charlie is still sad a lot of the time and he doesn't talk to Uncle Jude anymore, they fell out when I was a baby … and Daddy's worried about him because … Charlie, he's not really my uncle but Daddy loves him like a brother.'

'You don't miss a thing, do you?' Jessica said, and the little girl smiled again, this time her smile was full of mischief.

The man was feet away now, Jessica saw him and was struck by an odd sense of familiarity, she thought she vaguely knew him from someplace. *Come on Jess, engage your brain,* she thought to herself. *This little girl's mum is Becky Walker-Doyle. You recognised her from that documentary the Girlfriend Experience, which would make him…*

'Hank!' she said aloud. The man walking into the clearing looked up at the sound of his own name. It was odd, he wasn't what Jessica had expected, not from looking at his daughter. She had expected some young, fit, Adonis of a man, but here he was … very ordinary, slightly pot-bellied, brown hair that had the odd strand of white here and there, and a thick beard covering his chin. He was wearing a poncho, of all things. Its natural, colourful pattern was stained with splashes of paint. He had a large holdall slung over his right shoulder and a sketch pad under his left arm.

'Hannah.' he said, huffing and puffing slightly. 'Please don't run off, not everyone you meet in the woods can be trusted!'

'Yes Pop-Pop,' Hannah said, and her eyes went down to her shoes.

'Sorry,' Hank said, addressing Jessica. 'Don't take any offence to that … it's just my little girl, she's far too bold for her own good. Quite the opposite of shy kids like me and you hey? But my lord, you've gotten big,' he said gesturing towards Jessica with his head. 'I mean you've grown up well because you were always tall for your age, but you've grown into it so to speak.'

'Do you know me?' Jessica asked.

'Of course I do, you're old Owen's granddaughter … my old man used to work for him for a short while. Sometimes I'd come along and they'd use me as cheap labour … I think my old man used to make you nervous though. Anytime we popped around Owen's house you'd hide behind his leg. I can totally sympathise with that … my old man used to make me nervous too.' He let out a slight snorting laugh, thought for a moment and then said, 'But you said my name just now?'

'Oh, I recognised you from the telly.'

'Oh.' Hank replied. And then there was silence. Jessica stared awkwardly off into space, Hank looked to his daughter who was searching through the undergrowth at the base of the tree.

'Found one!' she exclaimed. 'A gift for Toskr.' She held a nut up in the air, presenting it to the adults, and then promptly threw it high into the branches. 'There you are you scoundrel ... now leave us alone.'

'Her godfather fills her head with nonsense. That's why we're here actually, you remember Charlie of course ...'

Obviously this was the Uncle Charlie that little Hannah had been talking about, but it wasn't a familiar name to her, at least not from her past, she couldn't recall ever knowing a Charlie back in the day.

But then something came back to her, something her mother had said. Prudence had seen her tatty copy of 'The Karaoke Glow' and started moaning about the trash book she was reading, then she had started ranting about how it was bad enough having the rock star living down the road, but the writer had brought a herd of slack-jawed gapers down upon them ... and yes, Prudence had then said that the writer was Tommy Walker's adopted son.

'Is Charlie the Charles Dunn who wrote "The Karaoke Glow"?'

'Yeah, that's him ... that's one of the good ones ... I mean I like them all but obviously I'm biased.'

'I loved "Karaoke Glow",' she said, and her eyes went glassy.

'I'm not allowed to read Uncle Charlie's books.' Hannah announced from halfway up the tree. 'They're for grown-ups so I think they must be full of rude sex bits ... I'm not allowed to go to

Daddy's studio either … most of the time there are naked people there.'

'You know, I remember thinking to myself, I'm going to be totally honest with my kids. I'm going to answer their questions and have proper conversations with them,' Hank said. As he made eye contact with Jessica he was blushing slightly. 'Well trust me, it's a mistake … when you have kids of your own never stop lying to them.'

Jessica laughed. She saw pride on Hank's face, it was there just under the rosy-cheeked embarrassment and slight frustration that came with raising a young, free spirit. They watched for a moment as Hannah scrambled up the tree trunk then reached out and hung on to a branch like it was the monkey bar in the local playground. She began to swing back and forth until Hank shouted for her to stop. She let go and landed on her feet like a cat.

'Are you walking back to the village?' he asked and gestured with his arm as if to say, 'come with us'. Hannah was already running ahead, and Hank had to shout to remind her not to get too far in front.

'Yeah, I guess so,' Jessica answered. 'I think I've satisfied my curiosity.'

'What did you come looking for? Were you chasing spirits?' Hank winked.

'No,' Jessica answered, she pushed a lock of her strawberry blonde hair out of her eyes and muttered to herself, 'only the Vodka variety.'

'Oh … do you mean the bear hunt, were you here for that? Aren't you a little old for that now? Besides, don't the kids usually do that with … you know … a group of friends?' he teased.

They were approaching the edge of the woods and Jessica could see the fields. She fetched up a deep sigh as she tried to frame an explanation that would obscure the truth.

'I never did it when I was younger you know? Did you?'

'No … you had to be popular to go on a bear hunt in my day,' Hank said, as he stepped out of the woods and into the field. Jessica had thought the use of 'in my day' was an exaggeration, that he was talking as if he was old before his time. But now in the glare of the afternoon sun, she saw a little silver in his mostly black hair.

'Well at any rate,' she began widening her stride to catch up with him, 'I was doing some chores for Granda' and then I thought I'd go for a walk to the Meridian.' At that, she saw Hank smile, but not knowing what to make of it she pressed on. 'And I just got to thinking about all the stuff I missed when I was a kid. I ended up coming down to take a look around … I guess to try an imagine what it was like to be …'

'What … popular, or drunk in the woods?' Hank asked jokingly, 'I guess it amounts to the same thing really. And to be honest, I think the whole popularity thing is overrated … I was an outcast at school and that mattered then, but now I have Becky and my kids, and I'm exactly what I set out to be … meanwhile, half the kids who terrorised me are behind bars or divorced, working dead-end jobs or just generally dealing with some fucked up situation that they've dug themselves into. Don't get me wrong, I'm not saying that to gloat, I've had my fair share of trouble over the years and I don't wish it on folk … but you realise … it doesn't matter what you were back then, what matters is who you are now!'

'That's very profound,' Jessica said. 'And I guess now that I think about it, very true.'

'Well … Hannah, not too far … it's knowledge I've gained by obsessing about my own childhood for so long.'

On the walk back to the village they made small talk about this and that. Hank asked after her Granda' and she told him he was his same old, brash, bold, stubborn, and lovable self. Jessica mentioned meeting Becky and baby Frankie at Jude's place and went on to tell Hank about how she would be helping her Granda' with the big project. By the time they reached the bridge over the Pickford stream they were back on the subject of Charlie.

'What's he really like?'

'Don't you remember him?'

'I don't think I ever met him.' Jessica said, she moved the hair out of her eyes again and took a moment to peer over the bridge at the babbling brook. She remembered when she was a little girl her Granda' told her that if she went paddling in the stream, she wasn't to drink the water, not under any circumstance. *'If you drink that water, you're as good as inviting the Pookas in,'* he would always tell her. 'I don't think I ever saw him with you and your dad.'

'You're probably right,' Hank nodded. 'I think by then he had his Saturday job working at Cactus Jack's.'

'So, what's he like?'

Hank sighed and ran his fingers through his beard. He turned and stared at her dead in the eyes and she thought she saw something there, maybe it was the way the light was hitting him, but for a moment she thought she saw flecks of purple in his deep brown eyes. As those purple flecks danced in his eyes, a sympathetic look washed over his face. For a moment Jessica felt like he was looking into the heart of her. It passed as he moved his head, breaking eye contact. The purple faded back into brown and the sympathy fell from his face.

'Why don't you come to dinner?' Hank said. 'Friday night, Charlie's coming over so you can meet him and find out for yourself.'

Jessica let out a snorting, sort-of giggle at the idea and then clamped her hands to her mouth.

'Really, you're not kidding me, are you?'

'Of course not, the more the merrier,' Hank replied as he walked over the bridge, leaving Jessica behind is a state of happy bewilderment.

'Oh, and by the way,' he called back to her, 'I've got a message for that old lech granddad of yours ... "does she want any welsh inside her",' he repeated, holding his fingers up in air quotes, 'he couldn't pull a rotten tooth with that line ... tell him: what's got two thumbs and is banging the prettiest woman for miles around?'

He paused and looked over his shoulder to make sure Hannah was far enough away that she wouldn't hear him.

'This bastard!' he said and pointed to himself with both thumbs. He laughed, turned and walked away. Jessica thought about the invite

116

and when she did, she felt butterflies in her belly. *It'll be nice to make friends,* she thought. *It will be nice to meet Charlie.*

.11.

De Niro-ing around

Charlie, dressed once again like a well-padded Eskimo, swung the axe up over his head and with one swift movement brought it down and split a log clean in two. Thankfully, by now he had gotten the knack of the thing and there was a little more muscle to his arms, making them feel a lot less like bendy straws under the weight of the axe. There was something pleasing about it, hitting the log dead centre and watching the two halves fly in opposite directions. It was a good way to work out his frustrations. He put his axe down by the side of the tree stump that served as his chopping block. With his gloved hand, he picked up a bottle of beer, nestled in the snow by his feet. He took a gulp, then another, then a third, then sighed with satisfaction.

Something he enjoyed about living in this frozen country was the beer. It was always cold and crisp. Drinking outside in the snow was like drinking inside a chest freezer, but then again, inside the cabin the beer was always cold as well. The cabin had an odd climate. All the rooms and corridors had electric radiators which, at best, took the bitter chill out of the room, but they never made it feel cosy. It was toasty and warm in the bedrooms and the living room because of the log fire, which Charlie kept burning practically all day long. Building the fire was usually his first job in the morning, something he attended to even before having a wash or cleaning his teeth. Once the fire was burning, he'd rush upstairs to the bathroom and jump into a hot shower. The saving grace of the cabin for him was that, thanks to the fancy electric combi-boiler, there was an endless supply of almost scalding hot water. He would have preferred it to be pleasantly warm, but the controls and settings were beyond him. He had given up fiddling with the buttons long ago and made do with either freezing cold or scalding hot. After his shower, he would normally dress, eat breakfast with Alison, and then disappear to his office to write. Some days he spent a good nine hours in front of his screen. On those days, however consumed he was by the story he was crafting, he still remembered to pop his head around the door every couple of hours and rebuild the fire.

In the afternoon, much like this afternoon, he took a couple of bottles of beer outside, planted them in the snow and set about chopping tomorrow's logs. Arguably, his afternoons outside with a beer and axe were a vital part of his writing routine. The physical activity, the cold crisp air, the wild beauty of the landscape, and yes, the alcohol, all helped. These things allowed him time to decompress from the day's scribbling and prepare for tomorrow's.

He had noticed that the beer tasted a lot better here in Húsavík. Here, it wasn't the corporate piss water they had back home, but rather an artisan brew called Saga. The logo on the front was the head and torso of a Viking woman in profile. She was sitting upon a shield, holding a drinking horn. The little Viking woman seemed to be smiling, at least that's what it looked like to Charlie.

He finished his Saga, then threw the empty bottle as hard as he could into the air. It spiralled up into the sky and he mimed shooting it with two fingers, made chubby by his thick glove. That was his third, but who was really counting? What was the harm in having an extra beer on a tiring day? No harm. Certainly, Alison didn't mind how much he drank. He was a lightweight anyway, and she had often laughed about how quickly he got drunk. A lot for Charlie was six, maybe seven pints, and today he had only drunk three small bottles so that would be just fine.

He was frustrated. He hadn't written so much as a word in three days, having chosen instead to nurse Alison through the disappointment of her period. He didn't resent her for monopolising his time, far from it. Although Alison had been racked with a heartache she was trying to hide from him, Charlie still found a deep-down part of himself enjoying the concentrated quality time, the part that wasn't entirely satisfied with sex alone. She was allowing him to take care of her again, and that pleased him. When they first came to the cabin, she couldn't bear for him to lift so much as a cup on her behalf. If she had been strong enough to handle the axe, it would have been her in the snow every afternoon chopping wood. Charlie thanked the Lord that in this instance she relented and allowed him to do the job. If he didn't chop the wood and build the fire, then what use would he be? It was as if she was determined to prove something. Maybe she wanted to prove that she could not only take care of herself now, but she could also take care of him, it was her turn. Alison had semi-retreated into the role of a Stepford wife and the work was divided up so that he did the writing, chopped the wood, and built the fires, and she did absolutely everything else.

The night before they had sat and cuddled on the sofa, eating their dinner from trays on their lap. Charlie had made baked ziti, which was more or less a pasta bake. He had glommed the recipe, and the fancy name, from watching 'The Sopranos', one of his all-time favourite TV shows, and every time he cooked it, he'd strut around the kitchen, acting like a mobster. By now Alison was on the inside of his routine, and while he 'De Niro-ed' his way around the kitchen, she did her own impression. Hers was half Harley Quinn, half vapid Jersey Shore gangster's moll. What this all came down to was Charlie trying to fit in the all-purpose phrase 'fuggedaboutit' into conversation as often possible, while Alison referred to him as 'Daddy'. It's funny how Daddy only sounded right in her gangster's moll voice. It was likely that Charlie would have thrown up in his mouth if she'd ever tried to call him Daddy in her own voice.

'I've missed this,' Charlie had said later that night after the cooking and eating was done.

'Missed what?'

'Just being ourselves,' he replied.

'We are ourselves, we're back to normal,' Alison replied, slightly baffled.

'Kind of,' Charlie took a moment to think of the best way to continue and then said, 'but up until now you haven't let me do anything for you … there's no debt to repay, you know that, right?'

Alison eyes filled with tears in response and then she buried her head into Charlie's chest. At that, he knew there would be no more discussion, at least not that night. Her gratitude still weighed far too heavy on her, for him to even say 'you owe nothing' was too much for her take. They spent the rest of the night sitting on the sofa, cuddling under the blanket, watching the TV without really concentrating on it. Charlie was smiling placidly and holding her hand, thinking about the words he wanted to say but couldn't. Not now ... this was frustrating but...

Now, as he stood three beers deep in the snow, next to a large pile of chopped wood, he realised where the frustration came from. It was born in the moment that Alison had looked up at him, just as they were about to have sex, and said, 'let's make a baby'. He had found it impossible to say, 'No, we can't'. Once upon a time there was nothing he wanted more than to be a dad, but he had already grieved for the loss of that ambition. Watching Alison fade during the dark days, he had put his dreams of fatherhood into a box and buried them deep within the ground. Even as she recovered, he had been reliably assured that there would be no children. No children, not ever, at least not with Alison. He had made an uneasy peace with this fact. He could sacrifice fatherhood as long as her suffering was done with. If the rest of Alison's days on Earth were spent in a state of dreamlike bliss, then what did anything matter? Given half the chance they could be happy together, and if he had anything to do with it, she would never know pain or heartache again.

A tear rolled down Charlie's face. He moved his gloved hand underneath his furry hood to wipe it away before it froze. He picked up the axe and carried it back into the woodshed, then returned to gather up the logs he had chopped. It struck him how, no matter what he did next, Alison would suffer. He felt stuck between the clichéd rock and hard place; tell her now and break her heart or say nothing and watch as her desire for a child slowly destroys her. Of course, he had been warned about this, he had been told to steer clear of the Midway. Bargaining with the Pookas was a tricky business. The deals always seemed to be fair but the devil was in the details, and the details were always stacked in the spirits' favour.

Standing at the back door he caught a glimpse of his reflection in a pane of glass. He looked pale and haunted. It reminded him of the face he wore in the cancer ward after creeping off to sit in the toilets, where he could cry without feeling guilty about it. He forced himself to smile, it looked ugly and unnatural at first, but after a while his face softened enough that he felt able to bend down and push the door open with his elbow, almost dropping the logs in the process. He kicked the snow from his wellies, then stepped in and made his way down the corridor to the living room, leaving a trail of wet footprints on the hardwood floor.

He found Alison lying on the sofa. The TV was on and she had a book in her hand, but she wasn't doing anything other than rubbing her belly and staring off into space. Charlie crossed the room and dropped his bundle of logs into the brass bucket by the side of the fireplace. The sound of it startled Alison so much that she dropped her book and rolled off the sofa, falling face-first onto the rug.

'Shit, are you alright?' he said as he rushed across the room to help her up.

He reached down with his long arms and took her hands in his. Smiling as he helped her back to the sofa, she nodded that yes, she was fine.

'I must have been daydreaming, I didn't hear you come in,' she explained. Instinctively, her hand returned to her belly and she began to rub it again.

'Are the cramps still bad?' he sat down beside her, still in his snowy, outdoor clothes that instantly left a wet arse print on the sofa.

'It's not as bad now,' her hand fell from her belly and she gripped his glove. After a moment of silence, she spoke again. 'I got my hopes up a little, didn't I?'

'Yeah, a little,' Charlie confirmed.

'Never mind,' Alison's voice sounded light and happy. She removed his glove and gripped his hand tightly. 'After all, there's always next month.'

'Fingers crossed,' Charlie replied, and as the words slipped off his tongue, he cursed his cowardice.

.12.

The Woman in the Snow

It was nearing the end of Jessica's first week of back-breaking work as an apprentice landscape gardener and every inch of her ached. She had pulled her weight, alongside her Granda' Owen and the extra labour he had hired, and proven herself up to the task. The labourers were Polish farm hands and worked like proverbial Shire horses. The pair had sniggered at her when she had turned up on Monday morning, following behind Owen in her brand-new overalls. By Wednesday they were giving her a polite and respectful nod every fifth time she passed with her wheelbarrow full of earth. On Thursday Bill – who spoke the most English – had come to congratulate her on all hard work.

'Is good work for woman yes!' he said as he patted her on the back. 'You work like English man, which like Polish woman.' He laughed then and turned to translate his joke for his friend Ben, who also laughed.

Of course, their real names weren't Bill and Ben, she had asked her Granda' Owen what their names were, and he had replied:

'Something unpronounceable, Strawberry.'

'You can't say that, Bampi!'

'I can … I just did.'

'Yes, but you shouldn't say that.'

At that, Owen had stopped dead and put his fingers in his mouth, blowing a loud wolf whistle. When they looked up, he had waved them over.

'Listen up boys … my granddaughter thinks I'm not respectful enough. Remind me, what are your names again?'

'Is okay Mr Owen … Is hard name for English!'

'Go on… for my granddaughter's sake.'

'Tymoteusz and Wojciech.'

'See!' Owen had said, 'They aren't names, they are losing hands at scrabble.'

Jessica laughed at that and her laughter marked the end of the argument. She spent the rest of the week referring to them as 'Bill and Ben, the flowerpot men'.

Now, as she lowered herself down into the hot bubble bath; gardening, Bill and Ben, and her Granda' Owen were the last things on her mind. She was thinking about her invitation to dinner the next night, and the dress she had liberated from her mother's house for the occasion. It was a blue polka dot halter dress, with a black ribbon tied around the waist. It was her dress for the university leaver's ball, or at least it was the dress she would have worn to the leaver's ball if Kelvin had allowed her to go. She had not long started with him back then, but he had gotten her under the thumb quickly. And so, the expensive dress that she had picked out, the one that Prudence had paid for with Daddy's card, the dress that had cost Jessica a whole day of criticism as they walked around the shops, had stayed in the back of her closet until this very afternoon.

That afternoon on the way back from the Valentine house she had made her Granda' pull up around the corner from her parents' house and, when she had seen the Benz pulling away, she had snuck down the drive and let herself in. Minutes later she ran back up the drive, the dress flapping behind her, the matching heels swinging back and forth and jumped back in her Granda's van.

As she sunk lower into the bath, she thought about that dress hanging on the wardrobe door and imagined herself wearing it at the dinner party.

The talk around the village according to her Granda' Owen was that they were doing quite well for themselves. Hank's was maybe not a household name yet, but his art sold for good money and Becky had just opened her second coffee shop. More than likely, Hank and Becky would live in Oakenbrook somewhere, probably not far from her parents and Jessica smiled at the thought of that. She liked to think of Prudence turning up her nose at the thought of the artist and the ex-escort living down the road and giving lectures at the golf club about how folk like that 'lowered the tone'.

Of course, the dinner party would be an elegant affair. All soft jazz music, champagne, and canapés, and likely a taster menu cooked by upmarket caterers. All the guests would be artists and writers, intellectuals, and bohemian types. She would sit opposite Charlie and undoubtedly she would be shy, but she would also intrigue him, she would be the pretty little mystery drawing him in with her demure glances across the table. At the end of the meal, she would wait and he would come to her and…

'Strawberry,' Her Granda' Owen yelled, banging on the bathroom door. 'Have you grown gills?'

Flustered after having been dragged from her daydream, Jessica shouted back, 'I won't be much longer Granda!'

'Good, because I'm gagging for a pint see, and I can't go out without a splash on my face. Not with all those widowers hanging around the Tiger's Head.'

'Yeah, alright Tom Jones, I'm sure they are all just dying to throw their pants at you.'

'I just hope they've dusted the cobwebs out first.'

'Oh, you're awful,' she laughed. 'Give me ten more minutes and I'll get out.' She heard him begin to make his way down the stairs when a thought occurred to her. She called out to him, 'Hey Granda', you know that Hank chap ... Big Tommy's son ... Where does he live?'

She heard him walk back up two or three stairs, followed by the familiar creak of the top step as he sat down.

'He bought old Mr Shepard's house, just down the road from the pub.'

'What in Castlegate? Not in Oakenbrook?'

'Oh lord no ... Big Tommy was a rabid socialist and it's about the only common ground he Hank ever shared.'

'You know them well then?' she asked, she could smell his pipe smoke creeping under the door.

'Well enough, Strawberry,' he mumbled. 'But it's village life, see, we all know each other ... probably far too well. The art of good neighbouring is knowing everyone's secrets and not saying a word about them … until you're behind closed doors that is.'

'What do you know now, Granda'?' she asked as she got out of the bath and wrapped a towel around herself. 'Is it more stuff like the bloke who ran the garden centre who was growing weed with old Mr Shepard helping him?'

'You can laugh all you want, Strawberry, you don't know what goes on around these parts.' He paused long enough to cough and then she heard the pipe go back in his mouth, 'I know secrets that would turn your red cheeks chalky white. You have your Gran'ma's flame in your hair now, but I could make it grey, I could. Take Hank's family for instance, there's a thick vein of tragedy in that family. There's one thing in particular that I wouldn't dare tell you about … something that happened when Big Tommy was just a nipper. And then there's the mystery of Hank's Granda'. Went missing he did … and right after that terrible thing happened. Everyone said he ran away, and maybe he did. But others say that Mr Shepard did him in, others say his bones are buried deep in Starkey's woods, and if they're right about that I wish I knew where they were buried … I'd happily piss on that man's grave.'

Jessica was sitting on the edge of the toilet lid, listening to her Granda's tale. He hadn't really told her much at all, but the deep Welsh valleys in his voice always made his stories hypnotic. She heard him groan as he stood up from the top step, she pictured him stretching out his back, the way he always did, and his groan turned into a sigh of relief. Somewhere in the back of her mind, she had noticed that there were far more aches in his bones these days and she didn't like that, not one bit.

'Best you not talk about this stuff, see. If truth be told I'm not sure how much Hank knows and it's not our place to tell him. It's good neighbouring, knowing about the pain of the folk next door and not talking about it. I told Pruney that much when she was a nipper ... I said "Pruney, leave the bones where they are buried girl! The dead don't haunt the living, it's the living that haunt the dead" ... but she didn't listen. Anyway, mum's the word about Hank's Granda' ... But it's odd, isn't it ... that he should end up buying old Shepard's house?'

'Should I believe any of this?' Jessica asked.

'Suit yourself if you don't, it makes no difference to me, Strawberry.' Owen answered. 'Anyway, you take your time lovely ... I'm going to go outside and take a piss down the drain. I'll freshen up in the kitchen sink and then be off to see to one or two of them dusty widows ... do you want a chippy tea bringing home?'

'No,' Jessica laughed. 'I'll find something healthy in your fridge.'

'No, you won't.' Owen answered as he made his way down the stairs.

Lying on her bed, wrapped in her towels, she stared at the dress hanging on her wardrobe door. She was in two minds about it now, half of her thought it would be overkill, maybe turning up to Hank's very normal house in a vintage cocktail dress and matching heels like an American sitcom wife circa 1960 was too much. The other half of her thought, *damn it, I'll wear it anyway ... I'll turn up looking immaculate and take Charlie's breath away.* She went to sleep thinking of that and dreamt…

… the night sky was painted white with a thick blanket of snow. There was snow at her feet, snow as far as the eye could see, and there, in the distance, log cabins built in concentric circles. She looked down at her feet and saw that she wasn't wearing any shoes. She lifted her right foot and wiggled her toes examining the snowflakes stuck to them. She felt the chill and at the same time, she didn't feel it, not really. Her foot wasn't numb, her skin wasn't tingling… it was as if the cold was distant and far away.

She put her foot back down into the footprint she had left and wiggled it around. When she lifted her foot again, she saw that it wasn't her footprint but rather animal tracks. She moved forward slowly, watching her feet puncture the snow and marvelling at the animal tracks – hoof prints, they were hoof prints – that she left behind.

Before long, she found herself in the middle of the village. She watched smoke rising from all the chimney stacks, and although curtains were drawn across all the windows, she saw lights shining out from each cabin, and noticed how they lit up the snow in oblong patches.

Jessica looked straight ahead and realised she was standing opposite a building that looked like a meeting hall. She heard music coming from inside, the strings of a violin, and a little girl giggling. Her hand reached for the door handle, but before she could take hold of it the doors swung open and a woman was standing before her. The woman had green-blue eyes, dimples, and chestnut hair done up in a braid. She was beautiful, and all Jessica could think to say was,

'The dead don't haunt the living, it's the living that haunt the dead.'

The woman responded by smiling. Jessica opened her mouth to speak again but the woman shook her head. She whispered something but the words were so quiet they dissolved in the air before they reached her ear.

'What was that, what did you say?'

The woman didn't answer, she just shook her head and stepped backwards through the door, slowly closing it in Jessica's face.

Jessica woke shivering on the bed at the sound of a door slamming. Downstairs, her Granda' Owen – now a little worse for wear – was singing merrily and trampling around the house like a baby elephant. She could smell chip fat wafting up the stairs and her belly rumbled. Realising she hadn't had any dinner yet, she decided to throw on some clothes and wandered down to beg a chip butty from him.

As she slipped on her jimjams she tried to remember the dream but it was broken now. Shards that didn't make sense, something about tracks in the snow that didn't belong to her. What stayed with her were her Granda's words, the ones she had repeated in the dream.

'The dead don't haunt the living,' she said aloud. 'It's the living that haunt the dead.'

Extrasensory Perception

Charlie was sitting in the office, leaning back in his chair. His hands were clutching the back of his head and he was staring blankly out the window. Somewhere beneath him Alison was busy with her tiny town, he knew she was down there because he could hear Pink Floyd through the floorboards, moreover he could feel it in his body. 'Shine On You Crazy Diamond' was reverberating through the bare floorboards, into the flesh of his toes, up his legs, and into his spine. Pink Floyd, it made him think of Hank, it made him think of home.

Hank had always been obsessed with Floyd, Zeppelin, and of all those classic bands. He loved stoner music but had never touched a joint in his life.

'It's not the thought of being high or out of control that bothers me.' Hank had once said, in response to Charlie's occasional requests to get stoned together. Charlie had argued that they were, after all, both creatives and that kind of made the odd smoke their birthright. Or maybe it was an inheritance, something won for them by the countless mad, genius, shamanic outsiders who came before, and pathed the way for them.

'No, it's not the thought of being high or out of control that bothers me. Or breaking the law, it's a stupid bloody law ... No, what bothers me is the thought of walking around, smelling like a combination of concentrated ball sweat and ditch water ... that smell turns my gut.'

Of course, there had been a time when Charlie had indulged himself in the wackiest tabacky in all of Warwickshire. He had been a lot younger then, on the cusp of eighteen and working his part-time job at Cactus Jack's garden centre. One day, he had happened upon Mr Solomon's private greenhouse and had requested a sample from his old hippy boss. Solomon had agreed to allow him a taste, but only under his supervision. A few nights later he had knocked on the door of the little cottage at the back of the garden centre and got good and stoned with his boss. Charlie spent the night lounging in a beanbag, staring at the ceiling, listening to his boss tell his stories about the Pookas. What he had discovered that night, and on several occasions since, was that the weed induced a delicious light and bubbly feeling. It was like a weight coming up off his shoulder, or a wall coming down. He felt able to talk about the things he kept hidden away without having to worry about his ego, pride or his sense of shame. It didn't make him anymore creative, it didn't inspire ideas that weren't already there, but on occasion, he thought it might have helped him see his ideas more clearly.

Now, as he sat in the office chair, he spun around and thought of Proust. That old French luminary had written a seven-book epic inspired by a single bite of a single biscuit, the flavour of which recalled to him a perfect memory of his childhood. As a writer, Charlie knew all about the power that the senses held in evoking memories – maybe not as well as Proust, but he knew it well enough.

He closed his eyes and felt the vibrations of Roger Waters' singing voice shoot up and down his spine. That voice cried the invocation, *'Come on you raver, you seer of visions, come on you painter, you piper, you prisoner and shine'*. He knew exactly who that prayer was offered up for. It was Hank's prayer, a prayer for the artist who had regularly hidden his light under a cloak of banality and blandness. It was a song for the ordinary little boy who was afraid to shine on. Not in reality of course, in reality, the song was a tribute to Syd Barrett, the one member of Floyd who was so wild that he was forced out of the band. Syd, who went from wild to wilderness, but that didn't matter. What mattered was what the song meant to Charlie, and to Charlie it meant Hank.

With his eyes still closed, Charlie could see his friend … brother, Hank was his brother. It had always felt that way and they had slurred as much when they were deep in their pint glasses. He saw those affable, chubby, hamster cheeks, the dark eyes that were almost lumps of coal. Over the last few years there had been flecks of purple in those eyes, not always, but sometimes in the right light, they were there. And why did that make him think of that old story about Puck, the one where the trickster cheated both Leofric and Godiva with the same crafty ploy? He saw Hank's beard, thick and black, and often scruffed up from his hand scratching eternally at his chin. Once upon a time he had sported a ponytail but then Becky had come along and tidied him up, and he looked all the better for it.

Charlie saw the way Hank walked, a slight hunch in his shoulders with his hands shoved deep in his pocket, his head pointed towards the floor. And then – almost as if to contrast that – he remembered that night in The Gluepot when a bunch of drunk numbskulls had been harassing them, two of them holding him at bay while the others had Alison and her friend pinned in the corner. Hank had come steaming over with his shoulders back, his head held high, a look of steel in his eyes and he had taken those boys outside and beat them. Charlie hadn't said anything at the time, but that night Hank had been the spitting image of his father, Big Tommy Walker. Of course, by that time Tommy had gotten sick, and Hank was nursing his not-so-secret aching heart. Hank was watching the colossus that had cast a shadow over his childhood slowly crumble.

Now with the gift of hindsight, Charlie thought that what his brother needed to hear in that moment was 'he would be proud of you'. No, that was a lie, hindsight didn't come into it ... even back then Charlie had known what Hank needed to hear. And it would never come from Tommy, Tommy could barely recognise his son's face anymore. But they were men, and even in this day and age, there was something ingrained in their nature, something that urged them to be strong, resolute and leave the powerful things unspoken.

Charlie was falling deeper into the song, and deeper into Hank with it. Hank was a map, a web of sensory stimuli linked to a thousand stories that all began 'remember when'. This was extrasensory perception, not mind reading or fortune telling. This wasn't some mythic sixth sense or an ability to know what couldn't be known. Rather, it was knowing clearly what could be known with the five senses you had.

Hank was the smell of oil paints and turpentine. The sound of scraping heels, caused by the feet that he dragged through the world. He was the firm grip that squeezed Charlie's shoulder or the feel of fingers brushing through his ginger hair. *He used to joke about my hair, he'd run his fingers through it and call it candy floss or a ginger cloud.* Hank was the comfort of that tatty, old, torn, Jackson-Pollock-splatted, leather sofa that sat in the corner of his studio on the Roman road. He was the soft texture of the stuffing in the rip of the cushion, and the sharp springs underneath it.

'Will you ever stop fingering my sofa you pervert?'

'Buy a new one.'

'Oh yeah, typical rich kid answer.'

The map of Hank was coming alive, burning across his senses and suddenly he remembered Donnie Jr.

Hank never really wanted to box, he had no interest in it. But for Charlie, there was a second encounter with that bulldog-faced bully years after the first. A month after Charlie came of age, he was leaving a bar a little worse for wear. Donnie was heading in his direction looking fatter, meaner, and greasier then he remembered him. In fact, Charlie didn't recognise him, not until they were standing level with each other, and by then it was too late. When their eyes met Charlie could see it; rage, the desire to lash out at the world, and if not the world then whoever was closest.

Charlie ended that night in a hospital bed, kicked, and punched black and blue, and bloody; his head stamped on. When Donnie Jr was caught the following day he was charged, put on trial, and received three years for gross bodily harm.

Hank hadn't been there that night, and when he stood over Charlie's hospital bed he had loudly blamed himself for his friend's ... brother's, sorry condition. Charlie had lain in his bed, watching a furious glare pass from father to son. Tommy didn't say a word, but the look on his face spoke up on his behalf. It said, 'What use would you have been if you had been there? You would have taken half the beating and ended up in the bed next to him.'

Deeper, deeper down into his trance, his memories, and Hank is the smell of sweat and the sound of his gloves colliding with the heavy bag. Charlie is there, in that gym, his face is still puffy and purple, and his ribs still aching. He can almost hear Big Tommy barking orders, shouting for Hank to move his feet, to breathe out on the punches, not after them, and the only word of praise that was ever offered up was 'better'. Not good, never good ... only 'better'.

'Of course I'm not starting to enjoy it.' Hank had said, after one training session. By then Charlie was more or less healed and Big Tommy had made them walk home. 'I know what I am, I'm not a bloke, I'm not a lad, I'm not one of the boys. Sometimes I think that you're the only guy I know who can understand that, but then other times I think, well no, you don't get it because you're not working-class ... you're our lovable cuckoo.'

'I might not be working class but I'm pretty smart, explain?'

'It's like this,' Hank had stopped dead and sat down on the curb. The bluebell road that lead from the boxing club was barely wide enough to fit two cars passing in opposite directions and the path was a slither of concrete. It meant that Hank was sitting in an awkward cramped position and as Charlie sat down next to him, being a good foot and a half taller than him even at that age, he looked even more ridiculous. In the fields beyond, the rapeseed was high, and in the heat of the day it was letting off its noxious, urine-like smell. For Charlie, this moment, this memory in the sensory map of Hank would always smell somewhat like piss and wildflowers.

'Growing up around here you learn early on that the worst thing you can be is gay because gay is not masculine.'

'But you're not gay, are you ... it doesn't matter to me if you are but ...'

'I'm not gay, not by your middle-class definition. You see, where you come from gay means "sexually attracted to men".'

'So, what does it mean around here?'

'Everything but that,' Hank had sighed. 'It's the opposite of masculine. It means you're an outsider, sensitive, creative, not obsessed with sport or looking like a hard-case all the time. Gay means that when you've been on the pints you don't shout, "Get your tits out!" every time a girl passes you by. It means that you're not made of stone all the way through, it means that some part of you is soft, some part of you feels. That's why Donnie beat you, because you're not masculine in his eyes. A lot of the time you get a pass Charlie, but there's an uglier side to that ... the people who'd abuse me for being unmanly will give you a pass because you don't even come close to measuring up to manhood in their eyes, you don't count enough for them to care about. Likewise, they wouldn't beat on a lad that really was gay as long as he was camp enough. They laugh at gay lads, they say, "ah he's alright for a poofter", or "I don't mind as long as he doesn't try and pull the stiff one eye on me", or "more totty for us".'

'Gay people get beaten up all the time for being gay,' Charlie had interjected.

'Of course they do, and posh lads get beat up for being posh, and black lads get beat up for being black. But you're missing my point, I'm not defending these people for picking on me because they think I should know better. I'm not saying that it's good that they leave gay guys alone. I'm saying it's awful that they look at these people and think, "they're nothing, they are beneath my contempt." Imagine going through life thinking so little of someone because of their sexuality or class that they are literally nothing to you. I get the abuse because I'm a reflection of them, I'm from their class, from their people and I have a softer side that's missing in them. They can't look at me and say he's gay so he doesn't count – although I imagine some of them do. Looking at me is like looking directly at what's missing from them. You see, I know these people, they're the guys who used to come to my old man's boxing matches. Not the boxing fans … just the handful who'd be up on their feet screaming "Kill the fucker Tommy!" … and if he was fighting a black man it wouldn't be fucker they'd shout. No, I'm not getting a feel for this, I don't have anything to prove to them. I don't like it, I don't like that my hands are sore all the time and that it's painful when I grip a pencil. Most of all I don't like that there's a chunk of buried anger in me that would relish in beating some prick bloody.'

'So, why are you doing it then?' Charlie asked.

'Because it's not about liking it. My old man's always lecturing me about how a man acts, a man protects his family, he keeps them safe and doesn't let them get pushed around ... it's been the same lecture ever since I was seven. Maybe it's not about masculinity, it's not about pride and proving I'm a hard case with a big pair of swinging bollocks. Maybe it's just about responsibility, I don't want to fight but I need to know how to ... A man does what he has to keep his loved ones safe. He doesn't stand by and let them come to harm ... it's not about masculinity, it's just about being a man.'

Down in the basement 'Shine On You Crazy Diamond' had finished and now Charlie could hear Lord Huron singing about being 'In the Wind'. This new song nagged at him, it called him away from Hank and pointed him in some other direction, some place far less comforting and life-affirming, Charlie resisted it. In the past when he daydreamed, his mind had been like a river turning this way and that, making its own course to the sea. But he knew – or at least hoped – that if he concentrated hard enough, he could direct the course of this river. He concentrated on Hank, he refused to let that chubby, affable face slip from his view, not yet.

Hank smelled of CK1, and Becky because they became inseparable. This is the way of things, of course, people are like patchwork quilts; little squares of personality, memory, and experience sewn together to make something bigger than one person. Becky would smell of ...

142

coffee, eventually, but before that she had smelled of perfume and sex, or had he just imagined that because Becky looked like sex? Of course, he knew her secret now, so maybe that old liar, hindsight, was altering his sensory perception. Hank called her his Lichtenstein blonde, his moonbeam, and when he spoke about her his face lit up with a bright white light, which was shot through with fear. Charlie knew that look, he recognised it from the mirror. It was a look he wore when speaking about Alison. It was a look that said, I adore her and I don't know what I'd be without her. Eventually, from Hank and Becky came little baby Hannah, his happy, little, gurgling goddaughter. Now the smell around Hank was his regular mix of odours with the distant undertone of breast milk and soiled nappies. The pair of them always sounded tired, but it was a happy sort of exhaustion, and the gurgling and the cooing, it was enough to melt your heart.

Hannah had been a babe in arms, a couple of months shy her first birthday, and Alison had insisted that they keep their promise, even after finding the lump. It had been her idea in the first place, and she had made the offer long before that black day had come along.

'We'll mind her, you go have your honeymoon and enjoy yourself. She'll be in safe hands with me and Charlie for a couple of days, and there's Hank's mum as well so between the three of us we've got it covered. We'll treat it as a practice run, we might want some of our own one day.'

'Don't tell them, Charlie,' she had begged. 'Don't ruin their holiday, it can keep until they get back.'

Like a fool, he had agreed to that and not long into the week he had found Alison sitting in front of her keyboard in the living room, holding Hannah in the crook of her left arm, and playing a lullaby with her free right hand. He had stood in the doorway and just watched because it was beautiful.

Moments later, they were both struck by the same idea at the same time. Charlie watched her stiffen in her seat and stare at the wall and he thought, *we may never have this.* As soon as that thought popped into his head, he felt a trickle of a tear roll down his cheek, and at the same time across the room, Alison burst out sobbing on her piano stool. He wiped his tear away and rushed forward to grab his goddaughter before Alison's sorrow overtook her, God forbid she drop that precious little kiddo on the floor. As he took the happy, gurgling baby, Alison drove her face into his belly and cried. He slipped his arm around her and watched as little Hannah reached up with her tiny hand and took hold of his shirt. It broke his heart, but it wasn't about him. A man does what he has to for his loved ones.

Hannah ... by the time Alison had got really sick, she was two and a half and a ball of energy. She had her father's chubby cheeks, but that was because of the toddling, podgy, age of her rather than any overt resemblance to Hank. She would grow into her mother's face, Charlie could see that much clearly. The last time Alison smiled in hospital, a proper honest to goodness happy smile, it was for Hannah. Hank and Becky had bought the little one to visit, she was all blonde curls and cute little dress, and at first, she had been nervous. She had run to Charlie and gripped his leg, not wanting to look at all the machines and Alison's gaunt appearance. Charlie had lifted Hannah and placed her on his hip, and after a moment the little girl had looked down at Alison and smiled.

'*Twinkle, twinkle, little star!*' Hannah sang as she reached out for Alison.

'That's right. Twinkle, twinkle.' Alison replied. 'We used to sit at my keyboard and play it together, didn't we baby?' At that, she lifted her frail arms and took hold of Hannah's full weight with a slight grunt. She lowered her to the space between her wasted body and the rail that ran around the edge of the bed.

Still sitting in his chair in the cabin in the frozen North, Charlie remembered being in that room, watching as, for a single moment, joy overtook the pain in his lover's face. He remembered feeling a hand close on his shoulder, and Hank's familiar, firm, brotherly grip. He remembered glancing over his shoulder, seeing past Hank to Becky who was standing, pale in the corner, quietly sobbing with her hands clamped over her mouth to muffle the sound.

'Don't bring her again.' Alison had told Hank shortly after Becky slipped away to the café with Hannah in tow. 'It did my heart good to see her, but I don't want her to see me like this. I'm only going to get worse and I don't want to end up being that little girl's nightmare, I don't want to be the thing lurking under her bed.'

Recalling those words forced Charlie from his seat. He paced the small width of the office, as the indivisible poison of sadness and anger surged through his flesh. He began to wonder, how long had they been in this cabin now, two years, four years, eight?

Time was funny in this place, he knew that, but what was time like outside of their little world? He wondered if somewhere out there Hannah was celebrating her tenth birthday? Or maybe now she was eighteen, a young woman in her own right, and Hank … would he have mourned for his adopted brother by now? How many sleepless nights would Hank have spent wondering where his oldest friend had disappeared to?

Charlie closed his eyes and leant his head against the wall of the log cabin. The wood felt cold and hard against his bald dome, he tried to anchor himself to that feeling, he tried not to think or feel anything. He had lied to himself, of course, he had told himself that he could change the course of the river, but the river and his daydreaming mind always made its own course out to sea. Now he was in the river with Lord Huron … 'Take your time let the rivers guide you in, you know where you can find me again. I'll be waiting here till the stars fall out of the sky.'

'Come home, Charlie,' the voice was in his head, or rather, in his imagination. It was the voice of subtext, the voice in between the lines of the song now playing in the basement. It sounded like Hank, it sounded like Becky, it sounded like little Hannah … it even sounded like Jude. 'Do what you've got to do and then come home where you belong. The dead don't haunt the living Charlie, it's the …'

'No!' Charlie yelled. He began to punch the wall, left then right, then left again. Every time his fists made contact with the wood there was pain and blood. He felt broken knuckles and split skin, but by the

146

time he pulled back his hands they were fixed and as good as new. 'No, I won't hear this … it's not enough.'

He moved to his desk, opened the drawer and took out a half-finished manuscript. The title page read, 'The Karaoke Glow'. He held it in his hand for a moment before opening the window and casting it out into the snow. He watched it fly, flutter, and flap before coming down onto the snow with a thump. But when he turned back to the desk, there it was staring up at him from the draw.

'Fine, have it your way,' he said. He sat down in the chair and turned on his laptop. He closed his eyes and concentrated on his sensory map of Hank. He opened a new document, set the title page as, 'The Boy Who Tamed the Bear' and began.

Old Starkey used to say that there was a bear living in the woods at the bottom of his farm. He said it was a beast the size of a hill with teeth like daggers and claws that glinted in the moonlight. Old Starkey told this story as often as he could and all of Castlegate laughed at him behind their hands.

Slowly the new story, the Hank, Tommy and Hannah story, began to unfold in his mind, the bones of a plot leaping up from the deep well of ideas in his mind. And, as his fingers began to move faster across the keys, he thought. *It isn't enough time, not nearly enough, not yet.*

.14.

Wish You Were Here

Jessica was ready, her hair pinned up, her makeup fixed, the day's ache eased from her bones, and the dress fitting like a glove. She looked in the mirror and smiled. It was one of those days when she could see a beautiful woman looking back at her. She picked up her clutch bag and made her way to the door. It was seven p.m. and outside the July sun was still setting, casting a warm orange glow over the green of Castlegate. It was such a warm evening that she decided to carry her little cardigan over her arm and walk the six streets to Hank's house. The cardigans arms trailed down over the supermarket bottle of wine she was carrying, partially obscuring it from view. As she caught a glimpse of herself in someone's window, she thought she looked just a little like a drunk trying to hide her alcohol problem.

While she walked, she rehearsed possible questions and conversations. She had told herself not to gush, to be cool, friendly, polite, and warm. No matter how eloquent she hoped to be, in the back of her mind she suspected that when she laid eyes on Charlie she might just start crying and rambling on about how important his book was to her.

Jessica heard a giggle and looked back over her shoulder to see Hannah. Hank and Becky's little Hannah was walking along the brick wall dividing two houses on her tiptoes with her arms stretched out as if she was a tightrope walker. Jessica walked towards her waving and smiling, and both were returned by the feisty little girl who jumped down off the wall and skipped through the grass to greet her at the fence.

'Hello, Twinkle,' Jessica said, then looking back over her shoulder. 'Am I going to the right house?'

'Oh yes, we're staying with Nanna Mary tonight ... me and little Frankie,' she looked at her feet and began to kick the grass back and forth. 'I wanted to come but Mummy said it was grownup time. I asked Uncle Charlie if I could come too ... I told him Mummy wouldn't let me because you were coming.'

'If it was up to me, I'd let you come.'

'It's alright,' she said, sighing deeply. 'Mummy says I have to learn that I can't have everything I want, she says little girls and boys who get their own way all the time grow up to be not nice people!'

'Well, she's probably right about that, Twinkle.'

At that, Hannah looked over her shoulder, through the window, and into her Nanna's living room. Jessica followed her gaze and saw a short thin woman holding up a leather-bound book. Without warning, Hannah bolted towards the back door of the house that had been left open for her.

'I have to go now,' she called to Jessica 'Nanna's found the old photo albums, and I'm going to see all the grownups when they were little like me.'

As she walked away, Jessica considered the little girl. There was something infectious about her, she was like a little ball of sunshine. Jessica found herself fantasising about Hannah's home life, she imagined it as a bubble of warmth and love, with structure and boundaries. Somewhere deep down inside her own heart a little jealous voice spoke up asking, 'why her and not you?', but as she knocked on Hank and Becky's door she dismissed it.

A moment later Becky answered wearing jeans and a shirt, looking effortlessly beautiful. Behind her Hank was sitting on the stairs, talking on the phone. Jessica watched as Becky looked her up and down and offered her a warm smile.

'You look beautiful,' Becky said. 'I love your dress.' She moved aside and waved Jessica in.

'Thank you,' she said, blushing. As she stepped over the threshold, she handed the wine over to Becky and her eyes flitted to Hank.

'Well, you gotta do what you gotta do buddy. If you don't feel up to it, if you're not ready than we completely understand.'

Becky sighed, rolled her eyes, and held her hand out for the phone. As Hank handed it to her, she tipped him a wink as if to say, 'don't worry darling, I'll deal with this'.

'Hello Charlie, it's me. I just want to ask you something … when was the last time you got a bit of a snog and felt a woman in your hands?' There was a pause as Becky waited for an answer and Hank and Jessica made awkward eye contact. After a moment, Hank stood from the stairs and, with a hand on her back, led Jessica down the hallway into the kitchen.

'No, I'm not saying she would let you, especially not after meeting her once … but that's beside the point isn't it!'

'That's where little Hannah gets her directness from.' Hank said, chuckling.

He gestured towards several bar stools set up around the breakfast island and Jessica sat down, looking around while Hank fixed their drinks. She noticed that the outside of the house didn't seem to match the inside. From the outside, it looked like an average, ex-coal-board, pebbledash and concrete, semi-detached house. The kind of house that was sometimes known affectionally as a 'slanty-shanty' by the folks who lived in them, because of how uneven the walls were. But on the inside, the house was decorated and renovated immaculately. The kitchen was all black laminate, white counters and tiled floors. The oven was up high, fixed into a cupboard, and something delicious and spicy was bubbling away on the hob in the middle of the breakfast island. An extension had been built onto the kitchen, creating an L-shape and giving them a small dining area. A glass conservatory had been built beside the extension which clearly served as a makeshift home studio for Hank, as Jessica could see bookshelves full of art supplies and an easel covered with a sheet.

'Pink gin and lemonade.' Hank said as he handed Jessica a glass.

'How did you guess?' she asked with surprise, taking a sip from the glass.

'You look like a pink gin girl.'

Becky was walking into the kitchen, the phone still pressed to her ear, her other hand, which was holding the wine, was pressed to her hip. It made the bottle stick out at an odd angle. Her brow was furrowed and a look of concern was plastered on her face.

'I know, we miss her too. But she's moved on, and she wouldn't want you to go on like this … well, like Hank said, take it all in your own time. And remember that we all love you. Remember that … okay, we'll see you Sunday … yeah, bye, bye'.

She hung up and shook her head at Hank, Jessica watched as a meaningful look passed between them. It was the type of non-verbal communication that can be present in any relationship that spans years but is particularly prevalent in a marriage. Hank sighed and shrugged his shoulders.

'Well, it looks like it's just going to be the three of us … are you okay with that Jess? Is it Jess by the way?'

'Oh yes, that's fine … and yes, Jess is fine.' She self-consciously reached up and touched her hair behind her ear and then, as casually as possible, added, 'Is he okay, Charlie I mean?'

'Yeah, he'll be fine,' Hank said. He took the wine from Becky and examined the label. 'I don't know why I do this, every time someone hands me a bottle of wine I look at the label as if I know what I'm looking for … Yeah, Charlie will be okay. Hannah let it slip that you were coming for dinner and he thought we were trying to set him up … and well … he's not ready to date.'

'But you didn't invite me to set me up with Charlie, did you?'

'Of course we did.' Becky answered. She hopped up on the bar stool beside Jessica and took her own gin from Hank. 'And we're not giving up on the idea either … we'll introduce you at some point … when Hank thinks the time's right we'll engineer a by-chance meeting.'

Jessica couldn't answer. Her cheeks burned bright red and her eyes fell to her hands, clasped tightly in her lap. Once she had noticed the silence it felt oppressive, the longer it went on the more she tried to force herself to think of something to say, something that would change the subject.

'Something smells nice.' She blurted, pointing at the pot on the hob.

'It's nothing special, Hank made lamb Rogan Josh.' Becky reached out and gripped Jessica's hand. 'Can I ask you something, what were you expecting from tonight? It's just … you dressed up so fancy.'

'I don't know really,' Jessica answered. 'It's just Hank invited me along and he's an artist, and you're so glamorous, and Charlie … well, I love his book, "The Karaoke Glow".'

'Books,' Hank interjected. 'There's more than one … remind me and I'll lend you a couple.'

'Don't interrupt … she was halfway through!'

'Yes, moonbeam.' Hank grumbled, he looked to Jessica and nodded for her to continue.

'Well … you have a lovely home, truly you do. But I guess I thought you'd have one of the big houses in Oakenbrook.' It was a lie, of course, or maybe half a lie. Her Granda' had told her last night where Hank lived. She had endeavoured to wear the dress so as to take Charlie's breath away. 'I thought that there would be all sorts of fancy people, you know, artists and intellectuals and all those sorts of folks.'

'Ha, not bloody likely!' Hank laughed. 'No intellectuals here, just us chancers and lucky fucks. But it's a shame Charlie isn't here, I'm sure you'd have taken his breath away the way you're all done up.' There was a knowing smirk on his face and Jessica had to look away from him.

'Ignore him.' Becky said, rolling her eyes. 'I have a suggestion. You're a bit taller than me but I'm sure I'll have something in my closet that will fit you … don't get me wrong you look fantastic. But maybe if you changed into something comfortable then you'd feel more at home here and we could make a night of it. With Hannah and little Frankie, we don't get many opportunities to have a drink and let our hair down these days … you could stay over if you don't want to walk home, the sofa in the living room pulls out into a pretty good bed.'

'That sounds lovely,' Jessica said.

As soon as she agreed, Becky took hold of her hand and whisked her upstairs, giggling. Becky – chatting the whole time – quickly found a pair of jogging bottoms and a T-shirt and handed them over. Jessica was waiting for her to leave before changing but when that didn't happen, when Becky instead sat down on the edge of the bed, Jessica turned away shyly and stepped into the joggers before reaching behind to try and fumble with the zip of her dress. She heard the bed creak and then felt Becky's hand pulling down the zip, quickly she pulled the dress over her head and threw the T-shirt on.

The T-shirt was black and featured a picture of two goldfish swimming around the edge of a bowl, touching each other, mouth to tail. The words above the picture read: *We're just two lost souls swimming in a fish bowl, year after year. Wish you were here.*

154

'This is pretty,' Jessica said, looking upside-down at the shirt. 'Where's it from, the words I mean?'

'It's a Pink Floyd song,' Becky said. 'I actually really like them. That's what happens when you marry an older man though, they open you up to things that you're probably too young to appreciate. He hates it when I say that though, he's only eight years older than me and he likes to point out that he's about twenty-five years too young for Pink Floyd as well. He says age shouldn't bar you from enjoying good music ... but I tell him that's something old people say, especially when they have hot, young wives and they're trying to stay relevant.'

While Jessica chuckled, Becky motioned for her turn around. When she did, Becky reached up and took the clips out of her hair, letting her strawberry blond curls fall down. She took a brush and a hair band from her dressing table and began to comb Jessica's hair back into a pony tail.

'I never had dolls when I was little ... ever since I had Hannah, I've discovered what I missed out on. There's nothing I love more than combing that little terror's hair.'

'She's a lovely little girl,' Jessica said. 'I saw her again tonight, she was tightrope-walking along your mother-in-law's wall.'

'She's always climbing,' Becky said, shaking her head. 'I was over the moon when we found out I was having a little girl, I thought it would be all tea parties and Disney princesses. But you know what she's like, she like that Tasmanian Devil from the cartoon, she's a tornado of chaos and mischief ... A few weeks back she punched a boy two years older than her because he called … Well, he said not nice things about me, so Hannah gave him a black eye. She's got too much of my fierceness in her, she's too wild for her own good.'

'No, I don't think so,' Jessica shook her head in disagreement. 'It's better she's wild than timid. Better she's handing out the black eyes rather than taking them.'

She said those words without really thinking about them. In an unguarded moment they rolled off her tongue and the instant she heard them her stomach twisted. *For God's sake Jess, don't unload your baggage at the first opportunity. Get to know them a little before you let them know how fucked up you are*, she scolded herself.

'That's true,' Becky said. 'Hank was over the moon with her, we got called into the school over it and on the way home, he bought her ice cream. He's been teaching her to box ever since. He says it's about discipline and knowing how to fight doesn't mean she'll go looking for trouble all the time. But I worry, you know.' Becky paused and looked at her feet. 'Anyway, we'd best go down, the little mister will cry over his ruined curry if we sit up here all night.'

Downstairs, Hank had served up his curry in stainless steel Balti dishes with rice and chips on the side, and naan bread, poppadums, and chutney in the middle of the table. Jessica had an idea of what kind of house she was walking into from the first time she met Hannah and Hank in the woods and she'd been right. True, she had assumed that they owned one of the big houses in Oakenbrook, but the size or value of the property made very little difference. You couldn't describe this place as a house, it was a home. And if Hank and Becky had lived in a palace or a shed then they would have made a home out of those places too. This was a warm place, a place where people were invited in and made to feel like one of the family. For Jessica, this was confirmed at the sight of that table heaving with food.

They sat and ate and drank, and in between mouthfuls of curry they talked and laughed in that polite, dinner chit-chat way, avoiding any big topics that may have required them to put down their forks. By the end of the meal, Jessica was nursing a satisfied after-meal podge.

'Thank God I changed.' She laughed, rubbing her belly and letting out a small burp.

Hank began to clear the pots and load the dishwasher. Jessica offered to help, but Hank insisted that she take it easy and let her dinner go down. Meanwhile, Becky disappeared into the front room and after five minutes she came back with tears in her eyes.

'How are they?' Hank asked.

'Mary says they're good. Hannah wouldn't go off without a story, but Frankie had his bottle and went off without any trouble.' She wiped a tear away from her right eye with the heel of her hand and then turned to Jessica. 'He's such a good little boy, he's 100% his dad. So happy and placid, hardly cries at all.'

She crossed the kitchen to stand where Hank was wiping down the counters and goosed him, before wrapping her arms around him and resting her chin on his shoulder.

'Can we have another one?'

157

'Well not tonight,' Hank said. He turned around in her arms and kissed her on the forehead. 'Even if we didn't have company tonight, I'm too full of curry and beer to be of any use to you.' He slipped out of Becky's grip, put his hand on her bum, and pushed forward. He looked at Jessica and smiled. 'Shall we go through to the living room?'

She followed them through into a cosy room with an L-shaped leather sofa and a La-Z-Boy armchair. The walls were lined with family photographs and a painting hung above the fireplace. In it, a little blonde-haired girl was sitting in the woods with a podgy baby sitting in her lap. Jessica studied the painting and noticed a face in the branches staring down at them.

'Who's that in the branches?' she asked, pointing at the painting.

'Where?' Hank asked

She moved closer to point out the face, but as she moved towards the painting she saw that the face was no longer there.

'That's odd, I thought I saw someone in the tree.' Her eyes moved from the painting to one of the framed photos in which she saw three couples smiling back at her. Hank and Becky to the left, Sophie and Jude to the right, and in the middle Charlie and a woman with chestnut-brown hair.

'That's Alison' Hank said. 'She's ... not around anymore.'

'You all look very happy here.'

'We were.' Becky replied.

'What's he like, Charlie, I mean?' Jessica turned around and saw Hank and Becky sitting together on the sofa. Hank was pouring more drinks and gestured for her to sit in the armchair. While she sat and took her drink Hank was fiddling with his phone, moments later there was music playing through a Bluetooth speaker.

'Charlie is ...' he paused and looked to the ceiling. 'A cuckoo. He came to live with us at the age of fifteen, just after his mum passed. He was this painfully middle-class kid, shy, and awkward but that's understandable when you consider what he was going through at the time. He had all that heartache and he walked into our house and the middle of all the drama we had going on. I was a shy kid too ... the difference between Charlie and myself is that he adapts to his surroundings. Within the year, he'd practically lost his accent and took on the Coventry drawl, but that's not all ... you see, we all build our walls, we all have those little character traits that work as a defence mechanism. Take me for instance, I have a hugely self-deprecating sense of humour. If you say anything nice to me, I spend half an hour joking about how shit I am ... and that's my childhood, I probably spent so much time chasing after my old man's praise that even now it feels odd when I get any. Charlie's defence mechanism was "the banter". He went around acting like a bit of a "lad", you know. Always taking the piss, always messing around, and he had a salty tongue.' He turned and looked at Becky. 'What was it he said to you when you met him?'

'His first words to me were: "so how long have you been fucking?"'

'Yeah, that was Charlie, salty as an old sea captain. You know how honesty is subjective, some people say the most vicious things they can think of to hurt someone and they call it honesty. At the same time, people tiptoe around the truth to avoid hurting anyone's feelings. Well, Charlie just used to take the varnish off, not to hurt anyone's feelings, just to get a rise out of you, just to make you giggle.'

'He thought he was Bukowski.' Becky chimed in.

'True,' Hank agreed.

Jessica had hardly finished her drink when Becky took the empty glass, refilled it, and handed it back. She took a sip and smiled, she was pleasantly tipsy now. Her eyes darted back to the group photograph hanging on the wall and the woman with the chestnut hair. Something from her dream came back to her then, something about snow and little wooden houses with smoke rising from their chimney stacks. She shook the dream off and looked to Hank.

'I take it from the way you're talking he's not like that now?'

'No, he's changed and changed again since then.' Hank replied. 'You see he fell in love and that changes a person, especially that kind of love ... I can attest to that.'

'What kind of love?'

Hank sighed and squeezed Becky's hand. She was leaning on him, her head resting on his shoulder when he pulled himself to the edge of the sofa and slid onto the floor. He sat between Becky's legs and stroked her knee. To Jessica it looked like something had come over him, he had a thousand-yard stare, it was as if he was seeing through the wall to some other time and place. As he sat there, a cacophony of ticking, chiming, and bell-ringing filled the room.

'Oh, listen.' Becky said, pointing to the speaker. 'This is "Time" by Pink Floyd.'

'It's an achingly beautiful song.' Hank said. 'You know there're videos on the internet of people listening to this for the first time and breaking down. Music, art, films, maybe even the odd book ...' he paused and pointed to a shelf where Charlie's books were lined up like soldiers. Jessica noticed a fresh manuscript lying face up at the end of the shelf. 'Sometimes they touch a deep part of you, they recognise your pain and that's enough to change you a little. Just to know that someone's felt the way you've felt, ached the same way as you, and then expressed that in words or music or dance or whatever... it's powerful. And not just the first time, I've listened to this song more times than I can count and it's beautiful every time ... I still feel the way I felt the first time I heard it, but it's a little distant now. There's a special kind of love that's exactly like that.'

He paused, took a drink to wet his mouth, and turned his gaze on Jessica. She saw flecks of purple in his eyes, flecks that she would have sworn weren't there a moment ago. She found his gaze slightly too intimate, slightly too sympathetic.

She turned away from him and looked again at the painting hanging over the fireplace, she saw that face in the tree once more. This time it wasn't looking down at the kids, but rather he was looking out at her. She thought she recognised that face, she thought that it looked like the man who had stopped her in the middle of town, the man who had told her 'it doesn't have to be this way'.

'That love …' Hank continued, 'It's the love between two people who have known pain. Two damaged souls who recognise each other's hurt and treat it with tenderness.' He paused. 'Alison was the best thing to happen to Charlie, she brought down all his walls and made him a fuller version of himself. He realised he didn't have to hide behind banter and piss taking … he could just be Charlie.'

'What happened?' Jessica asked. 'Why aren't they together anymore?'

'Well, it's this whole awful deal with …' Only the first few words of Becky's interjection were discernible. It was the strangest thing, as she was speaking her tongue seemed to swell in her mouth and her speech became impossible to understand. It was as if she had taken a shot of novocaine. She took a deep breath, looked at Hank, and when she spoke again it made sense. 'Are you kidding me, we still can't talk about this?'

'I guess not.' Hank replied, and then turning to Jessica, 'Alison has moved on … and that's taken a toll. He's suffering through the pain and trying to find his way back to himself.'

'And what, you want to introduce him to me because you think I can fix him?'

'Not precisely.' Hank replied.

Behind him, Becky began dozing on the sofa. Without saying a word, he stood up and put Becky's arm around his neck then lifted her into his arms. He left the room and Jessica heard him puffing and panting up the stairs. He was gone maybe ten or fifteen minutes. Jessica pictured him changing his wife into her nightie before putting

162

her to bed. When he came back downstairs, he had a quilt and a set of pillows, he dropped them on the sofa and gestured with his head for Jessica to come with him.

She got up and walked through the house to the back garden where she found him sitting on a small wall around a flower bed. Hank had taken off his slippers and now he was wiggling his toes in the grass. He took a deep breath of the midnight air and let it out slowly.

'Excuse the Mrs, like she said, we don't get many opportunities to enjoy a drink these days and it seems to go straight to her head ... It's not about fixing him, Charlie, I mean. Given enough time he'll fix himself. I just think if you were to meet at the right time and place then you could be good for each other.'

'And how do you know that?'

'I'm a good judge of character.'

Jessica laughed and sat down next to him. She had been barefoot ever since she changed out of the dress and now she was wiggling her own toes in the damp grass.

'I don't understand how you can know anything about my character. You hardly know me. Don't get me wrong, "The Karaoke Glow" meant a lot to me, and I'd love to get to know him, but I just don't know how you can tell.'

'I see you.' He replied.

From a sideways glance, Jessica saw those purple flecks in her eyes and she tried to avoid looking at him head on. She couldn't resist for long.

'I see you, I have this … I don't know how you'd describe it … ability, I guess. You know all those stories you hear about Pookas? Well, believe it or not I had a run in with one a few years back and now I see things … I see people's pain, I see their character, I see them for who they are.'

'Prove it,' Jessica said. 'Tell me about me?'

'Well, you feel unloved.' Hank said sighing. 'You grew up with parents who didn't treat you right. Your dad was uninterested, and your mum was cold, overcritical … then … then,' he began to snarl , 'He hit you … the guy you ran away from, the one you came home to escape. He wore you down into a husk and took to beating you, and you put up with it because you thought you were worthless. You're not worthless, you're a sweet, down-to-earth girl. You know the truth about Becky and me, you know how we met because you saw our documentary and you make no judgment about us. You long to be loved, you long to feel like you belong somewhere, to feel like you have real friends and …'

'Stop.' Jessica said sniffling. 'Please don't go on.'

They sat in silence for a long time, and then, in a clumsy attempt to change the subject Jessica said, 'So, when is the right time and place then, for me to meet Charlie?'

'Well, it's a bad idea to rely on someone to fix you. If it was go wrong or to end then you might end up worse off than when you started… I guess the right time is when you both feel ready. When you're both fixed.'

'I don't know if I'll ever be fixed,' Jessica said, tears rolling down her face. 'At least not completely.'

'No one ever is,' Hank replied. 'You just become fixed *enough*, strong *enough* to get by, the pain gets a little easier to deal with, you become a little happier day by day. Strength is the key ... I'm gonna help you there, I'm going to help you to reclaim your strength.'

'How are you going to do that? Jessica asked.

'Ironically, the same way my dad helped me,' Hank laughed and shook his head. 'I'm going to teach you to box.'

.15.

The Silver Stag

It is a universal truth that fate turns on the smallest of things. When fate is at work every creature that draws breath in the natural world falls back on its truest and deepest nature. Alison, for instance, was the type of woman who picked at loose threads, literally and figuratively. It was a compulsion. She knew that picking at a loose thread on a jumper would only cause it to unravel, but still she picked. Likewise, after being treated poorly by her first boyfriend, her relationships afterwards had unravelled because she couldn't help but pick at the flaws of lovers and friends. Over the years, she had grown to suspect that a saboteur lived inside her heart. Whenever she got too happy or comfortable, it began to pick away. Maybe it was a case of once bitten, twice shy.

When Charlie came along, she made a concerted effort not to pick when the saboteur spoke to her of her new lover's flaws. She told herself 'he's not perfect, but that's okay'. Over the years Charlie had become, not exactly immune to the voice of criticism, but rather stronger and more complete because of it. Unfortunately, the same could not be said about the world that existed outside of Charlie's body, heart, and soul.

For Alison, fate was about to turn and predictably it would turn on the smallest of insignificant things. Her true nature and, of all things, a slice of brown toast would begin to unravel the nature of her reality.

It landed on the floor butter side up. Probably two of the most tired clichés are that cats always land on their feet and toast always lands butter side down and if this is true, what would happen if you sellotaped a slice of buttered toast to a cat's back, then threw the cat out of a window? Would it fall, and inches from the ground, stop dead, and begin to spin around and around like a drill bit, never able to hit the floor? No, of course not. Obviously sometimes cats land on their backs and toast lands butter side up, but Alison had never seen it, not once. True, dropping toast was not a daily occurrence, but she was twenty-nine and just as capable of clumsiness as the next person. Until now, she had never seen the butter side of the toast staring up at the sky like that.

Alison bent down and picked up the toast, then, taken by some strange whim, her urge to pick at loose threads, she dropped it a second time. When she looked down, she found that she was staring at the butter side once again. She dropped the toast a further five times and each time she saw that butter side facing up at her, and her stomach turned.

It was slightly improbable, but chiefly it was an insignificant thing. So why then did it trouble her so much? This small thing, this little bit of nothing at all? The answer came like a sudden damn burst, a revelation that threatened to wash her away. Something was wrong. She felt that much in her bones. Likely she had always felt that wrongness and had mistaken it as some sort of hangover from the cancer. Something wasn't right, and the only way Alison could

167

conceptualise this feeling was to anchor it to the toast falling the wrong way time and time again.

She picked the toast up, and with a look of disgust plastered all over her face, she threw it into the pedal bin tucked under the kitchen counter. She crossed the kitchen to the sink and filled a glass with cold water, as she gulped it down she watched her hand tremble slightly. She put the glass down and reached up to her chestnut-brown hair. It was so long now that the night before she was finally able to braid it. As she ran her fingers through it, she noticed how thick and silky it felt. She had been able to look at herself in the mirror again lately. The signs of her once-upon-a-time sickness were invisible unless that is, you knew where to look.

Upstairs she heard Charlie's alarm clock going off. This morning she had woken before him and had discovered that her period was not passing but had passed. Just like that, she felt happier, lighter, and more optimistic. After washing and cleaning her teeth she had tiptoed downstairs to make Charlie breakfast and have it ready and waiting before he'd even opened his eyes. Over the last three days, she had soaked up the majority of his time like a sponge. He had barely written a word. Today she was determined to allow him his time, besides, she wanted to do everything she could to free him of distractions. Then she had dropped the toast and her mood had spiralled.

She began to move quickly. She emptied her glass then put it on the table with a second glass, two coffee cups, some cutlery, bowls, and plates. After that, she grabbed cereal and pastries from the

168

cupboards, milk and orange juice from the fridge, fruit from the counter, and finally, she flicked on the kettle. She arranged a spread of pastries and fruit, poured the juice, made coffee, then fixed a smile on her face just in time to greet Charlie.

'Morning!' she chirped, her voice diverting him from his usual routine of going straight to light the fire. He came to find her in the kitchen and she hugged him as he walked in. Then, she reached up on her tiptoes and kissed him, tasting the toothpaste on his breath.

'Morning,' he echoed. Yawning, he sat down at the table and poured himself a bowl of cereal. 'Early nights aren't good for me. The more I sleep the more tired I feel in the morning.'

'I think when it comes to sleep what matters is quality rather than quantity,' Alison replied. She poured her man a coffee, put it down in front of him, then rubbed his shoulders. She watched as his head drooped forward like an overcooked piece of asparagus. As her fingers worked their magic, he let out a contented sigh. At that, she released her grip on him and took the seat opposite. 'I think it's my fault. I've monopolised your time the last few days. You've probably got too many words and ideas floating around your head to sleep properly.'

'Don't be daft.'

'I'm not being daft,' she said, perhaps a little bit too sharply. 'It's back to work for you today. Back to this imaginary love triangle that's consumed you of late. I've got plans as well, I'm going for a walk down to the frozen lake, then I'm off back down to the grotto to carry on building Tiny Town.' She paused there and picked up a pastry, tearing

off a corner and chewing it. Her smile was still firmly fixed to her face.
'Soup and sandwiches alright for tonight?'

'Whatever you like, darling.'

'So, I've been thinking,' she paused and fixed her eyes on him, 'about why I haven't fallen pregnant yet. Sex is like sleep, what matters is the quality. So maybe we'll just cuddle for the next few nights hey, give you a chance to restock the tadpoles in your old love sack.'

Charlie laughed, and when he laughed he looked ten years younger. He pushed his empty cereal bowl aside and wiped his mouth with the back of his hand.

'I love your way with words,' he said, reaching for a banana.

They enjoyed a pleasant breakfast together, eating and chatting, towards the end of which Alison's smile felt more natural and far less forced. After they ate, Charlie went to build the fire and then sloped off to his office to write. Meanwhile, Alison left the pots exactly where they were, got dressed into her thermal clothing, and waddled out of the cabin.

Last night as they slept, a fresh fall of snow came hand in hand with a healthy wind. This meant that as soon as Alison stepped over the threshold and out into the snow, she saw that the world outside of their cabin had been made brand new, white, pristine, and untouched

Stepping forward, she looked towards the wall that circled the cabin. It had not been built from brick but assembled rather like a jigsaw puzzle made from oddly shaped stones, making a perfect circle.

It was like a pair of arms embracing the little log cabin and their 'just the two of them' world. The wooden gate in the wall was directly opposite the front door of the cabin, but the path that linked them had been made invisible by the snow. Slowly, and with steady feet, she felt her way along the hidden path, puncturing the snow with a satisfying crunch. Worried about the possible ice underneath, she held her arms out slightly to steady herself, like a tightrope-walker.

At the gate, something caught Alison's eye. The snow that lay outside the bounds of the cabin wasn't pristine. It had already been marked with animal tracks. Hoofprints made a circuit track leading to and from the line of trees at the bottom of the hill. She opened the gate, following the tracks down the path that snaked its way down the side of the hill.

As she walked, her mind flashed back to the toast and the wrong feeling that was anchored to it. Before long she realised that the wrong feeling had nothing to do with the slice of toast, and instead had everything to do with the world around her. She felt ambivalent about the world. It felt solid and full to her, yet at the same time it was so thin it was almost transparent. Alison thought she remembered everything since coming to Húsavík. Near enough every passing, perfect day was engraved on her mind, and yet, still there were gaps in her memory.

For instance, the first gap she found concerned the little town they now called home. She remembered what the town of Húsavík looked like. It was a quaint, little, chocolate box town built at the bottom of a rolling hill and directly at the side of the docks. There was whale watching taking place in the bay, a stuffed polar bear in the museum, and the prettiest little wooden church she'd ever laid her eyes on. Alison knew Húsavík like the back of her hand, but she couldn't remember the last time she had ventured out of their cabin on the hill and into the town properly. She must have been there recently. The cabin was still stocked full of food and drink and almost everything that they needed, but when exactly did either of them do a big shop?

This first hole in her memory led her to discover many more. She often remembered cooking, but not cleaning. She couldn't remember the last time she had hoovered, or the last time that the bins were emptied, or for that matter, how often the rubbish was collected. She knew she'd been living there for a year or more, but she couldn't recall celebrating a Christmas or birthday. Moreover, she knew that even this far north there were meant to be seasons. The snow was meant to melt during the summer, but it never did. The whole time they had been living in that little cabin, the snow had been their constant companion.

These thoughts about the wrongness of the world mounted, one on top of the other like a great house of cards. The whole thing felt ready to collapse at the slightest breath. In fact, as she thought about her life now, she came to the conclusion that the only thing in it that was truly stable all the way through was Charlie. He was his usual embodiment of strength and shelter, and she clung to that idea. It comforted her to know that no matter what was different and changing in the world, he at least remained constant.

Alison came to the bottom of the snaking path. She stood there for a moment, staring forward at the row of trees that separated her from the frozen lake, hidden behind them. Glancing down to her feet, she saw where the hoofprints began. As she was looking down, she caught something moving quickly out of the corner of her eye. A flash of something so white it was almost silver.

She looked up far too late. The silver thing was gone.

She decided to follow the hoofprints through the trees. Above her head, the hardy winter birds were tweeting. Although she couldn't tell one from the other, she did at least know the names of the Icelandic snowbirds now. The first time she had walked to the frozen lake and heard the birdsong she had been slightly shocked. She found it hard to imagine delicate birds thriving in these conditions. Most of the birds here were aquatic fishing birds like the Red-throated Loon and the Black Guillemot, but in the trees, there were crossbills, finches, and even the odd goshawk.

Listening to the twittering above her head and following the hoofprints, she found herself at the edge of the frozen lake. There, standing proudly on the middle was an ice white stag.

It was the same one from her dreams, the very same one. Tall and proud, with antlers like open arms. It spied her at the edge of the lake and slowly trotted towards her. Alison marvelled at how it managed to move across the ice without slipping. What's more, she wondered how it managed to walk without breaking through the patches of thin ice. You couldn't trust the ice in the middle of the lake. There it would be little better than a thin sheet of slush, and yet the stag walked proudly and easily across it, like the prancing prince of the wilderness.

Its progression was slow, and yet in no time at all, it was at the edge of the lake. It sniffed Alison and in return, she reached out gently to touch its muzzle. It drew back from her reaching fingertips and sniffed her again. Then, it stretched its neck forwards and licked her face from her chin, that poked out above the zip of her coat, up to her forehead that was crowned with the fur of her hood. The stag drew back again, and Alison was amazed to see it spit on the ground. It was as if her face didn't taste right to the beast. It shook its head from side to side, then nodded in the direction she had come from. It snorted and began to stamp its front, right hoof, then continued to nod to somewhere behind Alison.

'Go back?' she asked. 'Is that what you're trying to say?' The stag reared up onto its hind legs, then came down again. There was a glint in its eyes as if it was pleased to be understood. Although Alison knew what she had to do, for a moment she didn't move a single step back the way she came. She couldn't seem to tear herself away from this strange and beautiful creature. In response to this, the stag moved forward, lowering its head slightly and resting its antlers underneath her arms. It pressed its head against her belly and pushed her backwards. She took a few steps back and then fell into a deep bank of snow.

From there, she watched as the stag turned and galloped away over the ice and into the distance. It had all but disappeared before she came back to her senses and began to pull herself out of the mound of snow. She looked at the spot where the stag had been hidden by the horizon and once again she was struck by the wrongness of the world she lived in. That morning, staring down at the butter side of the toast had gripped her with fear. Now her fear had gone with the stag and something far more dangerous had taken its place. Alison had been filled head to toe with curiosity, and as she turned and walked back to the cabin, she wondered what would happen if she was to pull at this particular loose thread.

.16.

The Tale of the Murdered God

When Alison entered the living room, she found Charlie lying on his back next to the fireplace. With his right hand, he was holding a book above his face, and with his left, he was scratching his balls. She was just wondering how he was managing to read in that position when he turned to roll over onto his belly. As he rolled over, he spied her, stopped on his side and smiled warmly. She was still dressed in her winter coat, woollens, and wellies and they were still dusted with snow from her fall.

'Bloody hell, it's the snow queen!' he laughed. 'What happened babe, did you roll down the hill?'

'Something like that,' she replied. Alison unzipped her coat and struggled out of it. She draped it over the back of the sofa, then stripped off her scarf and gloves. In the corner of the living room there were two rocking chairs. She dragged one of them to the edge of the shag rug, collapsing onto it. 'Give me a hand with these will ya?' she asked, kicking her wellies off towards Charlie. He clambered onto his knees, crawled towards her, and set about yanking them off. She held her fingers and toes towards the fire and felt the warmth returning to them.

'Did you have fun out there today?' he asked. He threw her wellies aside, then turned and reclined at her feet, his bald head resting on her right knee. She reached down and caressed his dome, feeling how soft his skin was. His hair was already thinning when they met, but he had only decided to shave it bald after she grew ill. To begin with, it had been a sign, a mark of solidarity that said, 'we're in this together'. Now, after all this time, he had grown used to the look of it and shaving it had become a routine he couldn't quite break.

'Fun? Yeah, I guess you could call it that,' she said. 'Something kind of strange happened actually.'

'Oh yeah? What was that then?'

'There was a stag on the ice,' she said, pausing for a second to decide exactly what she was going to tell him. She decided not to mention the gaps she had found in her memory or her suspicions of the wrongness of the world that they lived in. She didn't want him to think that she was losing her mind. 'It was right on the centre of the lake and when it saw me it came trotting over. It got right up close and licked my face ... then it put its head against my belly and pushed me over.'

'Really?' Charlie asked, a hint of disbelief in his voice.

'Promise,' Alison replied. 'Cross my heart and all that stuff.'

'Erm,' Charlie grunted thoughtfully, 'maybe it was Baldr.'

'Who?' Alison noticed she was still stroking his head, like he was her lapdog or a moggy cat. She stopped with a slightly awkward, jolt. It was almost as if she didn't know what to do with her hands. After a moment or two, they fell to his shoulders, and when she started rubbing them her hands felt far more natural.

'You know, Baldr,' Charlie repeated, as if Baldr was a name she ought to know, like the name of the milkman, or the lead singer of a band, or maybe her pet rabbit from when she was a little kiddo. 'He's the old Norse God,' Charlie said completing his thought.

'Oh, of course,' Alison scoffed, 'why didn't I guess?'

'It's an old Húsavík superstition, the townsfolk often talk about it,' Charlie explained chuckling. 'They say the white stag that roams the hills, the woods, and the lake is the murdered God returned to life. That's why they never go hunting here. They don't want to offend the white stag.'

'Murdered God. That doesn't make sense. How can a God be murdered?'

Charlie moved his right hand onto Alison's knee, turning and gripping the side of her rocking chair with his left hand, and clambered to his feet. He took a moment to stretch, easing the ache in his lower back until it clicked, and then he let out a sigh of relief. He fetched the other rocking chair from the window and placed it next to hers. He sat in the chair and reached out his hand. Alison offered hers and felt it instantly enveloped. Seconds later, his thumb was tracing circles across her knuckles.

'Actually, gods dying or being murdered is fairly commonplace in mythology. The list of dead gods is as long as my arm. Osiris, Prometheus, Dionysus, Horus, and let's not forget JC, he wasn't the first God to die but I guess he's by far the most famous for it.' He leant forward in his chair, reached for a poker from the stand by the fireplace, and began to poke the fire.

178

'So, what's the story with this Baldr then?' she asked, watching as the log Charlie was poking cracked and split in two. He put the poker back in its stand and started to rock back and forth in his chair.

'Well, to begin with, the thing about the Norse gods is that, on the whole, they are a grim bunch.'

As Charlie spoke, Alison watched the flames flicker and dance. As the tale began to unfold, the fire captured her attention and drew her in. She could almost see Charlie's words being played out in the fire, smoke, and shadow.

They'd have to be a grim bunch, living in such a grim land. I think the land dictates the gods. In Greece, they may get endless leisure time to be drunk and debauched, to lounge around and womanise, but here in the North, the gods have real work. Here, they hold back the darkness, they wrestle with giants and prepare for war. Now, don't get me wrong, the gods up here are every bit as drunk as their Greek counterparts. It's just that here they multitask, meaning they tend to drink with one hand and fight with the other.

Everything is doom and gloom here. Everything is about the fast-approaching war, the war that has been said to wipe them all out. They know this. They know that in the end they are doomed, but still, they prepare for battle. It is for this reason that, although the gods here have their respective realms of influence, this far north they are all de facto war gods. All except Baldr.

Baldr is, or rather was, the one saving grace of the northern pantheon. He was the spirit of light, joy, beauty, innocence, and reconciliation. Baldr had healing hands that gave him boundless love and mercy for mankind. Not only this but, he was also the most beautiful God that ever walked the Earth and, even more than that, while he lived the great war could never come. All the other gods were destined to fight and die, but Baldr prevented this. He was a great shield, protecting man and God alike. Everything and everyone loved him, but it couldn't last, of course.

Baldr was troubled by bad dreams. Every night he dreamed of his death and the tragedy of the war that would come after his passing. It troubled him so much that eventually he went to his father Odin, and his mother Frigg, and told them of his dreams. Odin was wise, he knew what the death of Baldr would mean for them all. Immediately, he set about his plan to put a stop to this tragedy. He extracted an oath from everything in creation, from the air and the sea, to the earth and the rock, and the metal and the fire. From all the birds and all the beasts, the men and the women, and the dwarves, the elves, and the giants. He made them all promise never to harm so much as a single hair on his beloved son's head.

Of course, what he didn't know was that it was Loki, the jealous God of chaos, who had sent Baldr dreams of death. And while Odin was busy taking oaths from everything, he crept onto Earth and stole a sprig of mistletoe, which he kept hidden from the All-Father. The mistletoe couldn't make an oath, and so it became the only thing that could harm Baldr. Crafty Loki turned the mistletoe into a needle, which he hid in his sleeve. He transformed himself into an old crone and

made his way to Asgard where the gods were celebrating Baldr's
invulnerability, now that the prophecy of his dark dream was undone.

Being such a grim bunch of gods, they celebrated cheating Baldr's
fated death, first by tying him to a stake and then taking it in turns to
throw all manner of objects at him. Axes, swords, spears, uprooted
trees, rocks, balls of fire, great, jagged icicles, yet all of them bounced
off of him without leaving so much as a mark. The gods made a game
of it, laughing and drinking whilst aiming for his head, and all was well
for a while. Then an old crown crept up to Hod, the blind God of the
dark and cold, who lingered at the edge.

'Why don't you join in?' the Loki crone asked.

'I can't see where he stands, and I have no weapon to throw,' Hod
answered.

'Well, allow me to guide your hand,' the Loki crone offered, taking
the blind God by the shoulders and pointing him in the direction of
Baldr. 'And for the sake of comedy and high spirits, why not use my
sewing needle as a weapon?' The Loki crone put the needle in Hod's
hand and moved his fingers so that he clutched it like it was a tiny
dart. Together, the pair threw the needle and all the gods laughed as
it flew through the air. They stopped laughing when the needle landed
firmly in Baldr's right eye, causing him to slump dead against the
ropes that bound him to the stake.

The fire crackled and Alison jolted upright in her rocking chair. The
thought of a needle sticking out of Baldr's eye was deeply unpleasant
to her, when it came to eyes she was quite squeamish. As a child, she

used to watch her dad put his contact lenses in and it always made her shudder. She noticed Charlie was squeezing her hand a little tighter, so she turned to face to him and smiled.

'Are you okay?' he asked. 'You've gone a little pale.'

'I'm fine. Just you know, needles and eyes.' She shuddered again to display her disgust at the idea. Charlie leant across and kissed her forehead. He tried to draw back but she gripped the sides of his face and pulled him in for a real kiss.

The new policy of having quality sex over quantity was working, it had been like reliving their relationship from the beginning. Once again, they had gone through the stage of not being able to keep their hands off each other. Now, the sex was slower and more intense, every lingering touch was loaded with deep regard. In her heart, she just knew that her children would come this way, born of love rather than lust. Tonight, she would have him. Tomorrow, if the fates were kind ... well, she could only hope for that.

'What happened after Baldr died then?' she asked. She meant to have her man tonight, but first she wanted answers. After all, unfinished stories were nothing more than loose threads to unravel.

'Baldr, like everyone who dies, passed into the Kingdom of the Dead where the Goddess Hell rules. Odin went to her and begged her to release his son. She finally agreed on the condition that everything in creation shed a tear for him. Well, you can probably guess what happened next, everyone and everything cried for Baldr apart from one sour-faced, old crown who flat out refused to part with his tears. It all unravelled then. Baldr remained in the land of the dead and soon

182

he was joined by Hod who was killed for the sake of revenge and honour. Then, when it was discovered that Loki was behind the whole thing, he was punished severely.'

'How?' Alison asked. She wasn't entirely sure she wanted to know, but it was a loose thread and, slave to her nature as she was, she couldn't help picking at it.

'They took him and his family to a cave. Loki had many children, but only two boys by his true wife. The gods made Loki's eldest son rip out the guts of his younger brother with nothing but his teeth. They took the guts of the younger son and transformed them into a chain which they used to bind Loki to a rock. They wrapped a giant, immortal snake around a stalactite above Loki's head and nailed it there so that it could never escape. They forced the snake's mouth open with a spear, gave Loki's wife a bowl to catch the snake's venom, then covered the entrance to the cave with a great slab of stone. The punishment was to remain there together until the end of time, the eldest son driven mad and weeping over his brother's body, and the wife dutifully collecting the venom until her bowl was full, turning around to empty it, and, in doing so, allowing the venom to drip onto Loki's face. The agony was unimaginable, but what was worse than the pain was waiting for the bowl to refill. Waiting for pain is always worse than the pain itself, I think,' Charlie said, staring into the fire.

'Nice little story there, babe,' Alison said.

That afternoon they ate, drank, joked, and watched the fire grow small. As the flames died down, Alison felt Baldr's story fade from her mind. Now when she shivered it was because of the crisp air in the living room and not because of the grim story she had listened to. Before they went up to bed, Charlie threw another couple of logs into the fireplace and stoked the flames up a little. He didn't like to let the fire die out completely as he didn't like getting up in the middle of the night to take a leak, feeling like his piss was likely to freeze mid-air.

When the fire was rebuilt, Alison took her muppet man by the hand and led him through the living room, upstairs to bed. Passing the window on the landing, she smelt that familiar scent of lilac in the vase and a memory bubbled up inside her. She remembered their first dirty weekend away. A little run-down guest house in Devon where they pretended to be newlyweds so as not to upset the old dear who ran the place. Alison recalled she spent most of her time dressed up in various silk teddies, and she remembered how he had got so excited by that red number that, instead of removing her panties, he had ripped them in two. The sound of it had been delicious and thrilling, even now the echo of that ripping sound in her memory made her belly flutter.

She took him to bed, and under the thick, heavy quilt they made love. The quilt retained all their body heat which made the whole thing a sweaty and humid affair. About halfway through, as the pleasure was taking hold and her groans were building towards the big 'O', she was struck by a ridiculous idea. Isn't this always the way though? Leave a mind unattended for too long and it will think the silliest of thoughts at the most inappropriate times. Trapped inside that envelope of heat, sweat, and her wetness, with her man bearing

184

down on top of her, she began to wonder if this is what it felt like to be on the inside of a cheese toastie. For a moment she giggled, then quickly she rebuked herself for allowing that silliness to take hold. She concentrated on her man's movements, wrapping her legs around him so as to draw him in, closer and deeper. She heard the groaning in his voice, noticing the way it mirrored hers, the tremor contained in it. It was drawing ever closer to that great moment of gleeful exhortation. She bit her lip and held onto her pleasure, and when she felt him let go inside her, she let go too. His warmth flowed into her and she thought again of the pink and squishy baby she longed for.

Later, as they drifted off to sleep, a question came to her and she asked it before Charlie could even close his eyes.

'So why exactly do the townsfolk think that the stag is Baldr then?'

'I've no idea,' he answered in low voice. 'They say it's beautiful, maybe that's the reason.'

.17.

The Castlegate Boxing Club

Jessica was once again surrounded by snow, in the middle of all those log cabin houses. A crowd was moving around her. Wrapped up in hats and coats, scarfs and gloves, they went about their chores and side-stepped her without seeming to notice that she was there. She took a deep breath of the arctic air and felt the freshness of it in her lungs. It put the air in Castlegate to shame and made her feel like she'd been breathing exhaust fumes all her life.

She felt herself moving, not walking but rather being pulled forward to the edge of the circle of cabins. It was as if she was on a track, it made her feel like she was the camera in a movie, panning towards some mystery point in the distance. In this case, that mystery point was a long row of bars and restaurants at the edge of her vision. She looked down and realised that she couldn't see her feet in the snow, moreover, there were no footprints this time, human or otherwise. She wasn't really here. Of course, she hadn't really been here last time, it had just been a dream that dissolved into nothing on waking.

This time the dream was somewhat familiar, and maybe it was for that reason that she recognised that none of it was real. Most of the time this knowledge was enough to punch through the gossamer-thin nature of Jessica's dreams, but some part of her held on, some part of her wanted to see and know.

186

There was music coming from somewhere, the sound of violin strings playing some old rock and roll song that she must have heard before, or else it was one that was so well known that it had sunken into the collective psyche. But now, it sounded fresh and new and otherworldly, and she began to hum along to it.

As she moved along the street outside the bars and restaurants, she looked through the glass and saw happy people, drinking, eating, but most of all, laughing. It was a happy place, Jessica could feel that much in her bones, happiness seemed to radiate from the bricks, and the snow, and the air around her.

Ahead of her, Jessica saw the source of the strange violin song. The figure was standing beneath the awning of a cinema. The musician turned to face Jessica and instantly she recognised her, it was the woman from the previous dream, the woman from the photograph. Her chestnut-brown hair was down and a breeze was blowing it back behind her. Her eyes were bright this evening, when Jessica stared into them it was almost as if she could see starlight. The woman smiled and Jessica opened her mouth to speak, to repeat that line about the dead and the living, when...

... *Bang, bang, bang.* The hand knocking on her car window startled her and she woke with a jolt. By the time she realised where she was, the dream had slipped away, almost completely, the only thing that remained was that odd violin song.

'You were asleep,' Hank said, stating the obvious.

'It's been a long week I guess,' she replied as she opened the door and slid out of her seat. 'Too many early mornings.'

Hank responded with a nod and a grunt. He turned away, put his fingers in his mouth and wolf whistled and moments later Hannah came skipping down the road in her tiny little boxing shorts, vest, and trainers, her gloves tied, hanging around her neck. Jessica watched the little girl skipping down the road and then felt her gaze pulled towards the look of pride on Hank's face. She thought he looked different today, it wasn't the pride in his face but rather the sunlight on it.

The last time she had seen him had been the previous morning. She had woken up on his sofa bed to the pleasant smell of a cup of coffee, that had been placed on the table beside her, and bacon frying in the kitchen. Under the thick and oppressive cloud of her hangover, she pulled herself up, drank her coffee, climbed back into Becky's clothes and shuffled into the kitchen. There was Becky, dressed in her jim-jams, her blonde hair sticking up strangely as if a hairbrush had only passed through the air in its general direction. She was slumped at the breakfast bar, supporting her head with both hands and, every now and again, she let out a little groan. Meanwhile, Hank was standing over the frying pan, fully dressed, washed, looking as fresh as a daisy and sporting an apron.

Jessica had taken a seat next to Becky and eaten bacon batches washed down with orange juice, water, and more coffee. The three of them had a go at making small talk, but with Jessica and Becky's hangovers, the talk was so small it was almost monosyllabic. Hank was talking well, as he served, ate, and cleared away the plates, he looked fine. Jessica asked where his hangover was and he made some remark about being twice the size of them, and, of course, his family had Viking blood in their veins. Jessica didn't think he looked like much of a Viking, at least not standing at the sink, washing dishes and wearing an apron.

He didn't look different to her yesterday morning, not from under the cloud of her hangover. But now that she had slept, eaten, drank water, burned off the alcohol, and had time to think about some of the things he had said in the early hours of that Saturday morning, he did. Here was a man who, with a glance, was able to look at her and know her. He knew of the abuse, the black eyes, the sharp edge of her mother's tongue, and so many other, unnameable things. Here was a man who claimed to believe that he'd had a run in with a spirit, a Pooka, a pagan god. And, although his abilities could be considered to be evidence of this … could she really believe it? Everyone in Coventry knew at least five good Pooka stories, everyone had heard of that mythical place called the Midway, that place the Pookas called home, but no one really believed it … did they?

'Are you trying to work out if I'm mad?' Hank asked. When she looked at him, he had those purple flecks in his eyes again.

'No, of course you're not. It's just you look … well, not exactly look … feel maybe, you feel different now that I know …' she left her sentence hanging.

'Yeah daylight does that … some things are easier to swallow with gin and moonlight.' He smiled and it was familiar and disarming.

'Do you know everything that people are thinking?'

'Oh God, no,' Hank laughed. 'I just get glimpses, sometimes I try to see things, sometimes I see things when I'm not concentrating. Other times it happens when people have secrets they want to tell, they're the easiest to see. It's hard to surprise me these days.'

By now, Hannah had caught up and Hank was flashing Jessica a look as if to say, let's change the subject'. The little girl came skipping along and put her left hand into her Pop-Pop's giant paw. In her right hand, she had a bunch of bluebells that she had picked along the way.

'I stopped because the flowers were pretty today,' she said, presenting the bluebells to Jessica.

'Aw, are these for me?'

'Yes, I got them to make you smile. I told Pop that you had deep, down sad eyes like Uncle Charlie, and he said he knew. He said we're going to help you not be so sad.'

'Sorry,' Hank said shrugging. 'Just like me she sees too much, and just like her mum she doesn't know how to tiptoe around anything.'

'It's okay.' Jessica said blushing. She hated blushing, it made her look like ginger concentrated.

The sign outside the brick building had grown a green fuzz, though Jessica could still faintly make out the words 'Castlegate Boys Boxing Club' through it. Vines were growing from the corner of the left-hand side of the building and they stretched almost halfway across the wall, stopping dead at the door. The right-hand side looked as if it had been

190

freshly painted and, while Hank unlocked the door, Hannah explained that people had painted 'not nice things' on the building.

Jessica was surprised at what she found inside. Half of the room was as she expected, a boxing ring, punching bags, pads, and speedballs. The other half had been converted into a makeshift studio. Paintings lined the walls, some of them were portraits, others were of a more surreal affair. A number of them were scenes of a futuristic-looking, neon city, that somehow seemed familiar to her. Looking at those paintings was like remembering a dream of the future, or a place you had once visited in your imagination.

Jessica could see a work in progress set up on the easel in the middle of the studio. It seemed to be some sort of woodland scene, but it didn't hold her attention, not compared to the paintings of the neon city.

'This is where you work?'

'Yeah,' Hank grunted. 'I used to have a place in the city, just off the Roman road. But then when Hannah came along and we moved out here, I found out that this place was getting sold off cheap … and it meant a lot to my pop.' Hank pointed to a framed picture on the wall. Behind the glass, there was a picture of a man with a jutting, granite jaw, who looked to be built entirely from stone. She vaguely remembered glimpsing him from behind her Granda's legs.

'I had to buy the place. It's Hannah and Frankie's heritage, this place is their pop and their grandpop under one roof.'

'That's really sweet.'

191

Hank didn't answer that. Instead, he turned away and crossed the room to Hannah, who was putting on her gloves. He ruffled his daughter's hair and told her to 'work the bag' while he took care of Jessica, then he took off his jumper, picked up a pair of gloves, pads, and a head guard, and then waved Jessica over.

'This isn't "Rocky",' he said seriously, as he slipped the gloves over her hands. 'This isn't "Raging Bull", or "Million Dollar Baby".' He slipped the head guard on her and fastened it under her chin. 'I'm not making you a contender, or a fighter, I don't want you to be the best or the greatest. This is just about taking control, it's about confidence and not being afraid anymore … I don't want you to be the greatest, I just want you to do whatever you can, understand?'

'Yes!' Jessica said eagerly, there was a shiver running down her spine and she wondered if he had given Hannah a speech along these lines the first time he trained her.

'Good,' he said. He lifted her gloved hands and placed them so that her right hand was in front of her face and her left was extended out a little way in front. 'Lesson one, anytime you're not throwing a punch your hands are here, from here you can quickly bring them up and in to guard your head, and they're in the right place to jab and punch. Now, your feet.' He paused and scraped an imaginary line on the floor with his foot, then rearranged her feet in accordance with it. Her left foot was pointing into the line and her right foot was a little way back, pointed about ninety degrees out and away from the line.

'This is your stance, whenever you practice you get into this position first. You're standing slightly side-on so that you present a smaller target to your opponent. Eventually, you'll be light and springy on your feet and you'll be able to chase me around in that stance but we'll not worry about that yet.'

'Okay,' she said staring down at her feet.

Hank explained that for today, he was only teaching her to jab with her left. He said she should think of her left arm as a tool, a way of pushing her opponent away, keeping him off his rhythm, distracting him. It was her right arm that would eventually do the damage, but they'd worry about that another day.

'Watch me, extend your glove and at the same time rotate your shoulder,' he instructed. He made the movement in super slow-motion so that she could watch his fist move straight forward and twist so that his palm faced downwards. He held up his palm and told her, 'For now do it that slow.'

She took a breath, prepared herself, and then slowly jabbed at Hank's palm once, twice, three times. He stopped her, stood by her side, and placed both hands onto her hips.

'You're twisting,' he said. 'Do it again, slowly. Remember that the movement is in your arm, not in your hips. When we throw a punch we move into it and put our shoulder behind it but we don't move into a jab, jabs are built for speed, not power,' he explained.

She went again, and this time he held her hips and watched her movement. It had been a while since Jessica had a man's hands on her, Kelvin had lost his sex drive long before she left. Even so, there was nothing sexual about Hank's touch. To her, it felt brotherly.

That afternoon they spent two hours learning to jab. Once she had gotten the hang of the movement, Hank sped it up and taught her to breathe out sharply as she jabbed. 'Breathing right is important, it should make an "oofing" sound,' he advised.

As she jabbed at his padded hands, she watched as every so often he turned around to shout encouragement to Hannah. Before long, she was eager to hear him congratulate her and when he finally said, 'well done Jess, nice work,' her belly fizzed with joy.

By the end of the session, her left arm felt as heavy as lead while her right arm felt useless. She wondered if another boxing coach would have taught her to punch and jab side by side, or was he breaking it down especially for her? Sometimes she noticed a questioning expression on his face, it was almost as if he was asking himself, *is this how my pop would have taught her?* She thought that, maybe, the role of boxing coach didn't come naturally to Hank but still she appreciated his effort.

Hank undid the strap under her chin and took the head guard off her. There was a towel hanging over the edge of a bench and Hank picked it up and threw it to Jessica, but it slipped through the grip of her boxing gloves. She took them off, put them down on the bench, then bent to pick up the towel. There was a thick layer of sweat dripping down her head and her shoulder was aching a little.

'Sit down a mo',' Hank said.

She sat and Hank stood behind her, rubbing the ache out of her shoulder with the heel of his hand. She groaned with relief and tears blurred her vision. Jessica stared across the room and blinked to clear them, focusing on the unfinished canvas. On it, a bear was towering over a little boy who was wearing a wooden crown and holding up a wooden sword.

'That's cool,' she said, pointing over at it.

'Oh yeah, it's for Charlie … a cover for his new book. It's called, "The Boy Who Tamed the Bear".' With that, Hank stepped back, finished with her shoulder treatment.

'He's got a new one coming out?' she asked with surprise. Jessica stood up from the bench and wandered across the room to get a better look at the painting.

The bear and the boy were standing on a hill, half of a forest had been painted around them, the other half was yet to be completed.

'Yeah, in a couple of months' time,' Hank confirmed as he joined her at the easel.

'It's about my pop-pop!' Hannah shouted. Jessica looked over her shoulder at the little girl who was taking off her own gloves. 'That's why we were in the woods last week when we met you, Pop was doing some sketches for his painting. I'm allowed to watch him paint this one because there're no boobies in it.'

'You know, twice or maybe three times she's not been allowed to come here because I've had nude models in, and now the little madam acts like it's the Playboy mansion!'

'What's the playboy mansion?' she asked.

'Oh, if I have my way you'll never know the answer to that, Twinkle. If you live to be a hundred you'll still be asking that question!'

He rolled his eyes at Jessica and she laughed.

There was a moment of silence as the adults thoughtfully studied the painting and Hannah climbed into the ring and began bouncing off the ropes.

'Is his new story really about you then?' Jessica asked, out of the corner of her eye she saw him rock his hand back and forth in a 'sort of' gesture.

'It started off a short story in his first collection. It was based on the legend of the bear in Starkey's woods and Puck's daughter.'

'I only know about the bear, I don't know the rest of it.'

'Well,' Hank sighed. 'Charlie's better at telling the spirit stories, but basically Puck, the spirit of mischief, had this daughter. Some versions say she was an orphan, others say she was half spirit, half mortal ... but she fell in love with a man and left her father to be with him. When she got pregnant, the man got scared and ran away, Puck lost his temper and transformed the man into a giant bear, making him stand guard over the back door to the spirit world. The first time Charlie wrote it, it was just the bare bones of the legend ... now he's made it into a sort of young adult book ... and it's familiar, you know. I can't work out if I'm the bear or the boy ... maybe I'm both.'

Jessica was about to speak, but when she turned to look at Hank, she could almost see his anima leaving him. His mind seemed to be escaping through his eyes and going off to some other place far away. She watched and waited for him to return, his absence only lasted a matter of seconds, but it felt longer. When he came back to himself, he startled slightly and muttered something under his breath. Some

196

nonsense about seeing a boat washed into the harbour. Jessica decided to pretend not to have heard it, and when he turned to her she smiled pleasantly.

'Well I think we'll call it a day now,' Hank said. 'Are you free Wednesday evening?'

'Oh yes,' Jessica said eagerly. 'I can't wait.'

Outside in the car park, Hank locked the buildings doors and walked Jessica the ten steps back to her car. He dived into his shoulder bag and retrieved a plastic bag that he handed to her through her window.

'I forgot to give you this yesterday,' he said. 'That's Charlie's first book and the manuscript for the new one.'

'Oh, thank you,' she said, then looking up to make eye contact with him, 'thank you for everything, really.'

'Not a problem. Just remember what I told you.'

'Don't twist when I jab?'

'No,' he said.

Jessica was resting her hand on the car door and Hank reached down and squeezed it, again it felt like a brotherly gesture. She couldn't misconstrue the contact of his skin against hers because she had seen the way he looked at Becky with total adoration. When Jessica looked in his eyes she saw nothing but concern and compassion.

'It's not about being the greatest. It's just about taking control … it's about not being afraid anymore, understand?'

Unable to speak, Jessica nodded. She watched him as he took hold of Hannah's hand, waved goodbye, and lead her down the road.

I don't have to be afraid anymore, she thought to herself. *I hope he's right.*

18

The Art of Model Building and Denial

Downstairs in the grotto, Alison's little model town was coming along nicely. So far, she had built a total of fifty-six log cabins and had arranged them in concentric circles. The first circle consisted of eight cabins, the second sixteen, and the third thirty-two. She had placed the completed meeting hall in the middle of the town and flanked it with a couple of tiny trees. All of the previous week, her time had been spent on fiddly, little details. She had made bushes and placed them here and there in a seemingly random fashion. She had constructed telephone lines around the town and an electrical tower on the outskirts. Although all her cabins were hooked up to the mains, they also came with tiny generators. She had taken the time to build them all, fifty-six little generators just in case the weather in her Tiny Town ever got so bad that the power cut out.

So far, the thing that Alison was most proud of were the lanterns. In one unbroken line, they circled the rows of houses, their wires tucked under the white felt that served as the town's snowy ground. When she flicked a switch, two AAA batteries lit them up. Somehow those tiny, little lights made the town feel alive.

She was nowhere near done yet. The funny thing was, the more she built, the more models she found tucked away in the grotto. The folk who ran the Breidablik model company had an eye for detail and they certainly didn't lack imagination. In one large cardboard box labelled 'Main Street', she had found little models of various shops, a cinema, two different bars, a bowling alley, a restaurant, a little police station, and a fire station. She hadn't found a model of a doctor's surgery or a hospital, but she was okay with that. She decided that no one would ever get ill in her Tiny Town.

There was another box labelled 'big projects' that contained large and complex models including a train station with miles of tracks and four different trains. She had quickly put them to one side, she had never been a fan of trains. What interested her more was the harbour. What would an Icelandic Viking town be without somewhere to dock your boat. Also, she was taken with the functioning ski slope. It had a battery powered chairlift that picked up tiny model people, carried them up a mountain, then tipped them out onto a zigzag track for them to slide all the way down to the bottom.

At the bottom of the 'big projects' box, Alison found a mansion on a hill. Going from the pictures, it looked to be one of those minimalist palaces made of white stone and glass, the kind of place a rock star might live. The mansion was almost a perfect oblong, like a Lego brick. What made it interesting was the fact that the roof curved upwards to look like a ramp or a ski jump, that, and the fact that the back wall was made entirely of glass. This little mansion on the hill would be the perfect place to view the northern lights in her little Tiny Town.

As she sat building the miniature cinema, she also constructed a plan for the rest of the town. Main Street would be placed at the far west end and there would be one straight road for the little shops and bars, the bowling alley, and everything else the town needed. She would position the ski slope to the far east, the harbour would be in the north, and the mansion on the hill would be situated to the south where it could overlook everything. She knew, of course, that this wasn't how real towns worked. In real towns, the shops and the entertainment were always dead centre, and the houses were built around them. Not here though, here the people would be the heart of the town.

Alison smiled and rubbed her belly. Of course, it was far too early to get excited and carried away, but once again she couldn't help picturing a little boy with her face and Charlie's big, cow eyes. She had looked for strong Icelandic boys' names. The only ones she even remotely liked were Magnus and Johann. Maybe she would find something else, something a little more normal, maybe Magnus could be his middle name?

When it came to naming her potential child, the problem was Charlie's family name. Nothing really sounded right when paired with Dunn, there wasn't much romance in the name. Not that she thought her family name, Wheaton, was all that great. Of course, it was the trend now to have a double-barrelled surname but she cringed at the thought of it. *Look, there goes that little Dunn-Wheaton child. You know, the one with the mum who's got one boob bigger than the other, and the father who looks like a gangly Jim Henson puppet.* No, she'd just have to stick with Dunn otherwise it wouldn't be fair on the kid.

'Stop it,' she rebuked herself out loud. 'You're getting carried away again.' She had suffered four or five periods since they had agreed to officially start trying for a baby. The agreement hadn't been anything more than that one time she had said 'let's make a baby' during sex, and him not saying no, thus giving his silent consent to the idea. She had always been blessed with relatively manageable periods, but these last five, six, maybe seven times she had really suffered. Not because of the cramps, the bloating or the mood swings, but because of the sheer disappointment.

Since her brush with cancer, she was trying her best to live in the moment. It was easy here in the frozen North, living here was like existing in the 'in-between time'. Here and now was a perfect bubble at the end of one phase of their lives, but before the beginning of the next. The bubble would only last as long as it took Charlie to finish his book, then it would burst and they'd be swept back into the real world, where plans were stacked on top of more plans. For the most part, it was easy to be in the in-between and play in the snow, to drink hot chocolate by the log fire, to read and watch films and build models. All these things were easy, and Alison took to them well, but still...

Still, it was only human to wonder what might be. All who live and breathe think of the future. The happier the person, the more likely they are to daydream of what might be just around the corner. Alison was no different, except she was, she had come close to death. A couple of years ago there had been no future for her, then suddenly there was. Possibilities had come flooding in, filling the vacuum of her life, and although she tried not to, she planned her life the way she planned her Tiny Town.

Charlie would finish his second book and by then she would be heavily pregnant with her first child. There would be three in total, she hoped for two boys and then a little girl. But she would be happy with three no matter what the combination. They would go home to Coventry, get a nice family home on the outskirts of Castlegate or, failing that, a place in Pickford. She would get back to what she did best, teaching piano and violin. Maybe now and again she could get a professional gig, she'd love to play in a quartet again. They would have happy family holidays in warm places, and now and again they'd bring their brood back to Húsavík because it was a beautiful place. The kids would grow and thrive, and every day they'd make their parents proud. Eventually, they'd head off to university and the future would belong to them. A decade or so later, once they were sure that their kids were doing fine, they would retire to some place sunny, maybe the Umbrian valley in Italy. Hank had always spoken fondly of that place.

They would grow old together, but this time around she would nurse Charlie. Of course, he would have to pass away first. She wouldn't be able to bear that heartbroken look on his face again, once was enough for one lifetime. She'd be okay, she would come home to the kids and the grandkids who would take care of her and Charlie would never be that far away from her, she'd see him in her children's big, cow eyes and hear him in their laughter. This was Alison's plan, and it was a very good plan.

When it came to the loose threads and the wrongness that she had spotted in her little world, she had a brand-new policy. She was choosing to ignore it all, which meant fighting her deepest nature. The gaps in her memory, the things that didn't make sense, the way time seemed slippery. She just turned a blind eye to this and looked at her muppet man. She trusted in his solidity and his inner strength, and moreover in how happy she was. She wasn't about to let a piece of toast ruin what was virtually paradise for her.

Alison found that the trick was just to train herself to accept the strange and unbelievable. The days were distinct. The sun chased the moon and she could pick a single day out, point to it, and say to Charlie, 'remember last month when we made the snowmen and walked by the frozen lake?' She could pick out days, yet the seasons never changed. Birthdays were never celebrated, and Christmas never came. *Well fine, that's just fine,* she told herself. *Don't pay any notice.*

They ate regularly. She remembered cooking, she enjoyed cooking. Often, she watched Charlie cook as he rambled on about the latest development in his book. They would sit together and eat, talking about endless subjects. Afterwards, they'd put their plates in the sink and go about their day or if not, go to bed or sit in front of the fire. She never washed so much as a single plate or cup, they just appeared clean in the cupboards. Likewise, the fridge and the larder were always well stocked with food but she never went shopping. Besides, whatever they wanted to eat or drink was always in stock. If one of them had an odd craving for paella or pineapple upside-down cake, all the ingredients would be there, ready to go. *Well, that's just fine too,* she told herself. *We have the best maid service on the planet.*

Alison reached up and rubbed her temple to ease her throbbing headache. She got them a lot these days. It was probably the effect of using model glue in a poorly ventilated room. That, or the effort she was putting into controlling her reality. She didn't want to pick at loose threads anymore. It had become obvious to her that it wasn't a mystery she was unravelling, but her own sanity. Time wasn't slippery, food didn't just appear out of nowhere and dishes didn't wash themselves. The only logical explanation was that she was either losing her mind or she was losing her memory.

She could defy logic and say that the fault was not with her, but that it was the world around her that was wrong, and not just a little wrong, but big, big wrong. Wrong in a beautiful, magical, terrible way that obscures the small and mundane and denies the chance for change. It was like being trapped between a rock and a hard place. She knew she couldn't bear to struggle through another cruel sickness, nor could she live in a world that was so wrong. The only option was not to see but to pretend and make herself believe that all was well, and if she believed that then she'd be well. No longer would she be Alice, chasing the white rabbit down the hole, even if for her that rabbit was, in fact, a beautiful stag.

She glued the awning to the front of her little cinema and placed it on the table to dry. Another one done. It was really coming along now. Glancing at her watch she saw it said five p.m. so she decided to call it a day. Upstairs, Charlie would probably be lying on the rug by the fire, staring up through the sky and out into space. A full day in front of his glowing screen often left him feeling mentally exhausted.

She would go up and offer him a back rub in exchange for him returning the favour with her feet. As she stood, she heard a harmonica from a fragment of an old, familiar song, coming from the record player in the corner. *Did I put that on?* she asked herself. It made her think again of the white stag and that handsome nurse who took care of her once upon a time. She crossed the room and took the needle off the record, banishing the thoughts of the stag and the nurse, then went upstairs to spread her hands across her muppet man's back.

19

The Door That Never/Always Was

During the small, unguarded hours of the night, the sound of a harmonica rang out, filling the cabin with its forlorn notes that devoured the 'almost-silence' that they had grown accustomed to. The ticking of clocks, the wind rattling the glass, the logs and beams creaking like tired and painful bones. All these things gave way to a song that expressed heartache and loss, and something wonderful slipping just out of reach. Deep in their sleep, the lovers didn't hear the ethereal music, at least not in the depths of their minds. Charlie was busy dreaming of the plot hole he had dug himself into, and Alison was subconsciously pulling at loose threads. By day she could deny the truth and turn a blind eye to either the wrongness of the world or her loose grip on reality, but at night it was a different matter. By night her mind wandered of its own accord and saw whatever there was to see. Thus, tonight she dreamt of the geography of the cabin and thought, 'When is a door not a door?' *Eight. There had only ever been eight not nine. A door is not a door when it wasn't and never was there, but that's silly. Of course, it was always there. Doors don't just grow into walls.*

Meanwhile, as the lovers slept and dreamt troublesome dreams, something moved through their little home. The intruder was as pure white as newly fallen snow and crept through the corridor on its hooves. As it moved, its antlers scraped against the panelled walls without making a single mark or sound. One moment it was standing in the hallway, the next it was beside the bed where the lovers slept, then suddenly it was standing in the grotto sniffing at the little model town. It was the stag but, at the same time, it wasn't. In the exact same spot, superimposed over the stag like one photograph on top of another, stood a painfully handsome man. He surveyed the room and spied the record player in the corner. It was switched off and the cover was closed and yet, it still played for him. For him, it played the intro to a slow, sad song, one he knew all too well, one he had played himself in the key of C minor on his own Hohner harmonica. It had been this song that had summoned him from his place beyond, back to this cabin in the frozen North, where the writer and his muse lay in uneasy dreams. Still listening to the ethereal song, the handsome man bent over to examine the Tiny Town that Alison had been building. As he leaned forward, he seemed to be bathed in his own source of warm light. It was the broad gleaming, the Breidablik. Smiling, he reached out and lightly touched all the little cabins before examining the cinema and was pleased to see how well it was coming along.

Upstairs in her bed, Alison whimpered, troubled by the ninth door that was and wasn't, she seemed to be on the verge of waking up. Two floors below, the stag and the man that occupied the same space both looked up, seeing right into Alison's dream. She was still dreaming about the layout of the cabin that she knew like the back of her hand. Upstairs, there were two bedrooms and a large bathroom running alongside an internal balcony. Their bedroom was the larger of the two and was directly opposite the stairs. The chimney breast from the fireplace in the living room protruded from the walls in both the bedrooms, half in their room, half in the guest room, and the beds were huddled up to those brick breasts for the extra warmth that they radiated. The guest bedroom had never been used and was quite a lot smaller, practically a box room. It was very neat and tidy and contained a bed, chair, table, and nothing more. Between the guest bedroom and the bathroom was the small window and the vase containing the lilac. The bathroom was a fair old size and contained a sink, toilet, bath and a separate shower cubical.

If you peered over the balcony from the bathroom you could see the corridor at the bottom of the stairs. There were four doors leading off it, all opposite the staircase. Walking downstairs in the morning, the first door you came to led to the kitchen-cum-dining room. Next, there was the door to the large living room. This room had been built to focus on that roaring log fireplace. The deep shag carpet and the skylight next to the fire made it the perfect, little romantic spot to sit together. The next door on from the living room was the door to Charlie's office. There, he spent most of the day tap, tap tapping away. His office window overlooked the town of Húsavík and, in the distance, you could just about see the harbour. The last door along the corridor was the back door that led to the small woodshed at the end of the garden. The front door to the cabin guided you to the living room and was directly opposite the fireplace, the idea being that upon entering you would be immediately greeted by warmth, the heart of the home.

This was how the cabin had been built and it had always been this way, six rooms and eight doors over two levels. Then, of course, there was that ninth door, the one set in the middle of the staircase on the ground floor. Alison was absolutely convinced that the ninth door had always been there and, thinking that it was nothing more than a broom closet, she had just chosen to ignore it. That made sense. Quite often a person could see something but not really notice it. She had been happy believing this up until she had dropped that slice of toast butter side up and started pulling at loose threads. After that, she remembered looking at the panelled wall along the stairs. She remembered thinking that the point in the middle, where the door wasn't and had never been, would be a perfect place to hang some photographs.

But she banished that idea, dismissing it as nonsense. However, tonight, as she slept, her mind picked, and picked, and picked at it. Tonight, two separate and opposing memories had bloomed inside her mind, battling for dominance. She remembered slowly noticing the ninth door in half glances, day after day. It was small and slanted diagonally to fit under the stairs. Quite obviously, what lay behind was the junk hole where Charlie's agent stored all the knickknacks and bits of debris that he didn't want lying around the cabin. She had known this because there was a little pantry like that in her parent's house. There would be cleaning stuff in there as well, boxes of dusters and various products to use on all the different surfaces. If she opened that ninth door she'd feel compelled to organise the junk hole, then take all the extra cleaning stuff and polish the cabin from top to

210

bottom. She hadn't wanted to spend her whole time cleaning, and so she had decided to ignore the door. Day by day, she had trained herself not to look at it, because she was supposed to relax and convalesce, not sweep, mop, and polish. This was how she had managed to go so long before discovering her little grotto of entertainment.

At the very same time, she remembered looking at that stretch of plain, panelled wall and seeing no door, but rather an empty space to hang her pictures. If they were to be there for some time, she might as well make it feel like home. There was one picture in particular that she really loved. It was of the two of them, taken in the Cotswold village of Bourton-on-the-Water. In the picture they were sitting by the banks of the river Windrush, Charlie was dangling his feet in the water and she was resting her head on his shoulder. It was taken one late afternoon at the beginning of autumn and the trees behind them were bursting with reds and yellows. The sun was cresting behind Alison's left shoulder, casting a golden halo over them both. To Alison, this picture represented a beautiful time before they, as a couple, knew anything about pain, heartache and the fear of death.

They had gone to Bourton because Charlie had been booked for an appearance at the local independent bookstore. It was his usual dog and pony show consisting of a reading from his book 'Beta Male Fairy Tales', then a quick Q&A, followed by a signing and maybe an hour or so of hanging around for chit-chat. Alison was never sure if he enjoyed these appearances. He always looked as though he was having fun, but then he seemed relieved when they were over. Often, he made jokes about how these appearances were the price he paid for being the flavour of the month, or how he couldn't wait to slide into comfortable obscurity. Most of the time she went along with him, and they made romantic weekends out of it. Quite early on she realised she had become his silver lining. If she was in the audience, it made him feel a lot less like a performing seal. He spoke more naturally when he could catch her familiar and friendly eye.

When they went to Bourton, Charlie's agent had sent a photographer along. It was the perfect place to get some promotional pictures, both for the website and to use on flyers and posters for yet more appearances. Charlie quickly grew tired of posing. Alison watched from the bridge and saw him grow visibly more conscious of his body. From where she was standing it looked like he was bending over, trying to make himself look less tall and spindly. She asked the photographer if they could have some pictures together and the moment she stood by his side she saw the tension fall away from him.

Now in her dream, Alison stood in the corridor downstairs and watched as the ninth door shrank and collapsed in on itself. When she had seen that picture of the two of them by the riverbank for the first time she had thought, *this is the man I'm going to marry.* The memory of wanting to hang that picture on the section of wall where no door had ever been was powerful and connected to a reservoir of emotion. It was the stronger and truer of the two opposing memories, and it was devouring the false memory, the door that never was. She panicked, sensing all the holes that would open in the world around her, that would open up in her mind. She was at the very edge of madness now and…

Relief came as a beam of warm light shone through the cracks around the tiny door, lighting Alison's face. Everything fell away. She was standing in the middle of the frozen lake, staring as the northern lights swirled above her head. Out of the corner of her right eye, she saw the white stag standing by her side, and out of her left, she glimpsed the profile of a beautiful man. She couldn't get herself to look at him directly, as she thought her heart might burst if she was to see him in all his glory.

'Be still, dear heart,' he said. 'Truth is a fine and awful thing that is best served in small doses. It's acid and alkaline, do you understand?'

'Not really,' she answered.

'I mean, what does it matter if that pesky door was never there, always there, or only sometimes there? In the grand scheme of things that door, well … it's neither here nor there,' he smiled at his play on words and grew so bright that Alison had to hold a hand up to shade her eyes. 'It's not important because your picture … Wouldn't it look just as good if you hung it by the side of the door? Hang it twelve inches to the left and it solves all your problems, twelve inches to the left and the whole world won't fall down around you, dear heart.'

'Who are you?' Alison asked. She saw the beautiful man shrug as if that question had no importance. 'You seem so familiar, I think I've dreamed of you from time to time.' It dawned on her that she was dreaming of him at this very moment and she felt just a little bit silly. 'What are you?' she asked.

'I'm spirit made flesh.'

'Are you Baldr?'

'Well, it's a name,' the beautiful man answered in a vague and enigmatic tone. 'I prefer Jude though, I remember my friends just called me Valentine.'

'Like the band?' Alison said.

'Yeah, like the band,' the handsome man smiled again.

'Am I going mad?' Once again, the question rolled off her tongue before she could think not to speak. Jude, the handsome man, or Valentine, depending on how friendly you were with him, didn't speak for such a long time that she guessed the answer was yes, when he finally spoke again it was completely off-topic.

'Would you like to see some magic?' he asked. Not knowing exactly how to answer or, for that matter, what to expect, Alison simply nodded yes. 'Good. Stick your tongue out!' he ordered.

Alison stuck out her tongue as asked and the handsome man reached out and grabbed it between his thumb and forefinger. He gripped it just tightly enough that she was unable to retract it, but not tight enough to hurt.

'I learned this little trick from Puck,' he stated quite casually. 'You see, I hold your tongue and from this moment on you'll not be able to talk about me to anyone else or speak of my secrets or of any strange subject for that matter.'

'Thatsff stufid. It'sff not magif. You'ff juft pinfing my fong.' When she spoke it was sloppy and unintelligible.

'What do you want? Shall I start waving a twig around whilst speaking in pig Latin? Would that convince you?' He let go of her tongue and she drew it back into her mouth. 'When it comes to magic I'm a novice, but what I do know is that magic words, potions, spell books, that's all nonsense. It doesn't matter what words you say, what matters is how you say them.'

The white stag on Alison's right was growing restless, stamping its hooves against the snow and nodding towards the horizon. Slowly, she reached out a hand and stroked its fur, feeling warmth run up her arm and into her chest. Seconds later, a hand was gripping her shoulder, pulling her away, yanking her hand from the warm, white fur. Cold replaced the warm feeling that had been moving towards her heart. Out of the corner of her eye, she saw that the handsome man, Jude, was looking at her with a stern expression.

'Please don't touch him without permission. It's an intimacy I cannot afford you,' he loosened his grip on her shoulder and the sternness left his face. 'In answer to your question, you're not going mad at all ... but the world ... well, it has become a little stranger than I think you're used to.'

'What is it?' Alison demanded, her voice sharp and urgent. 'What's wrong with the world?'

'Slowly, slowly, slowly,' Jude replied, his voice not even the slightest bit sharp, urgent, or demanding. Instead, he spoke as if he was addressing a skittish horse. 'Too much truth is bad for you. A little at a time, dear heart, there's no rush.'

Alison was completely unsatisfied by this answer. Presented with a mystery, she could not deny her true nature and pull at the loose thread. The handsome man was talking to her, but his words went in one ear and straight out the other. She was busy scanning the swirling lights in the sky and the snow and rocks at her feet. It was as if she thought the wrongness with the world was so close that she would be able to see it as soon as she laid her eyes on it.

'Normally, when I speak people listen.' Alison stopped scanning her surroundings and turned her gaze back to him. She made the mistake of looking at him directly. It was like looking directly into the sun.

'I heard you,' she said squinting. 'You were talking about a tree.'

'Yggdrasil, I was talking about Yggdrasil.'

'You said a tree.'

'No, I said imagine a tree.' There was a humanising look of frustration on his face as he furrowed his brow and tapped his right foot impatiently. 'It doesn't matter, time is short now. Next time. I'll tell you next time.'

'I'm going to see you again then?'

'Yes,' Jude sighed. 'I fear I may have been a little neglectful. If I'd kept a closer eye on you then you wouldn't have gotten yourself into this panicked state. No matter, from now on I'll be in your dreams more often, I'll take you through the sky on the back of the stag yonder and tell you stories.'

At that, both the stag and Jude turned and walked away over the frozen lake. Alison noticed that it got darker around her as the two

216

figures moved away. After a moment or two, she chased after them. She felt like she was running towards the sun that was setting on the horizon, and if she could just keep up then the darkness wouldn't take her.

'Wait!' she shouted. 'What should I do now?'

'Be calm. You are well-loved and all is well, and all is well, and all manner of things shall be well,' his voice echoed from all around her. It seemed to be coming from the swirling lights in the sky, the snow, and ice at her feet, and the trees at the edge of the lake. 'Wake!' he commanded, and Alison woke.

20

The Remembrance of Things (Better Left in the ...) Past.
Part 1

Night has fallen over Coventry, and on this night the young lovers are 2,000 miles away from Húsavík, and two, or maybe four, or perhaps eight years before that frozen paradise began to unravel. This night is only ever really a breath and a heartbeat away. Charlie is walking the streets, aimless, and without direction. The white coats have numbered Alison's days, likely he can count them on one hand, certainly, he will not need two hands to count them. Time is so thin that he's able to see through it, and what he sees on the other side chills him to the bone. It isn't enough, it's not nearly enough time, how could you love someone completely in just four short years together?

The white coats have given up all hope, there is no medicine now that can save her, all they can do is ease her passing. That isn't good enough for Charlie, and because he was sent to Coventry as a young man he knows there are other ways, secret ways, old ways. Of course, the old ways are not really secret, the stories are prolific and likely he has heard them all. He is not quite sure he believes them. He is not a spirit chaser, just a story chaser, and these are the stories that he built his career on. In the end, belief is neither here nor there, because there's nothing he would not do, nothing he would not risk for a little more time.

He has been advised against this course of action. That nice male nurse, the ridiculously handsome one with the disarming manner. The one he thought he remembered from some other time and place, he said, 'Don't go, Charlie. Pookas, spirits, pagan gods. Whatever you want to call them, they're dangerous. You can't imagine what you're risking getting involved with the likes of them. Better to stay here, better to hold Alison's hand, say goodbye and then grieve for her.' The nurse's warning was wasted breath, words with no weight that just floated away on Alison's fading breath. There was nothing he would not do, nothing he would not risk because it was not enough time. It is for this reason that Charlie now finds himself standing in Broadgate, before the statue of Godiva at midnight. He falls to his knees, closes his eyes, and clutches his hand around a small object in his pocket. He mutters the words.

'I come in supplication to spirits beyond. Accept my token and open the way for me.' As ever, when it comes to real magic, what matters is not the words that are spoken, but how they are said. His are drenched in heartache and desperation, and these things are like food and drink to some of the more pestilent spirits. The veil opens, like a pair of curtains drawing back to reveal a different world. Charlie steels himself, and then leaps through into the Midway, the world that lies in between all worlds.

On the other side, it is vastly different from how he has imagined it. What he finds is a sprawling neon city built around an endless marketplace. It is the apotheosis and mix of all marketplaces, to his left, it looks like an Arabian bazaar, to his right it is Chinese, and from somewhere he hears a cockney barrow boy. He knows that the market stalls are where the lesser spirits ply their trade, as he makes his way through the swarm of bodies, he sees them. Glowing, magnetic beings, performing for, and making deals with, the little crowds gathering around their stalls.

Looking past the market stalls, he sees the neon signs hanging outside the buildings. On one sign below the word 'Nod', there is a man asleep on a turtle. Here is Somnus, the dream weaver, who is sometimes called Absolem, the truth speaker. Another sign depicts a woman stepping out from a clam, this place is called The Speakeasy and it is where the spirit of desire holds court. The third sign he sees shows a man standing on top of an elephant's head. This place is not named, but on the sign, there is a circus tent beneath the tusks of the elephant. Charlie knows this sign marks the entrance to Pandemonium, where Puck, the most tricksy of all spirits, resides. He knows better than to ask for help from Puck, and so he moves on, pushing his way through the bodies until he comes to a flashing purple lotus. Here is the home of Mephistopheles, who trades power for favours.

Through the lotus door, Charlie finds the spirit sitting on a throne at the centre of a derelict manor house. All about him lay the bodies of his worshippers, passed out on the floor, and staring through dead eyes at the ceiling. The power Mephistopheles offers is the drug Mana. It is a liquid he dispenses in small glass vials, capable of performing miracles. Mana is both extremely powerful and addictive, it gives you great power and yet, slowly, it steals your life away.

Charlie moves towards the figure on the throne, stepping over the bodies as he goes. He notices that the closer he gets to the centre of the room, the more sickly, and skeletal the bodies on the floor appear. A man nearest to the throne looks exactly the way Alison did when he left her side that evening. Seeing this, Charlie falls to his knees and tells Mephistopheles all about Alison. He cannot see the spirit's face, it's hidden in shadow, but nevertheless, Charlie begs for the life of his lover, offering up his soul in return.

'What have you got in your pocket?' The voice is rich and deep, with a trans-Atlantic twang to it. 'The token in your pocket, give it to me.'

Charlie slips his hand into his jeans' pocket and retrieves a champagne cork. It is the cork from the bottle he shared with Alison on their first date.

Black fingers shoot out of the darkness and pluck the cork from Charlie's hand. He watches as the cork is lifted high into the air and then drops into a gaping mouth. Mephistopheles swallows the cork whole and licks his lips.

'You're an idiot,' he says. Mephistopheles leans forward into the light and Charlie sees a black man dressed as a gangster rapper, in a white suit and white fur coat. He looks this way because this is how we assume he will look. Too many movies, TV shows, rap videos, and news reports have cast the African American man as a drug dealer. Thus Mephistopheles, Lord of Lotus Eaters, is bound to conform to the reality that we project. Expectation is everything and the flesh folk

have been trained to expect and fear the worst from strangers, minorities, and immigrants.

'You don't have a single idea of what a soul is, it's not something that can be sold like your second-hand crap on eBay. A soul is a place where character, experience, and intellect meet, mingle and do battle. We don't buy souls little, stupid man, here we trade in love and devotion. That's the only thing that counts with our kind.'

Mephistopheles steps down from his throne and circles Charlie, he makes no effort to step over the bodies on the floor, rather he steps on fingers, torsos, and a nose, which snaps and pours with blood. The owner of the newly-broken nose doesn't even flinch as he, her, or maybe now just it, continues to stare blankly at the ceiling. 'At any rate, there is no deal here. There is no Mana that can buy life, and for that matter, there is no amount of devotion that could settle the debt you'd owe me. No, there is only one thing that buys life, and it is beyond you.'

'Nothing is beyond me,' Charlie barks. 'There is nothing I wouldn't do for her!'

'Really?' The pestilent spirit grins then reaches into his coat pocket and takes out a flick knife. 'In that case, take this and kill. Murder is the only thing that buys life. It is your lover's time now but you want to defy that, you say "no, it's not enough, I need more." Take this knife and steal someone else's time, gift it to your lover by dripping blood on her tongue. Do this before the sun rises, and she will live.'

Charlie hesitates for a moment, then, swallowing hard, he takes the knife in his trembling hand. A toothy smile spreads across Mephistopheles's face, it is a grim thing, full of malice and hunger.

'She played it for you,' the spirit begins, tauntingly, 'Naked, on the edge of her bed, she played her violin and opened her heart. Well, it's your turn now muppet man! Play for her, play her a blood-red song. Open someone else's heart.'

The malicious smile spreads from the spirit's mouth to his eyes, as he swaggers over to stand by Charlie's side. Leaning close, he whispers in Charlie's ear.

'Sing her a switchblade serenade.'

21

Story Time

It was August in Castlegate, and Jessica was enjoying a rare Sunday afternoon of doing absolutely nothing. No gardening, no boxing, no chores, nothing but lying on a lounger beneath a parasol in her Granda' Owen's garden. Dressed in cut-off jeans, sunglasses, a large floppy sun hat, black T-shirt, and slathered in sun cream, she was doing her best to enjoy the sun without crisping up like pork crackling. As a pale-skinned, and freckled redhead, she had the same trouble as all of her kind. She didn't tan as much as she tangoed. Even so, she was making the best of it. There was a bucket full of Saga beer bobbing around in ice water on the grass beside her, and on a table to her left, a stack of books and a punnet of plump strawberries. Relatively speaking Owen's garden was bare, he was like a chef with a Michelin star who came home to eat pot noodles. There were a couple of plant pots and a hanging basket but nothing else. She had pointed this out to her Granda', she had suggested that she could help him give it a bit of a facelift in their spare time and he had laughed at that.

'Beaut, the last thing I want to do with my time off is more of what I do all week, only for free.'

And that had been an end to that.

She reached across and took another bottle of beer from the bucket, opening it on the edge of the table, the way her Granda' had shown her. She took a swig and placed it down on the table next to the books, then picked up a particularly succulent looking strawberry. She held it up to the light and examined it, large, and red, and shaped like a teardrop. When she bit it, the sweet tangy juice exploded. Her mouth was full of the taste of it, her nose full of the scent of honeysuckle and hyacinths coming from someone else's garden.

Inside the house, she heard the rumble of Owen's laughter. She had been showing him how to use YouTube on her laptop and now he spent all his spare time looking at old Monty Python sketches. He was a joker at heart, and he had always soaked up comedy. When he was a younger man it had been 'Hancock's Half-Hour' and Eric Sykes, nowadays he roared laughing at teen comedies and gross-out films. Jessica remembered catching him in front of the telly, chuckling at a young teen boy who had been caught by his father trying to hump a pie.

'I love the sense of freedom your generation has,' he had said with tears rolling down his face after watching that particular film. 'In my day we had to dance around everything, there was so much we couldn't say!'

'Like what?' she had mistakenly asked.

'Well, truth be told ... Fuck and cunt for a start.'

'Granda'!'

'What, I can't swear because I'm old, is it?'

'Yes Granda' ... you're very, very old ... why can't you suck Werther's and talk about how this all used to be fields?'

225

That little throwaway comment had prompted a lecture about how – just as Dylan Thomas put it – 'I'll not go gentle into that good night'. This quickly mutated into his opinion on the beauty of Welsh poets, and how he always used to tell his Irish wife that his lot had the edge in that department. According to him 'the Irish had nothing to teach the Welsh about poetry.'

At that moment, Jessica could hear her Granda' laughing at the election night sketch, in which the sensible MP's – who were all upper-middle-class Tory types – were losing out to loons with ever-increasingly elaborate, and wacky names. She picked up her phone and put on some background music to drown him out. She flicked through her library and stopped at Pink Floyd's 'Dark Side of the Moon'. She thought about the first time she had heard it and, of course, that had only been a couple of months ago at Hank and Becky's dinner party. Despite the pink gin haze of that night, she still remembered the strangeness of it, the laughter, the good food, the warmth of their welcome. For Jessica, rock bottom had come in Starkey's woods, where she remembered the coldness of a mother who could not comfort a crying child. She realised now that her first step up from rock bottom had been taken on that strange and wonderful night at Hank and Becky's.

The song 'Time' was reaching its conclusion and through Jessica's phone Gilmour was singing about how, when he was home, he liked to rest his bones beside the fire. She thought of that dream she kept having, the one she couldn't make sense of, the one where she was wandering aimlessly around a snowy, little town. She thought about

226

how wonderful it might be to one day sit naked in front of a fire with a loved one by her side. Maybe in a log cabin, on a snowy hill, overlooking a frozen lake and…

Halfway through that train of thought she shuddered with revulsion and shook off the idea of it. Her eyes fell to the books stacked on the table and the papers she had placed in between their pages.

Jessica had been doing a little bit of research. On her boxing days, Hank showed her how to be light on her feet and how to move quickly. He showed her how to put her shoulder behind her strong right fist and how to sway into her punches. During their training sessions, she made it a habit to ask him questions about Charlie. She had learned quickly that if she asked him direct questions about the nature of Charlie's heartache and why exactly Alison had moved on, he would avoid answering them. He stuck to his story about being unable to talk about it because he was under the enchantment of a Pooka. She didn't know if she believed it, but it became a little more credible every time she heard it.

'Anyway, it's Charlie's story … you should really hear it from him,' Hank had said, and she agreed with that. From then on, she had only asked background questions.

In the end, it was a Google search that shone something of a light on the mystery of Charlie. She had taken to searching his name and reading whatever the internet spat up about him. There were reviews of his books, interviews, articles about his style. All of these were accompanied by photographs of the man looking tall, ginger, and awkward, with that odd shooting star birthmark on his neck. One article, in particular, answered a lot of her questions, but not without raising just as many more.

The headline of that article shouted in block capitals: *CULT WRITER'S PARTNER DIAGNOSED WITH BREAST CANCER.* Underneath the headline there was a picture of Charlie and Alison, sitting happily together under a tree, by the banks of a river. She read every word three times over but in essence that article from eight years ago was summed up in the headline. Alison had gotten sick and then what ... what happened next? Seemingly eight years had passed since that article, and Alison and Charlie were no longer together. Jessica couldn't find another article online that filled in the gaps but she remembered Hank saying, 'Alison has moved on'. Moved on, not passed on ... To Jessica that suggested that Alison had beaten her sickness and then called an end to her relationship with Charlie. If that was the case, it would be all too easy to look at Alison negatively. But Jessica thought about the pressure of a long, grim illness, and how it was just as likely for a relationship to snap under that pressure as it would be to come out the other end stronger and more solid. If you have beaten death but, in that process, lost that spark of love, then don't you owe it to yourself to make a clean break? Don't you owe it to yourself to live again?

'Tarquin Fin-tim-lin-bin-whin-bim-lim bus stop F'tang F'tang Ole Biscuitbarrel.' Owen said, chuckling at the back door. 'I won't lie to you. Those Pythons crack me up they do.'

He crossed the garden, stepping around Jessica and bending to fetch a bottle of beer from her bucket of ice water. He sat himself down on his wall, grunting and groaning as his legs bent, then deftly popped the cap of the bottle off on a slightly jagged brick. He put the bottle by his side then filled his pipe and struck a match between his fingertips. Before long, he was puffing away, blowing out smoke circles and swigging the beer.

'That's a formidable stack of books you've got there, Michelle Tyson,' he said, pointing with his pipe. Lately, he had taken to nicknaming her after various boxers. Yesterday it had been Henrietta Cooper, tomorrow it might be Christine Eubank. Jessica didn't mind so much, it was all done in good humour. She knew him well and knew that he very rarely took anything seriously, not if there was a joke that could be made about it. 'Trying to read them all before your eyes drop out, is it?'

'I'm doing a bit of research Granda'.'

'About what, good girl?'

She picked up a strawberry and considered it, without really seeing it. She was looking past it, staring into the distance and breathing in the scent of those hyacinths. She popped it into her mouth and bit off the stalk.

'Remember when I was a kid,' she said chewing. 'You used to tell me those stories about the spirits?'

'Ah the Pookas, scared you they did. But you loved the stories all the same. Every time I told you one you'd have nightmares, and then

Pruney would be on the phone to give me an ear bashing ... that reminds me ... have you spoke to her lately?'

'Yes.' Jessica sighed. 'It was short ... I told her about how well I was doing with my boxing and how Jude's garden was coming along nicely ... I think just to get a rise out of her.'

Her Granda' Owen didn't respond to that. Instead, he just quietly chugged away on his pipe and drank his beer. Jessica turned her head to look at him and, in that light, she saw how old he looked. Of course, in the high places of her mind, she knew that her Granda' was getting on in years, but she hadn't been able to accept that in her heart until she had moved in with him. Up until then, she had secretly harboured that childish belief that her Bampi was solid and indestructible. That he would just go on, and on, and on, and never slow down, never stop. Since moving in – and moreover, since she began to work with him – she had witnessed first-hand his aches and pains, his breathlessness, and the occasional dizzy spell. What's more, he had noticed her noticing, and probably now they had both realised that enough was enough. She suspected that, after this final project for the rock star down the road, her Granda' would say he was done. If he didn't, well she'd just have to sit him down and have a little talk with him.

That was for later, right now she was concerned with the Pookas.

'Bampi?' she said in a questioning tone and he hummed in acknowledgment. 'Hank keeps talking about how some spirit intervened in his life, and these books ... they all revolve around spirits in some way ... but it's all nonsense, isn't it? I mean, lots of people around the city claim to have seen them … but it's not real, is it? It's all a weird joke, right?'

'Truth be told, I don't think it is,' he said and then he said nothing more for an age. Eventually, he pointed at the bottles of beer and said, 'Pass your Bampi another drink, good girl.'

She did as she was told and then watched him chip it open and glug it down, his giant Adam's apple bobbing up and down like fishing float. He finished the beer then wiped his wet mouth dry with this back of his hand.

'It's like this, see … your mama was a babe in arms when we came to Coventry. It was the five of us then, see. Little Pruney, your aunts, myself, and your Grandma Bridget. We'd hardly been here a month when it happened, we'd barely unpacked, barely got our feet under the table when your grandma passed, like that', he said and clicked his fingers. 'A vein in her head exploded while she was hanging out washing, and she was dead by the time she hit the ground. It was a Sunday afternoon; your aunts were out playing and I'd popped to the Tiger's Head for a jar. I came home first and found your grandma dead where she was lying, and your little baby mama lying asleep in her pram. Not crying mind, not making a blessed sound, just sleeping. I won't lie to you, my strawberry, at that moment I hated her. She was just a year old but part of me hated her for sleeping when she should have been upset. When your aunts came home, they cried, and even though it makes no sense I thought these are my lovely girls crying for their mama.'

Jessica stood from her sun lounger, crossed the garden, and sat on the wall next to her Bampi. She held his hand and felt him give it a squeeze. There was still some strength there, maybe he wasn't quite spent yet.

'There was a funeral, and then we went about life, but I was an awful father. It was your Aunt Alwena who took control, all of fourteen and there she was raising the girls and taking care of her Pa. I didn't want it, none of it, I couldn't live without my Bridget … and I'd heard these stories, see … there used to be a little Polish fella living in the village … Dobry something-or-other. He was always talking about the Pookas that lived in the woods, he said they were the trickster spirits … he told me there was a statue in the middle of the woods with an open mouth and a face faded away by the ages. He said, if I put a letter in the statue's mouth, the spirit would come to me at nightfall. One day, I took it to heart and I went in to see what I could find. Sure enough, at the heart of the woods, standing over the mouth of a stream, was the faceless statue. I put my letter in its mouth and came away before I had time to change my mind.'

'What happened next?' Jessica asked. There was awe and excitement in her voice.

'A spirit came to me,' her Granda' answered. 'I was asleep in my armchair, passed out with the booze if truth be told. I was deep asleep, but despite that, I had the feeling I wasn't alone, I felt like I was being watched and that was enough to wake me. When I opened my eyes, he was standing in the doorway as bold as brass. He was a willowy creature, pointy ears, and purple flecked eyes. He was smiling at me, it was this big crafty grin that lit up his face but I saw through it, and what I saw was a spark of anger. He held up my letter and said, "Owen Evans, this is unworthy, how dare you ask this thing of me", and that voice of his was light and bright but all the same it made me shudder!'

'What was in the letter?' Jessica asked.

At that, her Granda' Owen looked shamefaced and his eyes fell to his feet. When she looked at him now, he looked even older, it was almost as if this subject was aging him by the second. She turned away from him and her eyes fell to the bucket of beer bottles, now the ice had almost melted away and the water looked slightly murky, with the odd dead bug floating around on the surface. She took the two remaining bottles, popped them open, and handed one to the old man on the wall.

'It's okay,' she said. 'Whatever it was, it doesn't matter now.'

'Well, you see, I wasn't doing well without your grandma. My whole world had just disappeared, and I couldn't do it ... I couldn't be a dad, I didn't have the energy or the willpower. So, in the letter, I asked the Pookas to do a trade ... I asked them to take my life in return for Bridget. Let her live, let her be a mama to the girls and I'd just fade away.' He paused and swigged the beer, looking away from Jessica's sympathetic stare. 'That Pooka, he stood in my doorway and gave me a lecture about how life is pain, and if I can't deal with that pain, then I should laugh at it. "Sometimes the only sane thing to do is laugh at your darkness because laughter is a bright white light," he said. But I wasn't listening to him, not really, I was looking at his legs.

I'd noticed something, see … a face, there was a face peering out from behind his legs.'

'Who's face?' Jessica asked.

'Yours.'

Jessica was lifting the bottle to her lips and stopped dead when her Granda' confessed that detail. It was the last thing she'd expected to hear, and she didn't quite know how to react to it.

'Your little shy face, peering from behind that Pooka's legs. God love you, with those big eyes and your strawberry hair. You were the spitting image of Bridget, because the girls … your mother and her sisters … every bit of them was me. Seeing you there, a vision of the future … well, it was proof that a part of my Bridget was going to live on, and it made it easier for me to get by. I was still a lousy father though, useless with my girls … a joker but not a father. I was just killing time until you arrived … of course, I didn't know which one of my girls would be your mother … it had to end up being Pruney, didn't it?'

At that, Jessica snorted and spat beer into her lap. Having nothing to hand to dry herself with, she used the flat of her palm to brush the wet from her cut-off jeans. She realised that it looked a little like she'd had an 'accident'. She was about to point that out to her Granda' to cheer him up but now she noticed he looked even paler, washed out, and broken.

'Bampi,' she said softly. 'Please don't be too hard on yourself. You learned from your mistakes in the end … look how you were, no, still are with me. I can't imagine how bad my childhood would have been without you looking out for me. Without you, I wouldn't have had any warmth or love or ...'

'Oh, now, good girl,' he said interrupting her. 'It's truth you want from your Granda' today, is it? Then let's have all the truth and not just half ... because I've been lying to you, I lie to everyone... I say I don't know how Pruney ended up the way she did, but I know really. She grew up in a shadow, that's what did it for Pruney. You see your aunts knew what it was like to have a mother and father who loved them. Losing their mother was bad enough, but on the same day they lost their father in spirit if not in body, and that was worse. Even so, they were lucky, they could remember when they had a proper family. Pruney grew up not knowing what it was like to be loved by her parents, all she knew about the love of a mother and father she'd learned from scraps of overheard conversations between her sisters about the good old days before she was born. Those same sisters had been forced to grow up too fast and take care of her. They didn't want to look after her, they just wanted to be kids, and then young women. Even after seeing that spirit I couldn't manage to be a father ... I ached too much, I ached from the day your grandma died till the day you were born, and I poured all my effort into laughing at my darkness, just so that I could stumble from sunrise to sunset. Meanwhile, there was your mum growing up in that shadow, hating me for being there and not being there at the same time. Promising she'd be the exact opposite of me ... Not a joker, Pruney, no, not her. She was always so serious and severe. She wouldn't play with the little Castlegate girls and boys ... No, she made friends with the rich kids from the big houses, and she learned from them what she really needed to know … how to be the exact opposite of me. When you were a little kid you had a nanny, do you remember that Jess?'

'No.' Jessica said, fighting back the tears.

'This lovely, plump woman she was. Big, jowly, warm face she had, and grand pillows for breasts. Pruney had learned about nannies when she was a little girl playing with the posh girls and boys. Mostly, the nannies were Castlegate women, and if they saw Pruney around the village they barely noticed her, but at the big houses, they were smiles and sunshine. It was only natural that Pruney would take on a nanny, she had the big house, she had the rich husband, she had the baby, all she needed was someone to take care of it. Well, something happened … you fell and hurt your knee and the nanny picked you up and hugged you. That night, Pruney was tucking you into bed and you asked her if you could go away and live with your nanny. I know about this because she called me sobbing down the phone and I rushed around to see what was up. She told me the story … and even then, I couldn't find it in myself to reach out and say, "it's my fault Pruney, I was a horrible father, learn from my mistakes, be better than me". If I'd have done that then so much could have been different for you now.'

Owen stood slowly and stumbled towards the door, his feet shuffling through the grass, like a condemned man going to his death. At the door to his humble little house he stopped dead, gripping the door frame. He stared off to a point in the distance and took a few slow, deep breaths. Meanwhile, Jessica was still sitting on the wall,

236

desperately trying to think of something to say, something to make this better, words that would act as a healing salve for old wounds. She couldn't find any and, in the end, it was Owen who broke the silence

'It's a chain,' he said, 'and it needs to be broken.'

Jessica answered that by standing, crossing to the old man in the doorway and hugging him tightly from behind.

'I love you Bampi.'

'I know you do, good girl,' he said, patting her hand. 'But it's a chain, my girl. Your mother is the way she is because of me. You are the way you are because of your mother … it's up to you to break the chain.'

'How?'

'Live your own life, find your own happiness. You studied accounting to make your mum happy, you were a doormat and a punching bag for that shit of a boyfriend of yours, and now you're a gardener to spite them both. Your heart's not in my little strawberry, you enjoy it because you enjoy spending time with me, but you don't need an excuse for that … and besides, once we're done with Jude's garden I'm going to pack it all in. If your mother will still have me, I think I'll move in with her.'

'Are you sure, Bampi?' She asked, hugging him a little tighter. 'You don't have to move in with her, I can take care of you.'

'Live your own life, good girl. There's not much time left for me and Pruney to build our bridges. And besides, if I'm there it will be easier for you to build bridges of your own.'

'What can I do to make it better Granda'?' she asked and felt him shrug under her arms. He didn't answer but that didn't matter, as she thought she knew the answer, the only thing she could do was what he'd asked of her. 'Live my own life, find my own happiness.' Standing there in the doorway of the only place that had ever felt like a real home, she began to ask herself a question she had very rarely asked of herself. *What do I want from life, what will make me happy?*

22

The Remembrance of Things (Better Left in the ...) Past. Part 2

In a daze, Charlie leaves the temple of the lotus eaters and walks through the vast marketplace of the Midway, without paying attention to the hustle and noise around him. It's all nothingness to him, the lights, the smells, the sounds, he is numb to it all. All Charlie is awake to at this moment is the flick knife in his pocket, he feels it pressed, cold and heavy against his leg. On autopilot, he reaches the end of the market and passes through into the mortal world.

Here, faces pass him by, and he takes a moment to glance at each one. 'This one?' he asks himself. 'No, not that one. Maybe this one.' It goes on this way until he spies a homeless man sitting in a shop doorway. He tries to employ pure logic, he tells himself that if someone must die it should be someone who has nothing to live for. As he draws close to the desperate man, he feels the knife in his pocket and now it weighs about the same as a cannonball. It weighs him down and he feels barely able to take a single step closer. Charlie turns and walks away from the homeless man and the knife is as light as a feather.

Mephistopheles foresaw his weakness. Before Charlie left his temple the spirit told him, in no uncertain terms, that when it came down to it, he would fall short. He told Charlie that he was far too ordinary for something like this, too nice and prone to guilt. He said that the easiest thing to do to assuage his guilt would be to kill someone who deserved it and gave him a piece of folded paper. He told Charlie that it contained the details of a man who truly deserved to die. Now, as he wandered through the Lower Precinct, he felt that piece of paper in his clenched right fist. He unfolds it and reads the following disjointed words: The Meridian Hotel, gaunt and grey, slanted name badge, nightshift, murderer.

Staring at the paper, he feels sick. The idea of driving all the way out to the edge of his old stomping ground to kill someone, having all that time to think about them dying. Killing someone who would not only fight back but who also had more experience when it came to murder. In this instant, an idea occurs to him, a solution that is not ideal but likely to be the best he'll be able to manage for his Alison. Standing in the Lower Precinct he changes direction and heads to the taxi rank down by old Spon Street.

In the taxi on the way to the hospital he convinces himself that this new idea is the only real solution, and suddenly the flick knife in his pocket is so light that he can no longer feel it. At the hospital, he knows the route to Alison like the back of his hand. Without having to think about it, he crosses the foyer, takes a left followed by a right, enters a lift and climbs three floors to find her in her private room. He hears that beep, beep, beep and sees the wires. Although he's well used to it by now, his heart still aches just a little.

He walks to her side and holds her hand, it feels like nothing more than bone to him. He bends and kisses her forehead and tastes her sweat. He steadies himself, then reaches into his pocket for the flick

240

knife. He opens her mouth, then holds the knife to a vein in his throat. His finger lingers on the switch for a moment and then...

There's a blinding light and Charlie feels a hand on his wrist, pulling the knife away. The hand is strong, he struggles against it, but it's no use. The hand pulls his arm all the way down and a second one prises open his fingers, plucking the knife from his grip. He looks now and sees the male nurse, the nice one who has been taking such good care of Alison. The one who warned him against the Midway ... except it wasn't him, it was some golden being, a man bathed in light, radiating compassion and mercy. After a moment, the light died down and Charlie recognised a familiar face.

'Jude is that you ... All this time you were her nurse and I didn't recognise you ... you're a Pooka aren't you?'

'You can't do this thing, Charlie,' Jude said, not answering his question but rather addressing Charlie's actions. 'It's a cowardly act, it does her a disservice and she will not thank you for it.'

'I can't lose her,' Charlie pleads, 'It isn't enough, I need more time. I'd rather die than be without her.'

At that, Jude Valentine – Jude the Pooka – pulls Charlie into an embrace and allows him to sob on his shoulder.

'My friend, it will never be enough. All the time in the world is not enough time to love that woman.'

Charlie hears the heart monitor still beeping, and behind that, he notices the tick, tick, tick of the wall clock. He lifts his head up from Jude's shoulder and looks to the clock hanging above Alison's head. The time is three minutes to midnight. He watches as the second hand ticks forward, and then backwards, forwards and then backwards. He takes a step away and looks around him to see the room fading before his eyes. Suddenly the three of them are floating in space, Charlie and Jude standing on thin air, Alison still lying in her sickbed.

'How can you be a Pooka, you grew up in Castlegate? I know you, we drank together, we've laughed together ... you're just a man,' Charlie says. It's not a question but rather a statement of fact. He falls to his knees in front of the Pooka, Jude, and reaches out to him. 'Please,' he begs, 'Give her life.'

'You know that's beyond me,' he replies. 'I can't cure Alison or give her a second more life than is already owed to her, but I can do wonders still. I can make a space for you, a little world in a bubble, in the place in between. I can take Alison's last breath, everything that she is will be contained within it. I can give her breath form and set it beside you in the place I make for you. I can take a single moment, that moment being her last heartbeat, and stretch it to last an entire day. I can make that day repeat itself so that it may seem to the both of you that years have passed. But it will not be life, not as you know it. You will go on together, eat, breathe, drink and make love, but there will be no change. There will be no children, or travel, or change of the seasons. It will just be a moment, stretched out thin so that pain and misery can be forgotten, and you can say your goodbye. Is this what you wish of me?'

Charlie is smiling through his tears now. No matter what Jude says, it sounds an awful lot like life to him, or close enough. He looks to Alison who, in her sickbed, is no more than an ache and a rattling

242

breath. There is no doubt in his mind, he will strike this deal with the spirit ... and yet...

'Will she be well?' he asks. 'She won't still be in pain in this other world, will she?'

'She will be made whole, or at least near enough whole. There will be no more pain or suffering for Alison, all that is behind her now.'

'Then what do you want from me in return?' Charlie asks. 'Whatever you want, I'll do it.'

'I do require a service from both of you,' Jude says. He puts his hands on Charlie's temples and a sudden shock of electricity passes through his fingers and into Charlie's head. 'You will write my story.'

'And what do you want from Alison?'

'That's between me and her.'

'Don't tell her,' Charlie pleads. 'Let her think she's beaten it.' Charlie watches as Jude winces and turns away from him. 'If all we have is just a little time to say goodbye, then don't let that haunt her. I'll bear that burden, let her just be happy.'

'Okay,' the Pooka nods, 'we have an accord.' He offers his hand and Charlie takes it. 'Stand back,' he orders.

It begins. Jude holds his cupped hands out in front of him and begins to sing. Charlie does not understand the song, but it is beautiful, and he senses the power in it. He watches in amazement as a tiny cloud forms above the spirit's hands. It rains and fills the spirit's hands with water, which freezes instantly. Trees sprout up at the edge of the frozen water, and now it is snowing. Beyond the trees, there is a hill forming. On the hill, a log cabin magically appears. A bubble forms *around the little world in the spirit's hands, it floats out of his grip and begins to grow bigger and bigger until it fills Charlie's eyeline.*

'Step through,' Jude says. 'I will bring her to you.'

Charlie hesitates for a moment, but when his eyes fall on Alison again, he turns immediately and walks through the bubble. He finds himself standing in front of the cabin ankle-deep in snow, it is all so real, so vivid. The air feels cold and crisp in his lungs and there are swirling coloured lights above his head. He stands, staring at the lights, and sees a very strange sight, there is something small and pure white racing across the sky and down towards the cabin. As it gets closer Charlie sees that it's a stag, and on its back, he sees ... Alison. Alison, fast asleep with her head resting in the nook between its antlers, her arms gripping loosely around its neck. The stag gallops through a window on the first floor of the cabin, he passes through it and the glass doesn't shatter.

Charlie is pushing open the front door to the cabin, running through the living room past the empty fireplace into the corridor, up the stairs. His gut churns, he thinks, 'This is all some strange dream, none of it is real. I've fallen asleep by her sickbed, any moment now I will wake and things will be as bad as ever.' But now his hand is on the bedroom door, and as he pushes it open his doubt melts away because there she is.

There are no wires or tubes attached to her, no machines marking out the shortness of her life in flat toneless beeps. She is just sleeping, there's colour in her cheeks, meat on her bones, and hair on her head. She looks as beautiful now as the day they first met. Slowly, he crosses the room, he thinks to wake her with a kiss just like in the fairy tales, but when he kisses her she does not stir.

'She is not ready to wake.' Jude says from a shadow in the corner of the room. 'Besides, you have work yet. If you wish to conceal the truth from her you must concoct a tale, tell her how she came to be here, fit and healthy.'

'Where is here?' he asks.

'Nowhere in particular, from some of the windows you can glimpse the town of Húsavík, I suppose you could tell her you're there.' At that, Jude steps from the shadows, he looks tired and drawn, he walks to the bed and sits at the edge. 'She must be denied a violin or a piano, in time I suspect she will see through this world, playing music will only speed up that process. Music makes you feel magic, it helps you to see the magic around you as well.' He pauses and takes a deep breath. 'Remember, you owe me a service. Write your stories, as many as you like, but one day you'll write my story. Likely you will try to resist but you will be compelled to. Know that when you finish my story, this will all come to an end. Don't be fooled into thinking that this is forever, this is just a long goodbye Charlie.'

'I know that,' Charlie snaps, and already in his heart, he is planning to defy his friend. Sure, he will start Jude's tale, but what would happen if he never finished it? As the thought enters his head, he hears Jude let out a long, exhausted sigh.

'Whisper in your lover's ear, tell her how she came to be here. Then go outside and chop wood for the fire.' He produces an axe out of thin air and places it down on the bed beside Alison's feet. 'While you're out there she will wake.' The spirit stands, walks towards the window and disappears.

Charlie is alone with her now, his heart soars at the warmth and flesh he feels in her hand. He breathes in and smells green apples, the old familiar smell of her soap. It has banished the smell of death that had once clung so tightly to her. He thinks for a while, constructs a timeline in his head that explains how she beat the cancer and how they came to be in this cabin. He bends to her ear and whispers...

'Alison, you are better now, you've beaten it. The doctors trialled you on a brand-new drug that shrunk the tumour, and then they operated to remove it. You remember beating it, don't you? It was all just in the nick of time, you've gotten strong and healthy, and a few months ago you had surgery to reconstruct your breast, you insisted on it. There are no signs of your sickness now, all of that is behind us, and we have come away to relax and recover. My agent offered us his cabin in Húsavík, he says we can use it for as long as we like, just as long as I use the time to write. It's a beautiful place here baby, it's like a frozen wonderland. You could imagine Santa's workshop being here and all of those old Norse gods I told you about. We're gonna have a great time here baby, spending our nights cuddled up in front of the roaring log fire and, by day, we'll make snowmen and have snowball fights. I promise you'll love it here darling, I promise you will.' At that, he takes the axe in his hand and leaves the room. In seconds he is outside gathering wood, barely able to wait for her to wake up.

Alison is fast asleep, but in the moment Charlie's axe connects with the first piece of wood she springs bolt upright in bed, gasping for

246

breath. She is damp with sweat and dizzy with unreality. She has been
dreaming of her sickness and on waking...

23

Across Thin Ice

Alison stood at the edge of the frozen lake, watching Charlie struggling to stay upright and laughed. His long limbs flailed around in a way that made him look like a drunken spider, trapped at the bottom of a wet bathtub. The desperate clawing sound that his skates made against the ice, coupled with his height and thinness only served to make him look more ridiculous. As she stood laughing at Charlie's feet, which had been threatening to upturn him for quite some time, they finally went out from under him and he landed with some force on his back. Stifling her laughter, she skated over to him.

'Fucking hell,' he gasped, as the air slowly returned to his lungs. Alison bent and offered her hand to pull him up. She was still giggling as Charlie grabbed her and pulled her down on top of him, she came down a little faster and harder than he'd intended, and she bumped her chin on his bony chest. The physical pain of it felt very strange and unfamiliar to her. She couldn't quite recall the last time she felt pain, certainly not since coming to Húsavík. Here, she hadn't so much as stubbed a toe, banged her head, or cut a finger, in fact, the only pain she had experienced here were her cramps and the ache of disappointment. Yesterday, this realisation would have troubled her, but now after her strange dream of the stag and the handsome man, she was untroubled. He had told her that there was something wrong with the world and this was a source of great relief. She wasn't going mad, in time she would dream of him again and learn exactly what was wrong. For now, she could be satisfied with his parting sentiment, 'I am well loved, and all is well, and all manner of things shall be well'.

'What did you do that for?' she asked.

'I'm sorry babe,' Charlie said, his voice was sufficiently contrite. 'I was trying to be cute and playful and misjudged my strength.'

'It's not your strength that's the problem,' she said, as she rolled off him and sat on the ice. 'It's the fact that you're all skin and bones baby, you don't make a comfortable crash mat.'

Beside her, Charlie rolled over and clambered to his knees. He shuffled towards her, gently reaching his gloved hand under her hood to examine her chin which he found to be unmarked. Alison looked into his big, cow eyes and saw the ever-present ghost of concern.

'I'm okay,' she said. 'Just a sudden bang and a bit of a shock. It'll take more than that to end me.'

She looked around the frozen lake and spotted the gap in the trees that marked their way back to the cabin. This had seemed like such a good idea this morning. Yesterday afternoon she'd been daydreaming about ice skating on the lake and had coincidently found two pairs of ice skates buried at the bottom of one of the boxes in the grotto. She didn't question it, she just made a mental note to thank Jude next time he popped up in her dreams. She was convinced now that Jude, the handsome man, had snuck the grotto into their cabin and filled it with things to keep her occupied. The music, the movies, the books, and most of all, the models. She wasn't sure why exactly she needed to be occupied, but no matter, now she had ice skates as well.

As she sat on the ice looking to the treeline, it didn't seem like a good idea anymore. The prospect of supporting Charlie all the way back to solid ground wasn't exactly filling her with a sense of glee. They would have to make slow progress, him bent forward with his arm wrapped around her shoulder. She began to pull herself up onto her blades when she glanced at Charlie sitting on his bum, his hands planted on the ice, his gaze pulled towards the setting sun.

'You alright my muppet man? she asked.

'Yeah, I'm fine,' his voice was far away and distracted. 'Just sometimes you forget don't ya.'

'Forget what?' she asked.

'How beautiful it is here.'

Alison surveyed the horizon. The rugged landscape covered in thick snow and ice, an almost brilliantly white canvas now painted in many shades of orange and gold by the light of the magic hour. The sun setting over the frozen lake made it sparkle like it was made of diamonds. Yes, she supposed he was right, this was a beautiful place, savage but beautiful all the same. She turned and sat down beside him again, then followed his gaze to watch the setting sun. They sat in silence for a good while, until Charlie spoke.

'I don't think I would have chosen this place, not if somewhere else had been on offer.' His gloved hand reached out for Alison's, she took it and gripped it tight. 'If I'd had the choice, I would have picked someplace warm. Hank and Becky still rave about Umbria, Remember, when they got back from their honeymoon how they just seemed to glow with …' Charlie stopped dead. He had remembered what had happened after Hank and Becky's honeymoon; they came home to the news that Alison had cancer. 'Well, anyway,' he said, blurting on passed that jagged little detail. 'This place ... it has its charms.'

'It's as cold as hell, cut-off from the world and ...' Alison tried to say more, without thinking about it she was about to start talking about the strangeness of time, the lack of the change in seasons, and all the other things that were odd. The words were right there on the tip of her tongue but as she tried to speak them, she couldn't. She felt her tongue being pinched as if caught between a thumb and forefinger. What followed was a mushy-mouthed mumble.

'What was that?' Charlie asked.

'Nothing,' she answered, rolling her eyes. 'It's just like you say, we could be someplace warm, dangling our feet in a tropical sea, drinking cocktails out of coconut shells,' she paused and leant forward to rest her head on Charlie's shoulder. 'I like it well enough here, but I think when you're done with your work, I'll be happy to move on.'

The effect of her words was instantaneous. His body stiffened and when he turned to look at her there was that sadness in his big, cow eyes again. It was the same sadness she had seen there when looking up at him from her hospital bed. Of course, he had made some effort to camouflage it then, but now it was big and bold, and right out in the open.

'Baby, what's wrong?' she asked. An age passed as she watched the cogs ticking in his head, and a perfectly framed reply surfaced on his face.

'What if this is all there ever is?' he began. He paused and bit his lip. She saw the nerves in him, she saw him summoning up some measure of courage. All of a sudden, he began to talk very fast. 'If I could I'd give you everything, everything you want. The perfect life, children, sunshine and beaches, music, everything you could ever want ... but sometimes ... you know life ... it just doesn't work out the way you want, the way you plan. You make plans and the gods laugh, that's what they say, right?' He paused there and took a deep breath, once he was a little bit calmer, he continued. 'If this is all we have. Just me and you and this,' holding his hands up to the frozen horizon. 'Could it be enough, it's not how we saw our lives going, but considering how it could have gone, isn't this good enough?'

Instinctively, as Charlie spoke Alison's hand fell to her empty belly. Another month had passed and brought her blood. In fact, by now she had given up the pretence of trying to count all the months that had brought her blood. The first months had been agony, now they came and went and all month long she felt a dull ache in her heart. She was coming to understand that it just wasn't going to happen, and moreover, somewhere deep down she believed the problem was hers and not Charlie's. Charlie ... somehow, he had tiptoed his way to centre of her secret, not secret, heartache and presented it as if it was a side issue, a symptom rather than the sickness. He had gotten to the point, and at the same time, he had missed it as well.

'It's not all about me,' she said, annoyed. 'Sunshine, beaches, music ... kids ... happiness ... these aren't things I want just for myself, they are the things I want for you as well. If this is all there is ... just us and this frozen place, then so be it … but you'll never stop me hoping for more, we deserve more than this.'

'It doesn't matter about me,' Charlie replied, rushing on before she could interrupt. 'I mean it matters, but in another way, it doesn't. There is nothing I wouldn't sacrifice to be with you.'

More silence followed, more stiff posture and sad, cow eyes from Charlie, whilst Alison's heart pounded in her chest. Her daydream of their children was shrinking. She swallowed and felt the lump in her throat, a perfect ball of sadness that she was attempting to push back down to her belly where she could dissolve it. She turned her eyes back to the setting sun and wrapped the silence of that moment around her like a blanket. She sat still, and a memory surfaced inside her.

It's their fourth or fifth date, she had cooked him lamb tagine which they ate, accompanied by cheap wine and good music. Afterwards, they sit on the sofa comfortably, cuddling and talking. Already, Charlie fascinates her, beneath the slightly shy and awkward manner she sees a charming, funny, talkative man with big ideas. He talks about the places he's been, and all the places he'd like to go. He talks about the things that interest him, and, with his energy, makes even the dullest of them sound interesting. Most importantly, he listens, with a closed mouth he nods while she talks, and when she's done he remains silent for a moment or two before offering an opinion. She thinks he does this for two reasons: the first being that he's questioning what he thinks and feels about whatever it is that's just been said, the second, he is allowing some time to make sure she is finished before he talks. Too many people just wait for someone to take a breath, and then they jump in and hijack the conversation. Suddenly you're talking about something completely different, usually you're talking about them.

That's not Charlie's style. She talks about the future, about how years from now she'd like to be a mummy and have a big family. How growing up as an only child was a bit of a lonely affair. She had to resort to wandering the streets looking for friends. She says, two boys and one girl would be ideal because every little girl should have a couple of big brothers looking out for her. The more she talks, the more she realises that she probably shouldn't be saying any of this on a fifth date, but those big, cow eyes of his ... they are so goddamn disarming.

Charlie listens, waits, considers what he's heard, and then speaks. He talks about how his dad had never been on the scene, and how his mum passed away a few years ago in a car accident. He talks about how he craves fatherhood, but worries he'll make a useless dad. Never having one himself, he doesn't have an example of what to do or what not to do. There was Big Tommy of course, but maybe he wasn't the best example either as Charlie doesn't want to be the kind of father who's carved from stone. He says, he supposes when it comes to parenting, everyone has 'the fear'. Likely for different reasons and to different degrees, but surely everyone was just a little bit afraid, even if they didn't want to own up to it. He finishes by telling her, 'a large family sounds like a fine thing, three or four would be great.'

On the ice, the sun was clinging to the horizon by the skin of its teeth. Alison glanced back towards the trees and in the near dark, they felt further away from her now. She wanted to be off the frozen lake, she wanted to take off her skates, throw them back in the box in the grotto, then curl up in front of the fire. Because this was a cold place, not just physically but also emotionally. Here she was, sitting beside her man, while he painted a picture of a half-lived, unfulfilled life, which he claimed would be enough for him. She knew that to be a lie, and the only reason he ever lied to her was to save her feelings.

'Come on,' she said, getting up onto her blades. 'We should get back before it gets too dark.' She offered her hand and this time he didn't pull, instead, she steadied him as he pulled himself up.

Standing now, she took his arm and wrapped it around her shoulders, then wrapped her own around his waist. Slowly, they skated together towards the treeline at the edge of the lake. As they moved, she struggled to think of another subject, something other than this.

'How did the writing go today?' she finally asked.

'Not bad,' he answered. '2,000 words, 1,500 of them feel solid. I think it'll be finished in a couple of weeks, then probably a month to edit, then it can be sent off.'

'I'm looking forward to reading it,' Alison replied. He had explained the gist of the story to her but hadn't allowed her to read it yet. He was a bit protective about his work in progress, he said it was better to finish the thing before he cast it out for opinions. Too many times he had watched his stories die on the vine because of what someone else thought.

His story was centred around a musician who had fallen for a woman but she was slowly destroying him by sucking the life and joy out of him day-by-day. The musician's chance at redemption comes in the form of a beautiful young woman he falls head over heels for. The story describes his struggle to break free of the woman he once loved in favour of chasing that new love. It's an old, familiar story but Charlie says, 'The bones of all stories are old, and all you can do is dress them up some new way.' So, there would be a twist in the tail, Alison was excited to find out what it was.

They reached the edge of the frozen lake with their arms wrapped around each other and Charlie stooping to Alison's height. Now came the difficult task of walking up the S-shaped, steep, snowy path that led to the cabin. Worse still, they would have to walk it in those awkward bladed boots. Alison wanted to kick herself, she wished she'd bought their normal boots down to the lake and placed them at the edge for them to change back into. It had been difficult enough walking down the hill in bright sunshine with those skates attached. She dreaded to think how bad the return journey would be in the dying twilight.

Indeed, they both fell several times before Charlie shouted, 'Oh fuck it, I'm done with this!'

Alison watched as he untied the skates, pulled his aching feet out of them and threw them down the hill. He stood there in the snow, his thick woollen socks were the only barrier between his feet and the cold. In seconds they were cold, damp, and good for nothing.

'Hop up,' he said, 'I'll piggy-back you the rest of the way.'

She was going to argue with him, but the firmness in his face told her there was little point. He hunkered down and, being very careful about where she placed her blades, she climbed onto his back.

Once inside the cabin, she ordered her muppet man to get changed and then to sit on the sofa in front of the fire. She changed herself and fetched him a blanket, a mug of hot chocolate, and a bowl of warm water for him to dangle his icy feet in. She sat beside him and thought about their conversation on the ice. His question of, 'What if this is all there is?' had unsettled her, but conversely the news that the new novel would be done and dusted in more or less in six weeks lifted a weight from her heart.

On her way back up the hill, clinging to Charlie's back, she had been thinking about her model of Tiny Town down in the grotto. The houses and the meeting hall were finished, and so was Main Street. All the little shops and bars had been built and arranged in what she thought was the correct order. She was halfway through the ski slope, and after that, it was just a matter of building the harbour and the mansion overlooking the town. She thought that six weeks would be the perfect amount of time to finish her little project.

As soon as they were finished, him with his book and her with Tiny Town, they could leave this place. No matter what Charlie said on the matter, she was hopeful that there would be more to life than being here. This place was something, but it wasn't enough, not for her and not for him. Change was coming, she could taste it in the air. In six weeks, for better or worse, they would be done with this place, she felt that much in her bones.

Alison turned to Charlie and kissed him on the lips. She made note of the fact that it didn't feel exactly the way it always had, it felt a little heavier and darker than normal, it tasted almost bittersweet, and then a thought suddenly bubbled up inside her. *This isn't the last but...*

'I love you,' she declared loudly and with forced brightness. 'You know that, right?'

'Of course, I do,' he replied.

She climbed under his blanket and rested her ear on his chest to listen to his heart beating. She would sleep with him tonight, and not in the hopes of falling pregnant, just for the joy of the act. She would sleep with him, and then she would sleep, and instinctively she knew her dreams would bring her the stag and the handsome man. She didn't fear it, now as she approached the ending of this 'thing' this odd little 'just the two of them' world, and she rejoiced in the thought of what revelations she was about to discover.

.24.

The Well Running Dry

Charlie lay in bed, playing big spoon, with his arms wrapped around Alison. Her bottom was pressed up against his empty, aching loins, and she was grinding against him, trying her utmost to extract every last ounce of pleasure from him, to give him one last tingle before sleep took hold of them. Feeling her warmth pressed up against him, he reached his left arm under her body to cup her left breast and reached over her hips and covered her sex with his right hand. She groaned as he began to stroke.

'More?' she asked. 'Do you want more?'

'No, just you,' he replied, whispering the words in her ear.

Slowly, he worked her body, doing what he did best, playing her the way she had played her violin once upon a time. He listened to the music he was making from her, her shallow breathing, her groans, her exclamations of 'Oh Charlie', and 'right there'. He listened and thought of better times, before this cabin and the shadow of death that preceded it.

He thought of the little house on the edge of Coventry city centre, the one just off the Roman road. It was a little place, two bedrooms, one bathroom, a slither of a kitchen and a box of a living room. Of course, by then he had the earnings from 'Beta Male Fairy Tales' which was just shy of ninety grand, and there was the much more sizable inheritance left to him by his mum. He could have afforded one of the cookie-cutter mini-mansions in Oakenbrook, but Alison had insisted on something more modest.

As his fingers worked her slickness, Charlie remembered the day they moved into that little house. He remembered the boxes that lined the floor and the two sticks of furniture they had to rub together; the sofa from Alison's place and the bed from the apartment Charlie had shared with Hank. He remembered sitting on that sofa watching the TV, Alison perched beside him, straight-backed with one leg folded under the other. Her arm was resting around his shoulder, her hand stroking the hair at the back of his head. He remembered how her posture and breathing meant that her breasts were rising and falling in the corner of his eye, almost brushing against his cheek. He remembered how she had laughed when he turned his head and buried it in her cleavage.

'Thank God,' she had said. 'I thought you were going to take all night about it.'

Now, as he lay behind her, the big spoon bringing her to climax, he felt her reach back and stroke his smooth, bald dome.

'Kiss my neck,' she said, and he did just as he was told. He felt her spasm and quiver. He heard the cry escape from her and felt her clutch at his head, trying to get a grip in the hair that wasn't there anymore. After a moment, she was pushing him on to his back and taking him into her mouth. In seconds, she brought him back to a state of semi-arousal, but already he knew, it would do no good, his heart wasn't in it.

The pleasure was there, but it was far too distant and the wet, gulping, glottal-stop sound of it seemed overly loud in that quiet room. Charlie really noticed the silence in this place, the isolation of their cabin on the hill made it tangible, almost physical. It was the third person in the house, he always knew it was there and noticed the instant it was broken. Alison had noticed it as well, not long after they came to this place she had mentioned the wind, that it made her feel uneasy. She had told him that the wind haunted her dreams and made her think strange thoughts. He didn't think it was the wind exactly, he thought it was that silence, out here in the frozen wilderness it was so thick and oppressive that it gave power to the wind. There were no car alarms or squealing cats, there were no drunks or police sirens. Out here there was nothing, nothing but the wind and the noise they made to banish the silence.

What was funny to him now was how Alison had been disturbed by the silence for a short time in the beginning, and then she had quickly accustomed herself to it. Whereas he had enjoyed the deep peace and quiet in the beginning, but the prolonged exposure to it was unnerving him now. It made his skin itch and set his teeth on edge. Over the last few weeks, maybe months, he had begun to wonder if you could get a special kind of sickness from a lack of other people's company. He quickly came to the conclusion that, *of course you can, they even have a name for it. They call it cabin fever.* He had read that famous horror novel concerning cabin fever, read the book and watched the film, in fact. He always remembered that scene where the elevator doors opened, and a river of blood filled the corridor. He remembered watching it with Alison and snorting at the risqué joke she had made about how that scene would make a serviceable tampon ad.

'It would be better than those patronising ads they put on now. Hey girls, don't let your period stop you from going roller-skating or zip lining. I mean, it's crap, isn't it? I don't want to do that stuff any time of the month, let alone when I'm bloated, cramping, bleeding and emotional!'

Charlie closed his eyes and tried not to think about isolation, silence or Jack Nicholson bashing anyone's brains 'right the way in'. He tried to relax into it and enjoy the feeling of what Alison was doing to him. He recalled all the times she had looked at him with her 'come screw me' eyes, and all the sexy underwear she had bought and worn for him. He thought about all the times he had gone to see her play in her string quartet, sitting in the front row, enamoured with her talent. He thought about the way she looked the night that Hank moved into the big studio on the Roman road. Of course, that had been the night Hank had introduced Becky as the girl he was 'sort of seeing'. It was also the night that Alison was introduced to Jude Valentine; in short, it was the night that their circle of friends was fully formed.

Alison – who had confessed her love for Valentine's Day on their fourth date – had been giddy to meet both Jude and Sophie. Charlie remembered watching her talk to them about music with total passion, and in a complex way that he couldn't quite understand. It made her look so alive, so beautiful. Strange then, that she couldn't remember Jude and Sophie now. They had spent so much time together as a group but since coming to the Húsavík, Jude had been plucked from her mind. Was it a symptom? A side effect of the deal he had made?

'What's wrong?' Alison asked, her head popping from under the quilt. 'Are you not enjoying it?

'I think I'm too tired. Let's just call it a night, hey?'

'Okay,' she said, flopping on the bed next to him. 'Do you want to be the cuddler or the cuddled?'

'Cuddled.' He smiled.

She drew back the quilt a little and tapped at her breast – the right one, the one that looked as good as new to him. He rested his head there and she pulled the quilt up around him. He drifted away into sleep smelling her green apple soap and woke...

... not in Húsavík, not in Castlegate, not in Starkey's woods or the familiar dirty-grey concrete of his city. He woke on the grass, beside a river, underneath a tree. There was a man sitting beside him, a very familiar man, after all, Charlie hadn't forgotten him. He was sitting under the tree, balancing an acoustic guitar on his knees and plucking out melodic chords. When he sang, it was like silk.

'When you're down and troubled and you need a helping hand. And nothing, oh nothing is going right. Close your eyes and think of me, and soon I will be there. To brighten up even your darkest night,' he paused then and looked around at Charlie, turning those bright, blue eyes on him.

'You look so tired,' Jude said, putting his guitar down by his side. 'Rest a while, put your feet in the river.'

'I've been here before.'

'Is that a question?'

'No,' Charlie grunted. He refused to look at Jude, instead, he stared ahead at the river. 'I know I've been here before ... I came with Alison. It was a book reading, afterwards we sat under this tree together. We had our picture taken sitting right here and when I looked at it, I knew that ...'

'I know,' Jude said, interrupting him, saving him from the pain of those last few words. 'It's the river Windrush. Time, and time again, this is where you come in your mind. You come here to recharge your batteries ... so rest a while, lie down in the grass, and sleep.'

'Mind reader now,' Charlie grunted. 'That was quite a secret you were keeping!'

'It's no secret Charlie, at least not to the likes of you.' Jude said.

There was something moving down by the river bank. Something small that ran in a squiggly, almost serpentine manner. It weaved its way through the grass, this way and that, the brown of its body mostly hidden by the lush green. Charlie watched as Jude reached down and held out his hands. 'The Pookas walk amongst us, weren't they amongst the first words you wrote?'

'Yeah, but they're just stories, at least I thought they were.'

'No, you didn't,' Jude said contradicting his friend. 'You thought they were too good to be true, secretly you always hoped there was something more to it. Well, you were right, the Pookas are everywhere. They disguise themselves well, they could be the old man living down the road from you, your boss, hell, even your ex-girlfriend. They could even be this little good fellow here,' he paused and held out his arms. The brown creature running through the grass – which turned out to be an otter – jumped and Jude caught it in his hands.

'Hello, old friend,' he said addressing the otter. 'I'm impressed, this is one of your better disguises!'

At that, the otter squeaked and squealed, holding out a paw. Gingerly, Jude reached down and shook it as if he were greeting a friend or superior at work. The animal's high-pitched whining irritated Charlie, it was the sort of sound that rubbed a person up the wrong way.

'He says hello again,' Jude said, translating for the animal. 'He says you met him a long time ago, the night Hank had that fight with the gang of yobs in The Gluepot. He says, "he shooed one of them away" and now he's laughing.'

When Charlie looked at the otter in Jude's hands, it did look for a moment as if the animal was holding its paws over its mouth to cover its chuckling like Muttley, the dog. Charlie sighed and shook his head.

'I remember a time when all this would have seemed strange to me.' Charlie said, to no one in particular.

The otter jumped from Jude's grip, crossed the grass, and climbed up on Charlie's leg. It ran up the length of him and then stood erect on his lap so as stare into his eyes. It reached out with its little paw and squeezed Charlie's nose, squeaking again.

'Boop, got your nose,' Jude said, translating for the otter. Now the animal was squealing faster, gesturing with its tiny paws. 'He says that he asked me to bring you here. He wanted to talk to you. Well, not talk exactly, he just wanted to tell you a couple of things ...'

Jude paused and nodded his head while the otter was pointing first to Charlie's head and then to his heart.

'He says you know the truth about cabin fever now, and that the truth is more mundane and far more terrible than an axe-wielding maniac ... So, what is this truth you know about cabin fever, Charlie?'

Charlie paused and took a breath. 'The perception of isolation and loneliness is that people snap and do something terrible, but that's just the tip of the iceberg. Most of the time, when people are locked in routines and lacking companionship, they don't take a knife or a gun to people, they just wither away inside.'

The otter squeaked, and Jude translated, 'You thought she'd be enough, didn't you? You thought you could give up the world if you had her, but it isn't enough ... she isn't enough.'

'She is!' Charlie barked. 'She's all I want and need.'

'No,' the otter and Jude both insisted. 'She would be enough if things had worked out better. If you weren't trapped in that tiny cabin, if you could have friends and adventures then she'd be the only woman you'd ever have needed ... unfortunately, that isn't so, and soon you'll have to face the truth that ...'

The otter, continuing to squeak and howl in its disturbing high-pitched voice, reached out and put both its paws over Charlie's heart.

It pulled back then and drew a large circle through the air with its right paw. It looked over its shoulder at Jude, who sighed.

'Even after love ends life goes on.'

Charlie grabbed the little creature in his hands and, squeezing it tightly, he stood up to his full height. It nipped at his finger, but Charlie paid no attention. He held it out in front of him and then dropkicked it clear across the grass and into the river with a heavy splash. Blood was dripping from his finger and beside him, Jude was fetching up a heavy sigh.

'You've just hoofed the spirit of mischief into the river, I guess it's a good job he didn't come as a hedgehog or else you might have launched him into space!'

'You've done this to me!' Charlie shouted as he turned on Jude. 'You've manipulated me every step of the way, and now you're trying to take her away from me. I know you keep seeing her behind my back, she dreams of you and when she asked about the stag I couldn't help but tell her the Baldr story … you made me tell her that story.'

'I had nothing to do with it, you had to tell her because you went to that cabin to tell stories … stories hold up your universe.'

'No, no I didn't,' Charlie replied, collapsing into the grass. 'I didn't go there to tell stories, I went there to be with Alison … she holds up my universe!'

'Oh Charlie,' Jude said, his voice was soft and warm, and he reached out and put a hand on Charlie's shoulder. 'Let it come to its end.'

'No, you don't give up on the people you love. You do everything you can to keep them safe, Big Tommy was right about that and so was Hank.'

'Then why don't you let her keep you safe?' Jude asked. 'Let Alison save your soul. You still don't understand what a soul is Charlie. Mephistopheles had it half right, it can't be bought and sold but it can wither and die. It needs warmth and sunlight and laughter. It needs experience, knowledge, and adventure. Most importantly, your soul needs a draft of something brighter and happy. I'm afraid it won't survive on the bittersweet brew you're feeding it.'

When Charlie looked behind him, Jude was gone, and in his place stood the white stag. It pawed at the earth and looked at him with sad eyes. Charlie couldn't bear to look in those eyes and so he turned away and looked back to the river.

'You tricked me!' The words fell from Charlie like a whispering confession. 'It doesn't matter though, we had a deal ... if I don't finish your story, it will never end.'

'The well is dry my friend,' the voice seemed to come from all around him. 'You've delayed, written all the stories you could think to write, and now you're running on empty. You create with your heart and soul and there's nothing left but grief in yours.'

'You're not my friend, you tricked me.' Charlie insisted.

'Of course I'm your friend,' the voice echoed. The stag approached Charlie and he felt it snorting at his shoulder. 'I've been your friend ever since I've known you, and I didn't trick you, Charlie. Deep down you know that you tricked yourself.'

As Charlie sat in the grass, snow began to swirl in the sky above his head and the river in front of him froze over. In a matter of seconds, Charlie found himself standing in front of the cabin, far from the river Windrush and the happy memory that lived in that place. Charlie shivered and walked towards the door. It swung open for him, greeting him almost, and now Charlie looked at this place differently. It felt a little less like the place he had come to live with Alison, now it felt like a place that was slowly devouring him.

Jude's voice filled the air around him again, it talked to him all the way up the stairs and to the bedroom where Alison was still lying on her side.

'I'm not a trickster Charlie, I'm not a cheat. Long before anyone thought to call me Baldr I was just Jude. I'm your friend Charlie, and as a friend let me give you some advice ... This is a dead place Charlie, you can linger here for a while, but you can't live here forever.'

Charlie crawled into bed and took hold of Alison

'I can try,' he whispered to the dark.

The reply came lilting into the room, as soft as silk, as sweet as song, *'You just call out my name, and you know where ever I am, I'll come running, to see you again. Winter, spring summer or fall. All you've got to do is call ... and I'll be there, you got a friend.'*

25

The Mysteries of Yggdrasil and Tiny Town

Alison, dressed in her nightie, was standing barefoot at the edge of the lake as the white stag approached her. She understood that she was dreaming, as she couldn't feel the cold, not at all. It was a dream, but even for a dream what she was seeing was strange. She equated it to something like double vision because it was the stag, whilst at the very same time, in the very same place, it was the beautiful glowing man. The two figures approached her and then halfway across the lake their forms mysteriously combined to create a third figure, a new man. One who was neither stag, nor gleaming spirit, but rather someone who was flesh and blood. Someone who, although still devastatingly handsome, had wrinkles at his brow, the odd grey hair here and there, and all the usual signs of life.

She knew him, she wasn't sure where from, but she knew that she knew him. Glancing down to his feet she saw he was wearing ice skates, and sure enough, he was now skating across the ice with grace and poise. Twirling and jumping, making figure-of-eights in the ice and angling his body to hover inches above the ground. He looked like a professional with many years' experience behind him.

'You're good at that,' she shouted.

'Thanks,' he replied. She knew that voice, where did she know that voice from? 'This is my first time. It's quite fun actually.'

'I took Charlie out on the ice today, he fell flat on his back.'

At that, this new third man skated towards her, leaped into the air, spiralled a few times, and nailed a perfect landing in front of her.

'How can you be that good?' Alison asked.

'Well, the thing is,' he began. 'In this place expectation is key, if you expect to fall, you're gonna fall. And by the way, in short, that's what's wrong with the world. There's a gulf between expectations and acceptance, that's pretty standard wherever the flesh folk live and breathe and dream. But this place is built in that very gulf, so after a while, you're bound to see its strangeness.'

'What?' Alison asked. She looked baffled and felt like she had walked in halfway through a film. She watched as the handsome man ruffled his hair, he had a Jim Morrison mop of brown hair that looked both messy and purposefully styled.

'Sorry, I'm getting ahead of myself a bit.' He offered her his hand and she shook it. 'My name is Jude, we've met many times but you won't remember me, or you'll barely remember me. I've decided to come as myself tonight, it's hard to have a proper conversation with someone when they keep averting their gaze.'

He offered his arm to her and Alison linked hers around it. She noticed she was no longer standing barefoot in her nightie, now she was dressed head to toe in white fur and wearing Ugg boots. They walked in silence out onto the ice, to a point someway in front of them where the air shimmered. It was the exact point at which the light from the moon and the Aurora Borealis met. It looked otherworldly. Through that weak spot, she saw a mirage, a transparent town of log and brick cabins.

Jude broke away from Alison's grip and skated full pelt towards the weak spot. She watched him disappear and hesitated for a moment before chasing after him. She passed through and found herself standing in the middle of a familiar town. She was standing beside a meeting hall, and log and stone cabins were built all around her in circles. This was her Tiny Town, the very same one she was building down in the grotto. Her eyes darted back and forth and everything she saw delighted her. Here were the lanterns lighting the town, there were the bushes and trees she'd added, higgledy-piggledy. She even glimpsed the corner of a generator poking up from behind one of the cabins. When she glanced past the houses, she saw lights and realised it was the cinema's canopy. *That's west,* she thought, *that's where Main Street is.* Instinctively, she knew that if she walked in the opposite direction to Main Street, she'd find a half-built ski slope. There was no doubting it, this was her Tiny Town, and she was so happy to be here.

She noticed a signpost planted in the snow, one that she had not added to her model of Tiny Town in the grotto. The sign read: *Welcome to Breidablik, the broad gleaming*, this was written repeatedly in many different languages.

Moments later, the sound of music drew her attention away from the mystery sign and towards the meeting hall. She pushed open the doors and found a deserted room in which long tables had been set against the walls and chairs arranged in rows. At the far end, there was a stage. Jude was sitting on it, dangling his legs over the side. He had a harmonica pressed to his mouth and with that tiny bit of metal, he was playing an achingly beautiful tune. She recognised it, again she couldn't place it, but knew it was in her album collection. Not the one in the grotto but her collection back home in Coventry. She crept down the aisle of chairs and took a seat directly in front of Jude. She watched him sitting very still with his eyes closed, as the sad song played through the harmonica and showed on his face. After a while, he opened his eyes and slipped the harmonica up his sleeve.

'This is my song,' he said. 'It's the story of my life, my heart, and soul expressed in music. It calls to me from across worlds, wherever there is a heart that aches and calls for comfort I hear this song, and when I can, I go to them and offer comfort.' He paused and ruffled his hair again, it was a very human gesture. 'But you have questions don't you, ask away?' he invited.

'What's wrong with this Húsavík?' she asked. 'I don't know how long I've been here, the days change but the seasons never do. I can't remember celebrating any birthdays or Christmases but I'm sure we've been here longer than a year … and all of that is just the tip of the iceberg, there are so many little things that aren't right, but mostly I'm happy here, so at times it feels like I'm being torn in two … so, what is it, what's wrong here?'

Jude cocked his head and gave Alison a sideways glance, she saw concern and a great deal of warmth in his eyes. In that glance, she thought that she could almost recognise him. She had an image, or maybe it was a memory of him, dressed in white holding her hand and speaking softly.

273

"'Truth,' he said, considering his answer. 'Last time I came to you I came divided, a creature of pure spirit walking alongside a white stag, do you remember that?'

'Yes, you told me not to touch the stag. Why couldn't I touch the stag?'

'The stag is my human soul transformed,' he began. 'I was born a man, I lived and died and lingered as a ghost for a while and then became a spirit. How that happened is a long and convoluted tale, we won't get into that, even here time is short. Once I was transformed, a spirit made flesh, I couldn't stand to be without my human half so I transformed it so I could keep it near. Anyway, this is a digression. When I came to you last time, I tried to tell you about Yggdrasil, do you remember that?'

'Yes, the tree that isn't really a tree,' Alison replied. She watched as Jude rolled his eyes at her.

'Yggdrasil is everything,' he replied. 'It is made from every creature of spirit, every man and woman, every animal, every rock and plant, and drop of water. Yggdrasill is God, but it is a God that is mindless, or else a God whose mind has been shattered into countless, tiny shards. We tell you to imagine a tree because a tree consists of branches, leaves, acorns, bark, a trunk, and roots. Look at a tree in the wrong way and you can see many different things, but a tree is only ever one thing. This is Yggdrasil, Yggdrasil is the universe.'

When Jude stopped talking, Alison looked on, slightly bemused, she wasn't sure what point he was trying to make with this hippy drivel, it was lost on her. Everything was connected, and God was mindless, but how did that answer her question? She opened her mouth to ask as much, but he held his hand up to stop her interruption.

'Can you imagine what it's like to see Yggdrasil?' he said. 'To see everything, hear everything. Even the strongest of spirits have lost their minds by spending too much time staring into the infinite. Truth is the same, dear heart, too much can be a bad thing, better to take it a little at a time. Better to come to terms with this world slowly.' He jumped down off the stage and sat beside her. 'Out of interest, what do you think is wrong with the world?'

'Húsavík feels like a dream,' she paused and considered for a moment. 'I mean, when I'm asleep I dream and I know I'm dreaming. And when I'm awake I know I'm awake, but I still feel like I'm dreaming ... does that make sense?'

'Perfectly,' Jude answered, with a smile on his face. 'That was a very accurate and concise summary of your reality, well done you.' He ruffled her hair as if she was a child he was proud of. 'Yes, I imagine living in that cabin feels an awful lot like being stuck in a dream. In truth, of course, the cabin isn't in Húsavík. I believe that in the waking world there is a little town called Húsavík and from what I hear it is a beautiful place. The cabin you call home of late exists most precisely in the in between.'

'In between what?' Alison asked. For a moment Jude's only answer was to throw his hands to the sky, in a gesture that said everything.

'Well, then and now and what's yet to come, the world above and the worlds beyond; mainly it's between expectations and acceptance.

That cabin is where you go to make peace with the fact that life hasn't worked out the way you've planned.'

'Why do I need to make peace with that?' she asked, turning to look him in his eyes, which were not cow eyes but rather tropical, blue oceans.

'Oh, dear heart,' he reached across and put his hand on her back. 'You didn't.'

Just like that, she felt a churning in her gut. She hadn't been brought to this place in between for her own sake, she was here because of Charlie, there was something he couldn't accept, and she didn't want to know what it was. She leapt from her chair and ran towards the door of the meeting hall. Outside in the snow, she darted through the houses west towards Main Street, she wasn't paying attention to her direction, she just wanted to be away from that place and Jude, who was about to unsettle her old world. Again, she thought of that slice of toast landing butter side up, all of this because of something so stupid and small. Why couldn't she leave well enough alone, why did she have to pull at loose threads? She was happy not knowing, or rather happy enough not knowing.

Jude was waiting ahead of her, standing in front of the cinema, holding open the door. She wanted to resist him, she wanted to turn and run back in the opposite direction, but she couldn't. She felt drawn towards him, and when she looked at him she saw a measure of that otherworldly light around him.

'You're doing so well,' he said, as he beckoned her to come towards him. 'It's taken us a long time to get here, dear heart, but we're so close now. Don't be fearful, we're reaching the end of things.'

'Are you death?' she asked, tears welling in her eyes as she then asked, 'Am I dead?'

'No, dear heart,' he said. He stood aside to let her walk through the door and when she drew close he whispered in her ear. 'Listen ... your heart is still beating.'

Alison strained her ears to listen, first, there was only silence, as nothing moved in the town of Breidablik. Soon, she heard her heart beating in her own chest, and then on top of that, she noticed her pulse in her wrists and with these signs of life she gave a sigh of relief ... but then ... another sound, a sound that was sadly familiar ... it came from somewhere a hundred miles above her head. It was the sound of a steady and toneless beep, beep, beep. It was the sound she had come to equate with her sickbed.

26

Rise

It was a Saturday night at the end of August and Jessica was sitting in a booth in a corner of The Gluepot. An old Valentine's Day song was playing through the sound system and all the trendies dotted around the dance floor and crowding the bar were nodding their heads to the beat. Jessica turned away and glanced at her reflection in the window. Tonight was another one of those nights where she found beauty in her reflection. Moreover, she had begun to notice that, as time passed, as she got further away from her life with Kelvin and as she took more control over her own life, the days she saw a pretty face staring at her from behind the glass had begun to outnumber the days she saw an ugly one. *Ugly is just a feeling,* she thought to herself. *Like useless and worthless ... they are all just feelings.*

'Oh my god,' Becky grumbled. She put a fresh round of drinks down on the table and then slid in opposite Jessica. 'I hate hipsters. You know if you go to a dive bar and lads chat you up at least they're honest about what they what ... it's just like "cracking tits love, how about it?" ... I mean it's repellent but at least it's honest, I think I prefer that to what you get here!'

'Why, what's happened?' Jessica asked, she took her pink gin and sipped it, glancing across the room. There was a man slouching against the bar, wearing a hipster straw hat, and clutching a microbrew. As she made eye contact with him, he smiled and lifted his drink to toast her. She briefly smiled back and then quickly looked away. 'Was it him, the cat in the hat?'

'Yeah and don't look at him, he'll only come over!'

'Why, what did he do?'

'Hey sweets,' Becky said, mimicking the hipster's expression. 'I hope I'm not overstepping the mark here, but I just have to tell you how fine you look tonight ... do you do yoga? Because you're toned like you do yoga... I do yoga ... well, I'm an instructor, it's part of my whole healthy living regime. No animal products, no wheat, no sugar ... I promise you, living that way just gives you so much energy ... if you know what I mean!' At that, she reached out and gripped Jessica's hand and gave it a squeeze so as to demonstrate what the hipster had done at the bar.

'Ugh,' Jessica grunted.

'I know right, but on the bright side ... free drinks,' she said laughing. She grabbed her breasts through her white summer dress and gave them a squeeze. 'Thank you, girls.'

'You let him pay for our drinks?'

'I like to think of it as an arsehole tax.' Becky said smiling. She sipped her wine and tipped Jessica a wink.

'To the arsehole tax!' Jessica said, as she lifted her drink and clinked her glass against Becky's. 'I know what you mean though, I hate it when guys brag like that, it's like they don't know how to talk anymore ... just brag. What is it they call it, peacocking?'

'It doesn't matter what they call it ... whatever it is it makes my fufu dry up and close shut!' Becky replied

Jessica laughed again and snorted slightly. The sound of it surprised her, it wasn't a sound that she had ever made before. After hearing it she clutched her hand over her nose and blushed, making herself redder than usual. She glanced at the bar and saw the guy in the hat chatting to some other attractive and bored-looking woman. Now, he was taking his bank card out from his phone case and waving it to the bartender before pointing at the bored woman's empty glass. *He's going to pay the arsehole tax all night long,* she thought and then she snorted again.

Becky had followed her glance and when she saw the hipster talking to a new woman, who was already edging away from him, she smirked and then laughed herself. Over the summer, the two had become close. Whenever Jessica found herself at a loose end, she would accompany Becky to visit one or the other of her two coffee shops. Little Frankie was not even a year old, but still, Becky made it a habit to drop in and check up on her little empire. She made the trips pushing her pram, carrying a bag full of baby stuff that looked to weigh a ton. Jessica would follow behind, holding on to Hannah's hand if she was there, carrying the baby bag if she wasn't. On these trips, Jessica would sit at the counter and talk to Becky and the rest of the staff. They would laugh and joke, and Jessica would quietly admire the young, blonde tycoon. She had a girl crush on Becky, not because of how pretty she was, rather it was that aura of confidence that surrounded her. Moreover, despite the fact that Becky was married, had two small children, and ran two coffee shops she was still a free spirit, or at least, in part, she remained a free spirit despite all of her commitments.

Jessica had realised early on that the qualities she admired about Becky were the qualities missing from her own personality. Becky was how she wished she could be so maybe it was natural that she felt drawn to her, more so than she did to Hank. She liked Hank, he was friendly and affable, but time with Hank was time learning how to box and although that was satisfying, in some deep corner of her heart it wasn't quite the same. Hank's boxing lessons made her feel strong, but it was almost like he was polishing her, buffing out all her dents and marks. Time spent with Becky was fun time, time to giggle hysterically and be made strong in some other way.

She loved her coffee afternoons at the Ingle Nook and the new place which was called The Nighthawk. It was to be found down Far Gosford Street, slap-bang in the middle of the spiritual home for Coventry's hipster community. Jessica preferred the Ingle Nook, it felt cosier, warmer somehow. Although ... there was one thing she liked about the Nighthawk, and that was the mural that Hank had painted on the wall for Becky. It was a reimagining of 'The Nighthawks' painting by Edward Hopper, after which the coffee shop had been named. In Hank's version, all the people in the diner were his friends and family. In one corner Charlie had Hannah on his shoulders and she was reaching to touch the ceiling. His mother was sitting in a booth holding the baby, while Hank and Becky were sat at the counter making eyes at each other. Standing outside of the diner there was another figure. That figure was standing in a shadow, staring through the window, a strand of her hair was lit by a street light. When Jessica saw that figure in the shadows of the mural, her eyes were drawn it, she thought she recognised that shade of red.

Now, sitting in the booth of The Gluepot, she was daydreaming slightly. Staring at the ghostly partial reflection of her red hair in the glass, she found herself wondering if she was that shadowy figure lurking at the edge of Hank's mural?

She looked past her own face in the glass, to the street outside. Taxis were passing by and two drunks were arguing outside Abra Kebabra, one brandishing his doner kebab like it was an accusing finger while he screamed, *I know it was you, Fredo, you broke my heart'*. She watched as the kebab flapped, flopped, and fell apart in Fredo's face, but out of the corner of her eye she saw something else, or rather, someone else ... a sunken face hiding in the alleyway between the kebab shop and the newsagents next door. Glancing at it, she thought that whoever it was looked like death. She distracted herself by thinking about that mural in The Nighthawk. *How could it be me hiding from the lamp light?* she thought. *Hank didn't know me then.*

'I was saying,' Becky repeated herself. 'Jessy, where are you, babe?'

'Oh sorry, I must have spaced ... what did I miss?'

'Nothing really, I was just talking about Hank ... I was just saying, I'm glad I found a man with a personality instead of a "lifestyle", you know? Like right now he'll probably be sat at home, sneaking a drive-through burger and licking ketchup stains from his shirt. I know what people think when they see us together, they assume I'm a gold digger or something, but they don't get it ... there're no pretences about him at all ... he's just him, and every little bit of him is mine!'

'Anybody who spends any time with you can see you're meant to be together,' Jessica said while reaching over the table to give Becky's hand a comforting pat. 'If I'm honest it makes me a little jealous ... I've never had what the two of you have got. I've only ever had indifference and ugliness ... no, had it is wrong ... it's like I went looking for it, it's all I thought I was worth.'

Jessica paused, waiting for Becky to chip in, but the glamorous blonde sat mutely across the table from her with a pair of glassy eyes. She sniffed and the rested her head in her hands, waiting for Jessica to carry on with her story. So, after a moment or two, Jessica opened her mouth and spoke without thinking. The words came directly from her heart.

'I think that I've only just come to realise that I've always felt like I'm nothing, you know? By that I don't mean unimportant, well, I do but that's not all I mean. I mean that there's nothing about me, there's no depth to me, no hidden places or sharp corners. I've come to realise that all this time I've just been a vessel for other people. I was the object of my mother's criticism and the thing in the room that my dad tried his best to ignore. When I met Kelvin I gave it all over to him, I was the thing he fucked, his maid, his punching bag, his cash machine, his distraction from how fucked up he was and I just took it all ... And now my Granda', my Bampi ... I love him so much, he made my childhood bearable, you know? But even to him, I'm not me ... at least not entirely … for him I'm the living image of my Grandma, I prove that part of her still exists.'

At some point during this outpouring of heartache and truth, Becky got up and slid in next to Jessica. She wrapped an arm around her and pulled her into a sideways embrace. Jessica felt the hug, felt the warmth and shelter in it, and continued.

'But he's right, my Bampi I mean. We had this heart to heart the other day and he pointed this all out to me. He told me that he was an awful father to my mother and that's why she was such a bad mother when her turn came around. And then he made me see … I went to study accounting because it's what my mum wanted and then I went to work with my Granda' gardening to make him happy and to spite my mum. He says I should find out what I want to do with my life and do that, but I don't know what that is yet because I still feel like nothing.'

'It will get better,' Becky replied. 'You may not feel like that now, but I promise it will get better!'

'How do you know?'

'Oh, I know,' Becky said, snorting slightly. 'I know because I've been through it … not exactly the same maybe, but it amounts to the same thing. Charlie says there're no new stories, you just dress the old ones up. Life is the same, the details of our heartache may be different but it's the same basic story, just dressed in a different way. And not just for us two either, for Hank and Charlie too. Men and women all over the planet know what we've been through. I think the mistake is to think that people won't understand your pain. Most people do understand I think!'

There was a commotion then, a noise drew their attention to the bar where a trio of drunks were jeering and leering directly at them. One was shouting about a 'lover's tiff', asking if they were 'kissing and making up', the second was grabbing at his crotch and shouting across that he'd 'straighten them both up', while the third was flicking his tongue up and down in between the V of his fingers.

'Of course, not everyone understands,' Becky said, and at that, they both laughed.

They left the bar arm in arm, quickly making a retreat before the drunks could arrive, slobbering and swaying, at their booth. Outside, the night was warm and crescent moon shone down. The plan was to hightail it to The Nighthawk for one last drink, before calling it a night.

'What was Hank like when you met him?' Becky asked.

'Nervous,' Becky laughed. 'Like a praying mantis preparing for his honeymoon!'

'Oh, you're lying,' Jessica said. 'He's so chilled and effortlessly relaxed all the time!'

'Yes, now he is, but not when we met.' Becky stopped dead, took off her heels, rummaged in her handbag, and retrieved a pair of flats that she had folded up in there. She threw them down on the floor then slipped her feet into them. 'We were both different people back then though, both slightly broken in our own ways. He was so eager for tenderness and affection but worried it would swallow him alive and me... well, I felt used up. I had this idea about what men were and he changed that ... we fixed each other.'

'That's sweet,' Jessica said, she brushed her hair from her face and noticed the sound of footsteps following behind them. 'Do you think it's the age difference, is that why you're so good together?'

'Well, it's only eight years ... eight years isn't that much of a big deal really, it's just enough so I can take the piss out of him for being old though ... are you worried about age gaps?'

Jessica shrugged and heard those footsteps behind them again. Of course, it could be anyone, some passer-by, maybe it was the hipster in the hat, maybe one of those three drunks.

'Look, the thing is some older guys who go after younger girls are just pervs looking for something fresh and naïve enough to buy their bullshit ...'

'Yeah ... exactly, like Kelvin ... he was older than me!'

As soon as his name was over her lips, she recalled that that sunken face lurking in the alleyway. The one that looked like a mask of death, could that have been him? Could that have been Kelvin, the king of wasters? Is that how far he had come with his new drug, his Mana. Far enough to look like death on legs.

'Yes ... but some girls look for older men because they know that a certain type of older man ... well, it's a safe pair of hands. It's warmth and being nurtured, and given the space to grow. It's being loved without conditions or silly mind fuck games ... and it's experience, you know? A man who doesn't need an instruction manual to work a woman's body ... it's so much better when they've already had their training. I think that's what you'll get with Charlie … No, I know it is, I know the way he is with women.'

'You still think we're going to end up together then?' Jessica asked, and again she heard the scrape of a heel. It was closer now, that person behind. Her belly fizzed with nervous tension and automatically her right hand clenched into a fist by her side.

'Don't you want to meet him anymore?'

'No, I do. I love his books, and he's sexy in an odd sort of way.' She paused when she saw Becky nodding her head in an approving sort of way. 'But the way you talk about it, it's like you think it's fate. And I'm just not sure how I feel … I don't know if I'm ready for that.'

'Hank thinks it's fate, but I don't believe in fate. Someone told me once that there's no such thing as fate. Just what is, what could be, and what you want to make happen. That makes more sense to me. Anyway, you're stronger than you realise.' Becky replied. She turned to smile directly at Jessica. 'I've noticed that you're coming out of your shell a little more and Hank says you're coming on really well with the old boxing.'

'Yeah, but just because I can throw a punch and crack a joke doesn't mean I'm ready.'

And there was that scraping heel again, closer still. In her mind, she heard Hank saying, *'Remember to sway into the punch, put your shoulder behind it, and keep jabbing, your jab will keep him off guard.'* When she spoke again it was a little faster than before. 'I mean maybe your right, maybe we'd be great together and it would all be happily-ever-after but now I think I'm glad that I didn't meet him at your dinner party.'

'Dinner party!' Becky laughed.

'Well, meal then, whatever you want to call it. I'll be honest with you. I had visions of turning up all dressed up and sweeping him off his feet, having some mad love affair ... I don't know how I'd have managed that because I'm not a seductress, but if I had met him that night and we did start something, it would have been no good. I would have been swallowed up by whatever this secret heartache he's dealing with is. I didn't know how empty I was back then.'

'Come work for me,' Becky interrupted. 'Come work at one of the coffee shops, not forever, just till you figure out what you want to do with yourself. You get the odd arsey customer but most the time it's a good atmosphere and if you want to go back to university and study, we'll fit the shifts in around you.'

'Are you sure?' Jessica asked timidly.

'Of course I am, we'd love to have ...'

A dirty hand sunk itself into the back of Becky's hair, clutching it in a tight fist and yanking her to the right before letting go. Becky stumbled, spun around, and her head collided with a brick wall. She was out cold.

'Cunt!' Kelvin said. It came out like a bullet from a gun. 'You think you can leave me, you thought I'd just let you go!'

In the end, it was simple. Hank was right, it wasn't about revenge or anger, just strength, and control. Looking directly into his face now she found she wasn't afraid of him anymore. He was the weak one, he always had been, but now he had become weakness concentrated. He was a withered shambles, stinking of piss, a bag of rotten bones held together by yellowing skin, and a mouth containing all of five teeth.

He stepped towards her and instantly Jessica jumped back, stepping out of her heels as she moved and adopting her fighter's stance. When she held up her fists, he smirked at her.

'I'm going to fucking teach you, you ugly ginger slut!' he said as he moved in and lifted his shaking hands.

Jab, jab, uppercut to the solar plexus, and then her right fist was up and she was swaying into the punch, putting her shoulder behind it. It connected with his jaw and, without her gloves, her knuckles crunched painfully, but she didn't care because he was crumpling onto the floor. He was nothing, he had always been nothing.

She picked up her heels, stepped over Kelvin and moved to Becky. She knelt above her and saw a three-inch shallow gash across her forehead from where her head had connected with the wall. As she reached out to rouse her new friend, she heard another sound from behind her, not footsteps this time ... this time it was laughter, and someone giving her a round of applause. She looked over her shoulder and saw elfin ears and a puckish smile.

'Well done!' he chuckled. Stepping forward, he took Jessica's hand and began to pump it up and down in a manic sort of handshake. 'I'm proud of you, I told you, I was right, I said you didn't have to live that way and look at you now!'

'You,' she said, her voice was a whisper. 'You gave me the book, you signed it and hid the money inside for me to buy it … have you been behind all of this?'

'No, of course not.' he said, smiling his puckish smile. He was bending down now, taking Becky's head and supporting it in his right hand, he passed his left hand over her gash and Jessica was surprised to see it healed instantly, leaving no sign that it had ever been there at all. She looked behind her and saw the gash appearing on Kelvin's head. 'I wasn't behind any of this, you were … I may have pointed to the path in a few subtle ways but you did it all, and I'm proud of you.'

At that, he turned his attention back to Becky and flicked the tip of her nose. She came wide awake instantly, her eyes were clear and alert and they darted back and forth between Jessica and the fey looking creature holding her head.

'Goodfellow,' Becky sighed, 'was that you in the bar tonight, prattling on about yoga?' She began to pull herself up and dust down her clothes.

Goodfellow didn't answer, at least not in words. He answered with the glint in his eyes and the upward curl at the corner of his lips.

'I should have known it was you, you had that "I know something you don't know" look in your eyes'. She peered over Jessica's shoulder and saw the shabby figure lying flat on the floor. Seeing the cut on his head, she muttered, 'well at least it wasn't my nose this time!'

'You know him?' Jessica asked.

'Yes, I guess I best introduce you. This is Hank's ... well, I guess you'd call him a friend ... this is Goodfellow, the spirit of mischief and magic.'

At that, Goodfellow bowed deeply and then planted a smooth-lipped kiss on Jessica's hand. At the feel of his lips, she couldn't help but let out a little tittering laugh.

'Are you the same spirit that visited my Bampi, back before I was born?' Jessica asked.

Again, the answer came in the twinkling of Goodfellow's eyes and the upward curl of his lips. That slightest of smiles disappeared from the Pookas face almost as quickly as it appeared, and now as he moved passed Jessica and Becky and towards the unconscious body, there was a stern look on his face. It gave Jessica a chill.

'You,' he said, spitting out the word at Kelvin. He bent over the body and examined the bruise blooming on his jaw. 'Wake up!' he commanded, and Kelvin began to stir, opening his eyes and then letting out a groan. Goodfellow's hand shot out and his index finger covered Kelvin's mouth. He made a hushing sound and when Kelvin opened his mouth, he was unable to speak.

'That's right, not a word from you.' he crouched down closer so that their faces were inches apart. 'I freed Alison from your grip. She was meant to be giving a little boy a piano lesson, but I made him sick. Nothing serious of course, just a tummy bug. It was just enough to change fate, a little light touch of my finger, a little nudge in the right direction and she came home early and found you cheating. Once you were gone, she found herself a good man and had a wonderful, painful, beautiful life.'

Jessica tiptoed towards him, that name had drawn her. Alison, did he mean Charlie's Alison, the woman who had 'moved on', the heartache Charlie was still trying to recover from? When she was parallel with the spirit, she felt his eye dart towards her. Her belly churned and when he spoke again, she was sure it was for her benefit.

'I balance fate and free will with these hands ... and ... you know what I like? Symmetry, I like bringing the ending around to meet the beginning to form one unbroken circle. I like repeating myself, I like getting away with the same tricks over, and over, again and linking one circle with another!' At that, he made circles out of his thumbs and forefingers and linked them. 'But enough of fate and free will ... enough of you ... you had your chance to start again, and not only did you repeat past mistakes, you got worse. Just because I repeat myself doesn't mean you can ... And you won't ... Never again, I'm going to put you somewhere where you'll do no more harm!'

Goodfellow reached down, took hold of Kelvin and effortlessly hoisted him onto his shoulder, holding him in place with his right arm. As he walked away, Jessica thought that he looked a little less solid, it was almost as if she could see the street through him.

'Thank you!' Jessica shouted after him. He half-turned and waved at them, and then carried on walking, fading away with every step. She felt Becky's hand on her shoulder and turned to see her sticking her fingers in her mouth. Becky blew an ear-splitting wolf whistle and the spirit stopped dead, looking back one last time. Now, he was straddling the line between being there and not there.

'Oi!' Becky shouted. 'Stop teaching Hannah to climb trees. Every time Hank takes Hannah into the woods, he has palpitations. You've got him frightened that she'll fall.'

'Nonsense,' said Goodfellow, 'Henry was always one of my favourites. Let the girl climb, if she ever takes a fall I'll be there to catch her. You should know that by now!'

At that, he faded into some other time and place taking the limp body of Kelvin with him. It seemed to Jessica that the last thing to disappear was the twinkle in Goodfellow's eyes and the upward curl of his lips.

.27.

Euridice

In the near dark of the cinema, Alison sat next to Baldr, the spirit of mercy, who, in his mortal life had been called Jude Valentine. Even now, he still preferred that name. She sat very still and watched her life unfold on the screen in front of her, a little girl with chestnut curls is holding her daddy's hand and waddling alongside him on the way to feed the ducks. She watches and feels angry and disappointed, not with the girl on the screen, but rather with Charlie, who made some sort of deal with this spirit. Charlie who has lied to her and allowed her to go on questioning her sanity while pining for the children she could never have. How could he, how could he do that to her?

The little girl on the screen is laughing as the ducks swarm around her. The scene shifts and the little girl is older. She is wearing her uniform and attending her first day at school. As Alison watches this scene, she is struck by the tears in her mother's eyes. When she was the little girl on the screen, she didn't notice those tears, she was too concerned about whether the other boys and girls would be mean to her to notice them. The little girl in the uniform waves goodbye to her mummy, then files inside with the other children, as a single tear rolls down her mother's cheek.

The tableau of her childhood passes before her eyes and what really struck her were all those ordinary little kindnesses her parents performed for her. She had taken these things for granted the first time around, she said thank you at meal times, thank you for gifts and ice cream, but she didn't say thank you for the time they gave. All the times she sat on her father's lap learning the piano, and all the times her mum read stories to her or listened to her tell her own stories that never went away. She wished she could thank them for every second they had spent together.

Suddenly, the little girl on the screen with the chestnut curls becomes a beautiful, young woman who is leaving home to study music. As the young woman says goodbye to her parents there are tears, both on the screen and in the audience. The university years pass by in a stream of alcohol, late night studying, and trysts with boys who were never worth her time. Watching the whole thing from her cinema seat she is surprised at how gullible she was back then, she was a sucker for a pretty face and a half-decent smile.

'What is this all about?' she asks Jude. 'Why am I watching all of this?'

'Sometimes it's good to take a step back and take and look. It helps us to see how we've gotten to where we are.'

'So, what's your story?' she asked. In the movie of her life, she had finished university and was moving in with that king of wasters, Kelvin, whilst working as a temp in an office. She had no desire to witness this nothing stage of her life again, living through it the first time was bad enough. 'You said you used to be a man and now you're a spirit. How does a thing like that happen?'

'Through manipulation and interference,' he answered.

'Details, please?'

'If you wait a few more weeks, you'll be able to read all about it.'

'Charlie is writing about you?' she asked. She turned away from the screen, where her younger self was screaming at Kelvin, and looked Jude full in the face.

'It's part of the pact we made, I made a place for the pair of you and in return, I required a service from you both.'

'What did you need from me?' she asked, and then straight away she answered. 'Tiny Town, you needed me to build Tiny Town. It's going to be your home, right?'

'Not just mine,' Jude answered.

'How does that work? How does the act of me building a model town create this full-sized one here?'

Alison hears a door slam, and when she glances back to the screen she is storming out of the flat she had shared with Kelvin. She watched as she climbed into her little Mini and took the road home to her parents.

'I told you before, magic doesn't rely on what words you say, rather how you say them. It is the same for actions. While you were building your model town you were light and happy, as far away from pain and misery as it was possible for you to be. All you could think about was the little children who would enjoy this place one day and, because of that, there is now a town that exists in the universe that radiates happiness.'

Above them, Alison is sitting at the kitchen table with her mum, drinking wine, and setting the world to rights. She hears herself complain loudly that there are just no good men anymore and she cringes at the sound of it. But then she thinks of Charlie, and how she is still angry about what he did to her, somehow what he did feels like an intrusion to her.

'What's your story?' she asked again.

'Well, in essence, it's similar to yours, at least in certain places.' Jude ruffled his hair again and then leant forward in his chair. He planted his elbows on the chair in front and rested his chin in his hands. 'Once upon a time, I was a little boy. I lived in Castlegate and I had parents who loved me. A strange father, yes, but nevertheless he loved me. I grew into a quiet young man who had a natural aptitude for music. From an early age I learned first the violin, then the guitar, then the piano; before long I realised I could turn my hand to most instruments. When I left school, I didn't go on to university, I went busking and gigging, I wrote my own music and then formed a band …'

'Valentine's Day,' Alison interrupted. 'That was your band, right? I had your albums, I loved Euridice.'

'Thank you,' Jude replied, quite bashfully.

'I remember you!' she gasped. 'I met you at Hank's studio, you and Sophie … you'd hired the studio for him, you were paying him to create work for your new album and at the launch party you came to me, you whispered in my ear. You told me that everything would be well. It made me shudder … but there's more isn't there?'

'We were friends, the six of us, you and Charlie, Hank and Becky, myself and Sophie.'

'Of course we were ... I remember now. Why didn't I connect the dots? I should have known you the first moment I saw you.'

'I bewitched you with candle smoke. I didn't want you to know me, and so you didn't.'

'So, what happened then? Charlie's story is a love triangle story, so it's about you and Sophie and ... '

'Lexi.' Jude said, sighing heavily and looking down at his feet. He looked slightly shamefaced and didn't speak for a while.

On the screen, Alison saw herself sitting in the coffee shop. Charlie stands before the mic, reading from the book he has just had published. She looks at that younger self and sees she is in awe of this strange, thin, gangly, ginger man. Their romance starts to unfold and something a little magical happens. The hunk of anger she had been harbouring towards him began to dissolve. She had always understood how much she loved him, but again, she hadn't appreciated just how he loved her. Viewing their relationship from the outside she saw the way that they looked at each other, it was always right there out in the open, pure and mutual adoration. She watched as they sat beneath a tree by the banks of the river Windrush, and now there was not an ounce of anger left in her body.

'We were all manipulated from the very beginning,' Jude said, finally answering Alison's question. 'We were manipulated by several spirits and for many different reasons. Sometimes I wonder what might have happened if we'd we all been left to our own devices. Never mind, there's nothing that can be done about that now.'

On screen, the scene shifts. Alison is in the shower, her fingers graze across something that feels wrong in her right breast. Something that doesn't feel right at all, not a bit, not in her flesh, not in her gut, not in her heart and not in her mind. A lump that sends that wrong feeling shooting through her entire body. The Alison on-screen slides slowly down the shower wall and sits crying, whilst the Alison who was sitting in the cinema seat feels sick to her stomach, all over again. The scene changes again, and Charlie is now sitting beside her on their bed. Her younger self tells him about the lump and that paragon of strength and shelter pulls her into an embrace and tells her that everything is going to be okay. She saw it then, from her vantage point on the outside, from over her own shoulder she saw the colour drain from Charlie's face as tears first well up in his eyes and then roll down his face.

'I can sympathise with Charlie,' Jude said, the Alison on the screen had lost her hair and Charlie shaved his as a gesture of support. 'He watched as the love of his life was slowly devoured by cancer and I watched as mine was devoured by madness. Don't doubt for a second that I loved Lexi. It was no matter, I couldn't do anything to help her, I gave everything I had to make her happy and all she gave me in return was darkness.'

The movie of Alison's life moves into a montage, charting the progression of her sickness. What she comes to understand is that it is not her sickness but rather 'their sickness'. In her heart, she always knew this to some degree but watching it played back to her, the idea becomes solid and concrete. Charlie presents a strong façade, but regularly when she is asleep, or he is alone, the mask of strength falls away and reveals an emotional wreck, barely able to stop himself from crying.

'I couldn't help Lexi, so I stopped trying. Then, of course, I fell in love with Sophie, and she saved my soul. The rest of the story isn't that interesting, just death, and trickery, and bargains, it's not really important.'

Alison heard the words, but she didn't pay attention. On the screen, Charlie is in the temple of the lotus eaters and Mephistopheles is handing him a knife. When she watched him take it and slip it in his pocket, it sent a shiver down her spine.

'Oh God, no,' she gasped. 'What did you do Charlie?'

'What is important is the fact that I still love Sophie,' Jude replied, making no effort to answer Alison. Soon enough, she would see for herself what he did. 'I live a mortal life with her, and it is wonderful, but it is not permanent. Now, I can keep her in perfect health, I can stretch out her life and keep her young, but I can't make her go on forever.'

She watched as the Jude on screen sat on her bed and told Charlie not to allow her a violin or a piano. The spirit set out the rest of the rules and then disappeared through a wall. She watched Charlie whisper in her ear and she remembered hearing him whisper. After that, he left the room to chop wood, and when she woke and sprang upright, the cinema screen went dark.

'I needed a place for her when life was done. A place where she could be happy, surrounded by friendly faces. I needed the Breidablik, and what's more, I need you to be there waiting for her.'

'What?' Alison snapped.

'Your life in the cabin is coming to an end,' Jude said. 'For you, life is coming to an end and that's the way it should be, dear heart. This was never meant to be everlasting, it was only ever meant to be a long goodbye. The problem is, Charlie is crafty, he stretched this out far too thin. Since coming to the cabin, he has written twelve different books, my story is his thirteenth. This way, he has stretched a single moment and made it last twenty-four years. But time is so short now, soon you will have to say goodbye.'

'And what happens after we say goodbye?' Alison asked. Jude didn't answer, instead, he took hold of her hand and suddenly it felt like the world was moving around her. The cinema vanished, and they were zooming over a frozen wasteland which became a rough sea, and then a landscape of rolling hills and green fields. They slowed as they passed over a familiar, grey, dirty, concrete city and settled in a large square building.

They were standing in a brightly lit hospital corridor outside a private room. Jude was still clutching Alison's hand, and when she heard that familiar beep, beep, beep, louder than before, she squeezed it tighter. She felt her heart racing, and she marvelled at that because her heart wasn't in her chest; she knew now that her heart was in her real body preparing to beat its last.

'Is that me?' she asked. 'Am I in that room?'

'No.' Jude answered shortly. 'You asked what happens after you say goodbye. What happens is you have a choice to make. You can move on to whatever lies beyond, whatever that is, it's a mystery to me. Or you could take your place in Breidablik, it's a peaceful journey, not in the slightest bit scary. It will be like going to sleep again, and when you wake you will be on a boat. The last breath you breathe in life will fill the boat's sails and you will gently float into the harbour. You will come ashore, find a home, and settle down, and in time you will welcome others.'

'What happens to Charlie?' Alison asks. 'After I die, what happens to him, will he join me here one day?'

'I can't promise that.'

'Why not? What will keep him away?'

'Life,' Jude answers briefly. 'Life will happen, life will keep him away. After you say goodbye, he will grieve for you, and out of his grief, great art will be born. One day, he will start to live again, and with life comes love. He will meet a woman and marry her, and then become a father. He will be older then, there will be grey in his ginger beard when he holds his first child for the first time. He will grow old with a family around him, and when he passes, he will go to a different place, a place where his wife and children will one day join him.'

'And meanwhile I sacrifice everything!' she shouts, her face is red and her fists clenched by her side. 'I never know what it's like to be a mother and I never see the love of my life again. This is your plan for me, to sacrifice everything for your sake, so I can linger and keep your mistress happy when it's her time to join you. You deny me what you will never sacrifice for yourself!'

Jude pushed open the door to the private room; as he walked over the threshold his clothes transformed. Now, he was dressed in the white smocks of a staff nurse. *He was my handsome nurse,* Alison thought. *He held my hand and eased my pain.*

From the doorway, she watched as Jude crossed the room to the bed where a little girl lay fast asleep. The girl was frail and bald but not yet as ill as Alison was, or rather, still is. Jude reached to take the girl's pulse, and when his fingers touched her wrist she stirred and woke from her sleep. Seeing him staring down at her she offered a smile.

'Hello sugarplum, that's such a bright smile you have for me today. How are you feeling?'

'I'm good,' the little girl lied.

'Good, I'm glad to hear that. It's very early Cassie. Do you think you can get back to sleep? I think a couple more hours will do you the world of good.'

'I'll try.'

At that, Jude kissed his fingertip and placed it on little Cassie's forehead. Instantly, she fell back into a deep sleep. The second she did, he turned his face to Alison who saw just the slightest edge of anger in his face, it unnerved her.

'What would you prefer?' Jude snapped. 'Would you prefer Charlie to die by your side? I'm sure he wouldn't be opposed to the idea. Should he really be denied a life because you have been? If I knew you were that kind of woman, I would never have wasted my time on you.'

'I'm not that kind of woman, I just ...'

'Just nothing,' Jude interrupted. Quickly he strolled towards her, grabbed her wrist and pulled her into the room. He then marched her across to Cassie's bed and pushed her head down so she could really see. 'Do you want to know about love and life? They aren't fair, and no one ever promised you they would be. Life, love, romance, and all the fine things, they are only temporary, they never last and they go on without you.' He paused for a moment, and Alison could feel him soften by her side. When he spoke again his voice was warmer and far more gentle. 'Dying over lost love, that Romeo and Juliet stuff, it's all bullshit. Living despite your loss, moving on, living and loving again. These things, they are not a denial of how you once felt for someone, but rather an affirmation of it. If you let him go, one day Charlie will live again, and in part that will be to honour you.'

Jude slid his hand down from Alison's head to stroke her back. In the room, there was silence broken only by that beep, beep, beep. The sound of it didn't seem so harsh and cruel any longer.

'Meanwhile, there is this girl. One day she will pass, and I will bring her to the Breidablik, she should have someone there to take care of her.'

And there it was, at last, the baited hook. Just as she was the bait that reeled-in Charlie, this little girl Cassie was to be her bait. Of course, she would never be this girl's mummy, not in life and certainly not in death. But in an unfair universe, it seemed that this would be the best she could hope for. She thought of Charlie, she had felt angry and cheated by him. Not because he made a deal, but because he hid the truth from her, he lied and allowed her to fear for her sanity. Now she understood a little better, as she was already questioning whether she'd be able to tell this little girl the truth when the time came.

'Okay,' she said. 'I'm in, what do I do next?'

'Go home, back to the cabin, back to Charlie. Tell him nothing and prepare to say goodbye.'

Jude held out his hand and offered Alison a small gift box. Looking at it. she saw that it was the type of box that rings came in.

'It's a parting gift,' he said, as he held it out to her.

.28.

The Last Kiss

Lights twinkled around the tree in the living room, stockings were pinned to the fireplace and red, gold, and green paper chains had been hung across the ceiling. In the fridge, there was a rolled turkey breast filled with chestnut stuffing and wrapped in bacon, it was just big enough to make a nice lunch for the two of them. The vegetables had all been prepared and now they sat in pans on the stove. The table had been laid with crackers and cutlery, and there was a bottle of Prosecco, and half a dozen bottles of Saga beer cooling in the fridge. At long last, Christmas had come to the cabin on the frozen lake.

Alison was pleased with herself, it seemed that a little knowledge went a long way. *'In this place expectation is key'*, that's what Jude had told her. But he had also told her that time didn't work properly here. They lived inside a single moment, stretched out to last a day and set to repeat. Therefore, the seasons never changed, and Christmas never came no matter how much you expected it. Alison found the way around this was not to expect the coming of December 25th, which would never come, but instead to expect to find everything she needed to have Christmas on any old day.

It came to her last night as she sat in the grotto, putting the finishing touches to the mansion on the hill. It was her final model, the docks had been finished at the beginning of the week, now all that was left was to glue the roof on this last house. Her mind was wandering, she was thinking about Breidablik, and whether this mansion had already begun to materialise in that place. She realised that the goodbye was just around the corner, likely if she finished this model tonight then tomorrow would be the last day. She felt a great ambivalence wash over her, it was bittersweet, she was happy and yet, at the same time, inexpressibly sad.

Before she woke from that final dream, Jude had said something to her, something that struck a chord with her. *'All the time in the world is not enough time to love that man.'* Yes, that much was right, there would never be a good time to be parted from Charlie, and yet she would let him go. She understood now exactly what drove him to the Midway, it was the same impulse that drove her now. She would say goodbye to her muppet man knowing that she would likely never get to see his face again, not in life or death. But knowing that eventually, he would live again, there would be a new love, and children, and all the fine things her muppet man so richly deserved. How could she deny him that? Her last, almost-earthly desire now was just one, last, perfect day. One day to love him and commit the touch of his hand and the warmth of his smile to her memory. One last day to feed him, make him laugh, kiss him and feel him inside her.

'It has to be Christmas tomorrow, but I don't need it to be December,' she said aloud to herself. The roof to the mansion was now stuck firm and she was finally done with her little project. Alison closed her eyes and imagined a tree in the living room. It would have to go in the reading corner, adjacent to the fire, which meant she would have to move the rocking chairs, they could probably go against the opposite wall. She saw herself stringing lights around the tree and hanging baubles from the branches. She saw the paper chains, she always used to love making them as a kid, she saw herself on a stepladder zig-zagging them around the ceiling. She saw stockings above the fireplace, crammed full of chocolate and little treats. In the kitchen, she saw all the food already prepared and ready to go. When she came up from the grotto, she wasn't at all surprised to find everything exactly how she pictured it. She smiled at the sight of it, then skipped off to bed.

'Wake up,' Alison said, as she shook Charlie awake, 'Come see the surprise I've got for you.'

She watched as he slowly blinked open his big, cow eyes, and hesitantly scanned the room. As he turned his head, a shaft of light from the window hit him square in the face. He lifted a hand to shade his eyes then after a moment rolled onto his side as if to go back to sleep.

'Wake up, Charlie!' she shouted as she yanked the quilt off him and tickled up his sides. 'Come and see, I promise you're going to love it.'

Charlie suppressed a giggle, then swung his long legs onto the floor out of the opposite side of his bed. He sat hunched, rubbing his head, while Alison crawled across and sat next to him. She looked up at him and grinned a big toothy grin that spoke nothing of the lump in her throat.

'Why are you so cheerful today?' he asked.

'Just you wait till you see what I've got downstairs for you, my muppet man.'

'Muppet man,' Charlie grinned. 'You haven't called me that in a while, must be something special.' Alison answered with an enthusiastic nod of the head. 'Okay, fine. Have I got time for a shower first?'

'Why don't I join you?' she asked.

It seemed like a good idea at the time but once they were both inside there was barely room to manoeuvre. Charlie managed to scrub Alison's back well enough by stooping slightly, but when it was his turn he had to kneel so she could reach his shoulders. Despite the awkward manoeuvring, and the odd elbow nearly connecting with a face, it was quite enjoyable. It was an intimate start that set the tone for the whole day. Once they were dried and dressed, Alison took him by the hand and dragged him down the stairs. Pushing open the door to the living room, she revealed the Christmas she had prepared for him.

'Wow!' he said, slightly slack-jawed. 'How did you do this? Where did it all come from?'

'Well, all the decorations were downstairs in the grotto,' she lied. 'I dropped a piece of my model under the table and when I crawled under to get it there was a box full of Christmas stuff, including a stand for a tree.'

'So where did the tree come from then?'

'Well, like I said, I already had the stand, and it seemed like a shame not to have one ... so I went outside last night while you were asleep and chopped one down.' She wasn't sure exactly why she was lying but thought it essential to lie just a little. She thought that it would be best for him not to know the goodbye was coming until the last moment, the irony of this wasn't lost on her.

'What?' Charlie snapped. 'On your own?'

'No, of course not on my own … there was a choir of Canadian Mounties singing "I'm a Lumberjack and I'm Okay".' Despite himself, Charlie snorted at that.

'What if you got hurt though? What if the tree fell the wrong way?'

'Pfft … get hurt,' Alison sighed and rolled her eyes. 'You're out there swinging the axe every day, and I love you babe, but basically, you have the arms of an octopus and strength of a gerbil. If you can manage it so can I. Unless you're worried I'd chip a nail, or that my womb would self-destruct if I attempted a bit of manual labour.' He was laughing as she ranted at him, and yet she still saw that spark of concern in his eyes.

'I'm not worried because you're a woman, I'm worried because you went out alone in the pitch black with an axe. Anything could have happened.'

'Well, I could hardly wake you, one: you were dead to the world and two: it would have ruined the surprise.' She put her arms around his waist and strained her neck to look up at him. 'There's no harm done babe, so don't go grumping about this and ruining the day.'

'Okay,' Charlie said, rolling his eyes.

'Good,' she grinned. 'Now go get your stocking down from the fire.' As he walked past her into the room she turned quickly and slapped him on his bony bum. He looked back over his shoulder and she tipped him a salacious wink.

They spent the morning in front of the fire, eating triangles of Toblerone, and handfuls of nuts and raisins. At noon Alison put the turkey in the oven and that afternoon they ate one of the best Christmas lunches they had ever had. This was followed by a walk around the frozen lake hand-in-hand, watching as the sun made the ice sparkle like diamonds again. Before it got too dark, they climbed the hill back to the cabin and took their places on the sofa in front of the fire. It was then that Alison reached into her pocket for the little box Jude had given her, she had wrapped it and placed a tiny bow on top of the box. Or at least, she had imagined doing it and the magic of the world they lived in had done the rest.

'I got you this,' she said, as tentatively she handed him the box.

'I wish you'd have said something, I haven't got you anything.'

'Every day with you is a gift,' she said, turning bright red.

'Err … you've got feelings?' Charlie laughed and poked her in the ribs, 'You're sweet on me.'

'I am,' she grinned. 'Now open your gift.'

Charlie peeled the bow from the lid of the box and then unwrapped the paper, the box was so small that unwrapping it was a tricky, fiddly affair. Once the paper was off and the lid removed, what greeted Charlie was something that looked like a pale blue gem. He took a closer look and saw a flash of green running inside it, and something else, something smaller. He took it from the box and found a wooden ring, and on top of that ring, a gem, and inside that gem, a tiny arctic world beneath the Aurora Borealis, and right at the centre a little log cabin, their log cabin. Charlie examined it from every angle, the detail was incredible. When he turned to Alison his eyes were moist. She took the ring from his hand and slipped it on the ring finger on his left hand, she knew of course what this meant.

'We never bothered with marriage,' she said, noticing a tremble in her voice. 'It wasn't our thing, it didn't mean anything to us. But what I want you to know now is … well, you've always felt like the other half of me, Charlie Dunn. I never needed a ceremony or anyone's blessing to know that I was always Alison Dunn-Wheaton. I just never said it out loud because, let's face it, it's a bloody stupid mouth full isn't it!' She paused and watched Charlie simultaneously fight back his sobs and stifle a chuckle.

'I'd marry you now if I could. I want to spend forever with …'

'Stop.' Alison interrupted. 'Don't say anything else … just kiss me.'

He did just exactly as he was told and kissed her, she reached up and put her hands around the back of his neck and pulled him down on top of her. The kiss was long and deep, Alison tasted her sadness in it. Maybe this wasn't their last kiss exactly, but that last one couldn't be far away now. In her head she heard her inner critic asking, 'are you gonna sleep with him now, that's the traditional way of saying goodbye isn't it? One last fuck for the road before you …' She shook that voice out of her head and wrapped her legs around his back. Committing herself to the moment, she rolled so that Charlie toppled off the sofa onto the deep shag rug, taking her with him. She had a mind to end this all, in roughly the same place it began.

The whole thing was slow, intense, and full of heartache. At least for Alison it was, but then Alison knew. As he moved inside her she considered not doing what she knew she had to. But then she thought of that life that was waiting for him. And, of course, there was little Cassie who would be left alone in a strange town if she didn't go through with it. Cassie needed someone, someone who could care for her. More importantly, she needed someone who could sympathise with exactly what she had been through.

No, be here, feel this, remember it, she thought, rebuking herself for allowing her mind to wander again. For now, nothing that was outside mattered at all, all that mattered in the world was inside her. This man had been the great love of her life, and soon she would never see him again. She rolled him onto his back and took her place on top of him. She brought his hands up to her breasts. It's funny, but when she looked at them now they were both perfectly fine. Her right breast looked and felt the way it had before she had ever found that cursed lump. She realised that yet again, this was due to her expectations. Before she knew the truth of the world they now lived in, she expected to see the scars of her sickness. When she had looked at her right breast, she saw it reconstructed and smaller than her left. Now, she was finally done with sickness and free from the trauma it caused and so, when she looked at her body now, it looked the way it had when she was eighteen and in the bloom of youth.

Charlie noticed it, from beneath her he groaned and grunted and told her how beautiful she looked. Now, at long last, the sadness was receding, and she felt the pleasure in this. The light of the fire cast their shadows on the opposite wall and, from the corner of her eye, Alison watched. It was almost as hypnotic as the northern lights. The rhythmic fall and rise of her body and flicker of the flames made for a unique shadow puppet show.

It built to its natural climax, and she fell on top of him, tired, and for now, pleasantly numb in her heart. Before long, that bittersweet sadness would creep back into her, but for now, she lay, sweaty, feeling nothing. At some point, one of them reached over to the sofa and fetched the blanket. They lay together on the carpet beside the fire, beneath the blanket, and watched the colours swirl through the skylight. Once again, she felt like she was at the bottom of a deep ocean, her eyes felt heavy and slowly they began to close when … *No, now … do it now or you'll never do it.*

'How is the book coming along, babe?' she asked.

'Near enough done, just the closing paragraph to do now.' As he replied to her question, she felt him shiver beside her, probably at the thought of finishing it. She pulled herself up from his side and crawled over his body to reach under the sofa. She took out the manuscript she had placed there the night before and, clutching it tightly in both hands, she held it out to him.

'This is it, isn't it?' she asked, and watched as he pulled himself up to a seated position. He moved away from her until he almost blocked the light from the fire. 'There were twelve other manuscripts in your desk drawer, but this is the right one, isn't it … why don't you finish it now? If it's just one paragraph, let's finish it.'

'I can't do that … you don't know what will happen if I …'

'I do.' She took her right hand from the manuscript and reached across to grip his arm and steady his trembling.

'If you know, why would you ask?' he snapped. She had never heard so much anger in his voice, he was usually so placid.

'This has to end.'

Charlie didn't reply to that, instead, he sprang forward, grabbed the manuscript from her hands, twisted it awkwardly and threw it on the fire. Alison saw him visibly deflate as the flames refused to burn the pages, the fire only bent and twisted around the almost finished book like a nest of brambles growing around something discarded. Alison moved over to his side and placed a hand on his back. He began to cry out loud and she found herself wondering if she'd ever actually seen him cry in the flesh before. She knew now that during her sickness he had crept off to do all his crying alone, but she couldn't remember him ever doing it in her presence. She said nothing, she just stared forward at the fire that was burning around the book ... and then after a while, and without knowing exactly what she was going to say, she opened her mouth.

'I love you, Charlie,' she began, as that seemed like the right starting place. 'If I could keep you forever I would, but I can't. You know what happens if we stay here forever ... you fade away.' She wasn't entirely sure about that but once she had spoken the words they sounded right to her. 'I've treasured every moment we've spent together, both in life and in this place. But I can't be the reason that you're denied a life, I can't, and I won't be.' She paused again and reached into the fire to retrieve the book from the flames. She wasn't afraid, she knew the flames wouldn't burn her, nothing here could really hurt her.

'You know what Jude said to me?'

'Fucking lousy interfering Pooka.'

'I don't know Charlie, he feels like a good one to me, he's our friend ... I remember that now,' she said calmly 'At any rate what he said was true; he said Romeo and Juliet isn't romance. You fading away because you think you won't be able to live without me does me a disservice. It's like taking all my love for you and flushing it down the toilet.'

'How could you say that?' There was no anger in his voice now, just pure grief. 'What am I supposed to do, just clap my hands and say, "Well that's done, best move on ... Alison who?"'

'No.' She swallowed to try and rid herself of the sad lump in her throat, she had to appear strong now, it was her turn. 'Cry, kick and scream, swear at the top of your lungs, do whatever it takes to get through this, but get through this and learn to live again. Life isn't fair Charlie, love isn't either. Saying goodbye is agony, but it's part of it. It's divine agony to love someone and have to let them go, but it must happen, and it must be now. Because there never will be a good time. All the time in the world is not enough time to love you.'

When she finished there was an oppressive silence in the room. It squelched above their heads like a jellyfish, and for the longest time, they couldn't bear to make eye contact. Finally, Charlie lifted his chin and showed her those big, brown, cow eyes of his, she fell into them and when he reached out to cup her face, she felt electric in his

316

fingers. He leant forward and placed his forehead on hers, then let out a deep sigh.

'All the time in the world isn't enough time to love you either,' he said.

He took the manuscript from her hands and placed it on the floor between them, he flipped to the back page and then, out of nowhere, a fountain pen appeared in his hand. Alison's stomach turned over at the sight of it, she had to bite her lip and clench her fists as tightly as she could. This small amount of pain grounded her, it was the only thing that stopped her from yanking the pen from his hand and rushing to the door to cast it into the snow. She watched intently as Charlie's shaking hand pressed the nib of the pen to the page and wrote ...

Jude and the white stag – who were now one and the same – walked away towards the setting sun. He thought of 'she'. 'She of the heart-shaped face and soft voice', and when he thought of her, he saw her bathed in the neon, karaoke glow. Puck had gifted him the length of life to pretend to be a man, to live by her side, and love her. But what was one life measured against the eternity that stretched out before him. He found himself wondering if just one life would ever be enough. No, of course it wouldn't, likely all the time in the world would not be enough time to love her.

As soon as he put the pen down, they heard the wind roaring around the cabin. The windows began to rattle and the cabin groaned from the force of it. The lovers, kneeling naked before the fire, clung tightly to each other and Charlie grabbed the blanket and wrapped it around them. The wind ripped the front door of the cabin clean off, and the completed manuscript was carried out and away.

'Oh God, what have we done?' Charlie cried into the howling wind.

'Don't be afraid.' Alison felt the words vibrate in her throat, but she couldn't hear them. Just then, the windows shattered spraying shards of glass over them. Miraculously, they were unharmed, but then how much of a miracle could it be? This world had been founded and built from Charlie's love, even as it dissolved around them it wouldn't hurt them.

Alison took Charlie's face and yanked him down to kiss her, this would be the last kiss, the last ever one. It was as slow as molasses, bitter, like dark chocolate, and had the effect of downing a pint of vodka, Alison felt drunk from it. She gripped his face and ignored the chaos around her. They were at the height of the storm, and the beams, wood, blocks of stone, and shards of glass that had been the cabin moments ago, were now spiralling around them. She didn't see, she closed her eyes to this and thought about that time in Autumn when they sat beneath the tree by the banks of the river. That was the time, that was when she knew.

There was an odd sensation, something a little like falling, the feel and taste of Charlie's lips and tongue were growing distant, suddenly there was darkness, and after the darkness there was nothing.

The Resolution of a Dream

Jessica was sitting at the back of the bus resting her head on the glass. A slight shuddering vibration ran through her head and down her spine. It felt soothing, in an odd sort of way. Outside the window, the city was passing her by in a stream of grey concrete broken by the odd splash of colour, a tree bursting with green here, a flash of a red car there, and in the corner of her eye, a neon sign, its glow dimmed by daylight. She turned slightly to get a better look at the sign and saw a Chinese dragon clutching a bowl. The name above the neon sign proclaimed the building as The Hungry Dragon Chinese Buffet and Karaoke Bar. She chuckled to herself at the idea of it, a Japanese karaoke bar serving an all-you-can-eat Chinese buffet. *Only in Coventry,* she thought to herself, before closing her eyes and drifting away into last night's dream.

She was in the snow again, moving through the rows of houses towards the meeting hall at the centre of the little town. There were lanterns lining each side of the path, lighting her way to those big double doors. When she turned her head to look through the windows of the cabins, she saw smiling faces, waving to her. She smiled and waved back.

As she drew closer to the meeting hall, she heard music. The tinkling of piano keys accompanied by the strings of a violin. The doors opened of their own accord and she froze at the threshold and watched that brunette woman – Alison, of course it was Alison – play her strings while a happy little girl tapped away at the keys. After a moment, Alison looked up and seeing Jessica at the door, she walked towards her. As she moved, she put the violin down on a table then, reaching Jessica, she took her face in her hands and planted a kiss on her cheek. To Jessica, it felt like a blessing.

'Be happy,' Alison whispered, and at that, the dream fell apart.

The bus jolted her awake just in time for her to see that she was about to miss her stop. She leapt from her seat, threw her bag over her shoulder, and ran down the aisle. The driver pulled away before she could make it to the doors and she eventually got off one step further down the Roman road. It was fine, it was a lovely day and she didn't have much on apart from a speculative wander around Ikea, and there were some forms she had to drop off at the Ingle Nook. Apart from that, her time was her own.

Everything was different now, everything was new. Last week, they had finished the work on Jude Valentine's garden. She had stood next to her Bampi and watched as the big, foolish, wonderful man looked out with pride at his work. Not just in this garden, but rather the work of a lifetime that stretched out behind it. She had stroked his back and told him what a wonderful job he had done. He sniffled and wiped away a tear with a grubby hanky from his pocket. At the sight of Owen's sniffling, Bill and Ben slinked away. They were from the old country, of course, and they believed that a man should have privacy to shed his tears.

Two days after finishing work on Jude's garden Owen had packed up all his worldly belongings into two suitcases and three old wooden tea crates that he had stored away in the garden shed. The rest was piled up as junk for the charity shop or the tip, and after loading up his van to make the short trip up the Castlegate road to Pruney's annex, he had pressed his own house key into Jessica's hand.

'That's for you, my good girl, my little strawberry,' He had said, ruffling her hair. 'Do what you want with the place mind, and if you want to fix the garden up you know who to call don't you?'

'I'll call my Bampi,' she had said, fighting back the tears.

'No, you bloody won't girl!' Owen replied laughing. 'I'm retired now, or haven't you noticed that. If you want help tidying up this little eyesore, I suggest you call the flowerpot men. They work cheap see … they have all those kids back home to take care of mind.'

'Granda', you can't say that.' she had said, hitting his arm playfully, knowing after all that he was just trying to get a rise out of her.

'I can lovely,' he had said, climbing in behind the wheel. 'I just did see!' and at that, he pulled away.

Walking down the Roman road she had stopped dead outside the local bookshop, her eye drawn by the window display. She saw a cardboard cut-out of a bear standing on its hind legs, next to that there was a cardboard bookcase and at the far-left side there was another cardboard cut-out, this one of a little boy holding up a wooden sword and wearing a wooden crown. The cover of the book was Hank's oil painting, now complete, with a background and a title that read: 'The Boy Who Tamed the Bear'.

Of course, she had already read it, Hank had supplied her a draft months ago, but she thought that the right thing to do was buy herself a copy. She popped in through the chiming door and found a table just inside the shop displaying the book and a picture of Charlie. He looked tall and awkward, the ginger hair on his head was like candyfloss but his beard was thick, and lush, sporting the odd grey hair here and there. She opened the book and read the dedication.

To Hank, Becky, Mary, my second mum, and little Hannah and Frankie, it read, and then under that, *Twinkle, Twinkle our little stars. Never forget just who you are.*

Reading that little line of poetry brought Hannah into Jessica's mind. The little girl bloomed there, bright, and blonde, and beautiful, and with the image of that little girl came a memory of the weekend. She saw Hannah standing in Jude's finished secret garden with a letter folded up in her hand.

At the weekend there was a party, an informal, odd sort of gathering in Jude's new garden. Jessica had gone along, wearing that dress again, maybe she had been thinking that Charlie would be there, and maybe she had been thinking that if he was there then she still wanted to make an impression. Charlie wasn't there, and that was okay. The whole of the Walker tribe was there, Hank and Becky, Hannah, and baby Frankie, and Hank's mother Mary Ann. Her Bampi was there, sitting at a table smoking his pipe. Prudence was sitting on his left-hand side, looking all prim in her classic Channel ivory summer

322

suit with black trim, complete with hat and matching bag. On her Bampi's right side sat her father Andrew. He was sipping at a glass of Pimm's, the *Financial Times* not in front of his face today. Instead, it was neatly folded on the table so that Andrew could wear a veneer of sociability while still carefully examining the markets.

Bill and Ben the flowerpot men were there with their wives and children. They were smartly dressed, but they looked awkward and out of place. She had crossed the garden to say hello to them and Bill – the one who spoke the most English – looked up, saw her and met her halfway. He took hold of her hands and kissed her on the cheek.

'You is beautiful woman Jessy,' he had said, his accent making her name sound exotic. 'We never know this before.'

'Why thank you,' she had said. There was a compliment in there somewhere, and she was determined to take it. She stood for a while, making polite conversation with Bill, Ben and their families. Bill began talking in Polish, flexing his arms in strong man gestures. When he stopped, the group around them began to laugh and talk back and forth.

'I tell them all that you work hard like English man, which like Polish women,' He had explained. 'You remember this I say to you, yes?'

'Yes Bill, I remember … it was the proudest moment of my life, my greatest achievement,' she had clamped her hands to her heart at that and looked to the heavens in mock exasperation. Suddenly, Bill's wife was taking hold of her hands, patting them and speaking fast. When she stopped, Jessica looked to Bill for an explanation.

'My wife say, you is beautiful woman. Not English beautiful, but Polish and Irish beautiful. She say, maybe you not do this job anymore. Too much sun bad for pale skin and hard work give you hands of old Russian crone. Is not nice for pretty woman.'

'It's okay. I'm giving it up,' Jessica said laughing. 'I'm going to study again, I've found an Open University course, I'm going to study psychology and become a councillor.'

'What this for?' Bill asked.

'You know, a councillor …' she struggled to find a simple explanation and then came up with, 'I'm going to talk to sad people and make them better.'

'Is English thing, I think. Polish not have time for sadness, Polish work.' He had said with pride.

She had made her excuses and left Bill and Ben in order to say hello to Sophie, who was hosting. The singer was surrounded by people that Jessica knew but had never met. She had seen them on TV, and in the pages of newspapers, and had danced and sung along to their music. The guys and girls from Valentine's Day and The Origami Foxes, the bands that Jude Valentine and Sophie Mia Darling belonged to respectively, were gathered around the barbeque in high spirits. They were like one massive family, laughing, drinking, playfighting, shouting obscenities, singing, and talking about personal matters far too loudly.

As Jessica approached Sophie called her name, and the crowd around her parroted it, throwing open their arms and screaming, 'Jessica!' in a way that said, 'come in, you're welcome here.' She was passed around the crowd, she had her hand shaken, her back patted, her hair ruffled, and she was pulled into about half a dozen hugs.

'Hey, Hanky Panky!' someone shouted. 'Is this her, is this the girl that's going to fix our Charlie?' Hank, who was holding Frankie in the cradle of his right arm, answered by holding up his left hand and crossing his fingers. At that, the crowd let out a cheer and Jessica had gone bright red.

'Do you not think that you're getting ahead of yourself?' she had shouted. She looked at the mystery man. *Nimble,* she thought. *Lead guitarist in Valentine's Day.* 'I haven't even met him yet.'

'Yes, well, when you do meet our Mr Tickle, tell him we miss him. Tell him to come home to us.'

'Should I say hello first … or …' There was laughter then.

'Hey Jessy,' Sophie had taken her gently by the wrist and lead her down the path to the secret garden hiding behind the hedges. 'I just want to thank you for the brilliant job you did, it's beautiful. We really love it, and my fella wants to thank you as well.'

'Oh, he's home, is he?'

'Yes, he's home and done with traveling for a little while I think. He wants to thank you himself,' Sophie had said, pointing to the secret garden.

'Well, it wasn't just me,' Jessica had replied, blushing 'It was hardly me at all, you should be thanking my Bampi, and Bill and Ben as well.'

'He knows, he still wants to thank you.'

Sophie gestured to the archway and Jessica nodded and walked through it. Crossing over the bridge to the small island, she found

Jude sitting with his feet in the little moat. He had his jeans rolled up to his knees, his hands were pressed flat in the grass behind him, and he had neatly placed his Converse trainers and socks next to the leg of the table under the pagoda. He didn't see her at first, he was too busy staring at the water feature to notice her. Her Bampi had sourced it through his contacts at Cactus Jack's garden centre, the guy who ran the place these days knew a guy, who knew a guy, who knew a sculptor who specialised in bespoke water features. The one he created for Jude featured a stag's head, complete with antlers carved entirely from driftwood, set up on a rockery. The water trickled from the stag's mouth down the rockery, where it pooled and then drained into a bamboo tube. Once that tube was full, it emptied into the moat around the island before clanking against a stone. Jessica had been informed that this Japanese style of fountain was called a *'Shishi Odoshi'* or just simply a 'Deer Scarer'.

'It's so soothing,' Jude had said, and as she approached he ruffled his Jim Morrison mop of lush, brown hair. 'I loved touring Japan, Tokyo is the great neon city, it's all light and noise and the future bursting out from every corner … and then there are gardens as well, immaculate gardens …' at that, he had paused and pointed at the bamboo pipe slowly clanking back and forth. 'Do you know what these are for?'

'To scare the animals away, stop them eating up your flowers.'

'Right, exactly right,' he had replied, without looking up. 'It's beautiful isn't it, no need to lay out traps or poison. Not if there's a kinder way, this is the beauty of form and function going hand in hand.'

He turned to her then and smiled. She had seen him on the TV in his music videos. Even so, it didn't quite prepare her for how handsome he was in real life, he was the quintessential rock star pin-up. There was a hint of salt and pepper in his hair and the odd wrinkle by his eyes, but that didn't detract from his beauty, rather she thought it enhanced it. As he sat there, kicking his feet in the water, she thought how happy and peaceful he looked, it was almost as if he was glowing.

'Thank you, you all did such a wonderful job. You've created a place for me and the little lady to be peaceful, a little sanctuary. We're both very happy with it.'

'Well, as I was just telling Sophie ... it wasn't really down to me.'

'I know, but even so ... thank you for the part you played.'

'Can I ask you something?' She hadn't realised she was going to speak those words until they slipped out. Jude serenely nodded in a way that said, 'ask away'. She took a deep breath and then it came tumbling out of her.

'I know I've literally just met you, and I guess I shouldn't be sticking my nose in ... but how come you and Charlie don't get on anymore? I've seen the picture of you all in Hank's house. I get the sense that you were all close once?'

'We were, once' Jude sighed and then his shoulders sagged. 'He will tell you his story, it's not my place to tell it for him ... but ... well, the top and bottom of it is that he thinks I tricked him when what really happened was, he tricked himself'

'I don't understand?'

'No, but I'm sure you will.'

'Uncle Jude!' Hannah had yelled in excitement. Jude and Jessica heard her voice and then looked up just in time to see her come galloping over the bridge and launch herself at the rock star she called affectionately called 'Uncle'. It seemed that for Hannah, the words auntie and uncle did not denote blood relatives but rather just grownups she loved. Knowing that, Jessica wondered how long it would be until she was Auntie Jessy.

Jude leapt to his feet and caught the little girl mid-air, then swung her around laughing.

'I missed you lots!'

'I missed you too, little Twinkle,' he replied, putting her down on the grass.

'Are you back now? Forever back?'

'I think so,' he said. 'For a good long while at least. As far I know they are done with me for now.'

'Goooood,'Hannah had replied, stretching out the words to emphasise how good it was. 'Auntie Sophie missed you while you were gone.'

'I missed her too,' Jude said. He retrieved his trainers and then ruffled Hannah's hair as he passed her by. 'I'll leave you to it,' he said winking, before crossing the bridge barefooted.

'Your eyes aren't deep down sad anymore, are they?' Hannah stated, in a very matter of fact way. It was like she was saying 'your fingernails aren't pink anymore'. For a long while, nothing else was said, Jessica fell under Hannah's searching eyes and found herself almost hypnotised by them. 'Uncle Charlie's not as sad anymore either ... but I have something for you.'

Hannah rummaged around in the pocket of her summer dress and retrieved a piece of wrinkled paper. She took a moment to smooth out the wrinkles before holding it up to Jessica.

'What's this, Twinkle?'

'It's a gift from my Greatfather.' she replied.

'Do you mean Godfather?'

'No,' Hannah replied, rolling her eyes. 'Uncle Charlie is my Godfather ... I'm talking about my great, or Highfather, Uncle Goodfellow ... He's the Pooka in Starkey's woods ... he watches over our family ... he wants you to have this. I found it in the woods, it was crammed into the mouth of his statue.'

She took the paper, unfolded it, and found familiar, mannish handwriting. At the bottom, she saw her Granda's name, Owen Evans. She noticed that the 'S' at the end her Granda's name was smudged, as if by a splash of water, or maybe a tear. She read the letter.

To the Pooka in the woods.

I have been an awful father. I've let down my girls time and time again. Even after your intervention I've wallowed in my own pain and heartache and neglected my girls, I've laughed and joked away instead of facing my heartache and because of this, my Pruney has suffered most of all. I've made her cold and cruel, and she doesn't

know how to care for her daughter because I never cared for her.

Worse than all this, my little strawberry has gone away, she's shacked

up with some horrible man who mistreats her and she doesn't come

home anymore to show her face. She's jumped from the frying pan

into the fire and when she calls me she sounds sad.

Please help me, bring my little one home. Help me fix her, help me

make her happy, help me find her a good man. Help me break this

chain, help me make amends to my Pruney while I still can. I'm getting

old now and I don't want to die while she still hates me.

Owen Evans

'Uncle Goodfellow says this one was worthy. He says you should
show it to your mama,' Hannah said.

Jessica didn't speak. Quietly, she folded up the note and pressed it
against her body. She smiled at Hannah, her eyes glazed over with the
promise of tears yet to come, and she turned and walked away over
the bridge.

'Jessy!' Hannah shouted, and Jessica looked back over her
shoulder. 'Sometimes I dream about that snowy place in the north
and really real, I feel like I'm really there. I play with the little girl
Cassie, we have snowball fights and make snow angels and sometimes
Auntie Alison plays her violin for me … but I don't ever tell Uncle
Charlie about those dreams. Daddy says that when Alison went to the
snowy place, she took half of Charlie's heart with her. That's why he
was deep down sad because it's painful to regrow your heart … I like
going to the snowy place in my dreams but I don't ever tell Uncle

330

Charlie because I know it would hurt him ... Uncle Jude says that the dead don't haunt the living, the living haunt the dead.'

'I understand,' Jessica said, and she turned and walked away.

Crossing the garden, she had seen people revelling, drinking, eating burgers, telling jokes. From the corner of her eye, she spied Jude talking to Bill and Ben and she thought she heard Polish slipping off his tongue. None of that mattered, what mattered was her family still sitting at the table at the edge of the festivities. Her father Andrew was still examining yesterday's copy of the FT from sly glances. Her mother Prudence was still sitting prim and proper, with that expression on her face, that one that came from tasting or smelling something foul. In between them, there was her Bampi, asleep in his chair, his pipe had gone out and fallen from his hand into the grass. She walked to them and kissed the old, sleeping man on his wrinkly forehead.

'Oh, at last,' Prudence sniped. 'At long last, she deigns to speak to her family.'

Jessica had answered this by planting a second kiss on Prudence's head. It silenced her and wiped the foul-taste look from her face. Instead, she looked at her daughter with curiosity etched across her brow. Jessica pressed the note into her mother's hand and smiled.

'Read this,' she said. 'It's a letter, Bampi wrote it. It was found stuffed in the mouth of a statue in Starkey's wood.'

'Well, in that case, no ... if it's like the one I found when I was a little girl, I don't want to see it.' Prudence held it out for Jessica to take it back.

'Read it,' Jessica had insisted. She pushed it back in her to her mother's hand and pulled up an empty chair from the next table to sit beside her. She watched her mother read it, she watched the colour drain from her face, she watched as her mother reached out and gripped her Granda's hand.

Now, as Jessica approached the Ingle Nook, she thought about that moment, the moment her mother gripped her Granda's hand. Later that night there would be tears, heartache, the relief of letting go of something heavy. But it was that first moment that mattered, it was the moment when Prudence finally reached out.

Through the window of the Ingle Nook she saw people gathered around the tables, chatting and sipping their drinks. She pushed open the door and strode towards the counter, leaving her envelope of documents with the guy on shift. It occurred to her then that she could have dropped this stuff off with Becky at her house. She was just wondering why Becky had insisted that she bring them here when she turned around and saw him in the corner. He was sitting with his back to her, earbuds in, lost in his own little world. It was definitely him, and she felt butterflies in her belly as she approached ... Now was the right time to meet him, to say hello, to thank him for writing that book. She didn't know what would happen next, where it would lead, all that she knew was that it would begin like this, with her reaching out to tap him on the shoulder from behind.

As her hand made contact with him, she felt Alison's kiss on her cheek once again. *It was a blessing,* she thought.

.30.

Death After Life

Beep, beep, beep. The sound of it seemed overly loud, it rang in the centre of his head like an aching muscle that was out of the reach of a soothing hand. *Beep, beep, beep.* There it was again, even louder now, it made him queasy, he felt about ready to throw up all over the place. *Beep, beep, beep.* It was an alarm clock maybe, it wouldn't leave him alone and let him sleep. That's all he wanted to do, sleep, just that and nothing else. Not think, he certainly didn't want to think, not at all.

Beeeeeeeeeeeee ... the sound was now a flat and constant, monotonous drone that cast a fishhook into his heart ... *eeeeeeeeeep.* And when Charlie finally opened his eyes, Alison was gone. There was a female nurse standing over his lover. He watched as the nurse – a slightly squat woman in her early fifties – reached out and gently closed her eyes.

'She's gone now, Mr Dunn,' the nurse said. Charlie noticed that she had an accent that had all but faded. It sounded like there was a Geordie lurking somewhere in her. Of course, that wouldn't be a surprise, her lot had come to Coventry in their thousands to dig up coal long ago. 'I think she was hanging on 'til you were asleep.'

Charlie couldn't make any sense of it. His mind swirled with memories from the cabin. Twenty-four years of living, all crammed into one single moment. He felt like his head was about to split wide open, had it all just been some strange dream fuelled by heartache and grief? He looked down and spied the ring on his left hand, it was extraordinary, a little blue gem with an arctic world hidden inside. No, it was not a dream.

'I said, I think she waited Mr Dunn, 'til you were asleep, so you didn't have to watch her go.' The nurse repeated pointedly. He looked up and made eye contact with her and she crossed the room to stand by him.

'Yes, that sounds like her.'

'Is there anyone I can call for you, pet?' There it was, 'pet'. The emotion in the nurse's voice spiced up her accent, made it bold and full of flavour.

'No. Just give me a little time with her please.'

'Okay, Mr Dunn,' she took a step closer and squeezed his shoulder. 'I'll just be outside, you just be sure to give me a good, loud shout if you need anything and I'll come running. We'll take care of you until your family gets here, pet.'

As she walked to the door, he didn't answer her, he was too busy thinking, *what family?* There was Hank and Becky, of course, and his godmother Mary Ann. But in a very real sense, he was all alone now. However welcome they made him, however much he felt like Hank's brother and Mary Ann's adopted son, there was another secret part of him that felt like a cuckoo or an interloper. Alison had been his true family, she had made him feel like he belonged, and he never needed to question that fact. Alison's family would be here soon and Hank would come but really, he was alone now, and the thought of that scared him.

'Nurse!' he shouted. She was halfway out the door but stopped and turned back to him. 'Please, just call me Charlie. She always hated my last name, she said it sounded like an out of tune bell ... you know Dunn, Dunn.'

'Okay, Charlie,' she replied, and it was the sheer sadness of that tiny woman's smile that finally broke his heart clean in two.

He felt a great wave of raw emotion wash over him as he tried to make his legs work. They felt weak, and when he finally managed to stand, they wobbled under him. Surreally, cutting through the sadness he thought, *you look like a newborn giraffe*. He realised that would be exactly what Alison would say if she was ... he began to sob and clamped a hand to his mouth to stifle the sound.

He approached her body and bent to kiss her lips, the breathing tubes had already been removed by the nurse, now they lay by the side of her head. Her lips were still warm, and maybe that was the most terrible thing, or maybe not. Maybe there was still worse to come. His sobbing became a howl, and every passing second felt like something beastly clawing at his heart. Suddenly, he was aware of another body in the room. Charlie looked up and through teary eyes, he saw Jude in the corner of the room. He looked sorrowful, his hands were clasped in front of him and his head inclined to his feet.

'It wasn't enough,' Charlie managed to stutter through his howls.

'It never would have been,' came the solemn answer. 'You wrote my story, Charlie, you know it well … in a way you can be summed up in one line … you know what that line is?'

'Don't say it.'

'The dead don't haunt the living Charlie, it's the living that haunt the dead.'

'Go!' Charlie yanked the ring from his finger and threw it across the room at the spirit, who deftly caught it. 'Go, get out of here. You're no friend of mine Jude, I don't want to ever see you again. I renounce you, spirit!' By the end, Charlie was shouting.

Jude disappeared, he could do nothing other than go once commanded. Of course, it was not the words, but rather how they were spoken that did the trick. Charlie had filled them with all the power and pure rage he could muster. They pushed the spirit of mercy away, this was always the way with magic.

In the time between Alison's passing and her funeral, life for Charlie became very flat; everything was hazy and far away. It was not like being in a coma because he was aware of life going on around him. He just couldn't bring himself to care, or moreover, to interact. Sometimes people spoke to him and he mumbled responses, sometimes he ate, sometimes he drank, often, he slept, that was his favourite thing to do. Of course, sleeping meant waking, and every time he woke there were a few seconds of unreality where he expected to find Alison lying by his side. In this way, waking was like feeling all the stitches in his wounds being ripped open again.

The funeral happened around him, friends and family – her family – held him tight, they cried with him and remembered her, her wit and her smile were two very popular topics. People talked about how she lit up a room, and for Charlie, all of this fell short. For him, she was the room.

The fog didn't clear after the funeral, instead, it grew thicker. Days passed, followed by weeks, and months and life did not begin again. Charlie retreated into himself, his ginger hair grew back, only now it was joined by a messy, wiry beard. He ate, he drank, he slept, sometimes he washed, but nowhere near as often as he should have. He shaped his days around nothing, that is to say, he tried his best to be numb and not to think or feel. During rare moments of clarity when he did think, it was always about the ring. It had been a big mistake to throw it away, he realised that now.

Friends dropped in on him but he was no company at all, one by one they stopped coming. Of course, Hank, Becky and Mary Ann never gave up on him, they kept pulling him back into their family circle. And there was Hannah, of course, that precious little girl did more to keep him going in those first few months than anyone else. She was a ball of sunshine, a little twinkle of starlight. Every time he was bad company, every time he tried to kick out and push people away, there was Hank, handing him Hannah, forcing him to be true to his word. Forcing him to be the little girl's godfather, the giver of horseback rides, and the teller of fairy tales.

'Why haven't you given up on me?' he had asked Hank, one Sunday afternoon. 'I've been terrible.'

'I made a promise,' Hank replied. And that's all he would say on the matter.

Somehow a year passed. Charlie noticed the date on the calendar hanging on his bedroom wall and he thought, *a year ago today she passed.* Something felt wrong, something in his belly. The post came early that day and it was just one envelope. The envelope was completely blank, no name or address had been written on it, and there was no stamp or postmark either. Holding it, he noticed that it bulged in the middle, and there was a familiar scent on it. He held it to his nose and smelt green apples.

As he ripped open the envelope, he felt his heart pounding in his chest. This was the first time he had been aware of his own heartbeat in a year. He tipped the envelope up and caught the circle that fell from it. Wooden, blue at the top with a streak of green running through it, here was the ring he had rashly discarded, it was returned to him. He held it tight in the sweaty palm of his left hand and, with the thumb and forefinger of the same hand, plucked a note from the envelope. He unfolded it and found it was brief and to the point. It simply said, *Enough, time to live, time to write.* It wasn't signed, the handwriting was unfamiliar; he suspected it was from Jude, but it may as well have been from her. These would have been her words.

He slipped the ring back onto the ring finger on his left hand and felt something. It was raw and painful, but it was a revelation to Charlie, even feeling bad was preferable to feeling nothing. He was now able to comprehend that wrong feeling in his gut, it was guilt.

Guilt for the year he had wasted. How could he waste that much time when every second had been precious to Alison?

Life began there and then; it began with him showering, and then cleaning the house. Somehow, he had allowed dirt and dust to grow inches thick, and everywhere he looked there were piles of dirty clothes, unwashed plates and cups, and bins overflowing with rubbish. When he was done cleaning, he decided to take a second shower, he stood under the hot water and cried a little, it felt good to let it out.

It was nine p.m. and Charlie was clean but wide awake. Wrapped in his dressing gown, he took his laptop from his bag and set it up on the kitchen table. At some point during the day, he realised that he now had thirteen stories in his head, all itching to get out. Fourteen, if you counted 'their story'. It was hard at first, starting was always hard. Sometimes starting was like jumping into the middle of a mystery and then running to catch up on the why and how of the events occurring around you.

'I've written all these stories before,' he told himself, and then it became a lot easier. The words flew from his fingertips and he smiled as the first chapter began with: *It was midnight, and the rain and moonlight were drizzling onto the cobbled streets outside the faux-fancy apartment block.*

That year Charlie worked nonstop, completing three of the fourteen novels he had squirreled away. He was far more active, he took walks, got himself a bike. He joined a local archery club, mainly because he'd never be able to forgive himself if he took up golf out of boredom. He spent a lot of time with Hank and Becky, and Hannah, of course. Often, he couldn't help but feel like a third wheel but they were good people, and they always went out of their way to make him feel welcome. Sometimes he felt bad, sometimes he missed Alison like hell but there were other times he felt perfectly happy. Oddly, as soon as he became aware of these patches of happiness, he felt guilty about them. It was as if some voice inside was berating him for not grieving constantly. At times like this, he glanced at the ring on his finger and thought about what Alison would have to say about that.

Life went on and five years after Alison's passing, Charlie, now aged thirty-six, had written all fourteen stories and stored them away. So far, only seven had been published. His agent said that it was best to release them gradually, so as not to oversaturate his audience. His status as a writer had changed from underground cult favourite to a commercial hit; the critics were not his biggest fans but, to directly quote Hank, 'Fuck that bunch of sharp-nosed sourpusses'.

Life went on, but when it came to his love life, well, that moved more slowly. Over those five years there had been a few encounters, all of them one-night stands that left a bad taste in his mouth. He always felt somewhat guilty about them.

Shortly after the birth of Hank and Becky's little boy, Frankie, Hank had invited him to a dinner party. He was told to look smart and that made him a little nervous. Little Hannah had let it slip they were planning on introducing him to a woman. Charlie began to sweat, the idea of having to be charming and witty or worse still: 'interesting', gave him palpitations. He thought that somewhere along the way he had lost the knack. He called Hank and cried off, making some tenuous excuse. In truth, what he was saying was, 'I'm still not ready'. Never mind, he guessed all that would come in time, and if it never came ... well, he still had to live, he promised Alison he would live.

Of course, it came when he least expected it, in truth, he had practically given up on the idea. It was a month before the sixth anniversary of Alison's passing and four months before his thirty-seventh birthday. He was sitting alone at a table in the Ingle Nook, waiting for Hank and Becky to arrive with Hannah and the baby. Their little chap was six months old now, and they were still insisting on christening him Francis Arthur Walker-Doyle. When Charlie heard the name, he thought of Alison and laughed out loud. She had always found double-barrelled surnames slightly silly. On her behalf, he enquired whether they were planning on saving any names for the other babies, and then he had insisted he'd be calling the little chap 'Frank' or better yet, 'Fart'.

They were coming to see him today to ask him to be little Frank's godfather. It was meant to be a surprise, but Hank had let it slip accidentally-on-purpose to avoid any teary scenes in public. Charlie was glad that Hank had let the cat out of the bag. The last thing he wanted to do was run off to the toilet to have a cry, he was trying to put that stage of his life behind him.

Now he sat in the corner, minding his own business, and clutching his coffee. He had picked a point on the wall opposite, and as he listened to the music pumping through his earphones, he stared at that point with a pleasant but slightly vacant smile plastered all over his face. He didn't hear someone talking to him, but he felt her tugging at his sleeve. He turned sharply and saw…

'Excuse me,' she said in a small, shy voice. She was a vision. Big, dark eyes, ivory skin, bright red lips, and strawberry blonde curls that fell past her shoulders. He watched her as she began to ramble. 'I'm so sorry to disturb you, I know you were off in your own little world, and I know you're a busy man and must have people bothering you all the time … but I just need to tell you how much I loved your book.'

'Which one?' he asked, not from any sense of vanity but simply because it was the only thing he could think of to say.

'"The Karaoke Glow",' she replied. Charlie could almost taste the nervous tension in her voice and it baffled him. He never got used to the idea that some strangers were excited to meet him, it was a surreal, he was just a man who wrote words. It wasn't as if he went running into burning buildings to save kittens and babies. 'It meant so, so much to me, reading that book, it gave me the strength to get away from someone … someone bad if you know what I mean?'

'That's sweet of you to say,' Charlie began. He reached up and held her elbow and watched as she melted just a little bit. 'But I'm sure that you always had the strength. You would have found it by yourself, sooner or later.' He smiled his biggest, widest smile and watched as the mystery woman's pale cheeks reddened. There was a moment of silence in which Charlie realised that he was still holding onto her elbow. His hand shot back to him as if it was attached to a length of elastic.

'Oh, I have this' she said excitedly, diving into her bag, 'I've just bought it.' She retrieved a copy of his new release, 'The Boy Who Tamed the Bear', and handed it to him. 'Could you?' she mimed a signing gesture.

Charlie took a pen from his pocket, opened the book and paused.

'Sorry, what's your name bab?' he asked. He heard that 'bab' slip out and thought how funny it was that he always seemed to become more working-class and more 'Coventry' when he was nervous.

'Jessica.'

'Well, I'm meeting friends today, Jessica,' Charlie said as he signed her book. Looking up, he saw her face drop a little as she realised that she was intruding. He rushed on before she could get embarrassed and run away. 'But, if you want to meet me here tomorrow at twelve, we can have a chat and if you bring your copy of "The Karaoke Glow", I'll sign that for you too.'

'Oh, I'll definitely be here tomorrow!' she said. 'I start my new job here tomorrow.'

She smiled, thanked him profusely then turned and walked away. Charlie watched her leave and found himself wondering if her starting to work there was Hank and Becky's plan, had they arranged it? Was she the one they had intended him to meet over dinner? As he wondered about this, he realised that he felt something new. Or maybe it was something very old, something that predated his grief, his numbness, the dull ache, and the guilt that sometimes struck him simply because he was happy. This feeling was even older than the pure dread he experienced while watching Alison slowly sicken and wither away.

He felt a spark of electricity, and it made him feel warm inside.

.31.

Meanwhile

In the darkness there was nothing until there was something, that thing being a pleasant warm breeze. With her eyes closed, she smiled and rolled flat onto her back. What lay beneath her was stiff and solid, but that didn't matter, she felt perfectly comfortable. She noticed a gentle rocking motion, maybe it was this that was soothing her, making her feel calm and at peace. It reminded her of being an infant in her parent's arms, having them rock her to sleep and sing lullabies. Of course, there was that sound as well, it was peaceful, like that of waves gently lapping the shore.

Eventually, she opened her eyes and saw a beam of wood and a sheet of blue material flapping in the breeze. She sat up and found that she had been sleeping on the deck of a ship. It was a ship just big enough for one. From her new angle, she saw there was a shape painted on the sails, it was a white stag prancing across a field of blue. She smiled and leapt to her feet; she had travelled on this boat through the darkness and it had come to rest at the Breidablik harbour. Just as Jude promised, she was here in the town she had built with her own hands, and in minute detail. Moreover, she was here but all her pain, heartache, and sense of loss felt a million miles away, it was as if it had been left behind in another world.

Stepping down from the ship and into the snow, she examined the town and found that everything was the way she had built it. Every shop and house, every light and bush, everything was in the exact right place. She found that the doors to the meeting hall were wide open, and when she entered, she found a grand piano on the stage. Better still, on top of the piano, there was a violin case. She shut the doors behind her and rushed to the stage, within moments the violin was under her chin. As she played, she thought of the first time Charlie had stayed over, and about the morning after when she stood before him naked, serenading him with her own violin. It didn't make her sad, rather it made her smile a little bit broader.

That first day, she spent hours playing music, switching between the violin and the piano, and wishing she could play both at the same time. She found herself thinking, *when Cassie comes, I'll teach her, that way we can play together.* When it finally got dark, she left the meeting hall and pushed open the door of the nearest house. She found the walls lined with her photographs, and here and there were little trinkets and mementos. Upstairs, in the main bedroom, she found a wardrobe full of her clothes, and more pictures, and more mementos. There was a table beside her bed, and on that table, there was a lamp casting light on to her favourite picture, the one of her and Charlie sitting beneath a tree by the banks of the river Windrush. She crawled into bed and fell asleep smiling at the picture.

For quite some time, she was on her own in the town, but that didn't really concern her. She was content enough in her own company. She read, watched films, played the violin and the piano, went for walks and ate delicious meals. Mostly she waited for Cassie, she didn't know when the little girl would come but she knew that, relatively speaking, it wouldn't be long.

It happened maybe three months after she arrived in Breidablik or at least it felt like three months, time was tricky here too. It was early in the morning, and Alison was crossing the short walk from her new house to the meeting hall. In the distance, she saw the white stag. It was slowly trotting in the direction of the harbour when it paused and looked over its shoulder at her. Knowing what this meant, she rushed to the harbour in time to see the boat bobbing in the bay.

Cassie wasn't asleep, she was awake and peering over the side of the boat towards Alison. The little girl waved enthusiastically, and in that moment, she felt something click into place. She had been happy before but this was beyond happy, this was far above it. She waved back, and when the boat got close enough, she reached in and lifted the little girl down onto the dock.

Seeing Cassie there was not like seeing Cassie in her sickbed. In Breidablik, she was a very ordinary pretty, little eight-year-old girl. She had a tiny, little, button nose, fine blonde hair, and a round face. There were no lingering signs of sickness, pain, or heartache and Alison thought that was just how it should be. After all, she hadn't brought any of her troubles with her, why should anyone else?

'Hello Cassie,' Alison chirped. 'My name is Alison and it's very nice to meet you.'

'Is my mummy here?' she asked, in a 'just wondering' kind of tone.

'She isn't I'm afraid, sugarplum,' Alison replied. The nickname she had heard Jude use made the little girl smile. 'But she wants me to take care of you. So, how about you come home with me? We can have hot chocolate and cheese toasties.'

Cassie tilted her head and thought about it for a moment.

'Mummy and daddy say I'm not to go anywhere with strangers, but you're a good person, aren't you ...' It wasn't really a question but a statement of fact. 'Okay,' Cassie replied, slipping her little hand into Alison's grip.

From the very first moment, the two got on like a house on fire, practically like mother and daughter. Their time together was filled with laughter, snowmen, and snowball fights. There were music lessons, story times, and at bath times Alison washed Cassie's silky blonde hair. Everything was well and all manner of things were well. One day, Cassie pulled on Alison's sleeve and looked up at her with wide eyes.

'Did I die?' she asked. Alison's answer came through a smile.

'Yes, you did sugarplum but does that matter now?'

'No, I guess not,' Cassie replied, before wandering off to make a particularly big snowball.

Over time, the town began to grow and come to life. New people arrived every few months, and as they arrived the shops and restaurants opened. Some of the newcomers loved the work they had done in life so much that it felt right for them to continue it in the afterlife. Other newcomers abandoned their earthly careers and instead, did the things they wished they had done whilst they were alive.

Eventually, Alison met a man called Sam who she felt a connection with straightaway. It seemed only natural that there should be the chance of romance, why should anyone be denied a full life? She didn't wish a half-life on Charlie, and she certainly didn't wish

Time passed, and life went on, and suddenly one on herself. In no time at all, the three of them became quite the happy little family., six years on, or what seemed like six years on, she looked around and saw the thriving, little, paradise town.

She thought of Charlie, her one and only muppet man. Being parted from him forever wouldn't be so bad, as long as they could both be happy. She wondered if his life had begun yet. Of late, she had seen visions around Breidablik of a tall, beautiful, if not slightly awkward, red-haired woman. After a while, she realised that Jude had brought her these visions, she was to be Charlie's next love. Alison wondered if they had met yet? She hoped they had, she hoped it would go well for them, that they would marry and have lots of little ones to love and dote over. She loved him still, and part of her always would, but she hoped that she would never see him here. With all her heart, she hoped that he would find his very own paradise, no one deserved it more.

'Be happy,' she said, as she blew him a kiss across worlds.

About The Author

Jack A Rabbit was born in 1982 on the outskirts of Coventry in the UK. From a working class background and profoundly dyslexic in the early 80's he found it very difficult and received little to no support from the education system at that time. In deed he recalls being laughed at by his English teacher when confessing how he'd love to become a writer one day.

A lot of time has passed since then and Jack almost gave up on his dreams. If not for the love and support of family and loved ones he may have put them aside for ever. Thankfully he kept at it and today he has finished two novels and is working on his third. His message to anyone else in his situation: Never give up, never let anyone else define your abilities or limitations.

42232031R00207

Printed in Poland
by Amazon Fulfillment
Poland Sp. z o.o., Wrocław